TAMPERED

TAMPERED

A Dr. Zol Szabo Medical Mystery

ROSS PENNIE

ECW Press

Published by ECW Press, 2120 Queen Street East, Suite 200,
Toronto, Ontario, Canada M4E 1E2
416.694.3348 / info@ecwpress.com

LIBRARY AND ARCHIVES CANADA CATALOGUING IN PUBLICATION

Pennie, Ross A
Tampered : a Dr. Zol Szabo medical mystery / Ross Pennie.

ISBN 978-1-55022-936-3
ALSO ISSUED AS:
978-1-55490-936-0 (PDF); 978-1-55490-959-9 (EPUB)

1. Title.

PS8631.E565T35 2011   C813'.6   C2010-906697-9

Cover images: piano © Ryan Lane;
background © Roberto A. Sanchez (iStockPhoto.com)
Cover and text design: Tania Craan
Typesetting: Mary Bowness
Printing: Friesens 1 2 3 4 5

This book is a work of fiction. Names, characters, places, and incidents are the product of the
author's imagination or are used fictitiously. Any resemblance to actual persons, living or dead,
events, or locales is entirely coincidental.

This book is set in Bembo and Akzidenz

The publication of *Tampered* has been generously supported by the Canada Council for the
Arts, which last year invested $20.1 million in writing and publishing throughout Canada, by
the Ontario Arts Council, by the Government of Ontario through Ontario Book Publishing
Tax Credit, by the OMDC Book Fund, an initiative of the Ontario Media Development
Corporation, and by the Government of Canada through the Canada Book Fund.

 Canada Council Conseil des Arts
for the Arts du Canada 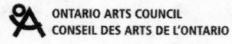 ONTARIO ARTS COUNCIL
CONSEIL DES ARTS DE L'ONTARIO

PRINTED AND BOUND IN CANADA

ECW PRESS
ecwpress.com

FSC
www.fsc.org
MIX
Paper from
responsible sources
FSC® C016245

This story arose from my affection for two people now well past eighty: Luise Denman, my godmother, and Reg Blundell, a longtime friend. Full of sparkle, Luise quotes Homer and Virgil, is still taking university courses, and is a whiz on the World Wide Web. Reg Blundell is a gentleman of the highest order. He is an accomplished artist who fought in the Second World War, helped build the telephone industry, and plays the piano with unabashed joy. I dedicate this book to all those who see the wonder in long lives well lived.

Although I wrote most of this book alone in the pre-dawn darkness when everyone else was still asleep, I had lots of help from the people I love and respect. Jack David at ECW Press continued his trust and mentorship. Peter Harcourt, Larry Kramer, Bob Nosal, Ken Stead, and Mark Walma critiqued my early drafts. Bev Haun came up with the title. Edna Barker guided me to the finish line with her unerring editorial insights. And every day Lorna was at my side, sharing the journey and making life worth living.

CHAPTER 1

Zol Szabo peered across the sea of silvery heads bobbing in the buffet line at Camelot Lodge. Usually, he looked forward to these monthly Sunday brunches with Art Greenwood, his ex-wife's granddad. Art, the only member of Francine's family who hadn't smoked himself into an early grave, sparkled with wisdom and wit in defiance of his age and physical restrictions. Best of all, Art and his tablemates never let political correctness get in the way of a candid opinion or a good story.

But today, Zol saw only clinical diagnoses smouldering through the retirement residence: the wobbly knees of rheumatoid arthritis, the stooped backs of osteoporosis, the trembling hands of Parkinson's, the vacant eyes of macular degeneration.

Zol forced another smile at Art, who was taking his place at the piano in the sitting room on the other side of the archway. Zol hoped Art was well enough to play. He'd looked pale and drawn when he'd greeted Zol a few minutes ago and confessed he'd been hit by another bout of fever and the runs earlier in the week. That made it his third bout in the past couple of months. And he wasn't the only one. Dozens of others had been hit with the same bug. Art denied any headache, thank goodness. When headache compounded the fever and diarrhea, the result was lethal. In the past month alone, two of the converted mansion's thirty-eight residents had died within hours of a blinding headache compounding their explosive stools.

Art warmed up with a few bars of "Bicycle Built For Two." His chording was tentative, not as sharp as usual. He switched to an improvised version of Beethoven's "Moonlight Sonata." Art played everything by ear. He couldn't read a note, but if he heard something once, he could play it forever. Despite the advancing muscle disease that had forced him into an electric scooter, he still glimmered with the genius that had made him an engineering whiz-kid in the telephone industry fifty years ago.

The understated elegance of the dining room's caramel walls and burgundy accents reminded Zol of a café in one of Hamilton's nicer hotels, except the bucolic vista through Camelot's windows was considerably more handsome than any view of the city's down-at-the-heels central core. Here on an elegant cul-de-sac a few blocks from downtown, stately homes abutted the woodlands at the foot of the Niagara Escarpment. Known locally as the Mountain, the imposing ribbon of limestone and old-growth forest snaked through the city like a giant's doorstep, its flora and fauna protected by the United Nations as a World Biosphere Reserve. Zol thought of his own renovated house a couple of kilometres above as the seagulls flew, perched on a generous treed lot on the Escarpment's edge. He was thankful once again for the two million in lottery winnings that had sent him to medical school and bought him such a gorgeous piece of real estate with its jetliner view. He could cope with Hamilton's overgenerous share of shysters and gangsters if, at the end of the day, he could tuck Max safely in bed, then sip a Glenfarclas while watching Lake Ontario shimmer in the ever-changing light.

Camelot's dining tables boasted smooth white linens, shiny cutlery, and imitation crystal that sparkled as brightly as the stuff his mother reserved for special occasions. Today's spread of poached salmon, eggs, bacon, French toast, salads, and gooey desserts looked a treat. As a former professional chef himself, Zol respected the care and effort that went into every dish. But as a public-health doctor, the table seemed to him less a chef's delight than a minefield.

Something nasty and undetectable — a microbe or a toxin — was poisoning the food. But intermittently. Not every dish and not every meal. As the Associate Medical Officer of Health for Hamilton-Lakeshore, second-in-command at the region's health unit, Zol's job was to quash epidemics, not wallow in them during Sunday brunch. Twice he'd sent his inspectors into Camelot. They'd examined every centimetre of the place with a magnifying glass. They'd collected scores of samples from the kitchen and dozens of specimens from afflicted residents. But they'd come up empty. The kitchen met all the health codes, and the laboratory detected no disease-causing pathogens.

Zol's friend and medical-school classmate, Dr. Hamish Wakefield, a savant in the field of infectious diseases, had raised the possibility of epidemic Norovirus. But even Hamish, an assistant professor at the city's Caledonian University Medical Centre, was stumped; he conceded there was no indication that anything as simple as the cruise-ship virus was the culprit here.

Zol helped the wait staff — invariably hesitant, awkward, and struggling with their English — park the walkers in a double row against the far wall of the dining room. He escorted the frailest of the gauzy-white residents to their seats, then joined the slow-moving buffet queue. He knew he'd soon be hunting down unsalted butter for one person and cholesterol-free scrambled eggs for another. He shrugged off the risk to his intestines and half-filled his plate with breakfast fare he hoped would be sterile: a rubbery fried egg, three crispy rashers of bacon, and a piece of charred toast. Bypassing the devilled eggs, sliced tomatoes, and potato salad, he took his place at Art's table where Phyllis and Betty were already seated.

Despite being past eighty-five, slow to move, and somewhat hard of hearing, Betty McKenzie and Phyllis Wedderspoon stayed fully abreast of the news. These days they'd be bursting with opinions on the latest Parliament Hill shenanigans and lamenting the deceptions that had triggered the stock-market crash now threatening their pensions.

Betty beamed at Zol, then peered over his shoulder. "Where's that handsome little man of yours, Zol?"

"Max sends his regrets," Zol said. "He's at a birthday party. One very brave mother is taking a dozen nine-year-old boys bowling."

"You tell him we missed him," Betty said. "And that his box of Godivas is here waiting for him. You will bring him next time, won't you Zol?"

"I'll have to check his social calendar. It's far busier than mine." It wasn't Max's calendar that would keep him out of Camelot until Zol got the place decontaminated.

He glanced at the buffet table. There was no one left in line. Earl Crabtree, a retired history professor, usually completed the table's foursome. Although Camelot's mealtime seating was officially open, Zol had noticed that most of the residents gravitated to their regular spots, like the four euchre-mad women, all former math teachers, who sat together and barely said a word to anyone else. Today, two of them were missing. And no one else had dared join them. Their intimidating impatience with forgetfulness, no matter how mild, was well known.

"Is Earl going to join us?" Zol asked.

"Not today," Betty said. "Dear Earl is staying in his room, close to the facilities." She gave Zol a knowing look and patted her abdomen.

Zol put down his fork. What must Betty and Phyllis think of him? Half their table was down with gastro, yet Zol and his staff were no closer to resolving the epidemic than they'd been two months ago. "Does he have a fever?" Zol asked.

"Just a gurgly tummy," Betty said. "And no headache. I made sure about that."

Phyllis lifted her chin and inspected Zol's plate through the bottom of her bifocals. "Well, Dr. Szabo, I must say it's a relief to see you're not a vegetarian, or even worse, a vegan. But what's wrong? Little appetite? You took barely enough to feed a chickadee. I trust it's not *your* belly this time."

"Let the good doctor eat in peace and not fuss about his tummy," said Betty, her voice a slight tremolo.

Phyllis lanced the yolk of her eggs Benedict. "I'm just saying that young people today are seduced by fads and schemes that distract them away from the tried and true. As I always say, *timeo Danaos et dona ferentes.*"

"For heaven's sake," said Betty, "we're not in your Latin class now. And there's no stranger with gifts we have to be afraid of here."

Phyllis was right on both counts: Zol was indeed an omnivore, and a Trojan horse was threatening Camelot's kitchen. He spooned strawberry jam onto his toast from a single-use packet and hoped the sugary hit would settle the disquiet he felt in his stomach.

From somewhere to his right came a sudden loud clang, the sound of metal bashing crockery. *Bang! bang! bang! bang!* Zol braced for shattered dinnerware skittering across the floor.

The more the clanging intensified, the louder Art pounded his rendition of "Camptown Races" from the sitting room.

Betty and Phyllis cupped their palms over their hearing aids and glared at the source of the unholy noise.

Eventually, the clanging stopped. Betty's face softened. "That's Bud," she said quietly. "Poor fellow. I do feel sorry for him."

"Poor fellow, nothing," Phyllis countered. "Bud doesn't belong here. Not anymore."

"He had a stroke, bless him," Betty explained. "And now he can't talk. Just bangs his spoon on his plate. It's embarrassing for his wife at mealtime. You know, with everybody watching."

Betty pressed her arthritic left hand on Zol's forearm. Despite her thinning hair and dorsal hump, she glowed with the grace and elegance she must have wielded forty years ago as the Prime Minister's executive assistant. Zol always found himself comforted by the quiet confidence of her presence. He'd never known either of his grandmothers, and as Art's girlfriend, Betty had become Zol's de facto grandma and Max's great-grandma. As a long-time widow, she understood Zol's years of single-parent loneliness. She'd coached him through it with more skill and empathy than anyone else. She'd really taken to Colleen, the private investigator he'd been dating since Christmas.

"Art plays our favourites so beautifully," Betty said, closing her eyes and drinking in the final chorus of "Danny Boy." The plump blue veins on the back of her hand, so clearly visible in their rich detail, reminded Zol of Gray's drawings in his anatomy textbook. Her skin felt warm and soft. "Without him, we'd never hear our kind of music anymore. They don't play our tunes on the radio."

"But Gloria should get that damn piano tuned," Phyllis said. "I've written to her about it over and over. It doesn't do the slightest good. The high notes are still flat."

In Camelot Lodge's well-defined hierarchy, Phyllis strutted in position number one. As the self-appointed grand peahen of the pecking order, she possessed a sharp mind and a strident voice. But the real source of her authority was her '72 Lincoln Continental. No one else had a car.

"None of us has a gramophone anymore," said Betty. She held Camelot's position number two, a status she didn't flaunt but that was hers nonetheless. "When my nieces and nephews moved me in here, they threw out all my seventy-eights and thirty-three-and-a-thirds."

Phyllis dipped her chin, her eyes piercing Zol over the top of her spectacles. "I believe you young people have taken to calling them *vinyl*."

Betty leaned toward Zol, still patting his arm. "Earl isn't the only one with a delicate tummy. I suppose Art told you. He hasn't been feeling himself the past few of days."

Zol stared at his plate and winced inside. He'd pleaded with Art to come and stay with Max and him until this gastro business got resolved. There was plenty of room in Zol's house for Betty as well. Zol had suggested confidentially to Art that the two of them could share a room or each have one of their own. Art had declined for both of them. It wasn't a question of the bedroom arrangements or the difficulty with the stairs. They would never abandon their friends.

Phyllis made a face. "No point in hiding it, Art has been down with *faeces liquifacti* for the past few days. I call it Gloria's Revenge. Montezuma had nothing on her." She stiffened and coughed into her serviette, as though forcing herself to stifle further criticism of the Lodge's manager, Gloria Oliveira. "But if we let the good doctor concern himself about Camelot's tummies, he'll have us in quarantine. Again. Every time we turn around, the place gets locked up like Fort Knox. No one in or out except the staff, who tiptoe around us as though we had leprosy."

"Now Phyllis, it doesn't help to exaggerate," Betty said.

Phyllis lifted a forkful of egg toward her mouth, studied it, then dropped it to her plate. "The Portuguese may be famous for their lace and celestial navigation, but they're hopeless in the kitchen."

"Zol has been doing everything he can to put a stop to our . . . our gurgly tummies." Betty dabbed her lips with her serviette and smudged her ruby lipstick into the wrinkles around her mouth. "Tummy troubles or not," she said, her tone of voice indicating she was changing the subject, "Art Greenwood is one of the best things to happen to this place. Just look around. Most everyone is smiling. Even the Mountain Wingers." She pointed to two tables at the far end of the dining room. "They've got their heads up."

Four of Camelot's Mountain Wingers were seated in wheel-chairs, terry-cloth bibs tied around their necks. They lived in the eight-bed infirmary on the second floor and were allowed out of the locked ward only on special occasions such as Sunday brunch. They ate puréed meals out of plastic bowls and were never given knives or forks. Around them hovered uniformed staff with the gentle movements, rich black hair, and almond eyes of Filipinas. Watching the aides spoon beige mush into the toothless mouths, Zol shuddered. He'd promised himself he would jump off the Skyway Bridge and into a watery grave in Hamilton Harbour the instant he was diagnosed with Alzheimer's, or anything like it.

"I'll grant you that," Phyllis admitted. "Arthur's playing is almost like magic."

"Of course it is," Betty said. "It lifts the heads of those dear souls like sunflowers tipped toward the noontime rays. They wave their arms, tap their feet, and sometimes sing along."

"Hardly," Phyllis corrected. "It's really just muttering."

"When they hear that music," said Betty, "their faces get so bright you'd almost swear they could partake in intelligent conversation. Until . . ." A look of sadness misted her eyes — or was it fear? "Until it's time for Art to stop playing and Gloria locks the keyboard."

Two men in dark business suits caught Zol's eye from the far side of the common room. Betty and Phyllis had their backs to them, thank goodness. The men were pushing a gurney, their passenger draped head to toe in a white sheet. To the right of the men, the wall of floor-to-ceiling windows lit the room and flanked the side door to the parking lot. A black Craig & Lafferty van was waiting on the tarmac by the exit, its rear doors yawning.

Once they'd negotiated the awkwardly narrow side exit and wheeled their client to the van, one of the men tapped the gurney with his foot. The wheels didn't fold as they were supposed to. He tried again. Still, the undercarriage didn't give. The other man tried with a swifter kick but the wheels didn't budge. The two men kicked together — at the wheels, the frame, the mechanism beneath. The stretcher rocked back and forth. The corpse's legs slid off and pitched precariously toward the ground. Suddenly, the undercarriage collapsed, and one of the men caught the body just in time. They hoisted the gurney and flung their reluctant cargo into the van, then jumped inside. The driver slammed his door, and the vehicle careened down the street.

Zol dabbed his mouth with his serviette, then wiped the sweat from his forehead. He stared at the bits of cold egg and charred bacon on his plate, his stomach in complete revolt. Betty and Phyllis started at the sudden chime from Zol's belt. He grabbed his BlackBerry, ready to silence it. Whoever was calling could leave a message. He hated cellphones in restaurants. Nothing in public health was so important it couldn't wait fifteen minutes.

But the phone's display said Peter Trinnock was calling. That was strange. Zol's boss never worked weekends. He golfed a lot, skied a little, and often got heavily into the sauce. If he wasn't on the slopes

today, enjoying March's last few weeks of spring skiing, he'd be into
his third martini by now.

Zol excused himself and strode toward the common sitting
room.

"Damn it, Szabo," Trinnock said, "where are you?" Zol pictured
his boss's piggy-eyed gaze, the veins on his cheeks flaring like a tangled nest of spiders.

"Brunch with my ex's granddad. Camelot Lodge."

"Then you know."

"Know what, sir?"

"About the Prime Minister's aunt. Nellie something." Zol heard
the shuffle of papers next to Trinnock's phone, then the yapping of
a small dog. Trinnock cursed through a partly muffled mouthpiece,
"Muzzle the damn dog, Marion. I'm on the phone." He paused and
took a loud gulp of something that sounded more like beer than
martini. "Nellie Brownlow, that's the name," Trinnock continued,
his voice again loud and clear. "Died this morning. At that Camelot
place. The Prime Minister's Office just called. The Prime Minister
is very upset. The woman was his favourite aunt. It seems she got
caught up in your epidemic. Stricken with diarrhea several times
since Christmas."

Bile burned the back of Zol's throat. The Prime Minister's
Office never interfered with health unit matters. "I'll . . . I'll look
into it right away."

"You've dropped the ball on this one, Szabo. The guy from the
PMO is saying people are dropping like flies at that Camelot place
and that our Hamilton-Lakeshore Health Unit is asleep at the
bloody switch."

"We've been doing everything possible to —"

"There are other Party favourites living at that place. The
Brownlow woman wasn't the only one. They may be retired, but
they're VIPs all the same."

Zol glanced at his table. He hardly needed reminding about
Camelot's connections to the country's ruling federal party. Betty,
Earl, and a couple of sisters named Maude and Myrtle were living

examples. Art stayed away from anything political, and Phyllis reck-oned that all politicians were tarred with the same unsavoury brush. She loved it when the press discovered any of them *in fla-grante delicto* and their careers got ruined.

"Any more of them gets wheeled out in a bag, an RCMP goon squad will be breathing down our necks." Trinnock downed another noisy gulp. "That's *your* neck, Szabo, now that the PM knows your name."

The Prime Minister?

The RCMP?

Zol imagined beer-bellied thugs in Kevlar vests waving fifty-thousand-volt Tasers.

He swallowed hard.

The force's boy-scouts-in-scarlet image had been shattered when shocking videos of RCMP brutality were broadcast to the world via the Internet. A brave guy with a video cellphone had recorded the nation's finest zapping a confused, unarmed traveller with a Taser at Vancouver airport. The guy died, right there on the screen. The scenario and the attempted cover-up had seriously jaundiced Zol's view of policing. Zol was sure many others felt the same way. The national anthem boasted that the True North was strong and free, but nowadays it felt like its citizens weren't safe if the RCMP took a sudden, arbitrary disliking to them.

"Does someone in the PMO suspect foul play?" Zol asked.

"You know these political types. Don't trust anyone. Which means you'll have to do better. Considerably better. And with due speed." Trinnock's English accent intensified when he got angry. "Shall I call in some assistance? Dare I say, our friends from Toronto?"

Ice filled Zol's veins. He pictured Wyatt Burr, the "consultant" who'd swaggered in from Toronto on his high horse and royally screwed up Zol's last big case. "I'd rather deal with our local experts. If you gave me the go-ahead to hire a couple more brains, I could —"

"Get the bloody thing fixed, whatever it takes. And keep us out of the papers."

CHAPTER 2

That evening, Max slurped from his Star Pirates mug at the kitchen table. "Can we have chicken noodle soup for supper every night, Dad?"

Dread hung over Zol, an anvil cloud that had hovered since Trinnock's noontime call. Such a reversal from yesterday's fun and adventure when life seemed full of promise. Zol and Max had taken Colleen and Max's school chum Travis to the Toronto Zoo for a Saturday filled with nothing more serious than home-cut fries, double-chocolate ice cream, and jokes about elephant poop.

Colleen Woolton first shined into their lives four months ago, and the bloom on their threesome was still in full glow. Every day with her was a treat. Quick and compact, with a long golden ponytail, Colleen radiated Rapunzel's innocence and Mrs. Tiggy-Winkle's kindness and wrapped them up with Barbarella's late-night passion. He closed his eyes and tried to let himself be stirred by the memory of the jasmine on her skin and the music of her soft South African accent whispering at his ear, but he was struck by recurring apprehension. Female anger and contempt seemed to evolve inevitably from early bliss. He wondered whether he possessed a flaw that drove women to nastiness. Alone in the dark he found himself desperate for things to be different this time.

"Dad-dy?" Max called. "Are you dreaming again?"

Zol forced a chuckle through his fears as he remembered Max giggling about oversized penises and excrement. The nine-year-old commanded an impressive knowledge of zoology — the finicky diets of aardvarks and the muddy habitats of tapirs. Did he learn those things in school, or was the Internet providing him with more than an unlimited repertoire of video games and downloads?

"Um . . . What's that, Max?"

"I said, can we have chicken noodle soup for supper every night?"

"Don't you think you'd get sick of it?"

"Never in a million, zillion years." Max looked at the empty place setting beside him. "Where's Colleen?"

"On her way. She had to work a bit late." Colleen had been delayed on a surveillance job. In true private-investigator fashion, she was tight-lipped about the details of her work. Zol knew not to ask but worried about her safety, despite her insistence that her clients were normal people with very ordinary problems, not gun-toting gangsters. "She'll be here soon. Ready for your next course?"

"What is it?"

"Another favourite of yours. Chicken pot pie."

Max made a face.

"Hey. We made it together. You chopped all that celery and cilantro." Max was becoming a whiz with his own kitchen knife — just the right size for a nine-year-old.

"Can't I just have chicken noodle soup? You said that's all *you're* going to have."

"If you're going to reach a million points on your new game gadget, you'll have to fuel up with high-test chicken pie."

Zol downed the rest of his soup, then pulled the pie from the oven. The doorbell rang, and Max shot to the front door with the speed of a Star Pirates lightsaber. The treatment he had received three months ago for his spastic left arm, the only part of him that cerebral palsy had made stiff and awkward, had improved his confidence. Having two upper limbs that functioned almost symmetrically made the boy feel like everyone else in his class. He was no longer the kid with the "special needs," a moniker that had rankled no matter how politically correct his teachers had been in handling him. Of course, Max had never needed handling.

Max's treatment, given by injection, wouldn't last forever. It needed repeating every year or so. Zol worried that the medication's potential toxicity, which had come to light since Max had received it, would mean he'd be denied another dose when the current one wore off. Then what?

But life was like that, wasn't it? You couldn't store the good times in the bank. You had to spend them while they lasted. Single parenthood, made possible by Ermalinda, Max's nanny from the Philippines, was a happier state than Zol would have anticipated, except for the gnawing loneliness and the guilt that Max might never know the warmth of a loving mother. Zol's marriage to Francine had lasted only twenty-three months, and less than half of that he could remember with anything approaching fondness. Was that the way it was going to be with Colleen? Would the smooth sailing they were enjoying be counted in months? He hoped not. Max was wild about her. And so was Zol.

Max bounced from the front hall into the kitchen, leading Colleen by the hand. She gave Zol a soft kiss on the lips.

"What's that new scent?" Zol asked as he took her coat and she set her Nikon on the desk.

"Can you guess?" she said.

"Let's see . . . there's a blend of floral and citrus — orange blossoms, I'd say. Vanilla. And another spice, clove. And . . . oak moss."

She only used a touch of perfume, savoured best during intimate embraces.

"It's lovely," he said, meaning it. And so was she. A batik silk scrunchy at the nape of her neck encircled her long, sandy-blond ponytail, which cascaded over her left shoulder.

"Oak moss? Heavens, you have such an imagination. I'll have to remember that one."

"Are you starving?"

"Haven't eaten since breakfast." She scanned the kitchen. "That pie smells too delicious. Is that one of *your* creations, Max?"

Max grinned, then pierced the crust with his knife.

"Let me heat your plate," Zol told Colleen.

"I don't need it heated."

"Sorry, I can't serve a home-cooked meal on a cold plate. Goes against all my instincts and training." His appetite suddenly restored, he put two more plates in the oven and cleared the remains of his chicken noodle soup from the table.

Max gobbled his dinner and asked to be excused — to the computer room, of course. Zol redirected him to his bedroom where his math homework was still waiting. Colleen perked Max up with the reminder that she'd be taking him for ice cream later, while his dad went to his meeting with people from work.

"Then you'll read me a story?"

"Certainly," Colleen said, her eyes crinkling warmly.

After Max shuffled off, Colleen eyed the Star Pirates cellphone consigned to the top of the refrigerator. Almost out of sight but certainly not out of mind. "How did it go? He seems to have taken it very well."

"The birthday party got him refocused. The tears didn't last long. He loves bowling."

Zol had opened Max's monthly cellphone bill on Friday. Sixteen hundred dollars in new charges. Convinced there was a clerical error, he'd phoned the company immediately. Eventually, a live voice came on the line. There was no mistake, the woman said. The charges were real. The service would be cut off if the balance wasn't paid by the due date.

Zol gave himself a day and a half to cool down before the inevitable confrontation. He and Max had their heart-to-heart this morning. Through sobs and tears, Max admitted that he and his friends had downloaded "a few" Internet videos from YouTube. He caught the significance of the sixteen-hundred-dollar charges when Zol explained the same amount of money could have taken the two of them to Disney World for a week. Did that mean he'd never,

ever get to go to Disney World, Max had asked, sobbing heavily. Zol hugged him and reassured him that Disney was still a possibility, but only for boys who learned their lessons about their cellphones, and for a certain boy who didn't whine, not even once, about his phone being off limits for the next month.

Zol and Colleen finished supper. Zol cleared the table, then Colleen handed him his scarf at the front door. She wished him good luck with the Camelot situation, then closed her eyes and kissed him. Her tender, lingering embrace held the promise of many more. He squeezed her hard and finally let her go.

Alone in the car, his stomach in knots over the Prime Minister's unexpected scrutiny, Zol thought of Art Greenwood's mantra: *Make every week count, son.* Art said not to worry yourself sick over any single day, but aim instead for a major satisfaction every week.

What Zol wouldn't give to get the gastro corked at Camelot Lodge in the next week.

CHAPTER 3

Zol pulled open the door of the Nitty Gritty Café, his office-away-from-the-office, across the street from the health unit on Concession Street. He stamped the March slush from his shoes on the way in.

In the back corner, Natasha Sharma and Hamish Wakefield were already at the table permanently reserved for health-unit staff. Here, amid the Andean décor — Machu Picchu travel posters and woven blankets — Zol and his closest colleagues did their best brainstorming and troubleshooting.

Natasha was skimming the froth from her latte. The young epidemiologist put down her spoon and rose from her chair as Zol approached. Her engaging manner and obvious skills made her the cornerstone of the health unit's Communicable Disease Division. She had an uncanny knack for finding the one smidgen of evidence that explained an outbreak of food poisoning or a cluster of unexplained deaths. She always smelled deliciously of sandalwood, and Zol knew she had a morbid fear of foam clinging to the down on her upper lip.

Hamish was frowning at his hands and rubbing them with a paper serviette. A sticky spoon protruded from the honey jar beside his mug of green tea. Hamish hated unresolved stickiness and tolerated it neither on his fingers nor in his clinical cases. He'd confided to Zol that things were sticky on the home front as well. Boyfriend trouble. Hamish had been out of the closet for only a few months, and the bloom was off the rose of his first love affair.

Zol greeted his associates and thanked them for coming at short notice on a Sunday evening, then settled in a chair and pulled out the loonie he always kept in the pocket of his blazer. The one-dollar coin was not for spending but for fingering whenever life's tensions mounted. It was much cleaner than his father's chewing tobacco and didn't cause cancer.

"We can't let this go on any longer," Zol told them. "Dozens of diarrhea cases in the past two months, and three deaths in the past two weeks, the latest one this afternoon. We have to give Camelot our full attention. Hamish, I need you in on this."

"Old people do die, Zol," Hamish said, passing his hand over his perfectly squared blond flat-top. "How bad is the gastro? Are you sure the deaths are related to it?"

"When the Prime Minister's favourite aunt dies during an unresolved epidemic, everything is related."

"Her death is more important than any other?" Hamish said.

"I didn't mean that," Zol said. "But it's turned on the heat. The Prime Minister now knows my name. I can't tell you how creepy that feels. At least the boss is giving me carte blanche to get this solved as soon as possible. And that means bringing you in as my number-one consultant."

"Whatever you need, just say the word. Only you've got to keep Peter Trinnock away from me. His eyes give me the creeps. Why are they always bloodshot? Anyone ever check his thyroid? Maybe he's got Grave's, or is it Sjogren's?"

Zol and Natasha exchanged glances but said nothing. Trinnock's two-martini lunches were an open secret at the health unit. And Hamish Wakefield's skills at spot diagnosis were legendary. Trinnock did indeed have Sjogren's, a syndrome that dried out his eyes and mouth. The discomfort made him permanently cranky.

"These are active, healthy seniors we're talking about," Zol said. "And their illnesses fit a pattern. Fever, vomiting, crampy abdominal pain, and diarrhea. After three to five days, the infection either resolves or results in shock and rapid death."

"Each of the deaths was preceded by two days of severe headache," Natasha said. "Including Nellie Brownlow, the woman who died today. I spoke with her family doctor this afternoon."

"Sounds like stroke," Hamish said.

"Not according to Dr. Jamieson, the family doctor who takes care of Camelot Lodge." Natasha said. "He filled out Nellie's death certificate, identified gastroenteritis as the cause of her death. And hasn't mentioned stroke on any of the other certificates."

"Any similar outbreaks in any other retirement residences or nursing homes in our region?" Hamish asked.

"Nothing this sustained or severe," Natasha told him. "Short-lived outbreaks of gastro, mostly viral. No increased death rates."

"I'm familiar with that Camelot place. Remember the bat-bite fiasco?"

Zol didn't need reminding. About a year ago, a bat got loose in the sitting room while Art was playing the piano for a singalong. Five or six of the residents and a couple of the staff got bitten. Hamish waded into the frenzy, calmed everyone down, and conducted a series of rabies vaccine clinics on site. It was ultimately determined that the bat was rabies-free, but by then the incident had caused an unholy commotion.

Hamish rolled his eyes. "The managers, a Portuguese couple, Gus and Gloria. They were hysterical. And totally disorganized."

"There's hysteria of some sort in their food-handling practices," Zol said. "But we can't pinpoint what it is."

"Well, it's obvious," Hamish said. "They're doing *something* wrong." He paused and looked into the unseen distance as if conjuring a recollection. "Of course . . . you *are* aware of the case I had last month." He paused again and lifted an eyebrow, then raised his slim, professorial forefinger. "An elderly Portuguese woman with listeria in her bloodstream — septic shock, intensive care, the whole bit. After the bat thing, I couldn't help noticing her high-class address. Camelot Lodge on Eaglescliffe Avenue. When her daughter stormed into our ICU, all tears and bluster, I recognized the woman immediately — Camelot's manager, Gloria Oliveira. In the end, the old lady did fine and returned home to the Lodge."

Hamish's eyes darkened and he continued, "We'd had another listeria a month before that, which was a bit strange. We usually see just one case a year. The earlier case had meningitis. He was a much younger man from a different demographic entirely."

Hamish shuddered, then massaged his neck and looked away. Zol knew that a delirious patient had grabbed Hamish by the throat a couple of months ago and gripped him in a choke hold until Hamish nearly passed out. Had that attacker been Hamish's listeria patient, deranged by meningitis?

After several moments, Hamish collected himself and coughed into a tissue, which he folded and tucked into his jacket pocket. He shot Zol a look that said *I know what you're thinking and don't ask,* then squared his shoulders and turned to Natasha.

"Listeria is a bacterium, of course," Hamish told her in his professorial voice. "It lives harmlessly in the gut until it sneaks into the bloodstream of anyone with a depressed immune system and causes —"

"It's okay, Hamish. Natasha knows all about listeria."

It bothered Zol that Hamish patronized Natasha because she wasn't a physician. In many ways she was better than an MD. She was committed to the job without pretence or ego. Since starting at the health unit two years ago, she'd proven herself repeatedly, but Hamish didn't get it.

"In fact," Zol continued, "your hospital lab reported both those cases to us." Doctors, hospitals, and laboratories were required by law to report every listeria case to their local health unit. "And with all that diarrhea going on at Camelot, we looked into them carefully."

"There'd been no reports of listeria at Camelot Lodge in the previous five years," Natasha added, her face the picture of sincerity.

"And we verified that Gus and Gloria were following Ministry of Health guidelines about not serving deli meats to seniors."

Listeria was notorious for contaminating cold cuts then infecting the frail, the pregnant, and the elderly. It was one of those quirks of clinical medicine, a food-borne illness that didn't cause vomiting or diarrhea. The germ went in for the big kill — bloodstream infection complicated by shock, meningitis, and organ failure.

Hamish swept the crumbs from the scone he had ordered into his napkin and folded the paper into a perfect square. He placed it on his plate. "So what's the explanation for all that food-borne illness at the Lodge if there's nothing wrong with the food? Is it the water? The staff? The cutlery? The china? A faulty dishwasher? A wonky fridge? A resident with a grudge? You've got to check out everything."

"Okay, okay," said Zol, exchanging glances with Natasha. "We know the drill. Been through it already." Hamish's input had been disappointing. No new ideas to chew on. "We'll go in again. Find what we've missed, one way or another."

"Try going in unannounced," said Hamish. "Catch them before they have time to clean up their indiscretions." He paused, as though struck by an idea. "You know, when I was there giving all those rabies shots, the old folks were always dunking their doughnuts in their coffee. I thought it had something to do with their teeth. But I tried a couple of honey glazed. Darn things were hard as rocks."

"Art Greenwood says the doughnuts at Camelot must have fallen off an ox cart, back in biblical times," Zol said. "He and his pal Earl only eat them when they're desperate. Usually, they send their friend Phyllis Wedderspoon out to Tim's for fresh ones. In her Lincoln."

Zol had told Art to ask Gloria to bring in fresher doughnuts, but Art was afraid of upsetting her. Beneath Gloria's smarmy smile was a tyrant. Zol could see how the residents wouldn't want to get on the wrong side of her, not when she lived on site and was watching them twenty-four hours a day. Gloria's husband, Gus, was another matter. He always seemed to have a genuinely happy grin on his face. Nothing was too much trouble for him, and he appeared incapable of passing judgment. Art said the residents loved the way he always called them Mister and Miss. A few times Zol had seen Gus look uneasily at Gloria, as if he knew the consequences of provoking her fury. Surely, he would stand up to her if he thought she were placing the residents at risk.

"Gus and Gloria are definitely getting their baked goods on the cheap," Hamish said. "Through a back door someplace. If they were younger and dressed like hippies, I might think they were freegans."

"Freegans? What's a freegan?" Zol said. "Is it a coincidence that it rhymes with vegan?"

Hamish smiled and nodded. "You'd never believe me. Look up it up on the Internet. Wikipedia."

Natasha frowned, then fingered the dark curls that draped the nape of her neck. "I never found any outdated items in Camelot's fridges. But it sounds like those doughnuts were past their expiry dates."

Like a few more of Camelot's residents, Zol couldn't help thinking, if he didn't get that place cleaned up in a hurry.

CHAPTER 4

The next morning, Art Greenwood dipped a fossilized doughnut, a sour-cream glazed, into his tea. He had always loved Mondays. During his thirty-seven years at Northern Electric, Mondays had promised a fresh start and the chance that a simple idea would spark a blaze of innovation. His role in the invention of touch-tone service had been exciting at the time, but the Princess phone was nothing compared to the BlackBerry. Now *that* was an impressive device, though altogether too intrusive. Too bad he was past needing one. At his stage of life it would be merely an affectation.

Twenty-one years into his retirement, Mondays held another sort of excitement — an afternoon of bridge with Betty, Phyllis, and Earl. They never missed, except when struck so badly by that gastro thing that they couldn't make it through a hand without rushing to the toilet. Last night, his belly had churned like a cement mixer. He lay there terrified he was going to be up and down again, soiling his bed, messing the floor, getting poop on his scooter. But nothing came of it. He'd managed toast and a bowl of the chef's lukewarm soup for lunch. One day, Art hoped, Nick would get it together and serve his soup piping hot.

He glanced out the windows at the ice and snow pushed into grimy piles at the edge of the parking lot. He rubbed his burning shins and shifted his feet on the footrest of his scooter. Winter made him wistful about his curling-club days, before he turned seventy and his knees went bad. He'd loved the heart-stopping strategy on the rink, the cold beers afterwards in the cozy bar. Too bad his local club had never taken up wheelchair curling. He'd love to try it. But not among strangers.

"Arthur? Arthur, stop daydreaming," said Phyllis in her best Latin teacher voice. "Are you going to answer my three hearts?"

"Ah . . ." Art sat up straight and studied his hand. He added up his points again. Not enough to counter with four hearts. It would be safer to let Phyllis stay at three. Yes, she could probably make three hearts. Not enough for game, but better to be safe than sorry when Phyllis was your bridge partner. "I'll pass."

Phyllis fixed Earl with her uncompromising gaze. "What about you, Crabtree?"

"I'll pass, too," said Earl.

Earl must have a pretty weak hand. He usually enticed Phyllis, who was competitive to the end, to bid higher than she should. Then he'd laugh when she started swearing, in Latin of course, at not making her contract.

A high-pitched screech pierced the air. Then another, then the jerky, low-pitched moans of uncontrolled sobbing. Art dropped his cards face down on the table. He didn't need to look to know what was happening at the far side of the common room. Melvin's outbursts were becoming more frequent these days.

The poor soul, his face black and blue from falling out of his wheelchair last week, was shouting through his sobs. Once he got started there was no stopping him. Always the same words, over and over, like a mantra. "Never saw them. Never saw them. I tell you, I never saw them."

Two aides rushed to Melvin's side. They shushed him, patted his hands, and smoothed his wild hair. The more they patted, the louder his mantra. The pair glanced nervously around the room.

They must be watching for Gloria, expecting her to sweep in and escalate Melvin's sobbing with her nursery-school patter. Her high-pitched prattle never settled anyone, just made them feel angry at being coddled. Art often wondered how Gloria ever got into this business in the first place. She had neither the temperament nor the organizational skills. She should have stuck with cleaning houses and keeping books. Her husband, Gus, was okay. His smile was genuine and he was an imaginative handyman. He could fix anything with a piece of wire and a roll of duct tape. Problem was, his low-cost repairs never lasted longer than a week.

One aide plopped Melvin's tartan blanket on his lap while the other wheeled him briskly around the corner toward the elevator and the seclusion of his room behind the Mountain Wing's locked door, one floor up. Art seldom went up there. The place was as bleak as a hospital ward and always smelled of poop. Its eight beds reminded everyone in the cozy Belvedere Wing that the next stage of the life cycle was waiting for them on the other side of the door — a linoleum-tiled purgatory at the brink of eternity.

"Poor Melvin," said Earl. "It rips me apart to see him that way." The look on Earl's face said, *We're all going to end up like that.* "Dementia is so demeaning. Maybe it's just as well they rarely let him out of his room."

Betty looked shocked at the remark. She opened her mouth as if to speak, then pursed her lips in diplomatic silence. During her thirty years as personal assistant to a prime minister and a string of federal cabinet ministers, she'd perfected the art of holding her tongue. In the close quarters of a retirement residence, diplomacy was a valuable skill. And, as far as Art was concerned, it added greatly to her charm. But still, she was no pushover.

Earl drew his hands to his vest and squared his shoulders. He read Betty's discomfort and his face softened. "Forgive my candour. But don't you think it would be awful if one of his former students stumbled in here and saw him raving like that? If it were me, I'd want to be kept well out of sight."

Art looked at Earl and nodded his agreement. For years Earl and Melvin, both professors, had offices in the same building at Caledonian University. Earl's specialty was European history. Melvin's had been the impact of war on civilian populations. The three of them, Art, Earl, and Melvin, had seen action together in World War Two. North Africa. Of course, everyone at Camelot had lived through the war — as combatants or munitions workers, wireless operators or distressed civilians. The conflict still stalked the halls like a permanent resident.

Phyllis studied the cards in her hand, too preoccupied with making her three hearts to voice an opinion. Bridge was the only thing that kept her quiet.

Betty lifted the spoon from her saucer. It tinkled against the china as she stirred her milky tea. "Shall we start? It's my lead." As soon as she'd placed her six of diamonds on the table, Art laid his dummy hand face up and left it to Phyllis to make their contracted tricks. He reversed his scooter and headed for the piano.

The keyboard was locked. Damn. It was supposed to be open every afternoon. Why did Gloria insist on locking it? It wasn't as though anyone would steal the ivories.

"Has anyone seen Gloria?" Art called to any of the dozen souls in the common room who might listen.

A few heads lifted from their jigsaws and knitting, but most eyes stayed closed in afternoon slumber. "What'd he say?" was the general answer from a few puzzled faces squinting from the sofas and wingback chairs.

A woman named Gertie, with fat red cheeks and an even fatter bottom, dropped her needles to her lap and said, "Honoria? She's gone, poor thing. Died last year."

The elevator pinged and Gloria appeared, leading two men in white shirts and black business suits. Art stiffened at the thought of what they'd be wheeling behind them. Earl had dubbed it running the final gauntlet: being wheeled out of the elevator, past the tall windows lining the far wall of the common room, and out the side exit. All in full view of your friends.

Gloria tugged at the lapels of her suit jacket as she strode to the middle of the room. Her lips formed a fake smile while her eyes scanned the faces as if looking for trouble. Then came that damn nursery-room whine. "I'm afraid, my dears, I am having some bad news."

Art scooted to the bridge table. It was better to be sitting close to your friends when Gloria made one of her pronouncements.

Phyllis put down her cards. "Are you going to tell us who that was on their way to Craig & Lafferty?"

"You know I'm not allowed to say, Miss Wedderspoon. It's our policy that —"

Phyllis rolled her eyes and muttered, "Of course, *res arcana.*" She turned to Art. "As always, the matter is confidential. We'll have to read about it ourselves in the obits."

Gloria crossed the room and stood beside Gertie. She never got any flack from Gertie, who'd been knitting the same purple scarf for the three years Art had been at Camelot.

Phyllis leaned into the bridge table and cupped her hand to her mouth. "Did you see that pair of legs dangling off the stretcher? It must be poor Judge Nesbitt in that bag. He was one long drink of water, and I know he had the runs. And a headache."

Betty shivered. When she clasped her hands together they looked like a pair of sparrows trembling on the table. In a deliberate motion, as if directing Phyllis to do the same, she set her jaw, turned intently toward Gloria, and awaited the announcement.

"As I was trying to tell to you," Gloria continued, "I need you to return to your suites. The health department informs me that we are now in a contact-isolation situation."

"Not again," said a tiny woman dwarfed by the cabbage roses of the loveseat.

"Is it influenza or gastroenteritis?" Art asked. Zol made sure he knew the difference between one type of flu and another.

Gloria hesitated as if wondering how much information was appropriate to divulge. "Gastroenteritis."

"I hope it's just in the Mountain Wing," said someone.

"How many cases so far?" Phyllis asked.

Gloria glared at her.

"I know," Phyllis replied. "You're *not at liberty to say.*"

"We have a right to know. How many people are sick?" Earl called above the hubbub.

"My dears, my dears." Gloria's nursery voice was gone, and with it all pretence of a smile. "Please. Calm yourselves. The situation, we have it under control."

"We'd better do as she asks," said Betty.

Earl put up his hand. "What about our supper?"

The same thought had occurred to Art.

"The staff, they are gonna serve dinner at four-thirty, as usual. Till then, please go to your rooms. No visitors in your suites. No outside guests, and —" Gloria pierced Art with her gaze, then turned it on Betty "— no fellow residents." She pointed at the dining-room entrance. "We're gonna have a hand-wash station over there. And don't forget to pump."

Art heard a noise at the rear door and turned to see the two men from Craig & Lafferty pushing an empty gurney toward the elevator. The taller of the two strode ahead, his eyes furtively sweeping the sitting room. He was trying to hide it, but there was no mistaking the black object folded under his arm. Body bag number two.

CHAPTER 5

Tuesday morning, Zol turned off Aberdeen Street into Eaglescliffe Avenue. And into Narnia. It might as well have been a fantasy world for all the resemblance the cul-de-sac bore to the rest of the lower city. Gorgeous mansions sat like haughty, overdressed dowagers at a nineteenth-century garden party. At the far end, the sheer face of the Niagara Escarpment defended the enclave from the riffraff to the south with its rampart of wooded limestone. Again, Zol felt uncouth driving his muddy minivan into such opulence. Everyone here would have a Porsche or a Mercedes tucked in the garage.

Camelot Lodge occupied one of the most well-known heritage structures in Hamilton. It had been built in the 1880s as a mansion for an industrialist's family. Now it loomed on a snowy island in the circular roadway, where it boasted three stories of intricate stone-work, a tall square tower, a round turret, and a forest of chimneys.

"I guess the previous owners didn't fuss over their vows of poverty," Zol told Natasha, who was beside him in the passenger seat.

"Sorry?" she said.

"I thought you knew. A few years ago it was full of nuns. A Catholic convent."

The massive slate roof capped the original structure and the boxy addition beside it, which included the elevator shaft and glassed-in fire escape. Despite its storied grandeur, the place looked drab in grimy, leafless March. It would look better in May when its lawns and trees turned green.

An anxious face peered through a mullioned upper window and quickly disappeared. A wild-haired soul in a pale nightgown rapped her fist at another window and called inaudibly through the triple-pane glass.

"Does your grandfather like living there?"

Art felt like a grandfather, so Zol didn't correct her. "He appreciates the company and the amenities, I think. A single room with his own bath and toilet. Says he's glad the Lodge is a small operation that doesn't feel like an institution."

Thirty active seniors lived in the original part of the building, known as the Belvedere Wing. It was a shame the renovators had removed the grand staircase, which Zol had seen in old photographs, to make space for an enlarged dining room and several more bedrooms.

"The common sitting room is just the right size," Natasha said. "Cozy but not cramped. And I love its chintz curtains."

Zol never noticed curtains and had yet to figure out exactly what chintz was. "Don't think there's any chintz in the Mountain Wing infirmary. According to Art and Earl, it's the dark empire on the far side of the moon. I've never had occasion to go in there."

Natasha pointed to the second floor of the addition and made a face. "You haven't missed much. Bare walls, ugly blinds on the windows. Eight patients, in four double rooms. All in various stages of dementia, poor things."

Zol thought of his parents, currently on a month-long golfing holiday in Florida. They lived thirty minutes west of Hamilton, off Highway 403. His dad was pushing seventy but still active on the farm and secretary of the Ginseng Growers Association of Brant County. He'd switched from growing tobacco to harvesting ginseng seven years ago, soon after Zol started his public-health training. Zol couldn't imagine his mother, so fastidious about her appearance, as anything less than a commanding presence in her own home. She was a super cook and a whiz at crosswords and Sudoku.

He had no warm and fuzzy illusions about nursing homes and retirement residences, no matter how many luxuries they purported to offer. He knew they were businesses, first and foremost. And visited by battalions who packed the parking lots: doctors, nurses, chaplains, chiropractors, chiropodists, physios, pharmacists, herbalists, hairdressers, and the delivery guys who lugged in everything from flowers to oxygen tanks. Today, only three vehicles sat in the lot: a blue Dodge van, a grey Chevy Malibu, and Phyllis Wedderspoon's long, snow-white '72 Lincoln.

The place was owned by someone offshore, a Taiwanese, Zol had heard. The Oliveiras were resident managers with their own apartment on the ground floor. Gus, who used to be in construction, did the maintenance. Gloria, who had once been a bookkeeper and office manager, was clearly in charge.

Zol read the closed-to-visitors notice on the front door as he held it open for Natasha. He'd ordered the Lodge quarantined the moment she'd told him about yesterday's deaths. Of course, no one used the word *quarantine* these days — too frightening for the sensibilities of the modern public, too much like the nineteenth century and its epidemics of smallpox and typhus. The politically correct term was *closed to visitors*, with instructions to take enquiries to the front desk. The elusive pathogen had become a vicious adversary, its power escalating. The damn thing had killed five people in the past two weeks. Zol found it impossible not to think of the Q-word. He pictured the Prime Minister's assistant at his desk beneath the Peace Tower, the name *Zol Szabo* scrawled on his to-do list.

Inside the lobby, Zol and Natasha pumped hand sanitizer onto their palms. Zol usually made a show of rubbing a double shot of the pungent antiseptic over every centimetre of his hands. But there was no audience to impress. The common room was dark and deserted. A ball of yarn sat forgotten on a sofa cushion, and pieces of a jigsaw puzzle lay scattered across a card table.

He waved away the smell of the alcoholic cleanser and swallowed a cough, then greeted the sombre-faced woman at the reception desk. He explained they were from the health unit, here for another inspection. Her name tag said Maria, and she was in no mood to offer a cheery welcome. She was probably frightened about coming to work, but had no choice if she were to put food on her family's table — tortillas and refried beans by the whiffs of cumin and chipotle that fought the lingering odour of the sanitizer. Zol's well-honed sense of smell told him more about a person's traits and habits than any photograph. He followed Natasha as the woman led them through the hollow, unlit dining room and into the kitchen.

The receptionist disappeared without a word, leaving Zol facing Nick, the chef. He of the lukewarm soup Art complained so much about. The man stood two inches taller than Zol, about six-three. He had a slim waist and the cultivated pecs of a cyclist or soccer player who did weights on the side.

Nick leaned against his counter, an act of possession. "None of this has anything to do with my kitchen," he told Zol. "Me and the boys, we run a tight ship. Eh guys?" His prominent brow and massive jaw framed a face that radiated too much confidence for Zol's liking.

Nick's three helpers, men in their twenties, were absorbed in the chopping, stirring, and plating of impending lunch for thirty. One man was tall and skinny with blue-black skin, perhaps a Somali, Zol thought; one short, Asian, with hooded eyes and a pockmarked face; the third, stocky with a gleaming white scalp. All three raised their heads briefly from their tasks long enough to gape at Natasha.

Natasha ignored the stares directed at her discreetly camouflaged cleavage and removed her clipboard from her briefcase, then set about her inspection. She checked the refrigerators and dishwasher for the required temperature probes and asked to see the logs that documented the twice-daily readings. She inspected both sinks and ran the water to be sure it got steamy hot. She checked every cupboard for general cleanliness, then looked more closely for signs of rodents — footprints and droppings. She opened bins of rice and other grains and probed them with a spoon for mould and weevils. She opened the refrigerator and looked in the crisper, sniffed every container, and examined every best-before date.

Meanwhile, Zol looked in a few cupboards, then dropped his doctor facade and tried speaking casually with Nick, chef to chef. It took some time for the man to loosen up, but eventually they exchanged details of their culinary training. Zol outlined his studies in Stratford, Ontario, before shifting gears and heading to medical school a decade ago; Nick talked about earning his ticket at Toronto's George Brown College. They traded stories of chefs who roared at their staff like boot-camp sergeants.

As Nick relaxed he pushed up his sleeves. He rubbed at an ugly patch of skin near his right elbow. Was it eczema? Psoriasis? Impetigo? The crusty lesion was perched at the crest of the tattooed waterfall Zol could see cascading down Nick's forearm.

"What are the Oliveiras like to work for?" Zol asked, finding it difficult not to gawk at Nick's forearm.

Nick caught himself scratching and quickly rolled down his sleeves. "Okay, I guess. But you know the Portuguese."

"Sorry?"

Nick shrugged and shifted his feet.

Zol raised his eyebrows and fixed Nick with his gaze.

"Skinflints," Nick said finally. "Never met a penny they couldn't squeeze into a dollar's worth of supplies."

"How does that affect you?"

"For one thing, they never let me do none of the shopping."

Zol understood that grumble. A good chef liked to choose his own quality ingredients, the cornerstone of a good meal.

A hint of pink flushed Nick's granite jaw. "Like," he continued, "I give Gus a shopping list and all, but he never buys me the best stuff. He snaps up the leftover baked goods and produce at closing time, when the store is practically giving them away."

"I see you've got a lot of no-name products."

"Nothing wrong with no-name. It's the wilted veggies I hate. Okay for soups and purées. But a nice Sunday dinner? Forget it."

Puréed meals would be the ultimate drag for a cook. No art in them, and little flavour. But that's all the Mountain Wing patients would be able to handle without teeth. And most of them had forgotten how to swallow. "I guess you whiz a lot of stuff in the blender in a place like this," Zol said.

Nick gave a rueful smile at being understood by a colleague. "I'll say."

Natasha pulled a large plastic bag from the bottom of a chest freezer. She grunted at the effort of dislodging it. Frosty condensation obscured the bag's contents, but Zol could just make out what appeared to be a jumble of vegetables — corn, celery, broccoli, and a couple of beets.

"What's this?" Natasha asked. "This stuff should be labelled and dated."

"Hey —" Nick chuckled "— we use everything up so fast we don't waste time with dating."

"But what is it?" said Zol. "At least the bag should be labelled."

Nick shrugged. "*I* can tell they're veggies."

"All thrown together?" said Natasha. She lifted out another bag. "And what about these?"

"Bread and baked goods. Gus puts everything in the freezer after his shopping trips."

Natasha replaced the heavy bags and shut the freezer. "Well, I suppose it doesn't matter if the vegetables are all mixed up if you're going to zap them in the blender anyway."

Zol fingered the loonie in his pocket as he watched Nick taste the soup the Asian man with the pockmarked cheeks had been stirring on the stove. Even if the Oliveiras did their shopping at the end of the day, and at down-market places like Food-Club and Price-Slashers, it wouldn't cause food poisoning. But it bothered him to see good food thrown carelessly together like that. Even if it didn't violate any regulations, it seemed a sacrilege. The quality of the meals at places like this was a constant preoccupation among the residents. And why not? They had a right to their money's worth.

"What about the meals in the dining room?" Zol asked. "Surely, the Belvedere Wing residents expect good food?"

"Yeah," Nick agreed, "they know a proper meal when they see one. Get gussied up for dinner every night. And won't touch slimy zucchini or mushy cauliflower, even with the brown spots cut off." He turned to his helpers and chuckled. "Gus's beaten-up broccoli comes back untouched every time, eh boys?"

The men nodded, tight-lipped, except for the Somali beanpole fellow whose toothy grin lit up his dark face. Zol pictured them scraping "untouched" vegetables off dirty plates and whizzing them into soup. It wouldn't be so bad if they boiled them before recycling them. Testing the soup for infectious pathogens was suddenly a top priority.

Nick chuckled nervously, a cast of guilt in his eyes. "Tranh hates the smell of broccoli no matter how it's cooked."

While Natasha checked out the pantry, Zol poked around the kitchen. It felt good to be back inside a professional place. His own kitchen gave him a great view over the city and the lake, but a home kitchen was small potatoes. This place had real muscle. The penny-pinching Oliveiras hadn't scrimped on equipment. The gas stove sported six turbo burners. The pots had thick copper bottoms. And the huge cast-iron frying pan gleamed with the beautifully cured surface only an expert knew how to care for.

Zol approached Tranh, the short guy standing by the stove, and asked if he could stir the soup. He'd always loved the satisfaction of swirling a wooden spoon through a hearty mix of stock, herbs, and vegetables. Soup could be difficult — it wasn't easy to strike the perfect blend of flavours. You didn't want it tasting as though you'd dropped a mess of leftovers into a pot, added salt and water, and stirred like hell. The only way to get soup right was to gradually adjust the seasonings as you tasted it. This one had the aroma of way too much cilantro, probably added to cover the bitterness of over-ripe broccoli. He pulled a clean spoon from a drawer and dipped it into the pot, but caught himself before putting the spoon in his mouth. The spoon felt barely warm. He looked at his watch. Eleven forty-five. This batch had a long way to go before it got hot enough for lunch. He took one of Natasha's specimen containers and filled it with a ladleful of soup.

They wrapped up their inspection with a look at the hot-water tank and a careful assessment of the staff toilet, then returned to the front lobby and asked the receptionist to locate the manager, Gloria Oliveira.

The woman at the desk looked no more confident at her station than she had forty-five minutes earlier. She picked up the phone as though it were a hand grenade, then mumbled something into it. "Mrs. Gloria say she down in a few minutes." The woman hesitated and stared at the closed-to-visitors sign beside her desk. Clearly, she had no idea what to do with visitors when none were allowed. She studied her fingernails, as if drawing inspiration from them, then pointed to a pair of wingback chairs in front of a coffee table in the common room. "Please, sit. Like a coffee?"

Zol stifled a shudder and turned to Natasha. There was no mistaking the look on her face. He shook his head for both of them. "Thank you. No."

They settled in the chairs, not for comfort but for the chance to talk out of earshot of the reception desk.

"Gloria Oliveira's got some cheek," Zol said, "keeping us sitting on our hands down here. Doesn't she know her licence is on the line?" He'd expected the manager to storm into the kitchen as soon as they arrived. He'd braced for her bravado and solemn assertions that *we take food safety extremely seriously here at Camelot Lodge.* What was she doing all this time?

Natasha tapped her checklist with her slender forefinger. "Nick isn't among her greatest fans, but he does run a tight kitchen." Natasha's parade of brightly coloured shoes had been the talk of the office ever since her arrival, fresh with her Master's. It seemed her latest indulgence was her fingernails. Today they were varnished the deep red, near purple, of a rich Shiraz. "A couple of minor deviations," she continued, "but no violations."

"I'm worried about the soup. We'll see what the lab has to tell us about it." He pointed to Natasha's case. "How many samples did you get in total?"

"About a dozen. The usual suspects — the ketchup bottle, mayonnaise jar, some slimy lettuce and broccoli from the crisper, a big thing of gravy from the back of the fridge, the drains from the three sinks."

"Unless things have changed since your last inspection, none of those cultures are going to show any pathogens."

"Won't even show any mould. We've been through every crumb in that kitchen before. Ever since their first gastro cases." She thumbed through her sheets, found what she was looking for, then added, "This whole thing started with four gastros on January eleventh. Total number reported now stands at thirty-one." She pulled at the curls beside her ear. "And five deaths."

Only three people had died at Camelot in the previous calendar year. It was a wonder the papers hadn't got hold of the story and done the math. They were bound to soon and shout from the headlines: *Cozy Camelot Turns Death Trap.*

"How many active cases at the moment?" he asked.

"It changes every day. But among the independent seniors on the Belvedere Wing, we know about four." She looked skeptically at her notepad.

Zol shared her skepticism. Unreported cases of flu, gastro, and other contagious infections were the bugbears of public health. Getting to the bottom of outbreaks in residential institutions — bringing epidemics under control by isolating their cases and pinpointing their sources — was close to impossible if many of the cases were not reported to the health unit. Even the most conscientious managers fudged the numbers. There was strong incentive for under-reporting: if cases weren't reported to the authorities, the outbreak didn't seem so bad, there was little for families to get upset about, life could go on as usual, and the problem might go away on its own.

"Did you notice that rash on Nick's arm?" Zol asked.

"That tattoo was gross."

"Dermatitis of some sort. And infected, by the look of it." He pulled two loonies from his pocket and juggled them. "You know, this could be toxigenic food poisoning — staph aureus from Nick's rash contaminating everything in that kitchen."

"He let me take a culture of his rash. But I don't think our problem is staphylococcus aureus. It never showed up in our previous samples. And doesn't staph food poisoning start with violent vomiting?"

"Hurling your guts out is the dominant feature. That hasn't been the pattern here, eh?"

"Abdominal cramps, diarrhea, and fever."

"Staph food poisoning doesn't cause fever," Zol said. "But we'll check it out." If the swab from Nick's arm did grow staph aureus, he'd have to ban the chef from the kitchen until the infection was controlled. "Until the results come back, he'll have to keep that arm covered."

Two minutes later Gloria Oliveira shuffled toward the side exit behind two men in black suits pushing a stretcher. A heavy sheet covered the unmistakable shape of a corpse. Zol watched Gloria's shoulders heave as she patted the body and watched it disappear into a waiting black van. Camelot's sixth death since January.

Dark circles ringed the woman's bloodshot eyes as she approached. She wiped the tears from her face, let out a few shuddering breaths, then smoothed her blouse. Zol's impatience melted at the sight of her distress.

"My mother," she said, blowing her nose. She turned and stared at the side exit.

"Your mother?" said Natasha, her eyes wide in disbelief. "Oh my goodness. How awful for you."

"I am so sorry," said Zol. "Here, you better have a seat."

Gloria sat down and the three of them stared at the carpet in awkward silence.

"She refuse to go back to hospital," Gloria said, finally. "Said she rather die."

"Was she ill for a long time?" asked Zol. It would be easier if the woman's death was one of those blessings, a release from a drawn-out, painful affliction.

"No. Until Christmas, she was perfect. Just a little arthritis and only seventy-six years old. Then, sick three times in one month. And two days ago, sick again. Refuse any doctor see her. Headache last night. High fever this morning. And then . . ." She covered her face.

Zol hated to rub salt into the woman's grief, but he had to ask. "Did your mother have diarrhea?"

Too choked up to speak, the poor woman just nodded.

Zol knew that Gloria had sponsored her widowed mother's emigration from Portugal a few years back. Raimunda Ferreira lived with Gus and Gloria in the manager's apartment. Zol had often seen her dusting the windows, even vacuuming the carpets. Natasha reminded him that Hamish Wakefield had looked after her at Caledonian University Medical Centre in February. She hadn't had gastro, but septic shock caused by listeria monocytogenes.

Zol thought back to a year ago when listeria had turned the country upside down. Two dozen seniors, mostly around Toronto, died after eating deli meats contaminated with listeria monocytogenes bacteria. The source turned out to be cold cuts prepared by a prestigious Canadian meat packer. Under the media spotlight, the provincial Ministry of Health and the federal Food Inspection Agency forced the company into acting swiftly. But it took weeks, and a growing string of deaths, to discover that the listeria was lurking deep inside the factory's meat-slicing machines. No one could promise that such contamination wouldn't happen again; it seemed that listeria in deli meat was almost an essential ingredient, like table salt and nitrites. Warnings went out that anyone with a compromised immune system — especially seniors and cancer patients —

should never consume ready-to-eat deli meats. But the damn bug was ubiquitous and impossible to avoid completely.

Gloria fixed Zol with her gaze. "Doctor — you must tell me where it comes from, my mother's infection. This fever. The doctors treat her and she get it again."

With Gloria following ministry guidelines about never serving deli meats, had her mother made clandestine trips for salami subs at a franchise sandwich shop? It looked like her final illness was either epidemic gastro that spun out of control, or a relapse of the listeria that had landed her in intensive care back in February. He'd ask the coroner to perform a post-mortem blood culture. If listeria had invaded her bloodstream again, it would show up there. It would be hopeless to ask for a full autopsy. Families never wanted them, and old people's deaths were never deemed suspicious without undeniable evidence such as neck bruises or gunshot wounds.

A few moments later they followed Gloria up the stairs and stood in silence while she unlocked the door to the Mountain Wing.

The place looked orderly enough, but the stench was horrendous. The air, thick with the smell of flatus and feces, hit Zol like a punch in the gut. The smell evoked a loathing he knew was bordering on pathological. One of the final torpedoes that sank his doomed marriage to the ever-flaky Francine had been her complete lack of sense of smell. Day after day he'd come home from work to the smell of Max's dirty diapers rotting in a pail, the house filled with that unbearable stench. And here it was again. He watched Natasha wince at the moaning coming from a room down the hall. The sound was almost as noxious as the smell. The cries told of loneliness and terror, unanswered except by tearful echoes from across the hall. Where were the staff?

A compact woman, no more than five feet tall, slipped out of a room. Her pastel top and matching pants had lost all semblance of crispness, and her sweaty brow was framed by strands of straight black hair escaping from barrettes askew on her head.

Gloria pocketed her Kleenex and straightened her shoulders. "Amelia," she called as the nurse dashed toward another room. "Dr. Szabo is here from health department. I want you to show him around." Gloria caught Zol's eye and continued, "Show him what a good job you girls do with isolation and hand washing." She flicked her gaze to the bottle of hand sanitizer on the wall.

The nurse turned and quickly pumped a measure into her palm.

Zol smiled at the diminutive woman staring at her shoes, clearly tired and apprehensive, yet rubbing her hands extra vigorously. He turned to Gloria and asked, "How many nurses do you have on this ward?"

"Staff of ten."

Zol looked up and down the hallway. This was a small ward with a pair of two-bed rooms on either side of the corridor, a nursing station at the far end, an alcove packed with supplies, a tub room, a staff toilet, and a couple of utility rooms. Where was the bustle? A staff of ten should make a lot more commotion than was evident here.

Natasha's eyes swept the bleak cinderblock landscape. "And how many are on duty at the moment?"

Gloria bit her lip. "Two. Amelia is the RN and we have Cora, fully qualified PSW."

Just one nurse and a personal support worker to feed and bathe and medicate and clean up after eight incontinent, elderly patients with the runs? It was absurd. And impossible.

The Mountain Wing was officially a nursing home that fell under a litany of regulations from the province's Ministry of Health and Long-Term Care. In contrast, the Belvedere Wing was officially a retirement residence; governments left those places alone, unregulated. It looked like Gloria Oliveira was playing loose with ministry staffing standards in the Mountain Wing.

"How many patients do you have here?" Zol asked.

"The ward holds eight," she said.

"And the beds are full?"

"One is free."

Natasha opened her briefcase and pulled out her pen and notepad. "And how many have diarrhea?"

Gloria looked to Amelia for the answer. "Three," Amelia whispered.

"We don't have reports of any of them," said Natasha. "Only the four in the Belvedere Wing."

Gloria bristled. "They just started this morning."

Zol studied the hallway again. There were no isolation carts outside any of the rooms. No easy access to gowns and gloves for the beleaguered staff rushing from patient to patient. No wonder gastro was flying through the Lodge. If he didn't get this place sorted out in the next few days, Peter Trinnock would see him dispatched to North Overshoe, if only to satisfy the Prime Minister.

"Where are the isolation carts?" he asked.

Gloria pointed to a doorway down the hall. "In the utility room."

"You need to put them outside every door," said Zol.

Gloria looked surprised at such a revelation. "We got only one cart."

"Ideally," said Natasha, "you should have four. One for each room."

"But this is small ward. Where we put three carts?"

"You could place the cart in the hallway where it's easy to access," said Natasha. "And make sure the staff always wear gloves when in contact with patients and their . . ." She paused, searching for a discreet way to phrase it. "Secretions."

Gloria frowned and crossed her arms. Zol sensed her tallying the cost of purchasing hundreds of vinyl gloves and laundering scores of isolation gowns. Infection control didn't come cheap, but this was a virulent strain. One that may have cost her own mother her life.

CHAPTER 6

When Art Greenwood asked Gloria to unlock the Heintzman's keyboard on Wednesday morning, he could almost feel the scowl in her response. In yet another of her edicts, she replied that a singalong was not appropriate, considering the ongoing *situation*. She was allowing the residents to use the common room this morning, but that was as far as she was willing to go. Eventually, he persuaded her that closing Camelot to visitors didn't mean the residents couldn't enjoy the piano; for heaven's sake, singing didn't spread disease. Of course, she knew damn well that the natives were getting restless and needed a boost in morale. None of them had ever seen such heavy body-bag traffic.

While shaving this morning he'd heard a piece on the radio, a song featuring Josh somebody-or-other. It was the sort of thing that Betty, Phyllis, and the other girls would love — soft and dreamy. Eager to keep the tune in his head so he could pick out the chording, he wrote down the first line of the lyric in his green notebook. Over the years, he'd nearly filled the book with first lines, organized by category. Show tunes, jazz standards, songs from the war, old favourites, and a few hymns and spirituals. All he had to do was read the words of the first line, and the entire melody would pop into his head. After that, his hands knew what to do. And as long as he took his Xanucox arthritis capsules twice a day as prescribed by Dr. Jamieson, the old fingers stayed limber enough.

He was fingering the melody of the new piece with his right hand when the sharp clatter of Phyllis Wedderspoon's footsteps announced her entry through the Lodge's front door. The keys to her Lincoln jingled in her hand as she stomped on the mat.

"Back already?" he called as she approached.

"The library is never busy on a Wednesday morning. The staff are just twiddling their thumbs until the onslaught of toddlers at one o'clock." She loosened her scarf and held up two books. "I found what I wanted: *The Secret Life of Goya*, and . . ." She shuffled the books and peered at the covers. "And . . . oh yes. *Understanding Dali.*"

Art chuckled. "I didn't know that was possible."

She paused, her face frozen in a rare look of puzzlement. Then her frown dissolved and she replied, "Oh, you mean Dali. Yes, quite. Our professor says to appreciate the paintings is to understand the artists behind them." The course in art history she was taking at Caledonian University was her latest preoccupation. Before that it had been conversational Spanish — or was it Italian? And before that, something about architecture. Phyllis did love her courses. And her daily trot inside Lime Ridge Mall, which she called her thirty minutes to strong bones and a sound mind. She told anyone who would listen about her three keys to aging well: academic classes to stretch the mind, regular exercise to tone the body, and friendships with younger folk to broaden the horizons. Of course, when you were eighty-three, ninety-nine percent of the planet's inhabitants qualified as younger folk.

Art pointed to the hand sanitizer on the piano, a reminder of the *new normal* at Camelot Lodge. "Now Phyllis, I didn't see you pump on the way in."

"I know," she puffed. She dropped her keys into her handbag and set her books on a side table. "There," she said as she pumped two dollops of sticky liquid into her palm. "Are you satisfied?"

"It's not me who has to be satisfied. They'll take away our in-and-out privileges if any more of us come down with the runs."

Art didn't mind the lack of visitors. In fact, it made for a welcome change of pace at the Lodge. He would hate, however, to give up their weekly trips to Tim Hortons. It was a struggle to transfer on his gammy legs from his scooter into the backseat of Phyllis's Lincoln, but it was worth it. When four or five of them sat parked in her vehicle, sipping coffees and munching fresh doughnuts from the drive-through, he felt like a youth again. It was sure nice to bite into a soft, warm doughnut that bore no relation to the biblical relics served at the Lodge.

He turned to the piano and started chording with his left hand and refining the melody with his right. Not bad, he decided. Betty would like this. A few minutes later he resolved the final chord, laid his hands in his lap, and was surprised by the clapping behind him. He turned to see an audience of four: Betty and Phyllis together on a loveseat, Maude and Myrtle seated at the card table, hunched over their jigsaw puzzle.

"That was lovely," said Betty. Her voice didn't sound right. It was weak and trembling.

He backed his scooter away from the piano and rolled to Betty's side. "You don't look too well, my dear," he said, taking her hand. "Something wrong?"

Betty looked down at their hands in her lap. "It's nothing," she whispered. "I'll be fine."

"That's not what Dr. Jamieson said," Phyllis corrected. "He's putting her on an antibiotic."

Art couldn't suppress the alarm he knew was lighting up his face. "Not another bout of —"

Betty shook her head. "Don't worry. No fever. And no upset tummy. Just . . . You know, bladder problems. A few days of antibiotics and I'll be fine." Her face brightened and she pointed to the front door. "Look. My prescription must be arriving this very moment. There's Vik."

Art watched Viktor Horvat, the owner of Steeltown Apothecary, standing beside the reception desk and rubbing sanitizer onto his hands. Vik arrived once a week with a cartful of medications arranged in those easy-open blister pack things that kept you from forgetting which pills to take at what time. He and the ever-canny Gloria had some sort of exclusive arrangement to provide the prescriptions for everyone at Camelot. Vik was a broad-shouldered fellow with a large Slavic head. He never wore a hat, and Art reckoned that was probably because he couldn't find one to fit. When Vik first started coming to the Lodge three years ago, shortly after Art moved in, he'd been jovial and charming, the steel cap on his front tooth flashing disarmingly when he smiled. Art hadn't seen a smile on that face for months, and the steel-capped tooth now seemed like a crudely fashioned weapon lurking behind his lips.

"He's starting to put weight back on," said Phyllis. "Lord knows, he needed to." Vik had spent a few days in intensive care at Caledonian University Medical Centre at Christmastime. He'd had some sort of dangerous infection. But he'd stopped smiling long before taking sick.

"He's been through a lot, poor fellow," said Betty.

"His English is atrocious," Phyllis said. "It's a wonder he can read the names of your medicines with any sort of accuracy."

Phyllis was proud of the fact she didn't need prescription medications and took only a baby aspirin once a day, which she purchased at Wal-Mart whenever she noticed the price was discounted.

"He deserves our compassion," Betty said. "Imagine losing almost your entire family to a hit-and-run driver and then starting your life over in a new country."

"It's all very well for us to take in these Balkan refugees, but it's another matter entirely to let them work at exacting jobs where . . ."

Art had become adept at tuning Phyllis out when she got going on her soap box. Betty was right. Vik did deserve compassion. From the recent stories on the front page of the *Hamilton Spectator*, it was clear he'd been having a year filled with misery and irony. His son — the only survivor of the car crash that had killed Vik's wife and daughters back in Yugoslavia — had been locked up for months in a Mexican prison, awaiting trial on drug charges. According to the *Spectator*, the young man claimed he was innocent, caught in the wrong place at the wrong time. But the news stories left one wondering what a young fellow was doing in Juarez, a city known more for drug deals than the tourist trade. No one at Camelot, not even Phyllis, had dared ask Vik for clarification.

No matter where the truth lay, Vik hadn't been himself for a long time. Art hoped that hadn't translated into any cock-ups with their medications. Except for Phyllis, almost everyone at Camelot took close to two dozen tablets a day, in a dizzying array of shapes, colours, and sizes. It was impossible to keep track of them all, especially when your eyesight wasn't what it used to be.

Art glanced around the room at his fellow residents, dozing and reading and chatting, trusting that people like Gus, Gloria, and Vik were taking care of them. He did his best to wave away a terrible thought by thumbing his notebook in search of a morale-rousing tune. But the thought kept coming back to him: if Vik, distracted by his son's tribulations, put the wrong pills into their easy-open blister packs, they'd never know it.

CHAPTER 7

At five p.m. on Thursday, Zol slid into his regular spot at the Nitty Gritty Café and caught the eyes of Colleen, Natasha, and Hamish, already sipping their lattes. It had been a long, painful wait — forty-eight hours — for the results of the Camelot samples they'd taken on Tuesday. Yesterday and today he'd thrown himself into the countless other matters stacked on his desk and in his email inbox, but found himself bracing at every knock at the door. He'd convinced himself the RCMP were on their way with orders from the Party's faithful to give his investigation some muscle.

"Thanks for coming, everyone," he said. "I know you've all put in a long workday already. I'm pleased to say that Dr. Trinnock is still in full support of your participation in solving what he calls *our situation*." His boss had even told him to offer the team a light supper at the health unit's expense. Nothing like the Prime Minister breathing down the old guy's neck to get Trinnock to loosen the purse strings.

"Don't tell me he approves of my involvement," said Colleen brightly, her hazel eyes dancing along with the glass-bead earrings she'd worn the first time he realized he was falling in love with her.

"Does he know she's a —" Hamish coughed, and his voice descended into the raspy whisper that appeared whenever he was anxious. "— you know, a private investigator?"

"Geez, Hamish," said Zol. "Colleen has professional skills just like the rest of us." He gave Colleen a reassuring smile. "And they come in very handy." Trinnock had no idea that Colleen was a private eye. She was on the books as a consultant to the health unit and that was good enough.

"Okay," Zol began. "Natasha is going to give us an update. Thanks to Hamish, we got the microbiology lab at Caledonian University Medical Centre to process our samples in record time." Normally, public-health specimens had to be sent to the government laboratory in Toronto. The people there worked at their own glacial pace, then reported their results by pony express. "What about the soup? Did it give us our pathogen?"

Natasha bit her lip and shook her head. "Afraid not, Dr. Zol."

He was disappointed but not surprised. Things never came that easily. "Oh well," he told her, "carry on."

Natasha had her clipboard and scribbler at the ready, but she didn't need them for reference. She kept everything in her head. "As of today, we've had thirty-five cases of gastro reported to us from Camelot Lodge since the outbreak began two months ago on January eleventh."

"That's an awful lot of diarrhea," Colleen said. "How many residents live at Camelot?"

"Thirty-eight," Natasha said.

"So all but three have had diarrhea?" Colleen asked.

"Natasha can give us the exact numbers," Zol said. "But I know that Art and Betty and Earl have had it two or three times. Which means that more than just three of the residents haven't been affected yet."

"Forgive me for stating the obvious," Colleen said, "but if residents are getting gastro more than once, the offending microbe isn't stimulating the immune system to protect the body from further infections."

Again, Zol was impressed how quickly Colleen caught on to the medical stuff. Without any formal training, she'd run her late husband's internal-medicine practice when they'd emigrated from South Africa. After his death, she'd not had the heart to cancel his weekly subscription to the *New England Journal of Medicine*. She read the editorials every week, filing the issues meticulously.

"That's what's got everyone at Camelot spooked," Zol told her. "They recover, think they're in the clear, then get sick with the same thing again. Or see their friends recover only to succumb the next time it hits them."

"Succumb as in . . . you know?" Colleen asked. She was a strong, practical woman, but she never used the words *death* or *dying*. Not even *passed away*. She'd been touched too many times by violent death. Her only sibling was killed on his motorcycle at age eighteen. And her parents were bludgeoned by burglars in Cape Town, murdered in their own home for a television set and the equivalent of fifty dollars cash. Then, after she'd started life over as a newlywed in the promised safety of Canada, her husband perished when Swissair flight 111 caught fire and came down off the Nova Scotia coast. She hadn't dated again until she and Zol met late last year.

"The outbreak is intensifying," Natasha said. "Four of the six deaths have occurred in the past five days. We're seeing a very high case fatality rate overall." She glanced at her scribbler. "Seventeen percent."

"Hell's bells," Hamish said. "That's worse than pneumonia or meningitis. Must be a high-grade pathogen."

Zol turned to Natasha. "What about the culture of Nick's rash? Any staph aureus there?"

Natasha shook her head, her mouth sagging in disappointment. "Just the normal bacteria you'd find on anybody's skin."

Hamish squinted in obvious puzzlement. "What's that about?"

Natasha explained their theory, now debunked, about staphylococcus aureus exotoxin making its way into Camelot's meals from the infected-looking rash on the chef's arm.

"What else have you got, Natasha?" Zol asked.

"We took twelve samples from the kitchen on Tuesday," she said. "Drains, surfaces, food. And at the same time, we collected seven stool specimens from the patients with active diarrhea."

"And?" Hamish said.

"No bacterial or viral pathogens in anything. Not even under the electron microscope."

"What about parasites?" Hamish asked.

Natasha shook her head. "Routine staining for cryptosporidium was negative in the hospital's lab. A parasite specialist next door at the university looked at the samples. Nothing."

"No amoeba, no giardia, no cyclospora cayetanensis?" Hamish said.

Natasha dipped her eyes. "I'm afraid not."

"What about C diff?" Hamish asked. "You *must* have looked for *that*."

"All negative," Natasha told him.

"You sure? What test method did they use?" Hamish asked. "Recurrent diarrhea among the elderly is C diff until proven otherwise."

Hamish was talking about clostridium difficile, C diff for short, a bacterium that lurked silently in the intestines. It caused explosive diarrhea when awakened from its slumber by antibiotics taken for unrelated infections. C diff epidemics raced through hospital wards and nursing homes, where it was particularly hard on the elderly.

Natasha looked at Zol as if to say, *Why am I taking the heat?*

"It's your university hospital's diagnostic lab, Hamish," Zol said. "We have to trust them to use the best test available."

Hamish shrugged then raised his professorial finger. "Mind you, the smell of C diff is very distinctive. You couldn't have missed it, Zol, when you were collecting your samples."

Zol hoped Hamish was right, but he got a sinking feeling at the memory of the nauseating odours on the Mountain Wing. Had he been so overwhelmed by the stench that he'd missed the telltale horse-manure smell of C diff?

"Moving on," Zol said, "any ideas about the vector of transmission? I know we have damn little to work with." They'd never bring this outbreak to a halt unless they could find where the responsible microbe was entering the Lodge's food chain.

"I keep thinking about those hard, stale doughnuts at Camelot," Hamish said. "Restaurants waste a lot of food. And I mean a lot. I bussed tables for a couple of summers at university. It's amazing what gets thrown out. Not just scraps. Entire meals untouched."

"Yeah," Zol said, thinking back to his days as a junior chef when he'd thrown out bins full of perfectly good food. "No one goes to a restaurant to eat leftovers."

"You started out by asking about the soup," Hamish said. "Is there a problem with it?"

"Hard to say." Zol looked to Natasha for confirmation. "We did wonder about the freshness of its ingredients and the fact that it never seems to get heated to a roaring boil."

"Homemade soup can contain almost any old scraps," Hamish said. He sipped his latte and held Zol's gaze, his eyebrows raised. "Did you look up freegans on the Internet, like I told you?"

"Sorry. Never thought of it again, till this second."

"Well, just think about," Hamish said. "Food is going to waste at the back of restaurants all over the city, we know that. Dumpsters are full of perfectly good but slightly wilted produce, day-old baked goods, and untouched full-course meals. On the other hand, you've got savvy entrepreneurs, like Gus and Gloria, feeding fixed-income seniors with poor eyesight and fading taste buds."

"Dr. Wakefield," said Natasha. She was hiding her smirk with her coffee cup, but her eyes revealed her unrestrained amusement at Hamish's theory. "You think Gus and Gloria are Dumpster diving? And bringing the stuff back to Camelot?"

"That's what freegans do. It's part of their manifesto. They refuse to shop in grocery stores because they're owned by hard-hearted, wasteful capitalists. Instead, they pull freshly discarded food out of Dumpsters and take it home. Claim they're saving money and the planet at the same time."

Zol looked at Colleen, who was covering her mouth with her serviette. He bit his lip. The last time Hamish approached him with a wildly eccentric theory, Zol had laughed it off, and Hamish stormed off in a major pout — stayed incommunicado for a week. It turned out that Hamish had been exactly on track and Zol had to eat his words. The guy had amazing instincts.

Zol stared at the foam on his latte. He remembered the large, unlabelled plastic bags of jumbled vegetables that Natasha had hauled out of Camelot's deep-freeze. He had to admit, those veggies could have come from a Dumpster. Who was to know? Suddenly, his coffee tasted cold and bitter. "Well," he said, breaking the silence around the table. "How do we investigate the possibility that the Oliveiras may have embraced the . . . the freegan movement?"

Colleen put down her serviette and nestled her cup onto its saucer. There was no hint of a smirk on her lips, just professional concern. "Sounds like this comes under my scope of practice. Who procures most of the food for the Lodge? The husband or the wife?"

"The husband," Zol said. "Gus does the actual shopping, though I imagine Gloria tells him exactly what to buy."

"Perfect," Colleen said. Zol loved the way her South African voice made the word come out like a purr: *purrr-fect*. She returned his smile. "I'll put a tail on our friend Gus."

He felt guilty that Colleen was being sent out on a fool's errand, but if that's what it took to keep Hamish in the game, so be it.

CHAPTER 8

At eight o'clock the next morning, Hamish felt an easing of the knot across his shoulders. No matter what, and especially on a Friday the thirteenth, a car wash was the perfect place to hide and meditate. Impenetrable to pagers and mobile phones, it provided a haven from an intrusive world. This was one of those automated jobs that left a lot of spots and was done in only a couple of minutes. Sadly, his regular, full-service place on Main Street West was on strike. It did a much better job and, more importantly, its twenty-minute cycle gave him plenty of time to practise his breathing exercises. During a stressful week, he'd visit the car wash half a dozen times. He hated the idea of mud spatters on the Saab's side panels, and going more than a day without his breathing exercises caused his anxiety to build almost to breaking point. He had no truck with all the yoga mumbo-jumbo that went with Pranayama breathing, but the exercises did put a rein on his galloping pulse and helped organize the thoughts that so often raced across his mind.

At the end of the cycle, he put the Saab into gear and eased through the car wash's narrow exit. He wasn't ready to face a long morning in his laboratory, verifying his research assistant's latest calculations. He parked at the curb, put on the CD of car-wash sound effects he'd downloaded from the Internet, and let the soothing vibrations sweep over him while he finished his breathing.

He hadn't missed the smirks last evening at the Nitty Gritty. Zol, Natasha, and Colleen had tried to hide behind their coffee cups, but he knew what they were thinking. They hadn't believed a word he'd said about the freegans. They were just humouring him. People did that. They humoured Hamish Wakefield, the prickly Sherlock, so he wouldn't blow a gasket. Well, sooner or later Zol would see that Hamish was right. Hell's bells, all Zol had to do was read the freegan article on Wikipedia.

He completed his exercises and killed the CD player. He turned on his cellphone. The display showed one voice-mail message from an unknown caller, left ten minutes ago. Unknown callers were usually anxious patients who blocked their identities. He wasn't on call for clinical cases this month. Someone else would have to handle it. He'd redirect them to the medical centre's switchboard.

The caller was elderly and not used to leaving messages. Hamish could hear that in his voice. "Dr. Wakefield . . . This is Art Greenwood, Zol Szabo's granddad . . . well, almost his grandfather. By marriage, if that counts after a divorce. Zol said it would be okay if I called you. Would you please return my call? We're really in trouble here and don't know where to turn." There was a pause while the phone rustled in the caller's hands and the man nearly hung up without leaving his number. He came back on the line, apologized again, and recited his number.

Fifteen minutes later, Hamish strode toward the large glass doors under the ornate wooden canopy at the entrance to Camelot Lodge. He could see an elderly gentleman sitting in a scooter by the reception desk. He had the crossword in his lap, but seemed more intent on scrutinizing arriving visitors than completing the day's puzzle.

"Thank you for coming so quickly, Dr. Wakefield," Art Greenwood said after introducing himself. "Zol said you were the best." He pointed to the coat rack in the corner of the common room. "Hang your things over there. They'll be safe. No one around but us old birds, and fewer of us than ever." He flipped the switch on his scooter and headed toward the elevator. "We'll go right up to her room."

"She's expecting me?"

"Of course. Dr. Jamieson left this morning for a week's holiday. We've had it with him, anyway. A pill pusher of the first order. No one's getting better. New cases keep occurring. As you youngsters would say, the shit keeps hitting the fan."

Normally, Hamish couldn't waltz in and write orders for another doctor's patients. But these weren't normal times, and he was now working for the health unit in an official capacity. The law provided for Zol's boss Peter Trinnock to appoint a team to plunge into any epidemic. This situation was going to take hip waders.

"How long has Betty been ill?" Hamish asked, rubbing sanitizer between his fingers as he strode to keep up with Art's scooter.

"Two or three days. Started as a gurgly tummy but Jamieson said it was a bladder infection. Treated it with antibiotics, of course. Then last evening she got hit with the runs. Told me she was up and down all night, poor thing. And she's got the shivers. I'm terrified she's going to get that terrible headache that often spells . . . well . . . you know . . ."

They took the elevator to the second floor. Art led the way to Betty's door. Hamish gave Art his pen and watch for safekeeping, then rolled up his shirt sleeves. There were no isolation gowns or gloves in sight, but he wasn't going in there unprotected. He pulled a pair of vinyl gloves from his pants pocket and put them on before knocking on the door.

The first thing he noticed was the pungent smell of commercial air freshener in Betty's room. He rubbed his nose against the sleeve of his shirt, forced a smile, and introduced himself. Betty smiled back and reminded him that he'd given her several rabies shots last year, during the bat-bite scare. He took a brief history and eased back her pink and green patchwork quilt.

Her thin, sparrow-like body was white from head to toe. Her forehead was hot, her pulse strong but rapid, her tongue glistening with moisture. No shock or dehydration. He fought to keep a neutral expression on his face as he checked for stiffness in her neck (it moved normally) and tenderness in her belly (it showed only slight discomfort). So far, so good.

"Do you have any headache?" he asked.

"A little, yes."

"How severe is it?"

"I don't like to complain. I know I'm not the only one who's got this."

He looked for signs of meningitis or a stroke, but her brain was okay — no confusion, slurred speech, droopy mouth, or weak limbs.

"I'm going to order some tests and a painkiller. Be sure to ask for it when you need it," he said and replaced her quilt.

"Really, Dr. Wakefield, can you tell me what's wrong? Do you have a diagnosis for me? When I had this before, no one could put their finger on it, though I must say I didn't feel this sick, or have this much tummy pain." Her pale grey eyes pleaded as they searched his face. "And what I'd really like to know is, how did I get it?"

Patients always wanted to know how they contracted their infections. More often than not, he didn't have an answer that made them feel any better. They never wanted to hear that their kids, their neighbour, their doctor, or their wayward spouse had infected them.

The answer to Betty's questions had three parts: *what*, *which*, and *how*.

What was easy to tell her — she had an infection, apparently of the intestinal tract, that seemed to fit the description of the thirty-some other gastro cases Natasha Sharma had documented in the past two months.

Which germ was making her sick, he couldn't say, though it was obvious Dr. Jamieson's antibiotic was ineffective against it. If the germ were a virus or a parasite, no antibiotic would help her. She'd need either tincture of time to let the infection resolve on its own, or exactly the right drug selected on the basis of culture results. Of course, her cultures were likely to be negative, just like all the other Camelot gastro cases.

How was impossible to answer. After two months of hunting, Zol and his team couldn't say how this infection was being transmitted. Was it the food? The staff? The other residents? The environment?

"At this point," Hamish told her, "all I can say is you've got an intestinal infection. As far as I can tell, your bladder's fine. And I'm working with Zol Szabo at the health unit to make you better and put a stop to further cases."

"Well, let me tell you, I was fine until I started writing my memoirs. Phyllis said I should start with a creative writing course at Caledonian University, so we enrolled together and . . ."

Hamish prided himself on being a good listener, but this sounded like a tangent that wasn't going to lead anywhere useful. "Yes?" he said, hoping she wouldn't go on much longer.

"And she was right. It was a lot of fun, and the instructor was a real hunk. Like our Dr. Szabo."

She shot him a look that said *Just bear with me, Doctor.* "I bought a notebook computer and I've written five stories so far — the humorous side of cabinet politics." She raised an eyebrow and fixed him with a coquettish gaze. "An insider's view. In the sixties and seventies I was the secretary to the Prime Minister and various members of his cabinet."

"What about the Official Secrets Act?"

"It was all a long time ago. I'm allowed to talk now."

"Do you think you've ruffled some feathers?"

"Earl Crabtree — he's one of our mates and a long-time Party insider — forwarded two of my stories to a friend in the Ottawa Press Club, across from Parliament Hill. The word is, the reporters think the current Prime Minister might not see the humour in my behind-the-scenes anecdotes of his predecessors. Afraid I might diminish the Party's carefully crafted image."

Hamish had no interest in government or politics and couldn't see any plausible link between memoirs and epidemic diarrhea.

Betty pulled at her quilt with her knobbly fingers and winced slightly. "I don't type as fast as I used to. It makes my arthritis play up. Thank heavens for those Xanucox pills."

"They help, do they?"

"On a good day, they work wonders. Raimunda used to share hers with me. I gather they're rather expensive. Vik provided them to her for free. You know, because she was Gloria's mother." She dipped her gaze, as if embarrassed at speaking out of turn about the recently deceased. "All in the family, if I can put it that way."

Camelot's residents, and so many others like them, would be on dozens of medications in a variety of eye-catching shapes and colours. Hamish could see how trading them could become an intramural sport.

Betty's face crumpled as tears welled in her eyes. "Poor Raimunda died on Tuesday. Such a shock. She was the strongest person here. She kept getting gurgly tummy, before and after she spent that week in the hospital. But I must say, neither her arthritis nor her tummy ever stopped her from helping Gloria with the cleaning."

Hamish handed Betty the box of tissues from the bedside table and watched as she dabbed her cheeks. "Don't worry, now, Betty. It's not Xanucox that upset your tummy or gave you the fever. The drug company is making a fortune out of the fact that Xanucox is easy on the stomach." Finally, an arthritis medicine that didn't induce ulcers or intestinal bleeding. And didn't cause strokes and coronary syndromes like its competitors. "But I need to remind you, it's not a good idea to share your tablets. You never know what that could lead to. If you think you need Xanucox, you should ask Dr. Jamieson about it."

He pulled off his gloves and asked her to drink plenty of fluids and stop the antibiotic that Dr. Jamieson had prescribed. It obviously wasn't working. He promised to check on her again soon and told himself that if she got any worse he'd send her for X-rays of her abdomen. He scanned the room for a bottle of alcohol hand sanitizer but couldn't find one. He hated washing his hands in a patient's bathroom. The inevitable clutter of pills and tubes and bottles around the sink gave the maneuvre an unsavoury ick factor. He had no other choice, so he carefully soaped and rinsed his hands, turned off Betty's taps with his elbows, and shook the water from his fingers. He couldn't bring himself to touch her frilly towels.

At the doorway, still shaking the water off his hands, something stopped him. A faint, unpleasant smell, rising above the scent of Betty's lavender soap. He closed his eyes and sniffed. Yes, there it was. Unmistakable. The textbooks said it smelled like a horse barn, but he'd have to trust them on that. It wasn't the normal odour of urine or feces you'd expect in a healthy person's bathroom, it was the odour of para-cresol. And it gave him Betty's diagnosis on the spot.

He returned to her bedside and kept his hands in his pockets.

"You found good news in my bathroom, Dr. Wakefield?" She hadn't missed the smile of success on his face.

"Absolutely. Tell me, have you noticed anything unusual about the odour of your stools?"

"Really, doctor," she replied with a teasing grin, "what a thing to ask a lady. Even the Queen doesn't pass lavender-scented motions."

"But I mean, do your stools smell any different with this illness than they did the other times you had gastro?"

"Well," she said, glancing at the floral-scented deodorizer on her night table. "It's not the sort of thing one brings up in polite company, but I did notice an unusual odour for the first time this morning. Brought me back to my childhood, my uncle's farm. In Manitoba."

"Horses?"

"That's right. How *ever* did you know?"

"And you're sure you haven't smelled that odour here at Camelot before?"

"Certainly not. Goodness, Dr. Wakefield, what are you getting at?"

"I have good news for you. Well, good news in the sense I know what's wrong and how to fix it."

"Don't keep me in suspense, Doctor. What is it?"

"Clostridium difficile. C diff for short. That distinctive horse-manure odour proves it."

She paused, as if trying to remember something. When it came, her eyes burned with understanding. "It's my antibiotic, isn't it? Just like in the papers. All those old people dying in hospital. They came down with C diff diarrhea after being plied with antibiotics."

"In your case, though, we've caught it early. You have a private drug plan, don't you?"

Vancomycin was very expensive — forty dollars a day, and the minimum duration of therapy was two weeks. Metronidazole, much cheaper at just twenty cents a day, was the government's preferred C diff drug. Trouble was, it often failed, and mild cases turned lethal. Vancomycin rarely failed if started early, but the provincial government's universal drug plan for seniors covered it only if C diff had taken the patient to death's door and back three times in the previous six months. It was a crazy false economy cooked up by heartless bureaucrats in a fancy office somewhere in Toronto.

"Oh yes," Betty said, "the federal government generously rewards its faithful servants when it puts them out to pasture."

"Good. We'll go straight to the best drug. Four capsules a day and you should be well on the mend by Sunday. Though I've got to warn you — you're still going to feel pretty rocky tomorrow." He hoped he wasn't being overly optimistic about how she'd feel on Sunday. "Be sure you keep up with your fluids, and I'll check on you tomorrow."

He passed her bathroom door, his hands still firmly in his pockets. The smell of para-cresol hit him again, this time with an alarming uneasiness. C diff in the elderly could be viciously unpredictable. The patient might not look too bad today, but tomorrow their large bowel could ignite into a lethal explosion of toxic megacolon — like those folks Betty had been reading about.

CHAPTER 9

It was almost nine on Friday night by the time Zol got Max home from indoor soccer after dropping Travis off at his house. As usual, Travis slipped away without a word, and no one greeted him at his front door. He was an unusual kid. A large, purple birthmark covered the right half of his face, and he lurched to the left when he walked. He never said a word to any adult, certainly not to Zol, and according to Max, not to his coaches or his teachers either. When Travis wanted something, he whispered in Max's ear and relied on Max to provide a simultaneous translation. The poor kid stumbled awkwardly on the soccer pitch, usually right in front of the goalie. Still, he seemed to love the game.

The two boys had been drawn together since kindergarten, each with a physical distinction that set them apart: Max with his spastic left arm, Travis with his birthmark. Neither considered himself sick or handicapped, but Zol had always sensed the bond of *the other* between them. Calling the dark purple nevus on Travis's face *the map of Norway* was Max's way of describing it in complimentary terms, especially since Travis claimed his mother was descended from the Vikings. There didn't seem to be a father in the picture. As far as Zol knew, there was nothing wrong with Travis's intellect. The boy was a great gamer and had pulled his weight when he and Max did a project together on the Inuit.

Max was so tired he barely balked when Zol scrubbed the post-game orange drink from his face and handed him his pyjamas. He fell asleep on the second page of tonight's installment of Lemony Snicket, just as Colleen pulled into the driveway. Zol eased off Max's bed and turned off the light. After soccer, Max was always down for the count.

Zol rustled up a corned beef sandwich and a green salad for Colleen while she put her feet up in the sunroom. He never touched canned meat himself, but kept a couple of tins of Fray Bentos on hand for her. She called it bully beef and said it reminded her of happy picnics with her family in the Drakensberg Mountains, on holidays from Cape Town. Zol handed her the sandwich and poured two fingers of Lagavulin for himself. He loved how her eyes crinkled when she smiled, and the girlish way she swept her braided ponytail off her shoulder as she snuggled beside him on the loveseat. With the lights turned down, her hair glowed more copper than gold. But she looked tired. Watching Gus must have kept her up most of last night.

"How's Betty?" Colleen asked.

"Not so good. Hamish went to see her today. Says she's got C diff from the antibiotic the Lodge's family doctor prescribed a couple of days ago."

"Is she going to be okay?"

"You know Hamish. Without ever saying it exactly, he lets you know he's prepared for the worst." In the bloodless tone Hamish used whenever he was concentrating or anxious, he told Zol that only time would tell how things would turn out. Either Betty would get better soon, or she'd go fast. That's the way C diff worked in the elderly.

Zol took a swig of the neat Scotch and swallowed hard. He closed his eyes and let the fiery wave of peat and iodine bathe his throat.

"Tell me about Gus," he said, after another scorching swallow. "You didn't say much in your phone message."

"To be honest, after he stayed home last evening and the entire night, I wasn't hopeful when I started out this morning. I knew he wouldn't be Dumpster diving in broad daylight."

"But?"

"Today he took me on a fascinating tour of the city. For three hours. First we went to Ancaster, for a stop at that coffee pub on Wilson Street — the place with the drive-through the neighbours made the fuss about."

"Delia's Donuts?"

"That's it. He picked up a box there. Doughnuts, I'd guess." She paused for a bite of salad. "And then he took the 403 down the Escarpment, got off at the Main East exit, and stopped at the Convention Centre and the Royal Hamilton Hotel. Then two more stops. The HamNorth Mission on Ferguson Street. And a nondescript house on Sanford Street North. The place has seen far better days."

First the trendy heights of Ancaster, then the true grit of down-town Hamilton. Life could get pretty rough in Hamilton's north end. What was the manager of an exclusive home for wealthy seniors doing at a homeless shelter and a place that sounded like a halfway house?

"Any idea what he was doing?" Colleen asked.

Zol sipped his Scotch and shook his head.

"Playing Robin Hood," she said.

"What?"

"Taking from the rich and giving to the poor."

"I don't get it."

"He collected food at the first three stops and dropped it off at the last two."

"He hauled it out of Dumpsters?"

"No, no. They gave it to him."

"Gave it to him? Just like that? What sort of food?"

"I didn't dare blow my cover by getting too close. But I managed a few pictures with my telephoto." She opened the bag at her feet and lifted out a camera. Not a point-and-shoot, but a hefty single-lens reflex. She pressed a few buttons and showed him the image on the screen.

"That's Gus, all right," Zol said. He was standing at the rear of his blue Dodge van and holding a large tray. "What's he carrying? Are those sandwiches?"

"It's hard to see on the screen, but yes, I'd say a gourmet assortment. This is taken at the service entrance to the Hamilton Convention Centre. He carried out seven similar trays — five of sandwiches and two of fresh fruit — and loaded them into his van."

Colleen pressed a button and up came another photo. This showed Gus Oliveira from a distance, carrying a large cardboard box toward the same van parked in a lane beside a large building. Zol recognized the striped green awnings of the Royal Hamilton Hotel. Colleen pressed the button again to show a closer view of the box. The photo angle didn't give a view inside, but the box was full, and silvery objects were projecting through the open top.

"It was a big box, and Gus was puffing quite heavily as he carried it. Looked like it was full of odd-shaped packages wrapped in aluminium foil."

"What did he do with this stuff?"

"He dropped the trays from the convention centre, and one of the boxes from the Royal Hamilton, at the HamNorth Mission. There were too many people milling around the sidewalks for me to take pictures. They were waiting for the place to open for lunch."

She pressed the button again. The next shot showed Oliveira on the front porch of a typical north Hamilton house. Battered wooden steps led to a cluttered porch; the roof sagged heavily to one side. Gus had two boxes in his arms. Zol could just make out a female face peering through the partly open door.

"She doesn't look too pleased to see him."

"I think it's a women's shelter. See the stroller and the tricycle in the corner? They don't have those in halfway houses for cons."

"What about the box from Delia's Donuts?"

She fiddled with the camera then showed him the screen. The shot caught Gus at Camelot's kitchen door. He had a large smile on his face and was carrying a colourful flat box and a large, foil-wrapped package. There was no mistaking the pink and green logo of Delia's Donuts, nor the packet from the Royal Hamilton Hotel.

"What's all this about?" Zol asked. "Doesn't sound like Gus is a freegan." He'd looked up freegans on the Internet, after Hamish had mentioned them for the second time. "They don't take handouts. They'd rather dig their food out of Dumpsters when no one is looking. Late at night, I imagine."

"I've got my hunches, and I'm going to keep following him. But first, you've got to let me finish my supper." She paused, her fork poised over her salad, then laughed. "Am I wise to trust the provenance of all the ingredients?"

CHAPTER 10

Hamish tiptoed into Betty's room on Saturday morning and opened the curtains a crack. Art said she'd fallen asleep barely five minutes ago after a restless night. Phyllis had sat up with her until dawn, helped her to the bathroom so many times she couldn't count. The air reeked of the para-cresol from Betty's C diff–infected stools. Her lips were dry, her eyes sunken, her pale face dissolving into the pillows.

Hamish lifted her bony hand and felt her pulse. The beat was feeble, her heart rate far too fast. Her vital body fluids, lost in all those liquid stools, hadn't been replaced. Too weak to drink, she was withering like the desiccated geraniums forgotten on her windowsill.

She needed IV fluids as soon as possible, before she slipped into shock and her kidneys shut down.

He called Reception and told the woman to page Gloria, tell her he needed to meet her in the Mountain Wing in five minutes. Art had said there'd been a death on that wing overnight. That meant at least one empty bed over there for Betty. He'd get some IV fluids into her immediately, then see about transferring her to a hospital bed at Caledonian University Medical Centre.

Fifteen minutes later, Gloria strode into the Mountain Wing. Dark circles ringed her eyes, and her hair hung limp about her face. Her blouse looked like she'd hauled it straight from the washer. According to Art Greenwood, Phyllis had heard the Oliveiras arguing about Gloria's mother's funeral arrangements, something about charter flights from Lisbon. The body was on hold in the funeral home pending the arrival of relatives from Portugal. It seemed Gus wanted to follow tradition and see his mother-in-law buried immediately, but Gloria insisted on waiting for her family to arrive. The strain of the delay was obvious on her face.

"I know you've got your hands full, Mrs. Oliveira," Hamish said, pointing to the charts scattered on the counter, "which makes me surprised Dr. Jamieson didn't transfer these gastro cases to Caledonian before he left on holiday." While he'd been waiting, Hamish had checked on the patients and found three of them, like Betty, dangerously ill, on the brink of organ failure.

"My staff do excellent job, Doctor. After Dr. Szabo inspected, we hired an extra nurse."

"That's still not enough. Your staff can't keep up with the workload." The poor fellow who just died would have consumed all the attention of the nurse and personal support worker on the night shift. "These patients need IV fluids. And so does Betty McKenzie. I'm bringing her over in a few minutes so we can get that started now."

Gloria crossed her arms and shook her head. "Intravenous treatment is against nursing-home policy. Nursing council says we can't do it."

"But you have RNs on duty."

"I cannot guarantee an RN for every shift."

Same old story: RPNs — registered practical nurses — weren't allowed to supervise a simple IV, no matter how experienced they were. "Well then, these people have to be transferred to Caledonian."

Gloria frowned and donned her reading glasses. She shuffled through the charts then held up two of them. "These clients have advanced directives — no transfer."

She pointed to the first page on the top chart. It read: *Routine care and oral medications where possible. No intravenous therapy. No transfer to an acute-care hospital under any circumstances. Above all, comfort measures. No resuscitation in the event of cardiac arrest.*

The no-transfer order certainly didn't apply to Betty, nor to the Mountain Wing's third dehydrated patient, who had crippling arthritis that kept her bedridden but didn't stop her solving stacks of Sudoku puzzles.

Hamish picked up the phone and punched in the number for Caledonian University Medical Centre's emergency department. He had at least two patients to send them, but if he didn't warn them, the nurses would have a fit and make things difficult the next time he showed his face there.

He asked for the MD on duty.

Jeff Suszek, the department's assistant chief, came on the line. "Hey, Hamish. What's up? Got a case headed our way?"

"I've got two for you, maybe more. Bordering on shock."

"You at a bus crash?"

He told Jeff the story.

"Can't help you, Hamish. Patients who fail the ministry's new CCAE policy have to stay where they are."

A new policy had started two weeks ago, on the first of March. Doctors and nurses had taken to calling it the Deep Six rule. A cohort study out of Toronto had shown that nursing- and retirement-home residents who were older than eighty, or had been hospitalized within the past twelve months, or were taking more than six drugs, were just as likely to die after transfer to an acute-care hospital as they would be if cared for in their residential facility. In the interest of saving money and hospital beds, and practising medicine based on scientific evidence, the ministry was insisting that the new Community Care Algorithm for the Elderly, the CCAE, be applied without exception.

"Your folks are over eighty, Hamish. So there's no way we can allow them in. Besides, I've got nowhere to put them. Our isolation rooms are full. Twenty-seven patients are lined along the halls of our department, waiting for beds upstairs. I spend the whole day running interference and —" A siren screamed in the background.

"Hell's bells, Jeff. These folks are going to die if they stay here."

"The ministry and the latest studies both say they'd be no better off if we take them. Why don't you shove IVs into them and give them your antibiotic *du jour?*"

"They don't do IVs here. Against nursing council policies. No trained staff, no supplies."

"Sorry, man. The dean, the CEO, and the VP Patient Services are all over us on this one. We gotta keep the beds clear for our elective hips and knees. And the new pancreas program."

The mandatory targets for hip and knee replacements, imposed by the Minister of Health, were sore points with everyone except the orthopedic surgeons who were putting new joints into vote-rich baby boomers. And the pancreatic islet-cell transplant program was the university's brand new poster child. Everywhere you looked there were ads asking the public for donations to *Help Cure Diabetes, the Epidemic of Our Age.* Pancreatic transplantation was a high-tech initiative, and purportedly revenue neutral: curing diabetes would stop the need for dialysis units filled with diabetes-induced kidney failure. Caledonian University was in a race with the University of Alberta to develop a slick, fail-safe transplant procedure that didn't require patients to take toxic anti-rejection drugs for the rest of their lives. Everyone knew that at least one Nobel Prize was on the line. A cure for diabetes would be huge.

"So what am I supposed to do with these people?" Hamish said. "Let them go into shock and die?" In almost every other country on the planet, there would be a private hospital down the street he could transfer them to. But not in Canada. In 1984 — had the irony attached to that year dawned on the country's politicians? — big-brother government had outlawed private health care, except for cosmetic procedures. When Canadians got sick, they got government-issue health care or nothing — unless they were rich and could make it to the States.

"Tell you what," Jeff said. "I'll send you a taxi filled with all the IV stuff you need. You find someone to look after the infusions. Here — I'll pass you on to the unit clerk. Tell her what you need."

Hamish looked around the Mountain Wing's nursing station in disbelief. Was he actually going to turn this place into an acute-care ward? He'd need backup. He couldn't manage a ward full of IV drips, day and night, for who knows how long, by himself. Jamieson's on-call replacement, Dr. Awad, wasn't going to be any help: Hamish had paged him three times last night, intending to tell him about Betty, but Awad had never answered. It was probably just as well, he figured. An office GP couldn't be expected to know much about septic shock, toxic megacolon, and running IVs.

One way or another, he'd have to handle this mess himself.

But sooner or later, if no one found the source of the gastro, the effluvium was going to hit the fan in the Belvedere Wing, and they all might need IVs.

CHAPTER 11

At eleven o'clock Sunday morning, Natasha stood in the front lobby of Camelot Lodge rubbing hand sanitizer between her fingers. She'd asked Maria, the anxious receptionist, to page Mrs. Oliveira. The buzz in the common room was subdued compared to last week. Fewer residents than usual were chatting on the sofas, their cardigans fastened tight across their chests. Two women stared intently at their half-complete jigsaw puzzle. Snow-capped mountains, Banff or Lake Louise, were emerging from the jumbled pieces. Dr. Zol had made it clear that Camelot's no-visitors status didn't mean no socializing among the residents, but there was no mistaking the pall of dread on every face.

It was hard to believe that nearly a week had passed since last Tuesday when she and Dr. Zol had inspected the kitchen. And still nothing to explain the cause or source of eight weeks of febrile gastroenteritis. Perhaps, she decided, Colleen was on to something. Those large bags in the deep-freeze could be leftovers diverted from shelters and charities. She shivered at the thought of food being recycled without attention to maintaining its temperature in the proper germ-free range: either very hot or suitably cold. And then she pictured Dr. Wakefield's freegans diving into Dumpsters at the back of the city's restaurants, hauling soggy meals out of the garbage. Her hands went cold.

The room pressed hot and dry on her face. She pulled off her winter things and hung them on the rack. She checked her watch and hoped it wouldn't be too long before Gloria made her appearance. Circling the room, she exchanged brief hellos with the residents, then studied the artwork on the walls. Half a dozen sentimental Trisha Romance prints glowed with portrayals of impossibly fluffy snow blanketing cutesy villages. Did little girls ever look that perfect at minus twenty? Why didn't the artist reflect the people of modern Canada? Celtic freckles might be adorable, but so was brown skin kept flawless with generous applications of shea butter.

On the wall toward the back of the room, she came across a painting that spoke to her instantly. It was an original, not a print, and it showed a soldier striding across a battlefield. Craters pockmarked a landscape littered with burnt-out Jeeps and tanks. A bundle of rags hung limply in the soldier's arms. The setting sun lit a background of jagged mountains in a spectacle of pinks and violets. She looked closer and saw that the soldier's dishevelled bundle was actually a child, her eyes round and wide. There was nothing the least bit sentimental about this artist's work. Its emotional tone reminded her of a Renaissance Pietà, but the vivid colours spoke more of the Hindu Ramayana.

Natasha tore her eyes from the painting and checked her watch again. Eleven-fifteen and Gloria still hadn't answered her page. They'd agreed to review the gastro situation and see what support Gloria needed for her infection-control measures. The woman did have her hands full. Maybe she was busy making funeral arrangements. Dr. Wakefield said they hadn't buried her mother yet.

At the far side of the common room, next to the tall windows, a scooter tire caught Natasha's eye. She peeked around the corner into the hallway leading to the elevator and saw Mr. Greenwood and a male companion standing at attention. They were gazing through the windows, watching two other men, from Craig & Lafferty, load a sheet-covered gurney into a black van. The elderly pair, dressed in flannel trousers and navy blazers, had their right hands tipped to their brows in formal salute. Natasha stepped back, hugged her briefcase, and stood still.

For a minute or more the two veterans didn't move. Tears spilled down their cheeks, but their salutes didn't waver. Even after the van driver bolted the vehicle's rear door and drove out of sight, the two men stood motionless. Finally, Mr. Greenwood began to wobble. He grabbed the handlebar of his scooter and dropped onto the saddle. His companion then terminated his salute with a crisp forward motion, closed his eyes, and briefly bowed his head before lifting his backpack from the floor. He pulled a hanky from a side pocket and wiped his face.

A few moments passed. Natasha wanted to slip away unnoticed, but decided she'd be less of a distraction if she stayed perfectly still. When Mr. Greenwood turned his scooter toward the common room, he halted immediately. "Oh goodness, Miss Sharma. I didn't see you standing there."

Natasha bit her lip, embarrassed at intruding on their private moment.

"Don't mind us," Mr. Greenwood continued. "We were just saying goodbye. To our dear friend Melvin. Gave them trouble right to the end, he did." He wiped his eyes and blew his nose with a tissue he drew from the basket attached to the handlebars. His light-grey eyes, though bloodshot, brightened. He turned to the gentleman standing beside him. "Have you met my very good friend and bridge buddy, Earl Crabtree?"

Natasha stepped forward and extended her hand. "Glad to meet you, Mr. Crabtree."

"Actually," said Mr. Greenwood, "it's *doctor*. The Ph.D. kind." He smiled at his friend and winked at Natasha. "Unlike Zol and Dr. Wakefield, he doesn't get his hands dirty. Professor of history."

"Emeritus, now," said Dr. Crabtree. "Retired years ago. Please, call me Earl. Though you'll hear Phyllis calling me Crabtree."

"She's one of our chums," Mr. Greenwood explained. "Phyllis Wedderspoon. Maybe you've met her already. Our chauffeur and

Internet hound. And former Latin teacher." He dipped his head and gave Natasha a look suggesting it was wise to watch your manners around Latin teachers.

"She hates losing at bridge," Professor Crabtree added with a chuckle.

"And paying for Internet service," Mr. Greenwood said. "She surfs online at the library, where it's free."

It was surprising how quickly these two had changed their tone. Maybe that's how you survived to almost ninety. A positive attitude gave you resilience. Natasha thought of her mother, only forty-six, prone to moping like a miserable crone. Mummyji could spend hours weeping on the sofa when Natasha refused to have dinner with one of the nerdy Indian guys the family had picked for her to sample.

Mr. Greenwood started rolling toward the centre of the common room. "So, Natasha," he called over his shoulder, "come and sit for a minute. Tell us what you're up to."

She offered to carry Professor Crabtree's sporty backpack as they filed behind the scooter, but he held it firmly and said, "No need, my dear. I'm fine as I am. Old age is contagious, you know. The more you let people do for you, the less you can do for yourself."

The three of them found a quiet corner. Professor Crabtree stayed standing until Natasha sat down, then invited her to describe how she approached her work.

As a field epidemiologist investigating any outbreak, she told them, her job was to track down every symptomatic case in a cluster and determine the common exposures among the people affected — foods, water, objects, places, other people. You did a blitz of the cases and the environment, matched the two, and usually found the offending germ and the contaminated agent carrying it.

Professor Crabtree massaged his knee with his palm, then winced as he shuffled his feet. "Now that the situation here has escalated, and we all seem to be at risk from an aggressive illness, what is your Plan B, Miss Sharma?"

"Ideally, I'd like to list, and cross-reference, every morsel ingested by every resident in the past two months."

"Good Lord," said Professor Crabtree. "My dear, you're asking the impossible."

"I know. A person would have to be a savant to remember what they ate the day before yesterday, let alone last week or last month."

Professor Crabtree smiled and tapped the side of his head. "Most of us are no longer pros in the memory department."

"Speak for yourself, my friend," said Mr. Greenwood. "Nothing wrong with my memory."

"Okay then," said Professor Crabtree. "Tell us what you had for lunch the Thursday before last."

Mr. Greenwood scratched his chin, looked up at the ceiling, opened his mouth as if to speak, then closed it again.

"There you are," the professor said. "Albert Schweitzer said that happiness is nothing more than good health and a bad memory. You've got a bit of both."

Natasha's gaze strayed to the painting of the soldier carrying the terrified child bundled in rags. She'd loved her university electives in art history more than any of the sciences she'd majored in. Her parents fretted that mooning over the paintings of dead artists could never be turned into a secure living. They'd insisted she continue with biology.

"I see you noticed my painting," Mr. Greenwood said, diverting the conversation from the competence of his memory. Had he noticed the work had set her heart racing, that it haunted and inspired her in the same breath? "What do you think of it?" he asked.

The piece must have come from a high-class gallery, the sort of place that didn't feature Trisha Romance. "It's very moving," she said. "Did you purchase it at an auction?" She'd always wanted to attend an art auction. They sounded exciting. And sophisticated.

"Auction? Heavens, no. I painted it myself. Acrylic on canvas." Mr. Greenwood dipped his chin and looked pointedly at his friend. "And from memory. North Africa. '43. Those are the Atlas Mountains."

Natasha's tongue went so dry she could hardly get the words out. "You . . . you painted that? You . . . you were there?"

"We both were," said Mr. Greenwood. "Canadian Army. Alongside the Gurkhas and damn good fighting men from India. We were seconded to the British."

She didn't know what to say. Her grandfather had fought in North Africa but spoke very little about it. He'd died at home in Delhi more than a decade ago. Had he met these Canadians, or others like them, during the war? These two gentlemen hadn't blocked their memories, and they still retained their sense of humour and a wholesome affection for each other. She wished she'd known her grandfather as more than a cheerless old man with a raspy cough.

The intensity of Art Greenwood's unexpected talent overwhelmed her. She stared again at the painting, then down at her notebook. It was several moments before any of the words on the page made any sense to her.

She forced herself back to her agenda, to reviewing the data she'd collected on her previous visits to the Lodge. She'd already gone for the obvious targets.

She tapped her scribbler. "There's obviously something I've missed. Something crucial. I just wish . . ."

"What about the soup?" Mr. Greenwood said.

"Oh, Art. You're always going on about the soup," said Professor Crabtree.

"Well, I can't help it. I hate cold soup."

"Like vichyssoise and gazpacho?" Natasha asked.

Mr. Greenwood thumped the handlebar of his scooter. "I mean soup that's supposed to be hot but is served barely lukewarm. In a cold bowl, to boot."

Natasha made a note about the soup, more to keep Mr. Greenwood happy than anything else. The lab had looked for pathogens in the sample of soup Dr. Zol took last week, but had found none. Of course, negative results on one batch didn't put Nick's soup completely in the clear. If soup was kept lukewarm for prolonged periods, and never heated above seventy degrees Celsius, it would be ideal for keeping microbes alive. Perhaps she could divide the residents into soup-eaters and non-soup-eaters, then compare the incidence of gastro in the two groups.

"I've been thinking about our pills," Mr. Greenwood said. "Vik Horvat, our pharmacist, has had more than his share of distractions lately. And that's got me worried."

"Come now, Art. Betty and the others have some sort of infection," Professor Crabtree said. "What's that got to do with Vik and our pills?"

"All I'm saying is that if Miss Sharma is interested in everything we put in our mouths, she ought to look at our pills. We sure swallow a hell of a lot of them."

"Viktor Horvat may have his troubles," the professor said, "and I grant you, his English is atrocious. But he's a damn good pharmacist." He waved a finger, reminding Natasha of Dr. Wakefield when he was about to make an important point. It seemed to go with the academic territory. Unlike Dr. Wakefield's, there was nothing sleek about Professor Crabtree's index finger. It was gnarled at the tip, like her grandmother's. "He keeps everything organized for us in those little blister things."

"He supplies your medications in convenience packaging?" asked Natasha.

Mr. Greenwood nodded. "Does it for everyone here, except for the three show-offs."

Professor Crabtree caught Natasha's puzzled look and explained that Camelot had three residents who made a big deal of not needing prescription medications. He tipped his head to the far side of the room where the two ladies were poring over their jigsaw puzzle. "The puzzle sisters — Maude and Myrtle — only take multi-vitamins. Those puzzle pieces are so damn small, good eyesight must run in their family."

"And Phyllis, of course," added Mr. Greenwood, "takes only a baby aspirin."

"Vik *better* do a good job of our pills," Professor Crabtree said. "Thanks to Gloria, he's got this place sewn up. Steeltown Apothecary has a nice little monopoly running here. Funded by the government, through Ontario's drug benefit program for seniors. Not bad for a guy who escaped from Sarajevo with not even a dime in his pocket."

"Speak of the devil . . . here's Phyllis," said Mr. Greenwood, looking in the direction of the reception desk at the other end of the room. "Better watch out. Looks like she's in high dudgeon."

Phyllis Wedderspoon stamped the slush from her boots on a mat near the entrance, then breezed into the common room like a ship in full sail. Her full-length fur coat glowed with the sheen and flow of real mink. Her dark felt hat, a cloche, was festooned with an extravagant yellow feather. The well-worn handbag dangling from the crook of her forearm looked like real crocodile, probably purchased long before Greenpeace and World Wildlife. But her plastic galoshes screamed Wal-Mart.

"There you are, boys," she called as she approached. "Take these, will you, Earl?" She handed him a cardboard tray supporting three Tim Hortons coffees with the red-and-yellow insignia of the chain's famous spring promotion. It was the season for Roll Up the Rim, the company's annual lottery that had everyone in Canada unwinding the rims of their cups to see what they'd won. Usually it was just an invitation to *Please Play Again*.

The professor took the coffees, set them on the table, then helped Miss Wedderspoon out of her coat. She draped it over the back of a nearby sofa, along with her purse. Mr. Greenwood made the introductions, and the sprightly woman dropped her slim frame into the wingback chair that Professor Crabtree pushed into their circle.

Miss Wedderspoon scrutinized her mud-spattered galoshes and seemed to find them wanting. "I hate the slush that March brings," she tsked. "But better than a blizzard, I suppose." She turned to Natasha. "Sorry, Miss Sharma, I only brought three coffees." She paused, then lifted the cup in front of her and held it out. "Here . . . If you can stand it with double cream, no sugar, take this one."

"I'm fine," said Natasha. "Thank you. You go ahead."

"Are you sure? You're welcome to it."

Natasha smiled and shook her head.

Professor Crabtree pried the lids from all three cups with his gnarled fingers in what seemed to be an expected ritual.

"Did you see Melvin off?" Miss Wedderspoon asked.

The light in the eyes of both men faded for a moment. Their lips tightened.

"Yes," said Mr. Greenwood. "The dear fellow's gone. They're going to hold his service on Friday afternoon. Wentworth United. His daughter was here earlier but she got called away."

"Her BlackBerry again, I suppose?" said Miss Wedderspoon.

The look on Mr. Greenwood's face said he was reluctant to admit the answer was yes.

"Don't knock them till you try one," the professor said.

"Don't tell me *you've* got one."

Professor Crabtree teased her with the sparkle in his eyes and didn't answer.

"Enough of that," said Miss Wedderspoon. "How's Betty?"

Mr. Greenwood's shoulders slumped. He stared into his coffee as though hoping it might portend better news. "Not much change. Still on IV fluids."

"She has to keep drinking," Miss Wedderspoon said. "I was reading on the Internet that the worst thing you can do with gastro is to stop eating and drinking. The bowel gets lazy if it's not stimulated. Just like the rest of the body, it needs exercise."

"I think Dr. Wakefield has everything in hand," said Professor Crabtree.

"He's sending her tomorrow to that clinic on Ottawa Street for X-rays of her stomach," Mr. Greenwood added.

"Emergency at Caledonian won't accept any of us over eighty with diarrhea," the professor told Natasha. "Something to do with practising medicine based strictly on scientific evidence, and a new rule they're calling Deep Six." He shook his head in disgust.

"Caledonian, my own alma mater, terrified we old geezers will contaminate the hallowed halls of their medical centre."

"Ridiculous," said Miss Wedderspoon. "You'd think we were fossilized freeloaders."

"We should march in there with our tax returns," Mr. Greenwood said. "Show them we still pay the taxes that keep that palace running."

Miss Wedderspoon scowled and shook her head. She blew on her coffee, then took a sip. "Is Gloria back from the airport?"

"Airport?" Natasha said.

The feather on her hat waved like a zany flag as she flicked her head and scowled. "She's picking up Joe, that lazy nephew of hers. We just got rid of him after Christmas. And here he is back again. He'll be canoodling with some girl on the sofa again. And snapping up the only tea-time goodies that aren't hard as Precambrian granite."

"His grandmother did just pass," said Professor Crabtree. "He's coming for her funeral."

"She didn't *pass*, she *died*. Plain and simple. Just like we're all going to do if Gloria keeps poisoning us."

"You don't need to worry. You seem to be completely immune," said Mr. Greenwood. "The good Lord gave you a cast-iron stomach."

She took a long draft of her coffee then gazed into some imaginary distance. "So far."

An idea was forming in Natasha's head. "I've done my best to pinpoint the source of the gastro, but it's proved impossible for me. It's time I tapped into your observational skills and insider knowledge."

The two men cooed politely, while Miss Wedderspoon put on her skeptical frown.

"You know all the residents and the habits that make them unique," Natasha continued. "People will tell you things they'd never tell me, a stranger."

She was never sure how much her youth and her brown skin were a hindrance here. Everything at Camelot was white: the hair, the skin, the servers' blouses, the table linens, the china, the mashed potatoes, the attitudes, the university degrees. It was time she harnessed *local knowledge*, as Dr. Zol liked to call it.

"We'll only solve this if we can figure out which foods are responsible for the outbreak," she told them. "Maybe we can't determine exactly who ate what, and when they ate it, but we *can* discover trends. People have strong likes and dislikes when it comes to food. Wouldn't you agree?"

"Certainly do," said Miss Wedderspoon. "And we hear about them ad nauseam. Like the puzzle sisters. So damn fussy they give me the pip. When I was a child my mother insisted I eat every morsel on my plate. I still do."

Mr. Greenwood leaned toward Natasha and patted her forearm. "That's not quite true. She never eats the soup."

"And you know perfectly well why not," said Miss Wedderspoon. She turned to Natasha. "It's always too damn cold, if you'll excuse my French."

The professor pursed his lips and aimed his concentrated gaze at Natasha. "Please continue, Miss Sharma."

With the two men running interference against Miss Wedderspoon's interruptions, Natasha explained what she'd like the three of them to do.

When they completed their game plan, there was still no sign of Gloria Oliveira. Professor Crabtree helped Natasha into her coat and escorted her to the front door. She promised to return in the afternoon with clipboards and questionnaires for their food survey. When she turned to wave goodbye, the three of them were rolling up the rims of their Tim Hortons coffee cups, eager to find a winner. She hoped her idea would be a winner, too.

CHAPTER 12

Hamish propped his elbows on the counter at the Mountain Wing's nursing station and rubbed his eyes. He could barely keep his head up. What day was it? He peered at his watch. Tuesday, the seventeenth, St. Patrick's Day. The end of another long night shift. His third in a row. The nurses had wakened him three times: twice when Betty's blood pressure dropped, and a final time when blood began oozing from her rectum. It didn't help that Zol had been calling every twelve hours for an update, and the news was more discouraging every time they spoke.

He punched Caledonian's number into the phone, pressed the receiver to his ear, and waited for Dr. Jeff Suszek to pick up at Caledonian's Emergency Department.

"What's up, Hamish?" Suszek said, breathing heavily, as though he'd run the length of his department. "You still at that nursing home?"

"Remember the woman I told you about, the executive assistant to a former Prime Minister? She's circling the drain. I filled her full of the IV fluids you sent me, but it's been four days now and the vancomycin still hasn't kicked in. Her fever's up, she's in and out of shock, and she's one step short of renal shutdown."

If Betty's disease got any worse, her colon was going to tear apart and all her internal organs were going to shut down.

"We couldn't do any better with her here," Suszek said. "And you've probably got a hell of a lot more space."

"But Jeff, I'm at my wits' end. She's a really fine woman who served her country well. Before this, she was in great general health. But now it looks like she's going to die on me."

"I'd like to help, Hamish. You know that. But I've got no wiggle room." Suszek cleared his throat and lowered his voice. "I already told you — the dean and CEO are adamant. No gastros from nursing homes when they fail the . . . you know, the ministry's Deep Six rule. We can't take the risk of a hospital outbreak when the evidence shows that hospitalization won't make them any better."

"How about a direct admit to intensive care?"

"You know we can't do that. Patients have to be assessed in Emerg before they're allowed upstairs. How old is she, again?"

"Um . . . Eighty-six. A good eighty-six. Still winning at bridge and writing her memoirs."

"Does she have an advanced directive?"

Hamish didn't want to admit it, but Betty had made it clear: no heroics, no life-support machines. Not under any circumstances. "I'm not sure."

"Check on it. If she doesn't want to be hooked up to a ventilator, there's no point in sending her to ICU. You'll just have to tough it out in the nursing home."

Hamish decided to try a different tack. "I need a surgical opinion. Her belly's very tender and it's blown up like a balloon. Maybe she needs surgery."

"Let me check who's on today." The phone clunked as Suszek dropped the handset on a desk. Hamish could hear coughing, crying, and beeping in the distance. Suszek panted into the phone a few moments later. "You're in luck. Josh Rooney's on call for general surgery. He visited my mother in her nursing home last year. Adjusted her feeding tube so she wouldn't have to make the trip back to the hospital. Give Josh a call. Look, I gotta go."

"But . . ."

The phone went dead in Hamish's hand. He pictured Suszek striding to his next case, sweat staining the back of his scrubs.

He documented the details of Caledonian's refusal in Betty's chart. Her parliamentary connections in Ottawa guaranteed that sooner or later the federal politicos would be calling for a public inquiry into the province's rule limiting the elderly's access to health care; it would be crucial to be on the side of the good guys when the lawyers ripped everyone apart and the politicians blamed the doctors for everything. He pocketed his ballpoint and looked toward the sound of approaching footsteps. Two figures emerged from the gloom in the hallway. He rubbed his eyes and heaved himself out of his chair.

"Zol. Natasha. What are you doing here?"

"Seeing what you're up to, good buddy," said Zol. He squeezed Hamish's shoulder. "How are you? Sorry. I shouldn't ask. You look like hell. And . . . I know you're doing the best you can for Betty. My boss tried to get Caledonian to take her. Even spoke to the CEO. But even Peter Trinnock couldn't get them to budge on their Deep Six rule. Her former connections to the Prime Minister's Office didn't faze them a bit. Too bad she's not a *provincial* VIP."

Hamish hated politics, especially the federal-provincial squabbling over health-care jurisdiction that threatened to grind the system to a halt. He ran his hand over his flat-top and tucked in his shirt. He knew he must look a mess. But what did Zol expect?

"Bet you haven't had breakfast yet," Zol said. "We stopped at the Nitty Gritty. Brought you a latte and a Brunch Bandit scone with all the trimmings. Go have a shower, then meet us downstairs. We've got something to show you."

CHAPTER 13

It was a tight squeeze, but Zol managed to fit five chairs around a card table in the common room, with just enough space for Art to roll in on his scooter. A quick shower had livened Hamish up, and he was nibbling on his Brunch Bandit scone. After each small bite he swept the stray crumbs off the wrapper and onto a paper serviette he kept to the side. It was the same way with clinical problems — Hamish tackled them one bite at a time, assembling the facts into a unified solution.

Natasha had assembled her three deputies, the Camelot Irregulars: Art, Earl, and Phyllis. Their eyes crinkling with apprehension, they sat with pens and clipboards poised. The yellow feather in Phyllis's hat fluttered with every dip and shake of her head.

"I gather your survey is complete?" Zol asked Natasha.

"Certainly is," Phyllis replied. "Maude and Myrtle finished the last of their assignments over breakfast this morning. We've now polled the eating habits of everyone in the Belvedere Wing." She peered at Earl over the top of her spectacles. "Some of us are very fussy and others of us will eat everything put in front of them." She paused as a self-satisfied smirk came over her face. "Within reason, of course. Out of politeness and good breeding."

"And lack of taste buds," Earl countered with a playful smile.

"Well," Natasha said, "I have to tell you. You people are amazing."

"You mean to say you're amazed that we old ducks could complete a simple questionnaire about what we like to eat?" Phyllis said.

"Heck, Phyllis," Earl said. "Just accept the young woman's affirmation."

"So what have we got?" Zol asked.

"To start with," Earl began, "the soup has turned out to be a *hot* issue." He looked at Art, as though sharing a confidence. "Or not so hot, depending how you look at it."

"Yes," Phyllis said. "We residents are deeply divided over soup. Some of us *insist* on it at every meal." She glared at Art. "Then complain about it incessantly."

"Others never touch it at all," said Earl. "Even when it's put in front of them." He motioned to Phyllis with his open palm. "A case in point, our dear Latin scholar. The puzzle sisters never touch it either."

Natasha's eyes brightened. She picked up her pen and turned to a clean page in her scribbler. "Any correlation between drinking the soup and getting gastroenteritis?"

"We haven't got that far," said Earl. "We thought that was more your purview. Perhaps it needs a computer."

"Except," Art said, looking straight at Phyllis, "we know that three of the healthiest people at Camelot never eat soup."

Zol took out his pen. "And who are —"

A rumble and crash echoed from the front door as two figures burst into the lobby. "Help!" It was more a moan than a shout. "Call an ambulance."

Zol could see that it was a couple, a man and a woman. Their faces were covered in blood.

Hamish was the first on his feet. He pulled a pair of vinyl gloves from his pocket and dashed toward the dining room. He grabbed two chairs from a table set for dinner and ran with them to the two bloodied figures standing hunched together by the reception desk. Zol joined him there.

Hamish's hallmark fussiness dissolved in the heat of the emergency. He yanked a second pair of gloves from his pocket and handed them to Zol. "Here. Put these on. We have to staunch the bleeding." He called to the receptionist, transfixed behind her desk. "Dial nine-one-one."

Zol pulled on the gloves, barely stretching them over his oversized fingers. The vinyl ripped at the cuffs, but would do the job. He helped Hamish settle the couple — blood-soaked and moaning — into the chairs. Then he steadied them while Hamish grabbed handfuls of linen serviettes from the dining-room tables.

The figures pressed the napkins against their bloodied eyes. Hamish folded one and held it against a gash spurting from the man's scalp. Zol did the same with the laceration running the length of the woman's cheek and jaw. When she'd dabbed the worst of the blood from around her eyes, Zol suddenly realized who it was.

"Mrs. Oliveira. It's you," said Zol. "What happened?"

"That bastard," said the man. "Going to friggin' pay this time."

Now that Hamish had the man's spurting scalp wound under control, Zol could see he was a generation younger than Gloria Oliveira. "You're Joe, aren't you?" Zol said. He turned to Hamish. "Gloria's nephew. From Portugal."

With his free hand, Zol felt Gloria's wrist for her radial pulse. It seemed about a hundred. And strong enough. Hamish examined the man with the swift, coordinated movements of a cellist. He checked the eyes, the nose, the jaw, then ran his hands over the four limbs, apparently looking for paralysis and broken bones. He felt the man's neck, looking for the pain of a cervical fracture, then the abdomen for signs of major trauma. Zol tried to do the same for the woman, but knew his technique couldn't match the elegance of his friend's.

"What happened?" Hamish asked when he'd satisfied himself that Joe's condition wasn't immediately critical.

Joe scowled and said nothing.

"Were you in your car?"

Joe shrugged, then stared at his blood-drenched sneakers.

"Almost . . . home," said Gloria. She could barely form the words. Her lips were swollen, and blood was oozing from around her teeth. It occurred to Zol that her jaw might be broken.

"Bastard side-swiped us in the Malibu."

Gloria's eyes filled with terror. "An accident."

Joe clenched his teeth. "No goddamn way it was an accident."

Hamish peered through the front entrance. "Is the other driver injured?"

"Took off. Just like those two other times," Joe said.

"You know him?" asked Hamish.

"Dark glasses," Gloria offered. "And black toque."

"You didn't see his face?" Hamish said.

"The bastard," said Joe.

"Was it someone you know?" said Hamish.

Joe turned away, then grimaced at the pain inflicted by the hasty movement of his neck and shoulders. He'd taken quite a blow to his head.

"Look," Hamish said, "either it was or it wasn't someone you know. Which is it?" He was trying to apply the same logic to a crime scene that he applied to clinical medicine. Zol figured it was a waste of time. They should let the police sort it out. Hamish pressed again. "Did you catch his licence plate number?"

"Um . . . a bunch of Js and a Y, that's all."

Natasha dipped a towel in the basin of cold water she'd brought from the kitchen and handed it to Joe. He rubbed at the blood on his hands, but it was going to take a lot more than a moist towel to remove all that blood.

An ambulance wailed in the distance, then roared to the front door. A pair of paramedics surveyed the scene, recorded the vitals, wrapped a pressure dressing over Gloria's wound, and strapped her to a gurney. They were taking her first because she seemed a lot more distressed than her nephew.

"I don't need that friggin' thing," Joe told the paramedic approaching him with a cervical collar. "And I'm not going to any hospital."

"You're banged up pretty bad, sir," said the paramedic. "You might have a neck fracture. And with a gash that deep in your scalp, you could have sustained a concussion or a fractured skull. But don't worry, they'll take good care of you at Caledonian."

Natasha stepped out of earshot and motioned to Zol and Hamish to do the same. "Joe's a visitor, not a taxpayer," she whispered. "He won't have an Ontario health card. Young guy, over from Portugal for his grandmother's funeral, probably didn't bother getting travel health insurance. That's what he's worried about."

"They'll treat him anyway," said Zol.

"Sure," said Hamish. "Then send him a big bill. CT scan and all."

"He really has no choice," said Zol. "As the paramedic said . . ."

Hamish stepped forward and rested his hand on Joe's shoulder. "Look, Joe. Don't worry about the cost. The hospital won't force you into the poorhouse. They never come after you if you can't pay."

Joe shot Hamish a look of surprise that suggested the fees had nothing to do with his reluctance to go to the hospital. He shrugged off Hamish's touch and started to stand up, but fell back onto the chair. At that moment, a second ambulance arrived. The backup team wasted no time in strapping on the cervical collar, maneuvering Joe onto a stretcher, and heaving him into their vehicle.

As they watched the ambulances departing, sirens blaring, Hamish turned to Zol. "You know, for a guy born and raised in Portugal, he speaks awfully good English." Hamish pulled off his gloves and tossed them into a wastebasket. "And his accent — you noticed it, eh? Pure Canadian."

CHAPTER 14

About eight that Tuesday evening Zol's front doorbell chimed and Colleen headed for the door. Max was absorbed in the computer room or he'd have been way ahead of her.

"You heat the plates," Colleen told Zol. "And I'll get Natasha settled in the dining room. You work her so hard, she'll be as hungry as I am."

"Hey," Zol said. "She works *herself* hard. I just reap the benefits."

By the time he arrived in the dining room with three heaping plates — chipotle spiced chicken wrapped in phyllo dough, vine-ripened tomatoes, and lamb's lettuce in Colleen's vinaigrette — the two women were engaged in lively conversation. Natasha's laptop case sat on the floor beside her.

"I took you at your word, Natasha," said Zol. "You said you ate chicken."

"At this point, I could eat a whole flock."

"You've been at it nonstop?" Zol said.

Natasha looked at her watch. "Since eleven this morning. Got started as soon as the paramedics took Joe and Gloria to the hospital."

That made it nine hours at the keyboard, entering Camelot's food survey data into her laptop. Thirty-some questionnaires, more than twenty fields each.

"But you're done?" Zol asked.

Natasha unfolded her serviette and laid it across her lap. "All set for the analysis. Any news on Joe and Gloria?"

"Treated and released. Cuts and bruises. How's Hamish?"

"Well . . . Do you want the honest truth?"

"Of course. I always do."

"He's completely exhausted," Natasha said. "And irritable. And can't go on much longer without any sleep."

"I found a medical student to help him. He starts tonight." Zol knew it wasn't only lack of sleep that was troubling Hamish. The poor guy was heartsick about Betty. Every day her state was more precarious. Zol's blood boiled at the thought of the ministry's Deep Six nonsense. But damn it, there was no getting around it, no matter what strings Peter Trinnock had tried to pull.

He turned to Colleen and drew in a long, slow breath. He always felt better after a dose of her nurturing aura. "You've had quite a day as well, though so far I've only heard the bare bones."

Between mouthfuls of salad and chicken, Colleen related how she'd followed Gus again, starting at ten o'clock this morning. He made pickups at the Royal Hamilton Hotel, the Mohawk Golf and Curling Club, and Four Corners Fine Foods.

"They never have day-old baked goods at Four Corners. Don't want to ruin their fine-food image," said Zol. "I bet it was artisanal bread and pastries he picked up there."

"Exactly."

"Where'd he drop everything off?" Zol asked.

"He didn't."

"Oh my gosh," said Natasha, "he brought it all back to the Lodge?"

"He took a call on his cellphone and the wheels fell off," Colleen said, then paused and waited for a reaction.

It took a few seconds, but the penny finally dropped. "Of course," said Zol. "Gloria and Joe."

"He'd already delivered two boxes to the HamNorth Mission on Ferguson Street and a couple of sandwich trays to the women's shelter. Then that call came and he took off. Roared up the Jolly Cut, hell for leather. Then screeched into Emergency at Caledonian."

Colleen chased the last of her meal with a long drink of ice water. She turned to Zol. "Tell me, how well do pastries freeze?"

"Depends. Creamy delicacies don't do so well, but pies, cakes, and croissants stay fresh enough if you keep them airtight. Why?"

"That's reassuring," Colleen said. A smirk crept onto her face. "After our friend left the medical centre, he drove straight to the Lodge." She paused and speared a forkful of lettuce. "With three boxes of Four Corners' finest. Someday, you'll see them at Sunday brunch. A little dividend after a hard day's work."

Without a word, Natasha finished her salad and lined her knife and fork in parallel across her plate. Something was bothering her, and it wasn't just the chunks of chicken she'd left on her plate.

"Let's have them, Natasha," Zol said.

"Sorry?"

"Your thoughts. What's bothering you?"

"It just bugs me, that's all." She tugged at the dark, fly-away curls at the nape of her neck. "Gus is stealing. And this can't be the first load of recycled baked goods that ended up at the Lodge. Dr. Wakefield first noticed the hard doughnuts six months ago."

"To be fair," said Colleen, "you can't really blame Gus this time."

"But we know this isn't the first time," said Natasha. "The other day, you caught him helping himself to a box of Delia's Donuts and a foil packet of something from the Royal Hamilton Hotel. What if he's bringing meat or dairy back to the Lodge after lugging it over hell's half acre in his unrefrigerated van? Maybe he's even been Dumpster diving at the back of restaurants, like Dr. Wakefield suggested. Who knows what bugs have been having a heyday right under our noses?"

Zol turned to Colleen. "You didn't see him hauling stuff out of Dumpsters, did you?"

"No, no," Colleen said. "His recycling seems perfectly respectable. In fact, it's part of a registered charity. I confirmed that this afternoon."

"What? You're kidding," Zol said.

"A charity?" Natasha said, her dark eyes wide, ready for the hunt.

"He works for an organization called Waste Not," Colleen explained. "Half a day, twice a week. As a registered volunteer driver."

"Waste Not?" Zol said. "What the heck's that?"

"Oh my God," Natasha said. "They're on my list. I knew something like this was going to happen."

"What list?" Zol asked.

"Our inspection list. We meet with them twice a year." Natasha grabbed her paper napkin and started picking it to pieces. "Every time it's the same thing. We bend the rules for them because they're a charity and because they threaten to make a huge fuss in the media if we give them a hard time. We back down because we're afraid of appearing heartless and draconian when we tell them they should use refrigerated trucks."

This was all news to Zol and none of it was making any sense. "Whoa," he said. "Back up a minute. How come I don't know anything about this?"

Natasha looked shocked. She sputtered then stopped, too steamed, or too embarrassed, to say any more.

"It's a food recycling service, Zol," Colleen said. "With an executive director and a proper website." She explained how Waste Not's team of volunteer drivers ferried leftover food — too good to throw out — from hotels, restaurants, convention centres, and food-processing facilities to organizations around the city catering to the needy.

Her napkin in tatters on her lap, Natasha found her voice. "I'm so sorry, Dr. Zol. I thought you knew all about them. It's always bothered me that Waste Not transports perishable food in private, unrefrigerated vehicles. They should know that the world is more complicated than it used to be."

The practice was a minefield of potential complications. And it seemed that Camelot was a living example. It was a good bet its residents were getting gastro from the past-their-prime leftovers Gus carted around the city before slipping them through the Lodge's back door.

But how to blow the whistle on a man like Gus Oliveira? Volunteers held a sacred place in society. Without irrefutable evidence of wrongdoing, any accusations could be interpreted as an attack on a saint who did nothing worse than help himself to a few discarded doughnuts.

"Well," Zol said, "I guess, Colleen, you'll need to keep tailing Gus, catch him with his hand repeatedly in the cookie jar without an iron-clad explanation. And the rest of us will have to prove that his Waste Not dividends are causing Camelot's gastro."

He stood up and cleared the plates from the table. "Okay, Natasha. Why don't you fire up your laptop. Maybe those food questionnaires have something to tell us."

Two hours later, Zol rubbed his back and heaved himself out of his chair. He paced the sunroom, working the cramps out of his knees. "Oh no, look at the time," he said. "Max should've gone to bed ages ago."

"Not to worry," Colleen said. "He's all tucked in with the light off."

"By himself? He's never done that before."

Colleen patted Zol's arm and gave it a squeeze. "Goodness — you really were absorbed by the data. I coaxed him into his pyjamas, supervised his teeth, then read him a chapter of Lemony Snicket."

Natasha had run her database program fifty different ways. It came up empty every time. Not a single correlation between the gastro episodes at Camelot Lodge and the dietary preferences of its residents. And whether or not residents ate Nick's lukewarm soup, made of potentially recycled ingredients, had no influence whatsoever on their risk of gastroenteritis.

"I feel like a fool for stating the obvious," said Colleen, "but we're missing something that's staring us in the face like a herd of zebras on the open savanna."

Zol shuffled Natasha's questionnaires. The residents' mealtime idiosyncrasies had sparked a chuckle here and there, especially the elaborations scribbled in the margins. One man had eaten vanilla ice cream with caramel sauce for dessert every night for the past four years. Another said he wouldn't touch soup if it were the last thing on earth. One woman only ate beef if you promised her it came from a cow named Angus. Myrtle and Maude, the puzzle sisters, appealed for brown eggs, brown bread, and brown rice.

"Are we looking for zebras when we should be just looking for horses?" said Natasha.

"Well," Colleen said, "are we correct in assuming the culprit has to be the food?"

"Fecal-oral transmission is classic for gastro," Zol said. "It's the cause of most outbreaks, from salad bars on cruise ships to contaminated raspberries in trendy restaurants."

"We checked the dishwasher," said Natasha. "The water's hot. The machine cycles properly. I watched the boys loading it — no worries there. The cutlery and dishes *must* be okay."

"And the residents are religious about the cult of the hand sanitizer," said Zol. "They can't enter the dining room without bumping into the dispenser."

"There's nothing wrong with the food storage at the Lodge," Natasha added. "The fridges and freezer are working perfectly."

"Is it worth looking at the dining-room seating arrangements?" Colleen asked.

Natasha riffled through the stack of questionnaires and pulled out four sheets. "Well, we could look at these four women. Retired math teachers. They always share a table and eat the same things. They choose the same items at breakfast, lunch, and dinner, and play euchre together almost every day. If you ask me, they're pathologically inseparable."

"And?" said Zol.

"Only two of them have had gastro." Zol could see an idea flashing into Natasha's eyes. "And they've had it repeatedly. Two or three bouts each." She clicked at her keyboard, paused for a moment, then clicked again. "This is interesting," she said, tapping the screen. "Look how many residents have had *recurrent* gastro. Of those with gastro, ninety percent have had it twice or more, and seventy-three percent have had it three times. One poor person has had it four times."

Zol rubbed at the ache in his lower back. The health unit looked at numbers of gastro cases when monitoring outbreaks at institutions; individual names were recorded but did not always figure in the analysis. Looking at each Camelot case as an affected individual might be important. Perhaps there was a subgroup of residents susceptible to the gastro and coming down with it repeatedly.

Zol returned to his chair and studied the chart Natasha had created on the monitor. "How many residents have come down with gastro in the past two months?"

Natasha's fingers danced across the keyboard, and a new table flashed on the screen. "Twenty-one, six of whom have died."

"In other words," said Colleen, peering over Zol's shoulder, "seventeen of Camelot's thirty-eight residents have never come down with the gastro." She gazed at the ceiling, and her fingers punched at an imaginary calculator. "Roughly half the residents seem to be immune to it, while the other half keep getting sick. Do I have that right?"

Natasha bit her lip. Zol had never seen her caught out before. She dealt more with numbers and risk factors than with patients. But now that the questionnaires had put names to the gastro cases, a pattern was emerging.

A trumpet blared from Natasha's handbag. She grabbed the purse from the floor and fumbled with the zipper. The blaring got louder and louder as she pawed madly through the contents.

Finally, she scooped the phone from the bottom of the bag and flipped it open. The racket ceased. "I told you not to call me tonight, Mummyji. I'm working." She scrunched her eyes and nodded. "I'm always okay, you should know that by now. We'll talk tomorrow." She closed the phone. "I'm sorry, Dr. Zol. She calls every evening at ten-thirty. On the button. If I don't answer, she sends my dad over to my place. One time, she called the police." She turned off the phone and held up the blank screen. "My little cousin must have fiddled with this again. He knows I hate those trumpets."

Zol smiled and did his best to stifle a yawn. "Sounds like we've come up with something to trumpet about, something creating two distinct populations within Camelot Lodge. Now that we know it must be there, we just have to find it." He covered his yawn with his palm, then added, "But we've done enough for one night. If I don't get to my bed I'm going to drop." He turned to Colleen and winked. He wasn't too tired to pay her some special attention.

CHAPTER 15

After breakfast on Thursday, and before morning coffee, Art Green-wood drove his scooter out of the elevator and headed for the Mountain Wing's nursing station. He and Earl had been up all night keying in their new data, and it looked like their efforts had paid off. It was time to tell Dr. Wakefield about it.

His spirits sagged as he passed that horrible sign on Betty's door. *Stop: Restricted Access, Contact Precautions.* It was as though they'd consigned her to a nuclear dumping site, a load of toxic waste. When he'd seen her yesterday, she'd looked sallow and wispy, as though she could dissolve into the bedclothes at any minute.

She wasn't the only Belvedere resident who'd been shipped over here to the dark side. One of the four euchre-mad math teachers had been wheeled here yesterday. Phyllis had scored a look at her in the elevator. Dry as a prune, she reported.

"How's my Betty?" Art called to Hamish Wakefield across the counter at the nursing station. The young doctor no longer looked like he'd just ridden three days across North Africa on a camel. Maybe he'd had a better night. Perhaps Betty, too.

Dr. Wakefield shook his head and lowered his eyes. "Just the same, I'm afraid. The antibiotic hasn't kicked in yet."

"But it's now six days. You said . . ."

The doctor's eyes darted evasively, their hallmark confidence nowhere in sight. "I know, I know. But Betty's colon hasn't been reading the textbook."

"Do you think today she'll . . ." Art picked at the spatters of dried acrylic dotting his handlebars. Sometimes hope was all you had left, even when you knew in your heart there was no cure. During the final weeks of Jeannie's breast cancer, they'd hoped for better control of her pain. When cure was impossible, you hoped for peace.

Art swept his tears with the back of his hand. "At least *you're* looking better today, Doctor."

Dr. Wakefield nodded solemnly and handed Art a tissue. "Zol arranged for a medical student to come and help me out. He arrived the day before yesterday and took a couple of the night shifts. He says this reminds him of his nurse-practitioner days in northern Manitoba — some frozen outpost this side of North Overshoe."

"That's all very well, but how come they sent you a student instead of a real doctor?"

"Todd's better than any resident. More experienced and far slicker at IVs. And you know the best thing? He never complains."

Dr. Wakefield made a face and straightened the crease in his trousers. "Mr. Greenwood, I feel terrible about Betty. I just can't understand why she's not getting better. I've done everything I can think of — blood work, X-rays, nasogastric suction, intravenous fluids, antibiotics."

"What if those things don't work, Doctor?"

"I . . . I really don't know."

Dr. Wakefield jammed his nose into a chart. Whatever anyone might say about the bluntness of his manner, this man could focus on a task like no one else.

Art dabbed at his cheeks until he was sure they were dry. He gripped his handlebars and said, "Dr. Wakefield? I wonder if I can show you something?"

"What's that?"

"When you're done."

"Sure. In a sec. Let me write one more order."

Dr. Wakefield finished with the chart and placed it in a rack beside several others. He closed his ballpoint and placed it in his shirt pocket. Then he fixed his blue-eyed gaze on Art's face as though no one else on the planet was worthy of his attention.

Art took a deep breath. "Earl got struck with a brilliant idea. So we've done a little sleuthing on our own. And remember, this is our home. We know this place inside out."

"You certainly do."

"What we've got is a little complicated. Better to show it to you than tell you about it. Has to do with our survey."

"I already know about your survey. Zol and Natasha went through those food questionnaires and said nothing turned up."

"But this is a different survey."

"Really? What's it about?"

"We have it laid out in my room. Can you come and take a look?"

"Give me fifteen minutes to finish up here."

Art reached over his handlebars and squeezed Dr. Wakefield's forearm. "Doctor, would you make it five?"

CHAPTER 16

Art's door was wide open, so Hamish knocked and walked in. The cinderblock walls, closed dark drapes, plain pine table, and gooseneck reading lamp gave the place the feel of a military outpost he'd seen in a movie.

Someone had taken down a painting and leaned it against the wall. It depicted the Normandy D-Day landing descending into a line of war graves blanketed with maple leaves. The artist's portrayal of malevolent power and raw emotion took Hamish by surprise, especially in the confined space of Art Greenwood's modest room. A plain whiteboard hung in the picture's place.

Earl hunched over the pine table. A laptop was open in front of him, and sheets of paper were stacked beside it. He touched the peak of his Blue Jays ball cap. "Morning, Doc. Hope you're full of energy. We've been up half the night, but we're still raring to go."

"He'll be up for this, all right," said Art.

"Up for what?" said Hamish.

The two men looked at each other, their impish expressions betraying a conspiracy they were dying to share.

Art picked up a pen and tapped the stack of papers. "You started it," he told Earl. "You tell him."

Earl pulled off his cap and scratched his thatch of thick silver hair. He replaced the hat, adjusted its position with both hands, then fixed Hamish with his pale eyes. "We need your appraisal of our analysis."

"What did you find?"

"Actually . . ." said Art. "We're not completely sure."

"Come on," said Earl, "we didn't pull an all-nighter for nothing." He patted his laptop. "Our electronic buddy here has done some heavy collating, and we've drawn one pretty solid conclusion. Natasha would be proud of us." He pointed to the empty chair to his right. "Have a seat and I'll show you what we've got."

As Hamish sat down, Art handed him a sheet from the stack on the table. It was a printed questionnaire, similar in layout to the one Natasha had used to survey the residents' food preferences. This one listed diagnoses.

"At our age," Earl began, "we're preoccupied with two things: our bowels and our medications. You already know too much about our bowels. Now it's time to take a look at our drugs."

"But we're talking about an epidemic here," Hamish told him. "Fever, diarrhea, and dehydration. I'm sorry, but that adds up to infection, not medication side effects."

"Maybe," Art said, "but a detailed exploration of our diets turned up nothing."

"I figure," Earl said, "it's like the Battle of Hastings. A thousand years of myth and erroneous assumptions buried the truth about King Harold's logistical failures. Same applies here." He frowned, shifted in his chair, then touched his belly as though gripped by some sort of spasmodic discomfort. After a moment his face relaxed. "We knew we had to start with a clean slate."

Art pointed to the paper in Hamish's hand. "Have a look at that," he said. "As a prelude to a survey of our medications, we started with a menu of our ailments: arthritis, bronchitis, cancer, diabetes, heart condition, high blood pressure, kidney problems, tummy troubles, and skin rashes."

"Did you include those who recently passed away?"

"Yes," Art said. "As best we could."

"Arthritis was tricky," said Earl. "Practically everyone has it. It's as natural to aging as wrinkles, so we weren't going to include it. But Phyllis suggested we break it into two groups: mild, requiring ordinary pain killers, and severe, requiring prescription medications."

"That turned out to be brilliant," said Art. He peered at his weather-beaten wristwatch. He always wore it over his shirt cuff, where it looked unfashionably gauche but was easy to read. "Where is Phyllis, anyway? She should be back from Tim's by now. I'm parched."

Earl's gnarled fingers clicked at his keyboard. No hunting and pecking for the professor who must have typed hundreds of academic papers and thousands of revisions.

A data table flashed on the screen.

"Natasha phoned me yesterday," Earl said. "Boy, she's keen. Told me to divide the residents into two groups: those who've had the epidemic gastro and those who've remained free of it."

"Just a lot of numbers that don't say much," said Art, his eyes twinkling.

Earl clicked again at his keyboard. "Until you turn them into percentages."

Art grinned. "That was my idea."

Another table flashed onto the screen.

	Gastro: 21 residents	Gastro-free: 17 residents
Arthritis mild	10%	82%
Arthritis severe	90%	12%
Bronchitis	29%	29%
Cancer	38%	41%
Diabetes	19%	24%
Heart condition	71%	71%
High blood pressure	86%	82%
Kidney problems	10%	12%
Tummy troubles (chronic)	38%	35%
Skin rash	43%	53%

Hamish ran a finger back and forth between the two columns — Gastro and Gastro-free — looking for a pattern in the data. "You've done a case-control study here."

Earl beamed and puffed out his chest. "That's what Natasha called it. Of course, she hasn't seen these figures." His hands darted over the sheets on the table. After a lot of muttering, and a couple of false starts, he found the page he was looking for and handed it to Hamish. "Here's our working copy."

The sheet was identical to the table on the screen, except that a pencil had scored out the diagnoses showing similar frequencies between the residents with diarrhea and the controls without it.

Only one diagnosis was left unmarked by the pencil: severe arthritis. Ninety percent of the gastro group were afflicted by it, but it affected only twelve percent of the gastro-free group.

"Have you verified your data?" asked Hamish. He'd visited his late grandfather in his seniors' home and watched the residents at mealtime. Communicating their choices from a simple dinner menu was a complicated process. Limited eyesight, poor hearing, and failing memory fuelled many a misunderstanding, ending with disappointment on the dinner plate. Did these Camelot questionnaires suffer from similar limitations?

"We've reviewed each questionnaire twice, and our data entry three times," Earl replied.

"That ought to be good enough," said Art.

Hamish raised his finger, saw the two faces beaming at him with the eagerness of first-year medical students, and dropped his hand to the table. He couldn't disappoint them.

"So?" said Earl. "What do you think?"

"This is a strong correlation. And it raises a number of questions. What sort of arthritis and exactly how severe? And what medications are they taking for it?" He let that sit for a moment while he thought about it. And then he said, "There are some heavy-duty arthritis drugs that make people vulnerable to unusual infections by weakening the immune system. Maybe you're on to something."

"We're not done yet," Art cautioned, then looked eagerly at Earl.

The professor pointed to the data table on the monitor. "We've designed another case-control study."

"Last night at supper, we got everyone's consent to enter their medications into our database," Art said.

"Vik from Steeltown Apothecary has us all in his medication administration record," Earl explained. "The nurses use it as a reference when there's a question about our meds. Your medical student showed us where they keep it."

"Can I see what you've got so far?" Hamish asked, amazed at the ingenuity of these two charmers.

"Afraid not," said Earl.

"The puzzle sisters are still entering the data," said Art. "They used to be keypunch operators."

"They're very methodical," said Earl. "We figure it'll be after lunch before we can have a look at the data."

Hamish answered a rap at the door. Phyllis stormed in pushing a wheelchair, its seat loaded with four Tim Hortons coffees and three paper bags filled with the smell of fresh baking.

"That place has a licence to print money," she huffed, "but Lord, they're slow. They make our dining-room staff look like *efficax exempoator*." She whipped off her scarf and peered at Hamish over the top of her spectacles. "And efficiency exemplified, they're not — believe me."

Phyllis blew the crumbs from a plate she retrieved from the windowsill, then opened the bags and laid out the snack: bagels, muffins, cream cheese, and jam. Hamish hoped he'd get to snaffle the bran muffin, protected inside its paper baking cup.

Phyllis pulled a hanky from her sleeve and dabbed the drops of wintry dribble from the tip of her nose. Her eyes narrowed and her hand jerked as she clutched her chest. "How's Betty?"

"Just the same, I'm afraid," Hamish said.

The others helped themselves to the bagels while Hamish washed his hands in Art's sink. There was no bottle of hand sanitizer anywhere in sight. Hamish took the unclaimed muffin and broke off a mouthful, taking care to leave the paper wrapping intact.

"Maybe you don't have the correct diagnosis, Doctor," said Phyllis. "My sister's pulmonary embolism was misdiagnosed by four different doctors before somebody got it right."

"For heaven's sake, Phyllis," Art said. "Of course Dr. Wakefield has got Betty's diagnosis right."

Hamish chewed on the muffin and said nothing. Maybe Phyllis was correct. Perhaps he didn't have Betty's diagnosis entirely correct. She did have C diff — the horsey smell of para-cresol in her room had been unmistakable, and the lab test came back clearly positive. But why was the vancomycin not working? Was old age slowing her response to the appropriate treatment? Or perhaps she had an underlying bowel disease — ulcerative colitis, diverticulitis, cancer of the colon?

"Earl," said Hamish, "let me see the names of the twenty-one residents in the gastro group."

Betty was on the list, of course. In fact, she'd come down with fever and diarrhea three times since Christmas. Art and Earl were there too, both hit by two bouts of diarrhea that were never as severe as Betty's. Phyllis, despite sharing their table at every meal, had stayed in the clear.

What had Earl said about the Battle of Hastings? Myths, assumptions, and logistical failures? Hamish wondered what false assumptions had been leading him astray.

Perhaps Betty hadn't told him her full medical history. The unabridged list of her medicines might point to a pre-existing diagnosis she'd failed to mention. Patients did that frequently. They came to you with fever and backache, and didn't bother to tell you they'd recently received six months of treatment for melanoma or bladder cancer. It didn't occur to them that the fever, the backache, and the cancer treatment were intimately linked.

"Tell me," Hamish said, "what's the name of the pharmacist who looks after you here? Did I hear you call him Vik?"

Earl nodded. "Vik. From Steeltown."

"He's foreign," said Phyllis. The word was a rebuke, not a description.

"Yugoslav," said Art.

"Croatian, to be exact," said Earl. "He has an interesting story. Came as a refugee from Sarajevo. Lost his family there."

"I find him rude and offhand," Phyllis said. "Delivers our medications, grunts a few words to Gloria and the nurses, then leaves."

"He loves hockey," said Earl. "Mention the Leafs and you'll get a big smile out of him."

Hamish's pulse quickened in his throat. He touched his neck. That sore spot was still there. "Was he hospitalized recently?"

"You bet he was," Earl said. "Intensive care at your place, and then off work for a few weeks. A Lebanese fellow delivered our pills for a while."

Hamish felt the blood drain from his face. He touched his neck again, then shuddered. He'd never forget the bear-like power of Viktor Horvat's paws digging into his trachea in the intensive care unit on New Year's Day.

The rage he'd seen in Horvat's face that day had seemed strange for a man askew on a hospital bed, one false step from death. Acute meningitis and septic shock robbed most people of their energy and emotions, left them pale and limp, past caring whether they lived or died. But Horvat's eyes had radiated a palpable fury.

"What?" Horvat shouted, a furious answer to Hamish's professional scrutiny. "You wanting I kiss your feet?"

Hamish held the bedside chart like a shield in front of him and tried to compose a response — a few controlled and empathetic words that would preserve the dignity of both doctor and patient.

Horvat bolted from his bed, oblivious to the dozen wires and tubes connecting him to the high-tech frenzy of intensive care. He flung his hand toward the door. "Goddamn soldier-doctor, get out."

No one had ever mistaken Hamish for a soldier before. It was true the precision of his blond flat-top, touched up by his stylist every ten days, might be mistaken for a military cut. But at five-foot-five, with a baby face and precious little fat or muscle on his frame, no one could mistake him for GI Joe.

Horvat scowled deeper furrows into the granite of his forehead then tapped his breastbone. "I am knowing." He turned his finger and jabbed it at Hamish. "You are soldier."

A second later, Horvat lunged. In an instant he had Hamish by the neck, his thumbs clamping Hamish's voice box in a vise-like grip, squeezing tighter and tighter. Bracing for the crunch of his crumpling windpipe, Hamish stared into Horvat's face. He read its hatred, knew the man was never going to let go. He pounded his assailant's forearms with an upward thrust. He'd been taught the maneuvre as a teenager by a Red Cross swimming instructor. It was supposed to break the stranglehold of the victim you were rescuing from drowning.

Horvat's arms didn't budge.

Hamish focused more intently on his own upper limbs: fists balled, elbows bent, arms stiff. Stars swirled in the consuming darkness. He heaved for his life.

Horvat's thumbs gave way. Wires flew, the monitor wailed, and Hamish stumbled from the bedside. He collapsed on a chair near the door and gasped. Lungful after lungful.

Three nurses stormed the room and flew into action, forcing Horvat back into bed and reconnecting his tubes and wires.

"Canada Army kill . . . kill . . ." Horvat bellowed. He pointed at Hamish's chest, his eyes as wide as gun barrels. "Goddamn maple-leaf soldiers." He bared his teeth, apparently incensed by the Canadian flag embroidered on Hamish's lab coat. "Always stinking drunk."

In the following days, Hamish had kept his distance and let the antibiotics do their thing for his delirious patient. Horvat recovered and was discharged home, though it had seemed strange for a previously healthy man to come down with listeria meningitis, a disease of the elderly and medically fragile. Hamish had chalked it up to one of medicine's inexplicables.

He stared at the empty muffin cup scrunched in his fist, then tugged his tie away from his throat and massaged his neck. A second case of invasive listeria was coming to mind — Gloria's mother,

Raimunda, infected a month after Horvat. She, too, had responded well to treatment. But a few weeks later she came down with gastro and died very quickly. Was it really gastro? Or had her listeria relapsed, caused an illness that mimicked gastroenteritis, and finished her off before any tests could be run? Zol had asked the coroner to send off a post-mortem blood culture, but it would be weeks before the provincial laboratory would report the result, and it would go only to the coroner.

The textbooks didn't consider listeria a proper intestinal pathogen. Laboratories looked for listeria in critical samples like blood and spinal fluid, but they never looked for it in stool specimens. Conventional wisdom dictated that detecting listeria in diarrhea stools was of no diagnostic value because the germ was present so often in the feces of healthy people.

Was that piece of conventional wisdom a myth, a medical old wives' tale that could lead to errors in diagnosis?

There was only one way to find out.

CHAPTER 17

Hamish dashed back to the Mountain Wing, grabbed the phone in the nursing station, and dialled the microbiology laboratory at Caledonian Medical Centre. He asked for Ellen Ballyk, the chief technologist.

"She's at a meeting," said the secretary who took the call.

"Until when?"

"I don't really know. A couple of hours, maybe?"

Hamish checked his watch — ten thirty-five. He wasn't waiting any two hours. "I need to speak to her now."

"Perhaps one of the technologists can help you."

"No, I only want to speak to Ellen."

"I'm sorry, sir. But she told us not to disturb her."

Hamish hated meetings. They were always getting in the way of the real work of looking after patients. "For God's sake, this is important."

"I'll put you through to one of the techs."

Before Hamish could protest, the line clicked, and Muzak exploded in his ear. Just when he thought he couldn't stand the screech of overly cheerful violins one more second, the line clicked again and a male voice said, "Can I help you?" By the man's no-nonsense tone, it was clear he'd been warned about the hostile caller on the line.

Hamish paused, rolled his eyes, then took a deep breath. "This is Dr. Hamish Wakefield. I understand that Ellen is in the middle of an important meeting. But I really need to speak with her without delay."

"Can I help you find a test result?"

"No, I don't need a result. I just need Ellen."

"The thing is," said the tech, "she left her phone and pager in her office. The best we can do is send someone to pull her out of the meeting."

"Now we're getting somewhere."

"It'll take a while. The conference room is in another building."

"I'll leave you my number. Have her call me as soon as she can."

Half an hour later, Ellen called him on his mobile. She sounded anxious and out of breath. "Dr. Wakefield. What's wrong? Is this a code indigo?"

"Indigo? Not that I know of. What's that?"

"Bioterrorism."

"No. But it is life and death."

"Jeez. This was a heck of a way to be sprung from a boring meeting. You really frightened me."

"Sorry."

"Never mind. How can I help you?"

"Do you still have all the stool samples sent to you this year from Camelot Lodge?"

"Of course. Until an outbreak investigation is wrapped up, we keep every sample frozen and available for further testing."

"I need you to culture those stools for listeria," Hamish said.

"You're not serious."

"Of course I am."

"But there's no validated stool-culture method for listeria." Ellen's tone was emphatic. She was never one to break the rules.

"I know, I know. It would go against the international lab standards."

"And for good reason. Listeria isn't a recognized cause of gastroenteritis."

She knew the conventional wisdom cold. But sometimes it paid to be unconventional. "That's the party line," Hamish said. "But maybe there's a listeria clone that's crashing the party. And causing the gastro that's baffling us at Camelot."

"And you want me to culture all those Camelot stools for listeria?"

"At this point, it's the best idea I can come up with."

"It would be a big job. And I'd have to get hold of the appropriate culture medium."

"How soon could you get it?"

"It would depend on my supplier. But I gotta tell you . . ."

"What?"

"It would to be an expensive project. And not just the culture medium. I'd need to pay overtime staff. Have you got a budget for this?"

Hamish thought about it for a moment, then nodded into the phone. "The health unit will pick up the tab."

"You're sure?"

"Of course."

"And will you take responsibility for reporting the results? As a technologist, I can't do that. Not with an non-sanctioned method."

"No problem."

"Well then, if the health unit covers the overtime, I might even be able to get started today. That is, if my supplier has the special medium in stock."

Hamish ended the call, sat back in his chair, and stared through the window toward the craggy face of the Escarpment. It was going to be tricky making sense of Ellen's results. No one had ever chased listeria as a credible cause of epidemic gastroenteritis.

And how forgiving would Zol be if this turned out to be an expensive wild-goose chase?

CHAPTER 18

At four o'clock that afternoon, Zol greeted the Camelot Irregulars at the door to the library, down the hall from his office. There was a gentle camaraderie among Art Greenwood, Earl Crabtree, and Phyllis Wedderspoon, but the concentration in their faces underscored the seriousness of their undertaking. They all shared the worry of Betty's precarious condition. And they knew any one of them could be next. Except Phyllis, perhaps, who seemed invincible.

"Nice view you've got here," Art said, pointing through the picture window. "Not much haze today. You can see the CN Tower."

From four floors above the brow of Niagara's precipitous escarpment, it *was* an impressive view — Concession Street's bustle at their feet, lower Hamilton's geometrical grid in the middle distance, and Toronto's towers across the lake, hovering like disdainful ghosts.

Art cupped his hands above his eyes and peered at the panorama. "I remember the day they opened the Skyway. Must be fifty years ago. That bridge seemed like a fantasy much more than an engineering marvel. And from here, the way it soars over the lake and Burlington Bay, it's still an awesome sight."

Natasha helped the visitors out of their winter coats and into chairs around the conference table. The look on her face was a mix of worry and excitement. Zol knew how she loved the hunt of an epidemiological investigation, but cared so personally about the outcome that worry lines were etching themselves deeper and deeper into her forehead.

Art wheeled to an empty place at the table and pulled off his well-worn gloves. "Dr. Wakefield sends his regrets." His eyes showed the seriousness of the situation. "The cases keep piling up on the Mountain Wing."

The feather in Phyllis's hat flashed a yellow alert as she dipped her nose into the quilted bag in her lap. She lifted a sheaf of papers from the depths of a patchwork of blue jays and daffodils. "I'll be taking notes, and be certain to keep him abreast of our proceedings." She exchanged conspiratorial glances with Art and folded her hands on the table.

Earl wiped the sweat from his brow with a handkerchief. Zol didn't like the pallor in the man's face. Either the medication survey had exhausted him or he was anxious about presenting their results. Zol wished the group had accepted his offer to meet at the Lodge. This trip looked like it was more than Earl could handle. And by the way his pelvis wobbled when he walked, his arthritis was acting up. Phyllis had insisted on holding the meeting at the health unit, confessing they needed the fresh air and exercise.

Zol extended his hand to the fourth member of the contingent, a woman he'd never met. "Welcome," he said, "I'm Zol Szabo."

"Myrtle Hastings," she replied. She'd dressed for the occasion in a royal-blue suit she complemented with a string of pearls and matching earrings.

"Myrtle and Maude keyed in the data," Art explained. "Maude would have joined us but she has another appointment."

As Myrtle beamed, Zol turned to Earl, who looked desperate for encouragement. "I understand the medication survey was your idea, Earl. Would you like to start?"

Earl wiped his face, then massaged the back of his neck with gnarled fingers. He was clearly flustered. "It's Phyllis who has the gift of the . . ." He seemed to catch himself, then continued in a quieter tone, "She's much more eloquent." He turned to Phyllis, his broad face pinched. "Please . . . You've got the papers. You start."

Phyllis looked surprised, but accepted the compliment with a proud smile. "If you insist."

She explained that when the kitchen at Camelot Lodge did not appear responsible for the ongoing gastro outbreak — more than thirty episodes since early January, she reminded Zol — they turned their attention to their medications.

"After all," Art said, "collectively we swallow hundreds of pills a day."

Phyllis eyed Art impatiently. She liked having the floor and didn't appreciate the interruption. "Some of us far more than others," she clarified. "We created a . . . you know . . . a whatchamacallit," said Phyllis, looking searchingly at Natasha.

"A database," Natasha said.

"That's it. Yes, a database. It lists every medicine taken by every resident in the past three months."

Zol couldn't help asking, "What does Gloria think about you doing this?" Nursing-home operators could be touchy when it came to anything that smelled of scrutiny, and they were expert at hiding behind the residents' confidentiality card.

Art waved his hand dismissively. "No one's seen her since Tuesday. She must be holed up in her apartment, nursing her injuries."

"We don't need *her* permission anyway," Phyllis said. "Just the residents'. And they gave it unanimously."

Zol knew it was unlikely they'd obtained consent to snoop into the records of the Mountain Wing residents incapacitated with dementia, but this was no time to stand on ceremony. As a public health official investigating an outbreak, he was permitted to look at all pertinent facts. If anyone asked, the Camelot Irregulars had been working on his behalf. "How did you enter the data so quickly?" he asked.

"The medication record was very helpful," Art said.

Phyllis stopped him with her *I'm-speaking* look, then bestowed Myrtle with her smile of approval. "Myrtle and her sister Maude used to be professional keypunch operators. And they haven't lost their touch."

Myrtle gave a shy bow, then held up her hands and wiggled her fingers. All those years at the keyboard and they showed no sign of arthritis. Was repetitive strain injury only a new-age condition?

"We divided ourselves into two groups," Phyllis continued. "Gastro-afflicted and gastro-free. Twenty-one in the afflicted group and seventeen gastro-free." She nodded toward Natasha. "We could never have analyzed the data without Miss Sharma's guidance. It's one thing to collect the information and type it into the computer, but quite another to make sense of it."

"Actually," Natasha said, "the relational database did the analysis. I just nudged it in the right direction."

"It doesn't pay to be too modest, my dear," Phyllis said. "You helped us draw some important conclusions." Her smile held the promise of a revelation as she passed around printed copies of a data table.

These folks were taking dozens of medications, presumably to keep their minds bright, their hearts ticking, their limbs moving, and their metabolisms under control. How much of this polypharmacy was necessary, Zol wondered, and how much was unbridled collaboration between doctors and drug companies? Which was the stronger motivation, profit or patient care?

"A penny for your thoughts, Dr. Szabo?" Phyllis said.

There were too many drugs and numbers to digest on the spot. No obvious pattern. "Well . . . I . . . I think you've done an impressive job entering all that data."

"Do you see any correlations?"

"Not yet, I'm afraid."

"Fair enough," Phyllis pronounced, then glanced at Natasha as though there was some sort of conspiracy between them. She dipped into her bag and pulled out another set of printed sheets. She handed one to Zol. "Now, have a look at this."

The page held another table, much shorter than the previous.

	Gastro-Afflicted: 21 cases	Gastro-Free: 17 controls
Any arthritis medicine	21 (100%)	14 (82%)
Allopurinol (gouty arthritis)	0	1 (6%)
Acetaminophen	17 (81%)	14 (82%)
NSAIDs (mild arthritis)	8 (38%)	13 (76%)
Xanucox (severe arthritis)	18 (86%)	1 (6%)
Durimab (immune inhibitor)	4 (19%)	0

Zol couldn't take his eyes off the last two lines of the table. "This is an impressive correlation." He looked at Natasha. "There's no mistake?"

"We went over it three times. Checked the numbers against the medication administration record. And I personally verified that those nineteen people have been taking Xanucox, and no one else."

"And the Durimab?" Zol said.

"That as well," Natasha said. She paused and scanned the faces of her four partners. "And there's more. Two of the four getting Durimab injections have died." She ran a finger down a page in her scribbler. "Nellie Brownlow, the Prime Minister's aunt. And Gloria's mother, Raimunda Ferreira, who recovered from invasive listeria, then got gastroenteritis and passed away last week."

Zol stabbed the data table with a forefinger. "We'd better keep an eye on those two others getting Durimab."

"You're ... you're looking at one of them." Earl's face, somewhat pale a few minutes ago, was ashen. He wiped his forehead, then balled his hanky in his fist.

A moment later, his eyes glazed and his teeth began to chatter. His knees and elbows hammered against the chair in a violent shiver.

Zol hadn't seen a rigour that severe since he was an intern. He felt Earl's damp forehead. It burned with fever. Natasha handed Zol a glass of water, but when he tried to press it into Earl's fist, it was as though someone had thrown a switch. Earl's shivering ceased, his arms hung limp, the light vanished from his face. He teetered for a second then slumped unconscious against the table.

Natasha grabbed the phone and punched nine-one-one.

CHAPTER 19

Late that Thursday afternoon,
Hamish handed Todd Jarvie a paper
towel after the two men had washed their hands at the sink in the
utility room next to the Mountain Wing nursing station. This was
Todd's third day at Camelot, on an impromptu medical-school
elective arranged by Zol Szabo. Todd, a senior student, had taken
the night shifts on Tuesday and Wednesday and was functioning
efficiently on very little sleep. He seemed made for this work.

"We make a good team," Hamish told Todd. "You haven't missed
an IV yet."

Todd tossed the paper towel into the wastebasket and smiled. He
rubbed his palm across the stubble of his unshaven cheek. Hamish
usually hated that raspy sound because it reminded him of his
childhood, of his father warming up for an outburst of fury. But
there was a mellowness about Todd, a kindness in his eyes that neu-
tralized the painful memories.

"Thanks, Dr. Wakefield," Todd said, "but we need a break." He
seemed to catch himself and smiled sheepishly. "Well, you a lot
more than me. You haven't taken a step out of Camelot in nearly a
week. Good thing you found that ICU nurse to take the night shift
tomorrow. How about you and me going out for a drink?"

"Tomorrow?"

Todd nodded. "Sure."

"I don't know. I'm not much into the bar scene."

"The Reluctant Lion can be a lot of fun, especially on Friday nights when it's karaoke."

Todd stood almost a head taller than Hamish and bore a handsome, square-jawed face, a thick neck, and the rugged build of a bricklayer. His arms and shoulders were no stranger to the weight room. His sandy-blond hair was naturally dishevelled, not studied or moussed. His moustache and goatee looked great on him.

"Why would a guy like you want to go to a place like that?" Hamish asked.

"Um . . ." Todd hesitated, then pressed on. "You're new to the game, eh, Dr. Wakefield?"

"Please, call me Hamish. We must be the same age, and you've been in health care longer than I have."

"I'd say your gaydar has a pretty narrow focus . . . Hamish."

"What do you mean?"

"Do I have to spell it out?"

Hamish swallowed hard, then looked around to be sure they were still alone. "*You?* You don't mean . . ."

Todd nodded. "Well, yeah. Sure, I'm gay."

"You look so . . ."

"Normal? Masculine? Could pass for straight?"

"All of those. Exactly."

"I've got my hang-ups. But I'm comfortable in my own skin."

"I've barely crept out of the closet. Only been to one gay bar. A place downtown, across from the library. Ken took me there a couple of times."

"I know the one. Lawyers and academics. Awfully tame, but a safe place to enter the scene." Todd scratched an itch behind his ear. "Ken's your boyfriend?"

Hamish's second thoughts about Ken were growing stronger every day. He'd come to realize Ken was more a mentor than a boyfriend. A few months ago, he'd dragged Hamish out of the closet and shown him the ropes. The validation had been liberating and the sex a fantastic revelation, but surely there was more to a relationship than that. They used to see each other almost every day, but now it was down to once or twice a week.

"Ken's a trial lawyer," Hamish said. "Emotional warmth doesn't come with the package."

"I know what you mean. My partner in Cross Lake was a constable with the RCMP. Talk about cut and dried. No shades of grey with those guys. He thought I was crazy for applying to medical school, said I was already making good money as a nurse practitioner, and working in the north gave me as much independence as a GP. He refused to follow me to the decadent south. At first, I thought I'd made a big mistake, but . . ."

"Did you find another partner?"

"A couple of guys for a few weeks, but nothing serious." Todd read the alarm clouding Hamish's face. "It's okay, Mr. Infectious Diseases Doc, sir. I'm a stickler for condoms."

Todd pulled on his lab coat, then glanced at his watch. "Time to make the rounds with the vanco." He grabbed the bottle of vancomycin capsules from the medicine cart beside him. "I'm helping the nurses. They get a kick out of the fact that I used to be one of them. But I draw the line at bedpans. I'm not getting myself eighty thousand in debt to keep wiping bums and sluicing shit down a hopper."

The sleeve of Todd's lab coat caught on the medicine cart's open drawer, and the pill bottle flew out of his hand. It crashed to the floor, scattering blue-and-beige capsules everywhere. "Shit," he said, retrieving the empty bottle. "Geez, I'm sorry. That must be a five hundred dollars worth of vancomycin."

"Or more," said Hamish.

"Can we apply the five-second rule?"

Hamish crouched beside him and started gathering the dozens of overpriced capsules. "We may have to."

Todd crept forward on his haunches, scooping up the pills. A crunch came from beneath his shoe. His ears turned crimson. He knew he'd just crushed fifty dollars' worth of medicine under his heel. He slowly stood up and eased backwards.

Hamish struggled to hold his tongue. It was going to be quite a production to get the insurance company to pay for more vancomycin. He looked at the five splintered capsules on the linoleum. There was something strange about them. No mess. No white powder. He picked up the fractured shells and held them in his palm. "Hey, look at these."

Todd lifted one of the broken capsules and pinched it between his thumb and forefinger. "I don't believe it." He took a second one and eyed it closely. "Holy shit."

"Holy shit, all right," Hamish said. "They're blanks."

Hamish drummed his fingers against the nursing station counter. He'd been forced to listen to three levels of phone-attendant automatons at Steeltown Apothecary, and a gum-chewing clerk had put him on hold until the boss was free.

He hadn't seen Viktor Horvat since the man had tried to strangle him from his intensive-care bed. His stomach churned as he pictured the man's powerful, stubby fingers counting Betty's pills.

"Can I helping you, Dr. Wakefield?"

There was no mistaking that voice, that accent, but Hamish had to be sure. "Is that Mr. Horvat?"

"Yes, this Vik."

"I'm calling from Camelot Lodge." Hamish could feel his vocal cords tightening. The best he could manage was a dry croak. "There's a problem with the . . . with the vancomycin capsules you sent over."

"Sorry. I not hearing."

Hamish repeated himself.

"Problem?" Horvat said.

"They're empty."

"Bottle not empty. I count myself."

"Not the bottle. The capsules. Not a thing inside them."

"I not understanding, Doctor."

What was there not to understand? Was Hamish's croaky whisper too much for Horvat's limited English? Or was the man playing dumb on purpose?

Hamish passed the phone to Todd. "Here, you tell him." He pointed to his throat and shook his head. "This always happens when I get upset. He'll understand you better."

Todd introduced himself and told Horvat about the capsules getting accidentally crushed, then found to be empty. He also explained how he and Dr. Wakefield had opened up twenty more vancomycin capsules and found every one of them empty.

Todd passed the phone back to Hamish. "He says it's not his fault. He didn't open the capsules."

Hamish scanned the counter. Sometimes a glass of water or juice soothed his voice. Nothing in sight, of course. The infection-control measures on the Mountain Wing had put food and drink under strict control. "Of course, Mr. Horvat," he said, forcing out the words, one by one, "it's not your fault. But you did send us dummies. No medicine inside."

"What you want I should doing?"

"Send me another bottle as soon as you can."

"I am needing permission from insurance company."

"Call your supplier, tell them what happened, and get them to send a replacement right away. They'll be happy to do what it takes, even send it by taxi."

"Taxi? From Toronto?"

"Sure. It's their fault. They sent you the empty capsules." Hamish had no idea where the empty capsules had originated — from Horvat himself or from a legitimate supplier. But this was no time to get the man's back up by accusing him of fraud. Especially a guy with an ugly temper. He glanced at the clock. Four-thirty. Horvat's drug wholesaler should still be open. They'd be mortified that a batch of empty capsules might have left their warehouse. And they'd move heaven and earth to deliver a new set today. They could get them here in an hour.

"And Vik?"

"Yeah?"

Hamish wanted to tell him that if he got the vanco delivered to Camelot by six o'clock this evening, they'd be even. But Horvat wouldn't remember him from the ICU. All Hamish could bring himself to say was, "Um . . . thanks."

At five-fifty-five, Todd dashed out of the stairwell and into the Mountain Wing nursing station. "Here you are," he said, handing Hamish a white paper bag with *Steeltown Apothecary* printed in large blue letters.

"Did you see Horvat?" Hamish asked.

"No. Some other guy made the delivery."

"What a royal screw-up. I hope he gave his wholesaler you-know-what."

Hamish washed his hands at the sink, then opened the bag and lifted out the white pill bottle inside it. He unscrewed the lid, pulled out the useless cotton batten that always found its way into medicine bottles, and peered at the two-toned capsules. They seemed darker in colour than the first lot of vancomycin.

He shook four capsules into his palm. "Wash your hands, then examine these carefully. Compare them with the others."

Todd washed and dried his hands, then shook out two capsules from the first vancomycin bottle, now marked with an X. He looked from his palm to Hamish's, examining the two sets of capsules. "The blue is the same, eh? But the brown looks darker."

Hamish rolled two of the new capsules in his fingers and held them up. "These have '125 mg' printed on them. And the brand name. Is there any printing on yours?"

"No."

"Put the imposters away, then do the honours with a few of mine."

Todd looked puzzled for a second, then said, "You mean, open the new ones?"

"Just a few."

"But they're so expensive."

"And useless, if they're empty."

Todd took one of the new capsules and tried to pull it apart. It wouldn't budge. "Is there a knife around here somewhere?"

Hamish opened a couple of drawers before finding a pair of bandage scissors. "Try these."

Todd snipped through the middle of a capsule, then inverted the two open halves. A tiny mound of white powder glinted on the countertop.

"That's more like it," Hamish said.

"Should I try a couple of others?"

"Before you do that, let's make sure they all look alike."

Hamish looked around for a dish. On the far end of the counter he spotted a plate under a bedraggled geranium. He washed the plate with soap and hot water, dried it, and lined it with a fresh paper towel. He dumped the sixty new vancomycin capsules onto the paper and raked them with his fingers.

"What do you think?" asked Hamish.

"They all look identical to me."

"Open two more."

Todd took the scissors, picked two capsules at random, and snipped them open. White powder puffed out of both of them.

"Should we taste it?" Todd asked.

"You can if you like, but I've got no idea what vancomycin is supposed to taste like."

"Never mind." Todd looked pensive for a moment, then walked over to the medicine cart and rummaged through its drawers. "Geez, where are they?" he said, after opening the fourth drawer. "The girls here are sloppy with their meds. Every drawer should be labelled."

"What are you looking for?"

Todd grinned in obvious satisfaction as he lifted a bottle of pills from the lowest drawer on the cart. "Here they are. Left over from a previous patient."

"What?"

"Metronidazole capsules," Todd said. "I know what *this* drug tastes like. Bitter as hell."

"We're not using it. Not worth a damn."

Todd took one metronidazole capsule from the bottle and snipped its green and grey shell across the middle with the scissors. There was a puff of white powder. As Hamish watched, Todd opened three more capsules.

White powder in all of them.

Todd licked his finger, dipped it in the powder, then touched it to the tip of his tongue. "Yup. This is bitter all right."

Hamish felt a hot wave of understanding rise from his gut into his throat. The empty vancomycin capsules were no mistake. Horvat had dispensed them on purpose. He hadn't wasted his time supplying fake metronidazole because the real thing only cost five cents a capsule. But at ten dollars each, vancomycin capsules were well worth faking.

Todd had come to the same realization. "If Horvat has clients all over the city," he said, "he's making some serious coin." His eyes grew distant, as though conjuring some half-forgotten image. He scratched his ear. After a moment he said, "Do you read the *Spectator*?"

Hamish shook his head. "Afraid not." He didn't have time to read newspapers. Not even the hometown rag.

"There's been quite the story lately about a local pharmacist — Viktor somebody. He's trying to get his son freed from a prison in Mexico."

"So?"

"He claims the charges — drug trafficking — are trumped up. Just a way for the Mexicans to make money out of an unsuspecting Canadian tourist."

"Extortion?"

"I guess. This Vik guy claims the Mexican judicial system is in the business of legalized kidnapping — charging him half a million dollars in lawyers' fees to spring his son from a rat-infested prison in Juarez."

"And . . . you think the Vik in the *Spectator* is our Vik from Steeltown?"

"Being held to legalized ransom would be one hell of a motive for selling fake drugs at ten dollars a pop."

Todd's eyes widened. He rose from his seat and began rifling through the medication cart again. He grabbed three patients' blister-packed medication cards and tossed them on the table.

"What?" Hamish said.

"Somebody needs to take a good look at these. Not the cheap generics, but the expensive brand-name meds. These packs could be full of counterfeits."

Hamish walked to the sink and turned on the faucet. He closed his eyes and splashed cold water on his face. He was way beyond his comfort zone.

CHAPTER 20

Shortly after six-thirty that evening, Zol hung up the kitchen phone and turned to Colleen. "Hamish is in a flap," he said. "He's coming right over."

Colleen frowned at him. "Oh no. Is it Betty?"

"No, she's just the same. Something else has got him worked up."

"Does he know about Earl?"

"Not yet."

Colleen touched Zol's arm and gave it a squeeze. He knew she shared his anxiety about Betty's condition and his anger that no hospital would let her in the door. Earl was lucky he'd collapsed at the health unit. The ambulance had no choice but to take him directly to Emergency at Caledonian.

Colleen smiled, her earrings glinting in the flood of the ceiling halogens. She turned to the stove and stirred the risotto. As with most things, she had just the right touch. A heavy hand could pulp risotto into ponderous porridge. "There's plenty of risotto," she said. "He can stay for dinner. Did he say what's wrong?"

"You know Hamish. He prefers the drama of the face-to-face disclosure. And when his voice gets like that, you can never tell on the phone whether he's angry or excited."

"The poor fellow has been cooped up in that residence all week."

Zol pulled the wide chopping blade from the rack, then opened the refrigerator for salad fixings. The sky was dark and wintry gusts were rattling the windows, but with the kitchen pot lights turned up high you could pretend it was spring in the Mediterranean. Greek salad, Italian risotto, and chicken roasted à la *Française* with plenty of garlic would do the trick.

When Hamish arrived half an hour later, stone-faced and subdued, he apologized for being late. He'd stopped at the car wash, which Zol knew was as much Hamish's meditative haven as a place to buff the salt and slush from his ever-shiny Saab. At the front door, Hamish performed his ritual alignment of his shoes against the wall, adjusted his tie in the mirror, and ran his hand across his flattop. In the kitchen, he lathered his hands at the sink with the diligence of a brain surgeon.

When Hamish had finished washing and drying, Zol handed him a glass of wine. Hamish seldom drank a full glass of anything alcoholic, but maybe it would throw a little colour into his cheeks. Zol closed the door of the computer room where Max was absorbed in his thirty-minute ration of pre-dinner video games. Whatever was bothering Hamish wouldn't be suitable for nine-year-old ears.

Hamish gulped the Chenin Blanc without showing any sign of tasting it, then he dropped onto a chair and blurted out the story of finding the empty capsules. He wasted no time in preambles, and his right hand was so busy clutching his wineglass that the professorial finger had no chance to make its appearance.

"You mean, nothing in them at all?" said Colleen. "Not even salt or sugar?"

"Nothing," said Hamish.

"Unbelievable," Zol said. "The guy's either incredibly bold or mighty desperate."

The flush was returning to Hamish's cheeks. "But . . . but what do we do?"

"Extraordinary," Colleen said. "Sounds like a matter for the police. But it's anyone's guess which force has jurisdiction — the city? the OPP? the RCMP?"

Zol shook his head. "Doesn't matter. It's impossible to get guys like these on criminal charges and make them stick."

"Come off it, Zol," Hamish said, his face crimson. "People have probably *died* because of those fake capsules. Betty's can't be the first case of C diff treated with Horvat's bogus vanco. He's got to be locked up — for fraud *and* murder."

"Attempted murder, or manslaughter, at the least," Colleen said.

"You'd think so," Zol told them, "but the RCMP — and the courts — were useless the last time. There were deaths then, too."

"*Last* time?" Colleen said. A pensive look came over her face. "Oh yes. That pharmacy in the north end. What was it they were dispensing?"

"Counterfeit antihypertensives," Zol said. He pushed out of his chair and retrieved his briefcase from the living room. It was loaded with dozens of reports he was supposed to read and digest — whenever he got the time.

He heaved a stack of papers onto the table. Halfway through the pile, he found what he was looking for: *Pharmacy Connection*, the official publication of the Ontario College of Pharmacists.

"It's all in here," said Zol, holding up the colourful journal. "Trinnock insisted I commit the circumstances to memory in case it happened again. Looks like the old bugger was right." He flipped to the dog-eared page he'd been reading before he was distracted by something more pressing.

He took a gulp of wine, read the summary, and paraphrased it for Hamish and Colleen.

After an alert from a sharp-eyed customer, the RCMP and a private investigator determined that a pharmacy in the north end of Hamilton was dispensing counterfeit high-blood-pressure tablets. The RCMP forensics laboratory established that the counterfeits, not quite identical in appearance to the real thing, contained no active ingredients. The brand-name manufacturer, a pharmaceutical giant, recalled and tested its tablets from pharmacies throughout the province but found no other counterfeits. The only fakes were in that pharmacy in Hamilton. The wholesale distributor was off the hook.

"It had to be an inside job," said Zol. "The two pharmacists involved were charged and taken to court. And you know what? They got off. Found not guilty of anything."

"You're kidding," Hamish said.

To drive home the point, Zol read word-for-word from the publication in his hands. "'The judge concluded that the Crown had not demonstrated beyond a reasonable doubt that the pharmacists actually knew they were selling counterfeit drugs.'"

"Horse feathers," said Colleen. "Of course they knew."

The wine's blush drained from Hamish's cheeks. Beads of sweat glistened on his brow. "What about the College of Pharmacists?" he asked. "Didn't they conduct an investigation? Subject the pharmacists to disbarment, or whatever they call it?"

Zol scanned the final paragraph of the case summary. "The pharmacists received an official reprimand and were ordered to take remedial training. They didn't lose their licences."

"How long was the pharmacy closed?" Colleen asked.

"One day," said Zol, "while the wholesaler cleared the entire inventory and restocked it with new."

"Outrageous," Hamish said.

"And it's happening again," Colleen said.

"Pretty good scam," Zol said. "Nicely lucrative, and only a slap on the wrist if you get caught."

Hamish, too edgy to stay seated, wiped the counter with a tea towel and leaned against the granite.

Colleen narrowed her eyes and ran her finger around the rim of her wineglass. She hadn't taken a sip since Hamish had started his account. "But still, it is a bit risky. After all, the pharmacists did get caught. What's Vik's motivation? It's got to be more than simple greed."

"Can I use your computer for a sec?" Hamish asked. "I want to Google a story that's been running in the *Spectator*."

Zol checked his watch. It was time to get the chicken out of the oven. "Sure," his said, pointing to the family-room door. "And tell Max I said it's time to get cleaned up for supper."

By the time Zol and Colleen had four dinners plated and on the kitchen table, Hamish was back. A look of satisfaction replaced his earlier outrage and dismay.

"Found something?" Colleen asked.

"I believe it's called a hat trick," Hamish said, holding up three fingers. "The same Viktor Horvat owns Steeltown Apothecary, nearly strangled me in the ICU, and has been raving in the press about his son being held for ransom in a Mexican prison."

Zol took a slug of his Chenin Blanc. "There must be a lot more to Vik than a bottle of empty capsules." He opened the side pocket of his briefcase and pulled out the medication survey that Phyllis and the group had presented that afternoon. "Look at this," he said, pointing to the bolded rows at the bottom of the page. "How do we explain the link between Camelot's gastro and these two arthritis drugs — Xanucox and Durimab?"

Hamish studied the sheet. Finally, in the monotone that came out whenever he was anxious or concentrating, he said, "Brings us back to money."

"How so?" Colleen said.

Hamish's professorial finger, freed from the wineglass, asserted itself. "Those drugs are really expensive. A month's supply of Xanucox runs about two hundred and fifty bucks. And Durimab is easily twice that. Neither drug is on the government's drug benefit list. To afford them, you have to be wealthy or belong to a generous private plan."

Zol eyed the plates steaming on the table, then winked at Colleen. "I hope the private detective assigned to the case this time is a lot smarter than the one who dropped the ball in the north end."

Max skipped into the kitchen, game gadget in hand. His eyes widened at the sight of supper on the table. Zol fastened the buckles on his briefcase and slid it under the telephone desk. It was time to put away the worries and enjoy the meal and the Chenin Blanc, at least for a few minutes.

CHAPTER 21

At eight-thirty that Thursday night, Art edged the foldable wheelchair, which he used for car-trip transfers, in through the front doors of Camelot Lodge. It took the last flicker of strength left in his arms. Phyllis was still parking the Lincoln, and Myrtle was striding to the elevator. He knew she was bursting to get to her room and share the afternoon's events with her sister Maude. The two were practically inseparable, and incredibly robust. They never got sick, never needed medication. What was their secret? Good luck or good genes? Art waved her on, explaining that he needed to catch his breath before transferring to his scooter and heading upstairs.

The afternoon's ordeal at Caledonian Medical Centre had been exhausting and humiliating. By the time Phyllis had found a spot to park the Lincoln in the visitors' lot, and Myrtle had lugged Art's wheelchair out of the trunk, poor Earl had been whisked into a treatment room in the dark reaches of the emergency department. He'd been consigned out of bounds, beyond the reach of three friends trying to find out what condition he was in, whether he was even still alive.

"Are you next of kin?" the nurse had replied to Art's first enquiry at the reception desk. She hadn't bothered looking at him, just kept writing on the forms it seemed she'd stacked on the counter to shield herself from an anxious public.

Art admitted that he and Earl were not related, but felt like brothers after a friendship of more than sixty years. The nurse tightened her lips and told him she couldn't divulge any information. Details about the patient's condition would be made available only to relatives. Phyllis tried her full-bosomed stance and crisp stare, but the nurse returned an equally stern glare and told them to take a seat in the waiting room. Some hours later, Art tried again with a different nurse, then pleaded with a baby-faced doctor, but was given the same unyielding responses. He and Phyllis finally returned with Myrtle to the Lincoln, forced to abandon their friend to whatever the system decided to do with him. On the ride home, none of them had the energy to speak.

Art set the wheelchair's brakes and transferred to his loyal steed waiting in the lobby. He thanked Phyllis and wished her goodnight as she came through the door, then rubbed at the burning in his legs. His neuropathy played up something fierce when he got overtired. After a couple of minutes the pain eased a little. He flipped the scooter's switch and drove into the common room. The walls of the deserted, tomb-silent room pressed in on him. They flooded him with memories of the funeral parlour after Jeannie's service, of his overwhelming desolation when the last of the guests had departed. It was then he knew he'd lost her forever to the pain and disfigurement of metastatic breast cancer. During his ten years as a widower, he'd become accustomed to living on his own and consoling himself with the notion that though death had changed his relationship with the love of his life, the relationship had not ended. He still had his memories of the wonderful times they'd shared, he could talk to her when he felt fearful or alone, and he could imagine her encouraging him at his easel and piano.

But then the peripheral neuropathy began to suck the strength from his legs, and his doctor took away his driver's licence. Being shut away in suburbia all winter without a car made him ache with loneliness. The move into the camaraderie of the Lodge had given new zest and meaning to his life. But today, with Earl and Betty fighting for their lives, and poor Melvin being buried tomorrow, the loneliness was palpable again and magnified with dread. As it had been in the suburbs, old age felt like a dry run for eternity: monotonous days of profound fatigue, relentless pain, tasteless meals, and fading eyesight stretching on for ever and ever.

Maude and Myrtle's jigsaw puzzle lay jumbled and abandoned on the card table. Gertie's knitting, a fixture on the blue sofa, had vanished — packed away or confiscated. All that remained was the imprint of her ample bottom on the cushions. Art scanned the room and found not a teacup, a paperback, a crossword in sight. Gloria had issued another quarantine order. Camelot Lodge was not a cozy home but an asylum, where inmates hid in their cells and ventured out like frightened rabbits, only at mealtimes. Art wanted to grab Betty and run, but who would take in a desperate elderly couple tainted by a deadly plague? Zol had offered the run of his house, bless him, but the bedrooms were upstairs, as inaccessible as Everest. And it wouldn't be right to abandon Phyllis, Earl, and the others.

The confidence of youthful footsteps approached from behind him. Art turned to see Joe, Gloria's accident-prone nephew, carrying a bottle of beer in one hand, a full plate in the other, and a second beer tucked under his arm. His right eye was black and swollen as a result of the other day's hit and run. A line of blue stitches scored the skin above his right eyebrow.

Art gestured toward the double-decker sandwich piled on Joe's plate. "Feeling better?"

"I guess. But Jesus, I ache all over."

Art smiled and nodded. "They say the third day is the worst. You feel like you've been run over by a steamroller, but then it passes. How's your aunt?"

"Who?" Joe looked puzzled for an instant, then chuckled at his momentary lapse in concentration. "Oh, yeah. She's okay. Says it's all my fault."

"Your fault? I thought it was a hit and run."

Joe took a swig of his beer then wiped his mouth with the back of his hand. He strode to the sofa and dropped into Gertie's spot. "Long story," he said, setting the beers on the table then biting hungrily into his sandwich.

Art said goodbye and headed for the elevators. Betty had looked rough this morning. And gaunt. She hadn't eaten a thing in almost a week, and it was showing in her face. He scrunched his eyes and allowed himself a little prayer: *Please may she look a tiny bit better tomorrow.*

As he waited for the elevator, Art pondered the tattoo he'd just seen on Joe's bicep. What was a Portuguese fellow doing with a tattoo of a maple-leaf military crest and the words *Jason Argylls Forever* below it? The men of the Argyll and Sutherland were Canadian soldiers, based in Hamilton. In Art's day, soldiers tattooed the names of their sweethearts on their arms. Was this a sign that Joe entangled himself romantically with men? These days, you never could tell who was who and what was what — not a bad thing, he supposed. They called it diversity, and if it made for a better world, then Art was all for it.

Joe had made quite the scene at the time of the accident. He'd gotten riled up when Dr. Wakefield had asked if he knew the identity of the hit-and-run driver. Joe had intimated the car crash was intentional, that something similar had happened before. Was this a grudge match in the wake of a failed liaison with a soldier named Jason? Is that why Joe was so tight-lipped about the circumstances of the accident?

Raimunda's funeral was set for Saturday afternoon. After that, her ruffian grandson would be catching his return flight to Portugal and taking his vendettas with him. And good riddance.

CHAPTER 22

At ten-forty on Friday morning, Natasha's heartbeat fluttered in her throat as Colleen drew the Mercedes to a stop on a quiet side street two blocks away from Steeltown Apothecary. Natasha had awoken at six with a stomach full of butterflies — heck, they were cockroaches — and hadn't been able to face breakfast.

In about five minutes, she'd be walking into the strip mall at Mohawk and Magnolia, into Viktor Horvat's lair. Colleen had shown her photos of the man. He looked surprisingly ordinary — forties, medium height, short brown hair, beefy face and hands.

Colleen killed the ignition and unlocked the doors. She touched Natasha's arm and told her to take a few deep breaths. "Honestly, you look fantastic, like you just stepped off the last Air India flight."

Natasha checked her *tilak* in the rear-view mirror. The dot of red kumkum was positioned exactly where it should be, in the *Ajna Chakra*, the space between her eyebrows. "You're sure the hair's okay?"

"It's perfect. Looks a hundred percent natural. And that sari's a stunner."

"Not too stunning, I hope. It's my cousin's. She said the yellow and green were suitably subtle. Told me mine were too flashy for a trip to a pharmacy." Her cousin Anjum had fifty saris, one for every occasion, including spying on villains, it seemed. Natasha had only three, in fuchsias and blues with gold trim — strictly for weddings and Hindu celebrations like Diwali.

"You better ditch the shades," Colleen said. "With that trench coat over your sari, and that long gorgeous hair, you look enough like a Bollywood star."

Natasha pulled off her sunglasses and gripped them in her fist. "But . . ."

"Much better. You don't need them. Even your best friends wouldn't recognize you today."

Colleen looked in the mirror and straightened her Ray-Bans, then tucked her ponytail under the wide-brimmed Tilley hat that dwarfed her face. In her denim jacket and jeans, and rubber boots from Wal-Mart, she looked like a farmer — one of those organic types who cruise the shelves for natural supplements and herbal remedies.

She cracked open her door, then paused. "Remember, give me three minutes. I'll be scouting inside when you arrive. And whatever you do, don't pay me any attention."

"But what about the red hanky? You said —"

Colleen's face looked taut and serious. She wasn't wearing a speck of makeup. "Don't look at my face." She tapped her jacket's breast pocket. "Just a quick glance here."

They'd agreed to abort the mission if the red hanky was showing. If Natasha saw the signal, she was to casually exit the pharmacy without approaching anyone.

The three minutes alone in Colleen's car felt like three hours. Natasha held the key fob of the Mercedes in her fist and practised her script, unsure whether she felt more frightened or excited. She'd never expected that a Master's in epidemiology would lead her undercover into a crime scene. Stuffy lectures, case-control studies, and statistical formulas seemed light-years away.

She stepped out of the car, taking care with the long, flowing hem of Anjum's sari. She clicked the door locks and pocketed

Colleen's fob in her trench coat. The other pocket held her sunglasses — just in case.

She started striding toward the strip mall and tripped on a piece of ice. She caught herself in time without falling and forced herself to slow down. South Asian women were supposed to take dainty steps. Bold strides were for Canadian women wearing jeans or short skirts. As her mother never stopped harping, stepping lightly was part of knowing your place. Natasha dodged the icy patches on the sidewalk and concentrated on her footwork. She could feel her cheeks flush at the thought of those two pharmacists in north Hamilton last year, duping the vulnerable with fake medicines and getting away with barely a rap on the knuckles from the College of Pharmacists. Well, Viktor Horvat was going to get nailed.

When Dr. Zol phoned her last night, he confessed that the case seemed more like a police matter than a public health concern. He'd described how useless the RCMP counterfeit squad had been last time and reminded her that catching Horvat in the act required the same scientific vigour they used at the health unit when sleuthing out food poisonings and streptococcal epidemics. Nursing homes came under the jurisdiction of the Ministry of Health, which meant that health-unit staff were responsible for addressing breaches in the legislated codes. It looked like Viktor Horvat had been breaching umpteen codes at Camelot Lodge. Catching him willfully dispensing counterfeit medications was truly in the public interest. When she'd volunteered last night to play her part, it seemed the natural thing to do. Today, she felt anything but natural.

As Steeltown Apothecary came into view, past a dry cleaner's and a pizza place, she closed her fists and reminded herself that she was not doing anything criminal. She was just running an errand at a drugstore, while wearing a long black wig, a *tilak*, and a sari.

She stepped into the store and felt a wave of panic rise from her chest. It was a fairly small shop, and she couldn't see Colleen. There was no way she could do this without Colleen watching her back, ready to pounce to her rescue. She turned to dash from the store — to heck with the dainty steps — when she saw the top of

Colleen's hat in the vitamin aisle beside the far wall. At barely five feet tall, Colleen could make herself almost invisible. When she turned, she ignored Natasha completely, apparently absorbed in the process of choosing among bottles of bee pollen and shark cartilage. There was no red flag in her pocket.

Natasha tugged at the lapels of her trench coat and pulled out her sunglasses. She stared at them for a moment, took a few deep breaths, then returned them to her coat pocket. Yes, she could do this.

She picked up a shopping basket and headed for the hair-products aisle. The familiar bottles of shampoo and conditioner made her feel at home. She strolled in the direction of the dispensary at the rear of the store, keeping one eye on the hair stuff and the other on the pharmacist's counter a few steps away.

The only person visible in the dispensary was a woman in her thirties. She stapled a receipt to a paper bag and passed it to a customer. The phone rang beside her. She spoke into it briefly, then turned and called, "Dr. Carter on the line."

Natasha grabbed a bottle of her favourite shampoo and pretended to study its label. Out of the corner of her eye, she saw movement at the counter. She gripped the bottle and turned for a better look. A man in his forties was standing there, drying his beefy hands with a paper towel. There was no mistaking his identity from the photos Colleen had shown her this morning. His grim face with broad forehead, large round cheeks, and flat dark eyes set her heart racing faster. He'd be a formidable opponent in any showdown.

An unholy crash thundered at her feet. The cardboard display and its dozens of shampoo bottles tumbled to the floor, the avalanche triggered by her coat sleeve.

Horvat looked up. He frowned. His dark eyes pierced her face, memorizing its features so he could point her out in court when he sued her for damages. Oh shit!

He finished drying his hands, then pressed a button on the phone and picked up the receiver. As he spoke, his head bobbed, and the stainless-steel cap on his front tooth flashed in the harsh fluorescent light of the dispensary. He pulled a pen from his lab-coat pocket and scribbled on a pad.

She stood there dumb and helpless, staring at the mess of shampoo containers and feeling hotter and hotter under the ridiculous wig. Finally, a skinny teenage boy sauntered down the aisle carrying a mop.

"I'm so sorry," Natasha said, squatting to recover the bottles.

The boy righted the display without comment. None of the containers had broken. Soon, everything was back in place. The boy took off, leaving Natasha with panic washing over her again. What should she do? Had she drawn so much attention to herself that it was impossible to go through with her mission? Colleen appeared like a genie at the far end of the aisle, apparently ogling the fair-trade coffee. Still no red signal in her pocket.

Natasha grabbed bottles of shampoo, conditioner, and hair gel and tossed them into her basket. She scanned the aisle for Colleen's reassuring presence. Her mentor was gone. Oh my God, she was on her own. Was that a good sign? It better be. She straightened her shoulders and pushed annoying strands of wig hair behind her ears.

Viktor Horvat was off the phone and counting tablets on a tray when she approached his dispensary. She fished in her trench coat for the prescription Dr. Wakefield had written out for her earlier this morning. Oh no, she'd lost it. Her knees felt like rubber. Where was it? Oh yes, now she remembered. She'd put it in the outer pocket of her purse. She must look a sight — embarrassed and terrified. Maybe that was okay. She was supposed to be a recent immigrant picking up a prescription for her grandmother — brand name Zytopril.

The medication survey had shown that eighty percent of Camelot's residents were taking Zytopril for high blood pressure. Dr. Wakefield said that if Horvat were running a counterfeit substitution scam, Zytopril was a perfect target: it was covered by the government's drug plan for seniors, Dr. Jamieson prescribed it like candy, and the high price of the originals made for high profit margins on the fakes.

Horvat gave her a knowing look that quickly broke into a mocking grin, hardened by the steel tooth. "How many you break?"

"Pardon?" she said, forgetting to put on the just-off-the-plane Indian accent that always made her friends laugh. They wouldn't be laughing at this.

"Hair stuff displaying. Company is giving us that. Fall down always. How many you break?"

"Um . . . none, sir."

He scowled at her skeptically. "Okay. What you want?"

She handed him the prescription. "For my grandmother, sir. Her blood-pressure medication." Her accent was on track.

Horvat took the paper, studied it, then shook his head. "I not knowing this name. Is customer here?"

Natasha's mouth felt as dry as sandalwood. She hadn't expected the third degree. "I am sorry, sir. I am not knowing."

Horvat turned to his computer and clicked at the keyboard. "Address and phone number."

"My grandmother's?"

He looked at her as though she'd just grown a beard. "Of course."

She hesitated, frightened to give Horvat her grandmother's personal details. All of a sudden, her entire family seemed at risk. Would he come after them? Dr. Zol said this had to be a bona fide transaction if they were to catch Horvat willfully selling counterfeit meds. It had been Natasha's idea to come here undercover; Dr. Zol had tried to talk her out of it. And now it was too late to turn back.

She told Horvat her grandmother's real address and phone number, then stumbled over the postal code.

"Date of birth?" he asked, squinting at the computer screen.

Natasha had to think for a moment, then forced herself to recite what seemed like the greatest violation yet.

"Then she a senior," he concluded. "Over sixty-five. Need health card number."

In what felt like a final act of betrayal, Natasha pulled a photocopy of her grandmother's Ontario health card from her purse. The only consolation was that the copier did such a poor job of the photo that her grandmother was unrecognizable.

Horvat shook his head. "Need to see card. Copy no good."

"But . . ."

Horvat sighed heavily, his metallic tooth a piece of machinery between his heavy lips. He took the photocopy and seared her with a stern look. "This real? You sure? You people . . . always try to cheating."

Natasha squared her shoulders. How dare he? She opened her mouth, steadied herself for a sharp retort, then dropped her gaze. She studied her size-six Stuart Weitzman pumps. Dainty steps today, she told herself. If she did this right, the cops would be stomping all over Horvat by next week — Canadian strides in sturdy leather boots.

"I am sorry, sir," she said meekly, concentrating on the authenticity of her accent. "She is always keeping card in handbag." She pointed to the crinkled photocopy. "That is proper number from goh'ment."

Horvat huffed and typed the number into the computer. The printer beside him spat out a label, which he detached and tossed into a basket on the counter. "Ten minute."

CHAPTER 23

Ninety minutes later, having ditched the wig, the sari, and the *tilak*, Natasha stepped into the staff room at the Lakeview Pharma on Concession Street, a good three dozen blocks east of Steeltown Apothecary. She felt safe in this part of town, up the street from the health unit. She took a seat next to Todd Jarvie, the medical student helping Dr. Wakefield at Camelot Lodge. Todd's uncle, Wayne, closed the door behind him and dragged a chair in front of it.

A hesitant smile lit Wayne Jarvie's face as he slid into the chair opposite Natasha. Wayne and Todd looked more like brothers than uncle and nephew — same neatly trimmed moustache and goatee, similar mid-brown hair, though only Wayne's was highlighted. Wayne lacked Todd's muscle-man shoulders. As the owner of a chain of drugstores throughout the Hamilton region and a high-profile Rotarian, he wouldn't have time for toning his pecs. Still, he looked fit and had the healthy glow of a recent few days in the south. He seemed too earnest for tanning salons. His delicious cologne wafted her way. How wonderful to own the store and wear any perfume you wanted, on the house.

"It's very good of you to help us out, Mr. Jarvie," Natasha said, lifting her briefcase onto her lap.

"Todd said it was important," Wayne replied. He glanced at the door. "And very hush-hush. But please, call me Wayne."

Todd pulled his chair closer to the table and turned to his uncle. "I know how pissed you were about those two guys operating that counterfeit drug scam on Barton Street."

"Bad news for pharmacists everywhere," Wayne said. "They tainted all of us, made us look like charlatans. It took six months before my customers stopped looking at me sideways."

Natasha undid the toggles on her briefcase, then hesitated before revealing its contents. "I'm not sure how much Todd told you on the phone, but —"

"I'm all ears," Wayne said. "So go ahead and start at the beginning."

Natasha told him about the empty vancomycin capsules on Camelot's Mountain Wing, her trip to Steeltown Apothecary to fill her grandmother's Zytopril prescription (she left out the part about her disguise), and the sampling of Zytopril tablets from among the eighty percent of Camelot residents who were taking it.

"Eighty percent of them are on Zytopril?" Wayne said.

"Does that seem like a lot?" Natasha asked.

"Sure does. Most people do fine with tried-and-true generic antihypertensives. Zytopril is new and expensive. Government reimbursement kicks in only if the doctor verifies that cheaper drugs haven't worked or are contraindicated." He examined his nails and absently twisted the large black opal on his left hand. "I can guess who prescribed it," he said softly. "Dr. Jamieson, eh?"

"Hey," Todd said. "How did you know?"

"In this city, he's Zytopril's biggest fan. I see more prescriptions from him than anyone else."

"An early adopter?" Todd suggested.

"I suppose," Wayne said. "But it could have something to do with his sister being the regional sales rep."

Natasha pulled out the bottle of Zytopril blood-pressure tablets Viktor Horvat had handed her at his dispensary. She set it on the table and shivered at her grandmother's name glaring from the label.

Wayne dipped into his lab-coat pocket and pulled out a large white plastic bottle. The drug company's logo beamed from the label, and under it *Zytopril 50mg*. Natasha knew the logo well; she saw it every morning when she shook a pill from her birth-control dispenser. She figured any company that saved her from mortal shame and the eternal condemnation of her family was a lifesaver.

Wayne opened his jumbo bottle of Zytopril and shook a dozen tablets onto a small plastic tray. "Let's have a look at these first. As far as I can tell, they're the gold standard. I trust my wholesaler."

Natasha picked up three of Wayne's brand-name Zytoprils and examined them. Each tablet was round, about four millimetres in diameter, and a pretty shade of turquoise. *ZYT* was printed on one side in bright white letters, and below it, *50mg*. The obverse was blank.

"Okay," Wayne said, "now let's look at what Natasha got today from Vik Horvat at Steeltown."

She opened her small bottle and poured a few pills onto a blank sheet she tore from her notebook. Her heart sank in disappointment as she studied the tablets. They looked exactly like Wayne's, the gold standard. All that sweating under a silly wig to catch Viktor Horvat deceiving the public had amounted to nothing.

Wayne examined her tablets carefully then shot her an inquiring look. "What do you think?"

"They're the same as yours," she said, feeling defeated. "Identical in every way."

"Yeah," Todd said. "But . . . could they be knock-offs anyway?"

"It's possible," Wayne said. "Counterfeits often look perfect, though occasionally the printing may be slightly off. The fakes from Barton Street looked perfect, except for the printing. You had to look closely to see that the letters weren't uniformly crisp and the ink wasn't quite the right colour."

"Can we look at these?" Todd asked, holding Mr. Greenwood's blister card from Camelot.

Wayne pulled a magnifying glass from his coat pocket. "Sure."

Each compliance-enhancing blister card was the size of a sheet of letter paper and contained a resident's weekly allotment of pills in a four-by-seven matrix of easy-to-open blisters: four times a day for seven days. The cards made it convenient for nurses to dispense drugs accurately in nursing homes and for independent residents to manage their own medications. Dr. Wakefield had obtained a dozen cards from Camelot this morning and given them to Todd. Narcotics were kept under lock and key at the Lodge, but the other drugs were readily accessible from the Belvedere residents themselves.

"Do you provide these to your customers?" Natasha asked Wayne.

"Sure do. For over twenty institutions — retirement residences, nursing homes, group homes."

"Wow. How many clients does that work out to?" Todd asked.

"Oh, about fifteen hundred. Steeltown has a good deal more. I know, 'cuz the bugger often underbids me."

"You have to bid for the institutions to give you their business?" Natasha asked.

"In a backhanded way," Wayne said. "In general, pharmacies make so much money on the dispensing fees that nursing homes expect a kickback for granting them access to their residents."

Kickback, thought Natasha, what a nasty word. Entirely out of place in health care and so unexpected from the mouth of the genial Wayne Jarvie.

"Can I ask," Todd said, "how ... um ... how much coin a pharmacy brings in a month from providing prescriptions to a place like Camelot?"

Wayne smiled. "Don't need to be bashful about it, Todd. We're all grown-ups." He pulled out a pen and jotted down a few calculations. "Each retirement-home resident is on six to twelve different medications at any one time," he explained. "The pharmacy's dispensing fee, paid by the government, is eight dollars per month, per medication. That's for each resident, of course. But if the person is a patient admitted to a certified nursing home, the dispensing fee is even higher — twenty dollars per month."

Natasha was amazed at Wayne's final calculation. A pharmacy with fifteen hundred elderly clients, twenty percent of them in nursing homes, took in $125,000 in dispensing fees every month.

Wayne saw the amazement on Natasha's face. "That goes to the pharmacy as its professional fee. Putting together the compliance packs is labour-intensive," he said, a tinge of defensiveness in his voice. "The drugs are extra, mostly covered by the government with an eight- to twenty-percent mark-up for the pharmacy. Fifteen hundred residents, each taking eight medications, would bag the pharmacy an extra $25,000 per month."

"Big business, when you add it up," Todd said.

"You could say that," Wayne said, then chuckled. "Are you sure you want to stay in medical school, Todd?"

Natasha removed a Zytopril blood-pressure tablet from Mr. Greenwood's Camelot blister card and examined it under Wayne's magnifying glass. Same size, shape, and colour, same crisp white printing as those from Wayne's bottle and her grandmother's Steeltown prescription. The real thing. She looked at Todd, who made a face. He was as disappointed as she was. They each took another card and popped out other Zytoprils. The pills were perfect.

Wayne studied the Zytoprils from four other Camelot cards under the magnifying glass, then grinned and raised an eyebrow. "Have a good look at the blank side. What do you see?"

The tablet in Natasha's hand had a scratch on it, but that was it. She could see no differences between Wayne Jarvie's Zytoprils from Lakeview Pharma and Viktor Horvat's from Steeltown Apothecary.

After a few moments, a quizzical look came over Todd's face. He pointed to twelve of Horvat's tablets, six from Camelot and six from Natasha's bottle. "All of these are scratched," he said. "But Wayne's tablets are not. Does that mean anything?"

Natasha looked again. "The scratch marks are identical on every pill."

Wayne shook his head. "Those aren't scratches. They're a mark from the stamping machine used to make the tablets. Comes from a blemish inside the equipment. Whoever made these has an old machine, probably snapped up on the cheap. Or retrieved from a dump site. In Turkey or Mexico. Or even Congo."

"Congo?" Natasha said. "They make pills in Congo and ship them to Canada?"

Todd popped the Zytoprils from four additional Camelot cards and examined the blank side of each tablet. His eyes twinkled as he raised his fist in victory. "Got him."

Natasha wasn't so sure. They still had to prove these were counterfeit and not a legitimate but cosmetically wonky batch from the brand-name company. She opened her briefcase and pulled out the cards from the nineteen Camelot residents taking Xanucox for severe arthritis. "We'd better look at these, too," she said. "Out of the nineteen people on Xanucox, eighteen have had epidemic gastroenteritis."

"Xanucox is a heavy-duty anti-inflammatory," Wayne said. "I'm amazed that Jamieson has so many of your Camelot residents on it. It's pretty hard on the immune system." He popped three maroon-and-white Xanucox capsules from their blisters, turned them over in his palm, and examined them closely. He popped out three more. Then he pulled two of them apart and shook their powdery contents onto a sheet of paper. He licked his index finger, picked up a little of the powder, and placed it on his tongue. "Hmm," he said, screwing up his face and spitting into the waste bin. "Like many drugs, it's very bitter. That's why Xanucox is formulated as a capsule, not a tablet. Must be the real thing. And just as well — they're eight bucks each and paid for by the ministry only under their limited-use directive. You could make a fortune selling counterfeits of these if you figured how to bypass the red tape."

"How much would he make from scamming the Zytoprils, Uncle Wayne?" Todd asked.

"Hard to be certain. But he'd be sharing in the seventy-five billion dollars the World Health Organization says changes hands in the counterfeit drug trade every year."

"Seventy-five billion!" said Natasha.

"And growing at twice the rate of *legitimate* drug sales. You can thank the Internet for that. And criminal gangs. And governments that have no stomach to put a stop to it."

"And Horvat's take?" Todd pressed, as amazed as Natasha at the huge money involved.

"Let's see," Wayne said, "you told me eighty percent of the residents at Camelot are taking Zytopril for their blood pressure. That's how many people?"

"Thirty-eight residents," Natasha told him. "And eighty percent makes . . . thirty."

"That's . . . nine hundred tablets a month," Wayne said. "At three-fifty a tablet . . . that's thirty-one hundred dollars a month, billed to the government as brand-name Zytopril."

"How much would the fake ones cost him?" Todd asked.

"Most counterfeit tablets have little or no active ingredients. Usually just talc, brick dust, or floor polish. And they're made in developing countries where labour is cheap. The cost of production might be ten cents a tablet. The cost to Horvat would be triple that or more, after a couple of middlemen take their cuts. Let's say he pays fifty cents each if he buys in bulk."

Wayne scribbled a few calculations on his notepad, then fixed Natasha with his clear brown eyes. "That's twenty-seven hundred dollars a month in profit."

"Not exactly a fortune," Natasha said.

"But," Wayne said, "that's just from one facility. Horvat has arrangements with at least five old-folks homes, and signed contracts with ten nursing homes, most of them three times the size of Camelot. Zytopril-friendly Jamieson is the doctor for many of them."

Todd was doing the arithmetic. "If Horvat is doing the same at the other places, and only a third of the residents are on Zytopril, he's scamming . . . $40,000 a month . . . that could be half a million a year."

"Plenty of bucks for prying his son out of that Mexican jail," Wayne said. "You read about him in the *Spectator*, eh? He's their celebrity *du jour*."

"Maybe his legal bills led him to scamming in the first place," Todd said.

Wayne pocketed his pen and pad. "Maybe."

Natasha found herself boggled by the amount of money involved and disheartened at the difficulty of proving that Horvat's actions were both intentional and criminal. Last year, the pharmacists covered their tracks at the first indication they were under suspicion, then pleaded ignorance. "We've got to prove for certain the Zytoprils are counterfeit, *and* that Horvat knows it," she said. "And whatever we do, we can't tip him off."

Wayne pushed his chair away from the table and crossed his legs. "Well . . . not to put too fine a point on it, but I do have contacts. When you own four of the largest pharmacies west of Toronto, the drug companies court your attention. I'll call the firm that makes Zytopril. Their head office is in Montreal. The VP of medical affairs will want to get these tested pronto, even if they have to be couriered to Switzerland."

Natasha was still worried. "But will they do it quietly? I mean, we don't want Horvat covering *his* tracks, hiding his involvement, then getting off with a silly warning."

"The company will want him nabbed and fully prosecuted, that's for sure," Wayne said. "And they'll want to track down his supplier." He checked his watch and stood up. "Look, this has been very enlightening, but I've got to get back to work. Those prescriptions don't fill themselves, and we're short-staffed today."

He led them out of the staff room and smiled warmly as he shook Natasha's hand and offered her his business card. "Anything comes up you need my help with, call me on my cell. Day or night, doesn't matter. Don't be shy."

As Natasha did up her coat and put on her gloves, a key question niggled her. How had Dr. Jamieson come to prescribe Zytopril to eighty percent of Camelot's residents — and, if Wayne was correct, countless others across the city? Was he convinced that Zytopril, used by other doctors for special cases only, was absolutely superior to every other drug? Or was he trying to help his drug-rep sister earn her annual bonus? Or perhaps the state of his wallet superseded family ties and he'd gone in with Horvat for the tax-free bonanza.

One thing seemed sure: the drug company wasn't getting a nickel from the "Zytopril" dispensed by Horvat, and sooner or later that would show up in its bottom line.

CHAPTER 24

At four o'clock that Friday afternoon, Zol hung up the phone in his office and said a prayer of thanks to the inventor of call waiting. Arlene Novak had rung off to take another call coming in at her end. Despite all scientific evidence to the contrary, the woman was convinced that her children's school was wrapped in carcinogenic asbestos and toxic mould. She wanted the building condemned and rebuilt on a brand new site where the basement was certified free of radon gas. During Mrs. Novak's daily calls, Zol considered it a point of honour to stay calm and keep his tone measured. No matter how shrill her voice, how outlandish her claims, Zol challenged himself to maintain his cool while not giving in to her exorbitant demands.

He gazed out of his window at the parking lot and its scrum of dented garbage cans. The gritty view was a poor inducement for daydreaming. It kept him focused on the stark matters at hand, like catching Vik Horvat with his fingers on the counterfeit meds he was dispensing to dim-eyed seniors. Natasha told Zol about Steeltown Apothecary's suspicious blood-pressure tablets when she'd called on her cellphone. As a good citizen, and a trusted public servant, Zol knew he should blow the whistle immediately —

inform his boss Peter Trinnock, the RCMP, the Ontario College of Pharmacists, Gloria and Gus Oliveira at Camelot, and the residents themselves. But he was going to sit tight and wait for the drug company to analyze Horvat's tablets. If the meds were fake, the bastard truly was putting seniors in jeopardy all over the city. Rushing in with no hard evidence against the man would accomplish nothing but front-page drama and another black mark against everyone in the health care system. Zol prayed that Horvat's clients could live with poorly controlled blood pressure for a few more days.

He turned to his computer screen, intending to see what emails had piled up in the past hour, but his door swung open and Colleen tiptoed in carrying two coffees and a Nitty Gritty bag of pastries, which she handed to Zol.

"Thought you could do with a Friday afternoon treat," she said, closing the door.

Colleen herself was treat enough. Without a second thought for the computer, he set the cups and pastries on his desk, then greeted her with a squeeze. She had the knack of appearing exactly when he needed her most — professionally and emotionally. She lifted her face and offered a warm, full kiss on the lips. He drank in the arousing hints of jasmine and mandarin enveloping their embrace.

He finally let her go, then took her coat and hung it on the rack. He felt suddenly hot in his blazer and shrugged out of it.

"Mmm," he said, ripping open the paper bag. "Marcus's famous raisin scones." Not only did Marcus run his Nitty Gritty Café like a well-oiled machine, he was a cheery barista and a talented baker. "Already buttered. Fantastic. Thanks."

"Have you noticed? Marcus only makes them on Fridays."

"Really?"

"Like DeBeers and their diamonds."

"What? DeBeers only mines diamonds on Fridays?"

"No, silly. But they lock most of them away. Then dribble them slowly onto the market. To preserve their allure and prestige. And bolster their price, of course."

"Then I better do the same with my thin-crust pizzas. Seems to me I've been serving up my *quattro stagioni*s far too often. A certain person could start taking them for granted."

"I didn't say that." He loved the way her eyes crinkled when she laughed.

He removed the lid from his coffee. "I gather things went well at Steeltown this morning? Any problems? Natasha hasn't been in the office all day."

"Not to worry. She was brilliant. Should have been an actress."

"No way. I need her here."

Colleen gave him a detailed account of their trip to the pharmacy. Zol wished he'd witnessed Natasha's authentic South Asian accent and mannerisms. She really was a good sport. And deserved a lot smarter boyfriend than Bjorn, that goofy Swedish stockbroker she'd finally had the sense to dump. Dating him was such an obvious rebellion against her parents. Brown or white, she needed someone her intellectual equal, not a guy who played only on the strength of his looks.

Of course, who was he to talk about the suitability of love mates? He should have anticipated from the beginning that Francine, as flaky as a Parisian croissant, would be a disaster as a spouse and mother. Her last phone call had been from an ashram in India. In eight years, she'd never seen, never spoken to her son. Colleen on the other hand . . .

"Zol?"

"Sorry." He gulped his coffee.

"I said, that's not the only mission I had today on your behalf. Gus made his rounds again. Right on schedule."

"For Waste Not?"

"Pickups at the Caledonian's faculty club, and —" She stiffened, and the twinkle in her eyes dissolved at the sound of a brisk rap at the door. He'd noticed that about her before. She bristled at unexpected knocking. Three times such knocking had signalled stone-faced police officers on her doorstep, mouthing shattering news.

"Yes?" Zol called.

"It's me."

When Zol opened the door, Natasha was standing breathlessly. Her pupils were huge, and red blotches sprouted on her neck. She looked like an exhilarated huntress who'd chased her prey to within pouncing distance.

"Goodness," Zol said. "What's up?"

"Ellen just called. From microbiology. At Caledonian."

"With results?"

"Doozies." She gaped at Colleen, the Nitty Gritty bag, and the pair of coffee cups. She realized she'd walked in on a tête-à-tête. "Oh, I'm sorry. You're busy."

"No, no," said Colleen. "I was just updating Zol on your fantastic performance this morning."

After further encouragement, Natasha took a seat and held her notebook in her lap. Once she'd caught her breath, she asked, "Did you tell him about the shampoo?"

"All part of the authenticity you brought to the role," Zol said. "Now, tell us. What did Ellen have to say?"

"Earl Crabtree's blood and cerebral spinal fluid — they're growing listeria monocytogenes."

"That's bad," Zol said.

"And it makes two from Camelot in the past month, both with bloodstream infections. Earl Crabtree and Raimunda Ferreira, the manager's mother."

"How's Earl doing?" Colleen asked.

"All Ellen knows is he's still in the ICU."

Natasha clearly had more on her mind than another case of meningitis, important as that was. She investigated these mandatory notifications of reportable illnesses routinely without getting breathless over them. These Camelot cases were getting to her personally. He should talk, he told himself — he was losing sleep over Art's and Betty's safety.

"Ellen dipped into her deep-freeze," Natasha continued. "Retrieved the three dozen stool samples submitted so far this year from Camelot's gastro cases. On a hunch, she cultured every one of them for listeria."

"But what's that going to tell us?" Zol cautioned. "You can find listeria in almost any normal stool. The experts say it's pointless to look for it, except in blood and spinal fluid."

"She ran controls as well. Samples from diarrhea patients who don't live at Camelot." Natasha flipped through the pages of her notebook until she found what she was looking for. Then she paused as if to say, *I hope you're ready for this.*

Zol said nothing. He just let her enjoy the drama of the occasion. She really should have been an actress.

"Ellen tested thirty control stools. And she found listeria in two of them."

Okay, thought Zol, *I guess listeria isn't that common.*

"And," Natasha continued, "from thirty-five Camelot gastro samples, she recovered listeria from . . . twenty-eight."

Colleen grabbed the empty Nitty Gritty bag and worked out the math on the back of it. "That's ten percent in the controls, and . . . eighty percent in the Camelots. Extraordinary."

"Mother of God," Zol said.

CHAPTER 25

At nine on Friday night, Hamish followed Todd out of the parking lot at the corner of James Street North and King William. Hamish's stomach churned a toxic brew of nerves, hunger, and sleep deprivation. After Ellen's call this afternoon, he'd told Todd he wouldn't be joining him at the Reluctant Lion's karaoke after all. Suddenly, there was a lot to do, and it didn't seem proper to go out drinking as soon as they got their first break in the case. Discovering that listeria was the gastro-causing culprit they'd been looking for all along put a whole new spin on Camelot's outbreak, and on Betty's illness.

No wonder she was so sick. She was infected with C diff *and* listeria. Vancomycin — even the bona fide stuff — would never cure both infections on its own. She needed treatment with two antibiotics, and he'd wasted no time in getting the second one started.

He'd called Caledonian University Medical Centre and asked the pharmacy to send him a large carton of saline solution, syringes, and ampicillin. The drug was one of the few antibiotics predictably effective against listeria, and he needed enough of its intravenous formulation for everyone at Camelot with gastro. He'd had it with pills. He could trust only injectable ampicillin, where he could watch the drug going straight into his patients' veins. Local pharmacies would have lots of ampicillin on hand, but only in capsules. Caledonian was the only local source of the intravenous form.

The pharmacist refused Hamish's order, saying she had no authority to dispense drugs outside the hospital. The matter got settled only after Hamish phoned Jeff Suszek in Emerg and threatened to load every Camelot resident who had diarrhea into a van and park them in the hospital's ambulance bay. Suszek got the pharmacist to see things Hamish's way, and the ampicillin had arrived within the hour. The ICU nurse, whom Gloria had agreed to hire for twelve hours each night for two nights, got the IV ampicillin into the patients in record time. After that, Todd convinced Hamish that the best thing for his patients was a clear-headed doctor. He said if Hamish took a couple of hours off for R and R, everyone at Camelot would benefit. It didn't have to be a late night.

So here they were, trudging through the wet snow.

The wounded heart of Hamilton gave Hamish the creeps. He rarely ventured north of King Street after dark, and he wished they'd taken a taxi to the door instead of leaving the Saab in an outdoor lot. Wet snow was falling, and it would probably turn to freezing rain. In an hour or two he'd be assaulting the Saab's windshield with an ice scraper. He hated that.

The streetlights, half of them burnt out, lit the graffiti scrawled on the abandoned storefronts along King William Street. Hamish knew this strip of gashed doors and boarded windows was a Canadian reality, but his heart ached at the way it taunted his own picture-postcard version of his country. It was hard to believe that only three blocks away City Hall flaunted its polished floors and the Sheraton its Egyptian cotton sheets.

He gave a wide berth to two winos sprawled on the sidewalk. They dozed against the pockmarked brickwork, their tattered shopping bags piled beside them. Labelling them *homeless* didn't begin to capture the complicated stories he'd heard from men like these when he'd worked his shifts in Emerg. He glanced at his car and pressed the lock button on the key fob for the fourth time, then edged closer to his well-muscled protector.

"That's the place," Todd said, pointing to a black facade half a block ahead. The Reluctant Lion proclaimed itself in gold letters painted above the door. It looked too nice a place for this neighbourhood. The clientele must not be hung up on geography. Hamish wondered how far the *Wizard of Oz* theme would be carried inside the bar. Would the bartenders be Munchkins?

A tall, square-jawed man, mid-twenties, greeted Todd at the door with a high five. He wore a white shirt with the cuffs rolled back and a black waiter's apron over blue jeans. His short haircut glistened with gel; Hamish was relieved it wasn't dyed pink or magenta. In fact, the few patrons at this still-early hour looked like regular guys. Hamish felt the weight of the waiter's scrutiny as he swept the snowflakes from his flat-top and stepped around a stain on the hardwood. Introduced as Conor, the man led them past the stand-up bar to a two-man booth in a quiet rear corner.

Hamish pulled off his coat and slid onto the bench. Conor wiped the table, handed them menus, then posed for a moment, his hairless pecs peeking between the unfastened buttons at the top of his shirt. He flashed Hamish a smile along with that look of recognition Hamish often got but tried to ignore. In here, he decided, that look was okay. Here, it was safe to be himself. He hoped the place didn't fill up with in-your-face drag queens when the karaoke got going.

"I'm starving," Todd said. "What do you feel like? They don't have full-course meals, just killer appetizers."

They settled on nachos with all the fixings and a double order of deep-fried zucchini, Cajun style. When Todd ordered a pint of local draft, Hamish asked for the same, his pulse quickening at his bold choice of beer over Pepsi. This place felt edgier than Ken's matronly Town and Gown. And light-years away from the hospital cafeteria where most nights Hamish dragged his supper out of vending machines.

Conor delivered the beers almost immediately and explained that he'd be right back with the nachos, but the zucchini would take longer.

Todd raised his glass. "Here's to finding the listeria."

"And to following hunches," Hamish added. "Let that be a lesson."

They clinked their glasses, and Hamish took a sip, then gulped eagerly. This stuff was good. No bitter aftertaste. He pulled his scribbler from his briefcase, asked Todd to repeat the name of the brew, and wrote it down. He hoped they had it at the Town and Gown.

"And," Todd continued, "to Betty McKenzie looking a bit better by tomorrow."

"I didn't know how I was going to face Zol if she . . ."

"I checked her abdomen before we left. Still tender, but less distended than yesterday. I'm not sure her diarrhea is any better, but she did manage to keep down a can of that high-protein shake. She's one feisty lady. Told me she doesn't dare go yet — hasn't finished her memoirs."

"I like your optimism." There was a lot to like about Todd — tons of positive energy and intelligence packed into a great-looking body. Too bad he was off limits, at least until he graduated. So much of Ken's energy was negative. All that courtroom bickering, week after week.

Hamish checked to be sure no one was watching, then placed Ellen's one-page fax of Camelot's listeria results on the table. "We've spent so much time this week on Mountain Wing reacting, but too little time thinking." But what could he expect with half a dozen critically ill gastro cases and almost no support. "This listeria thing may seem like the breakthrough we've been hoping for, but Zol's gang has been through the Lodge on their hands and knees. I don't see how listeria can be coming out of that kitchen."

"I'm puzzled about listeria turning up in all those stool cultures. I thought the bug wasn't supposed to cause gastro."

"It's there in the textbooks, but in really fine print. Filed under 'febrile gastroenteritis.' But I agree, as a clinician, I never think about listeria causing diarrhea. Ellen used a selective culture medium she ordered specially, otherwise she'd never have detected it."

"How many residents have been affected?"

"That's the strange thing. The gastro episodes have been reoccurring over and over in the same twenty-one residents. Seventeen others have remained completely unaffected."

Todd peered at the rough notes in Hamish's scribbler. "Did all twenty-one have listeria in their stools?"

Hamish looked carefully at Ellen's fax. Not every stool sample submitted from Camelot contained listeria, but all twenty-one residents with gastro had at least one sample that was positive.

"Correct," Hamish said. "But we don't know yet if it's the same strain each time, or a series of different strains. Ellen's going to tell us next week after she genetically fingerprints the listeria in each specimen. We'll need those fingerprints to definitively link the cases to the source." He smiled ruefully. "When and if we find it."

"Sounds like Ellen's got a lot of work ahead of her."

Conor set a mountain of nachos on the table, and both men dug in. Hamish was amazed how great the salsa and guacamole tasted with the beer, which was going down very quickly. Good thing Conor had brought two more pints. The stuff was getting more delicious with every swallow.

"Tell me," Todd said, "how does listeria tie in with those heavy-duty arthritis meds?"

The medication survey showed that officially, eighteen of the twenty-one residents with recurrent febrile gastroenteritis were taking the arthritis drug Xanucox. Only one of the seventeen gastro-free residents was taking it. Unofficially, Betty had been taking Xanucox from Raimunda's supply, which put the real figure at nineteen, or maybe even higher if other residents were sharing their medications. Hamish couldn't help wondering how many residents shared their pills the way Raimunda had done. Perhaps there was so much pill swapping at Camelot that the medication survey was too inaccurate to be useful.

Todd smiled as he washed down a mouthful of nachos. "Is it possible that many of the residents have been silently infected with listeria, but only those taking Xanucox have been getting obvious symptoms?"

Xanucox, a remote cousin of aspirin, was a second-generation NSAID, a non-steroidal anti-inflammatory drug that fought arthritis by tinkering with the body's immune system. When reined in by a drug like Xanucox, the immune system lost a lot of its punch.

"I suppose the Xanucox could be inhibiting the immune response enough to allow the listeria to go a bit wild in the gut — stir up fever, nausea, and diarrhea. But not wild enough to kill anyone."

"But," Todd said, "Durimab is the true blockbuster, eh? Controls rheumatoid arthritis by stopping the immune system almost dead in its tracks. I noticed that four of the residents have been on it."

When the body's inflammatory response was paralyzed by a drug like Durimab, the pain and swelling of arthritis quickly vanished, and microbes had a heyday. Germs usually too weak to cause even minor illness became a major threat because the body couldn't fight them. "You've been doing your homework. With Durimab on board, a bout of listeria could progress from mild gastro to life-threatening meningitis overnight."

Applying the theory at Camelot would be impossible to prove this long after the two Durimab deaths.

Todd took a swig from his glass then smiled shyly. He toyed with his coaster for a moment, then raised an eyebrow. "You know . . ."

"What?"

"A couple of days ago, I snuck into Camelot's reading room. It's a cool place. Top floor of the turret." He mimed an arc with his hands. "The walls and bookshelves curve all the way around. I shooed two bats out the window."

"Yeah. Those bats are a major pain. Thousands of them in the neighbourhood."

"In the middle of the city?"

"They live on the face of the Escarpment, in the biosphere reserve. Under the protection of the United Nations." Hamish had learned last year how the bats squeezed through the holes in the rooflines of all the houses in the area. "Zol is always getting reports about bats in those mansions. The price you pay for living at such a fancy address, I guess. The owners worry about rabies every time their kids chase after a bat. You didn't get bitten, did you?"

"Not even close."

"I've never heard of bats transmitting listeria."

"It's not the bats that worry me. It's the cold cuts."

"Don't worry. They don't serve deli meats at Camelot. Natasha's been through every millimetre of that kitchen."

"Well, they serve afternoon tea in that reading room between three and four o'clock. Along with dried-out salami sandwiches on really stale bread."

"Salami! You're kidding."

"Had to dunk my sandwich in my tea. But what the heck, I was starving."

"All this palaver and you happen to stumble upon a plate of past-its-date deli meat? I wish you'd told me before."

Todd dipped his gaze. "Sorry, Hamish. At that point, we didn't know about the listeria. And with all that's been going on this week, I forgot. I guess I didn't want to be too much of a buttinski."

"You can buttinski all you like. Looks like you've cracked a giant piece of the puzzle. We'll have to track down that meat and get it tested for listeria. There's gotta be a stash of it at Camelot somewhere."

"Gus and Gloria live on site in their own apartment," Todd said. "Maybe they keep it there."

"And trot it out at tea time — against ministry guidelines — for residents with a hankering for deli meat?"

Hamish grabbed his cellphone. Zol needed to know about this, pronto. Zol's machine picked up. Hamish primed himself to leave a message, but snapped the phone shut without saying a word. Zol wouldn't hear him over the bar's increasing hubbub.

Todd licked a glob of sour cream from his thumb. "Uncle Wayne says the Zytopril blood-pressure tablets are on their way to Montreal. The company's giving them number-one priority. Going to test them on Monday."

"I can't see where the Zytopril fits," Hamish said. "Counterfeit antihypertensives can't have anything to do with listeria."

Todd raised an eyebrow. "And what about the empty vanco capsules? They don't make any sense either. If you're running an old-folks home, epidemics are bad for business, right? The place gets closed to new admissions and when your residents die, the empty beds don't generate income."

"Good point," Hamish said. "And if you're the pharmacist dispensing empty capsules to your patients with a contagious, life-threatening condition such as C diff, sooner or later you'll have no market left for your counterfeit Zytoprils." There had been eight deaths at Camelot in the past month: six in the past couple of weeks, starting with the Prime Minister's aunt the Sunday before last. He steadied himself with a swig of beer. "There's more than medication fraud going on at Camelot. But I can't put my finger on it."

"When will you get the results of the autopsies?" Todd asked. "Maybe they'll show something helpful."

"You must be kidding. Old folks in nursing homes almost never get autopsied. By the time they make it to the funeral home, no one cares exactly why they died. The doctor puts *congestive heart failure* on the death certificate, the local coroner is happy, the bureaucrats are happy, and that's the end of it."

"Even the Prime Minister's aunt?"

Hamish shook his head. "The coroner said he had no reason to suspect foul play so he didn't order a post-mortem. And the family didn't ask for one. Said her arthritis had made her suffer long enough." Hamish hated the lunacy of thinking an autopsy could inflict suffering on a corpse.

Todd caught the waiter's eye, pointed to his empty glass, and held up two fingers. "Don't you think it's odd that no one has made a fuss over Caledonian's refusal to accept Camelot's diarrhea patients?"

"I did my best, I really did. But it didn't get me anywhere. They won't budge on the Deep Six rule. Ministry's orders."

"Back in Manitoba, when I was working on the rez at the health centre, we called that HLI — high level interference. I've been thinking — acute-care hospitals are choked to the rafters with old folks who belong somewhere else, like a nursing home. As a result, acutely ill patients are lining the hallways of emergency departments, waiting for beds upstairs, right?"

"That's why they brought in that awful Deep Six rule."

"And it's never going to work because there's nowhere for the old folks to go. The government isn't building nursing homes nearly fast enough." Todd paused, his eyes dead serious. "These days, space only gets freed up when someone dies." He paused again, then continued. "One way to accelerate the flow out of the hospital and into nursing homes is to . . . well, speed up the nursing-home deaths."

"You mean . . . No, you're not serious."

"Well, yes, I guess I am."

"You mean someone could be cooking up a scheme to clear elderly patients out of acute-care hospital beds by freeing up spaces in old-folks homes like Camelot Lodge?"

"My uncle Wayne says Horvat provides the drugs for fifteen nursing homes. Given the right monetary incentive, he could knock off a lot of people and create plenty of space on the acute-care wards at Caledonian."

Hamish rubbed at the condensation on his fresh glass of beer. Todd's idea was too fantastic — more the movie of the week than real life. An institution with the prestige of Caledonian University, famous for its pancreatic transplants, couldn't get itself mixed up with a desperate pharmacist whose son was locked up in Mexico on drug charges.

"Nah," Hamish said. "You can put your imagination back in its cage. Caledonian's senior leadership lets a lot of money slip through their fingers, but they're a long way from criminal."

After Hamish had consumed half a plate of zucchini sticks and another beer or two, the Reluctant Lion buzzed with chatter and dance music. Everyone was competing for the barman's attention except for the foursome dancing to something loud and fast coming from speakers in the ceiling. To Hamish it sounded like an unholy union of Kylie Minogue and Michael Jackson. He could barely make himself heard above the noise. Todd did most of the talking. He spoke of his life in Cross Lake practising seat-of-the-pants medicine as a nurse-practitioner. The guy had more guts than most doctors in the south. Up north, he'd had to stay in the closet. Would there come a day when a gifted, openly gay doctor found total acceptance in small-town Canada? Or could you only be free within the anonymity and wider mores of the big city? Hamish wondered what Todd would think of family practice if he got stuck in a strip-mall in Scarborough or a concrete canyon in downtown Toronto. After the rushes of adrenaline served daily in Cross Lake, he'd find the snots and shots of big-city practice a major downer.

Hamish watched a young guy — bald, hoop earrings, black pants, matching T-shirt — set up a microphone, speakers, and a carload of gear. This was Hamish's first time at karaoke, and he wondered how far he could shrink into the booth if someone started hauling audience members onto the stage. As a boy soprano, singing in public had been second nature, but long ago he'd abandoned that stunted, awkward child who hit high C like a crystal bell. Nowadays, though he felt less like the ugly duckling, he croaked like the frog prince.

A fit-looking man, late twenties, wearing a pressed white tee and designer jeans, stepped onto the impromptu stage and stamped his gleaming black brogues against the raised floor. The dance music stopped, and he waved at a group hooting from the window table across the room. He took the microphone in both hands and nodded to the black-T-shirt guy seated behind more electronic gizmos than you'd need for a Mars landing. Hamish recognized the Andrew Lloyd Webber introduction with the first three chords. The racket ceased as the audience dropped into their seats.

The handsome guy behind the mic lit the room with as moving a rendition of "The Music of the Night" as Hamish had ever heard, and he'd seen *Phantom* five times in three cities. What a set of pipes!

At the closing chords, the audience erupted in whistles and cheers. The singer bowed to calls of "Encore! Encore!" and the place hushed again as the sound man nodded and a familiar melody flowed through his speakers.

For a time in the seventies, Hamish's mother had played Don McLean's "Vincent" over and over on the living-room record player while doing her much-hated housework. It was weird to hear that song again without the skips and scratches in the vinyl that back then had seemed integral to the score. But the immediacy, the raw emotion of the live voice on the stage quickly wiped out any memories of Don McLean and Hamish's lonely mother.

Hamish leaned across the table and spoke into Todd's ear. "That guy's amazing. Better than Josh Groban. Who is he?"

"Al Mesic. I'll introduce you."

"You know him?"

"Sure. He's here every Friday night. Always gets the karaoke started."

"I could listen to him all night."

Todd shook his head. "Not here. He does two songs, and that's it."

"I'm sure he never has to pay for his beer."

Roaring cheers morphed into general clamour as the singer stepped off the stage and joined his supporters at the window table. Todd finished his lager and slid out of the booth.

"Where you going?" said Hamish, anxious at the thought of being left alone.

"Gotta take a leak." Todd headed toward the front of the room, in the opposite direction to the washrooms. He stopped at the window table, spoke to the singer, and shook his hand. Then Todd looked back and pointed at Hamish. The singer smiled and seemed to nod in agreement before Todd disappeared around a corner.

Two minutes later, Al Mesic strode past the stage, now occupied by a squat fellow wearing a black cowboy hat. The guy was making a hash of a Johnny Cash hit. Al slid into the booth opposite Hamish, put out his hand, and introduced himself. He spoke fluently, with a slight accent and rhythm that Hamish couldn't place — Czech? Hungarian? Balkan? His face was as gorgeous as his voice. He had the kind of bristly haircut that turned Hamish on, and perfectly trimmed sideburns extending a fraction below his earlobes. But it was the colour of his eyes that held Hamish in rapt attention. Wide black pupils floating in rings of light amber.

"You're a doctor, eh?" Al said.

That line was always a spell breaker. What was such a big deal about being a doctor? Hamish wanted to be a regular guy with a couple of beers buzzing in his head and delicious eye candy seated opposite him. He'd hidden his briefcase under his coat. He forced a smile, then made the face he used to discourage further medical questions. "What's the title of your album?"

"Sorry?"

Hamish leaned forward and repeated the question.

Al laughed and waved his hand dismissively. "I don't have one. I sing only for fun."

Singing for fun. What a concept. Hamish had spent his boyhood singing in church choirs, not for fun, but because he was forced to by his mother.

"What do you do when you're not singing?"

"I report from City Hall."

"For the *Spectator*?"

Al raised an eyebrow. "I'm your eyes and ears, watching the city manager and his gang."

"As far as I can tell, they don't get much done." It had always been that way in Hamilton — the political machine ate up taxes and produced little to show for them, except the current extravagant facelift of City Hall's exterior.

"Don't kid yourself," Al said. "They do a lot of things. But mostly for themselves."

Hamish was entranced by Al Mesic's accent. His English was perfect, his grammar impeccable, but the sexy lilt in his phrasing was mesmerizing. "Where are you from?"

Al finished off his beer in three speedy gulps. "The former Yugoslavia. Actually, I'm Bosniak. My mother pulled me out of Sarajevo when I was fourteen." He waved at the barman and held up two fingers.

Hamish finished his pint and thought for a moment. Al would probably know the answer to a question that had been bugging him since New Year's. Again, he leaned in close. "Tell me, what sort of name is Horvat?"

Mesic pulled back. Fire lit his eyes. "Croatian. Very common. Like Smith in English."

"You don't like Croatians?"

"When you're Bosniak, *all* Yugoslav Christians treat you like shit, even if you're more atheist than Muslim." Al paused, looking searchingly at Hamish. "You know someone named Horvat?"

"A pharmacist I've been dealing with."

Conor collected the empty glasses and set down two fresh beers. "From your fans at the window table," he said, then posed for a moment, smiling at Al. He shot Hamish a look that seemed to say, *Aren't you lucky to be sitting with our star, especially since you're new to this scene.*

"You mean *Viktor* Horvat?" Al said, once Conor was out of earshot.

"You know him?"

"There's a lot more to his story than makes it into the paper."

"That's *you* reporting on Horvat in the *Spec*?"

"My editor won't let me. Says I lack the necessary objectivity. Horvat is also from Sarajevo, but the war turned Bosniaks and Croats into . . . um, shall we say angry brothers?"

Hamish stared at the frosty beers on the table. He wanted to find out more about Horvat, but his bladder had been demanding to be emptied for the past twenty minutes, and he really had to go. He hated to leave Al alone; someone was bound to steal him away. Besides, the stories of the antics in gay bathrooms terrified him. He'd never used the toilet at the Town and Gown. What would he do if he walked in on two guys with their pants down, making out? Or worse, what if he got propositioned at the urinal?

He saw the foam cascading down the beer glasses like a waterfall and he knew he couldn't hold it much longer. Maybe the full beers on the table would make it clear Al wasn't sitting alone.

When he got there, the washroom was blissfully empty and quiet. Everyone was dancing to the throaty Bette Midler who'd replaced Johnny Cash. At the urinal, Hamish unzipped his fly, then closed his eyes to the lewd graffiti and braced himself against the wall. He'd never been this beer-dizzy before.

"You and Todd — you guys an item?" Al's voice startled him from the adjacent stall.

Hamish said nothing. He'd always been too embarrassed to talk to anyone taking a leak — not his dad, not the boys at school, not the kids peeing into the bushes at Y camp. With the alcohol spinning in his head, he finished up and staggered to the sink where he steadied himself with both hands.

Al finished off and joined him. "Sorry. A reporter's habit. Always asking questions."

"No problem," Hamish said.

Al raised his eyebrows. He was still looking for an answer.

Hamish reached for a paper towel. A cartoon of an erect penis was scrawled beside the dispenser along with a list of phone numbers. "No. Todd's just one of my students. We came for a drink. After work. That's all."

Al looked pleased. He checked his watch. "This place gets very noisy after ten. Too noisy for talking."

"You're right." Would Todd mind, or even notice, if he slipped home? "I should be going."

"No, no. That is not what I meant." Al raised his left eyebrow again and reached for his belt buckle.

Oh shit! Mesic was going to drop his jeans. *Oh my God*, thought Hamish, *I've given some sort of signal. I should've gone home after the first beer.*

Hamish gripped the counter, his head reeling. How many had he drunk? Two? Three? Four? Next time he'd stick to ginger ale.

Al straightened his buckle and smoothed his T-shirt over his board-like abdomen. He turned on the tap. His pants were still up, his fly closed. He began washing his hands, like any guy in any normal washroom.

"My place is only a few blocks from here. James South. Let's go back there. I make pretty good espresso."

He read the hesitation on Hamish's face. "Don't worry about Todd. Now that he's started dancing, he'll be here all night. Do you dance?"

"No."

"But surely you drink coffee? Or would you like something else, more satisfying?"

Was that another code? Did he mean sex? Al was hot. And seemed kind. He'd lived through a lot but had a cultured manner. Hamish tried to suppress a sudden image of Al's trim body, naked, aroused, standing in a top-floor apartment singing Josh Groban like a nightingale. He'd never had casual sex with anyone. Ken was his first and only partner. But these days, it didn't feel like a partnership. More like an awkward acquaintance bound by green tea, stir-fry meals, and fast sex.

He knew he was too buzzed to drive for the next couple of hours. So, what the heck? He'd say goodbye to Todd, walk over to Al's for a coffee or two, then drive to Camelot after he'd sobered up. That ICU nurse's shift didn't end until seven in the morning.

But how long would the Saab be safe in the parking lot? The rims and stereo would be gone if the poor thing stayed there much past midnight. He wouldn't let that happen. Two coffees and nothing else.

They exited the washroom, their arms brushing together in the narrow doorway. At such close range, Al's sweat and cologne were suddenly more intoxicating than any beer.

CHAPTER 26

At about seven-thirty the next morning, Zol pressed a mug of coffee into Hamish's hand. He'd never seen his friend in such a state. Dark circles rimmed his bloodshot eyes, and his cheeks were wet with tears. His hair stuck out every which way. He smelled of beer and vomit and sweat — or maybe that was sex.

Zol glanced at Max and Colleen. They were too busy at the stove to worry about Hamish. Max was showing Colleen how to make Saturday-morning pancakes shaped like Mickey Mouse. His cellphone peeked proudly from his hip pocket. Their dust-up over the phone was almost forgotten, but Zol hoped the lesson would be retained. Max hadn't whined about his cellphone once in the fourteen days since Zol had taken it away. Max's inscrutable poise while his friends worked their phones stirred Zol with pride at the little guy's grit. Zol had returned the phone to Max first thing this morning, two weeks early, and they'd reviewed the rules of usage in detail. Zol found himself wondering again why a nine-year-old needed to be in instant communication with every friend and acquaintance, twenty-four-seven. He did admit that the phone's GPS locater function gave him peace of mind when Max went to a neighbour's house and forgot to report in.

Colleen's movements at the stovetop entranced Zol with their fluidity. He felt himself stirred at the memory of last night, her delicate fingers dancing across his naked skin, the warmth of her compact body nestling so neatly into his private spaces.

But then the stench of stale beer came wafting on the steam from Hamish's coffee.

Zol rubbed his nose. "Come on," he told Hamish, "we'll go into the sunroom."

Hamish followed Zol to the rear of the house. It was a glorious, haze-free day, but Hamish showed no interest in the million-dollar view.

"That's one hell of a hangover," Zol said, throwing a protective towel over the loveseat. "You taken an aspirin yet?"

Hamish eased onto the towel, his back to the window. He put down his coffee and held his head in both hands. "I'm never drinking again."

Zol cracked open a window and gulped in a breath of fresh air. "How many did you have?"

"I dunno. Three. Four. Maybe five." He made a face, embarrassed at getting this sick after only four drinks. "I'm not used to it."

"You've been out all night?"

"At a friend's. He was asleep when I left."

"What about Ken?"

"What about him?" Hamish flared, clearly touchy over Zol's innocent inquiry. Had Hamish and Ken broken up? Was that how this had started? Had Hamish been drowning his sorrows?

"I just thought —"

"He's away for the weekend. A conference in Vancouver."

"Are you two . . . you know, still an item?"

"At this point, I couldn't care less. All I can think about at the moment is my Saab."

"Are you sure you looked for it in the right lot?"

Hamish let out a groan. "It's gone, all right. Being picked to pieces in some chop shop in Brant County. I'm such an idiot. I should never have —"

"We'll call the police after breakfast, once that coffee takes effect." Hamish was in no shape to file a coherent complaint. No impatient cop would take him seriously if he blubbered into the phone. "Listen, go upstairs and take a nice long shower. I'll put out a clean shirt and jeans." Zol stood up and took a swig of his coffee. "But first, let me get you an aspirin."

"Please, Zol. Sit down. Got something to tell you. About Camelot."

Zol hesitated, then sat down. Poor Hamish, his life was consumed by work, even during a personal crisis.

"Todd found the listeria."

"What do you mean?"

"He found its source. At the Lodge."

"You serious? What'd he find?"

Between sips of coffee and moaning about his headache, Hamish explained how his medical student came across a plate of salami sandwiches in the reading room.

"Hot damn! Colleen's gotta hear this. She's been following Gus all over the city."

"Not so loud. My head."

"Sorry, buddy," Zol whispered. "Look, go jump in the shower. We'll report the stolen Saab and talk deli meats as soon as you're cleaned up and . . . and feeling more like yourself." It would be a relief when Hamish stopped reeking like the porta-potties at Oktoberfest.

Twenty minutes later, Colleen handed a freshly scrubbed Hamish a glass of orange juice. The scent of oil of bergamot trailing him into the kitchen was a huge improvement over eau-de-hangover.

When Max started to giggle at the sight of Zol's long jeans rolled over Hamish's stubby ankles, Zol stopped him with a quick frown and pointed upstairs. "Time for Saturday morning cleanup, my good man."

Max pulled a face. "Can we have lunch at Four Corners?" He hated missing out on adult conversation. Sometimes he eavesdropped from the top of the stairs, then asked searching questions later. A journalist in the making?

"You know the drill: bed, desk, closet, floor. And collect your dirty dishes. When your room passes inspection, we can go to Four Corners. We have to be back by one o'clock, so make it snappy."

Max took his game gadget from the counter and slunk out of sight. Zol listened for footfalls on the stairs and upper landing before easing into a chair opposite Hamish.

"I understand you found Gus's cache of sandwiches," said Colleen, pouring herself another cup of coffee. "I knew they had to be somewhere. Though I thought maybe he kept them for the family — a personal dividend for his voluntary efforts on behalf of Waste Not."

"Does Gus bypass the main kitchen when he carries the stuff in?" Hamish asked. "Take it straight to his apartment?"

"Looks like it," Zol said. "Otherwise, we'd have found his stash of deli meats by now." Zol cursed himself for not thinking of inspecting the Oliveiras' private quarters.

"My guess," Colleen said, "is that whatever baked goods and sandwiches Gus and Gloria can't eat get set out later for the residents."

"Where the listeria have a heyday," Hamish said, "doubling in population every twenty minutes at room temperature."

"I can't believe it," Zol said. "Looks like the monkey may be off our backs. Trinnock, too."

"Let's hope," Hamish cautioned. "We still have to prove there are live listeria in the sandwich meat. That may be a hit-and-miss effort. We can't expect every piece of salami to be culture positive."

"Fair enough," Zol said. "We'll make a surprise visit today and seize all the deli meat we can find. I sure hope we get a hit, 'cuz that's going to be our only chance. Once Waste Not gets wind of Gus's misappropriations, his Robin Hood days are going to be over."

"I've got pictures of him carrying food trays into the Lodge," Colleen said. "The same trays he picked up at the Royal Hamilton. Mind you, my telephoto isn't good enough to capture the filling in the sandwiches. But tell us, how's Betty?"

"I called the Mountain Wing from your upstairs phone," Hamish said. "She's asking the nurses for chicken noodle soup."

Colleen smiled. "That sounds encouraging." She got the orange-juice carton from the fridge and refilled Hamish's glass. "But how did she get infected with C diff in the first place?"

Zol closed his eyes and took a deep breath, relieved that Betty was finally improving. C diff was everywhere. Normal people carried it in their stools. If they didn't wash their hands after using the toilet, every surface they touched could have live C diff bacteria on it.

"The source of C diff isn't the real problem," Zol said. "It's the empty capsules that Horvat's been dispensing for treating it."

"Todd, my student, has a theory about that," Hamish said. He paused and looked around as if to be sure no one was eavesdropping. "It starts high above Horvat in the medical chain. And really, it's a bit over the top."

Hamish explained Todd's hypothesis that someone at the hospital had engaged Horvat to free up acute-care beds by killing off nursing-home patients. When he was done, Zol held his tongue. Hamish could get touchy when you challenged his ideas. He coped well with frank discussion, but he'd pout for a week if he sensed he was being targeted for ridicule, no matter how mild.

"Extraordinary," said Colleen, her hazels wide.

"Hmm," Zol said, playing it safe. "I don't know what to say."

"Medical people have done worse things, I suppose," Hamish said. "Look at that guy in England. Dr. Shipman, was it? How many elderly patients did he knock off for their life savings?"

The theory *was* way over the top. How far was an associate medical officer of health supposed to stick out his neck? Zol wished Peter Trinnock was the sort of boss he could brainstorm with. Solving something like this needed creative thinking, a heart-to-heart with a confident mentor. But not much creative thinking went on inside Trinnock's office. These days, the chief was paving a flawless highway to retirement, not tackling issues that led into minefields. Trinnock's mantra was FMG: follow ministry guidelines. Sticking to policies and procedures kept the city manager and his purse strings happy, and kept the health unit out of the media's hot seat. There were no ministry guidelines on catching high-profile administrators murdering nursing-home patients. Or pharmacists selling empty capsules.

"We can start with Horvat," Colleen said. "He's a softer target than the hospital's bigwigs."

She's right, thought Zol. *Catching Horvat is the key*. The medical establishment wouldn't circle its wagons around a pharmacist with a thick accent whose son was in jail on drug charges. They'd leave him out to dry.

"I've been watching him," Colleen continued. "I know from my sources that he allowed his burglar alarm contract to lapse. The security company's posters are still on Steeltown Apothecary's doors and windows, and the hardware is still mounted on the wall near the front door. But it's all just for show. Nothing's connected to the police or a private firm. He must be saving every penny to pay for his son's Mexican lawyers."

"Going without an alarm," Hamish said, "that's awfully chancy. Think of all those narcotics asking to be stolen."

"He's got a huge strongroom at the rear of his shop," Colleen said. "Behind a heavy steel door that's controlled by a combination lock — one of those push-button jobs."

"I'd love to be a fly on the wall inside his operation," Zol said.

"Operation?" Hamish asked.

"All those blister cards he produces for two dozen nursing homes — he must have some sort of production facility."

Colleen nodded. She'd been thinking about this too. "If we find his workshop, complete with fake capsules and counterfeit tablets, we've got him."

"Well," Zol said, "we'll have to prove that Horvat *knows* he's dispensing fakes. Without that, the police won't be interested. They'll figure a judge will let him off as not criminally responsible, the way the courts let the others off last year."

Colleen held Zol with her incisive gaze. "All the more reason for us to have a good look at his operation. Without him knowing, of course."

Zol waved his hands. He'd spoken too hastily. He still had night terrors about the last time he and Colleen had inspected an illicit operation in a remote location. They'd barely come out alive. "No, Colleen. *Please.* We can't. Not this time. Too dangerous. We'll lay the groundwork for the RCMP, but we're not going into Horvat's lair ourselves. None of us."

"So what are you saying?" said Colleen. "You don't want to know what's inside that windowless building attached to the rear of his pharmacy? The one that looks like a large garage, and has 'Jack the Printer' scratched on the side?"

"I can't wait to see what's in there," Zol said. "But we're only going in with a police escort. And that will be after we hear for sure that Horvat's blood-pressure tablets are counterfeit." He glanced at the clock above the stove. "Please, Colleen. Have I made myself clear?"

Colleen nodded but didn't smile, her face neutral. She looked out the window, the way she did when she was concentrating. He prayed that meant she was plotting an alternate strategy for nailing Horvat. One that didn't involve breaking into his hornet's nest. Finally, he caught her eye. "If you help Hamish inform the police about his Saab," he said, "Max and I can get going on our Saturday-morning errands."

"All part of the service," she said, and fished her cellphone out of her handbag.

Zol downed the last of his coffee and pushed away from the table. "They say funerals make good scouting grounds for unsolved mysteries. Let's see who turns up at Gloria's mother's service this afternoon."

"Two o'clock at Craig & Lafferty," Colleen said. "Their Main East location. I'll bring my camera."

The Oliveiras are feuding with someone, Zol told himself. When Gloria and her nephew had staggered bleeding and banged up into Camelot's front lobby, Joe had hinted at two other so-called accidents involving the same hit-and-run driver.

"Good idea," Zol said. "There's more going on in Camelot than dodgy food and fake pills."

CHAPTER 27

"Crocodilae lacrimae," Phyllis Wedderspoon pronounced loudly from her seat in the pew beside Zol. She pointed her finger at Gloria Oliveira two rows in front of them. Zol hunched forward, desperate to crawl through a hole in the floor. The preacher stiffened, clamped his Bible with both hands, and finished the benediction that signalled the end of Raimunda Ferreira's funeral service. Phyllis's voice, echoing into every corner of Craig & Lafferty's chapel, reverberated off the brick walls and stained glass. Stuck between Art Greenwood in his wheelchair and Phyllis Wedderspoon on the pew, Zol had no escape.

Gloria Oliveira flinched visibly at the outburst, then rose to follow the casket and the preacher down the centre aisle toward the back of the chapel. Flanked by her husband and her nephew, and followed by two look-alikes in polyester dresses who could only be her sisters from Portugal, Gloria looked a sorry sight. The car crash had made a mess of her face. Steri-Strips criss-crossed her jaw, her right eyelid was almost swollen shut, and her cheeks bloomed as purple as eggplants. She crushed a Kleenex in her fist and stepped behind her mother's casket, which was being wheeled in full retreat.

The service had been plain and brief, reflecting the family's abandonment — according to Phyllis — of both the Catholics and the Jehovah's Witnesses. After an opening hymn and two Bible readings, the preacher had said a few words, but kept apologizing that he didn't know the deceased very well. After stumbling over her name a few times, he'd given up and referred to her as *The Deceased*.

Zol felt the collateral sting of venom when the procession reached his row and Gloria pierced Phyllis with a killing stare. As always, Gus's face was a blank canvas reflecting the mood of the others around him. Zol wondered whether an original idea had ever entered Gus's mind, or was he one of those people who went through life doing as he was told without giving any thought to the consequences. His nephew Joe looked like a black-eyed boxer. A dark crust slashed his forehead where dried blood and stitches covered the gash that had pumped like a fire hose three days before.

Ahead of the sombre trio, two black-suited funeral directors, trained to turn bland eyes on every sort of funeral-service outburst, guided their cargo toward the front door without missing a step.

Only slightly cowed by the look on Gloria's face, Phyllis leaned into Zol's ear. "Those were crocodile tears," she said, her voice echoing again, but perhaps not quite so loudly. "They didn't get along, you know."

Art tapped his lips with his index finger and glared at Phyllis. Then his eyes softened as he caught Zol's eye, and the corners of his mouth hinted at a smile, which he covered with his hand.

Zol wished he could ignore Phyllis, pretend she wasn't there, but he knew if he didn't provide some sort of response, she'd come out with another, louder bombshell. The next time it might not be in Latin.

"I see," he whispered. "Let's talk later. In private."

He took her by the arm and steered her into the procession, well behind the family. Colleen, sitting by herself at the back of the chapel where she'd been observing the service in her professional capacity, caught Zol's eye and grinned. She'd heard Phyllis's benediction, that was clear. Colleen could smirk all she liked from the safety of the rear pew. He was still ready to drop through the floor.

The guests filed out of the chapel and into an adjacent parlour where solid women, bursting out of their black dresses, poured coffee and juice behind tables draped in white linen. Phyllis dashed off, either to the ladies' or in search of a cup of tea. With the change of venue, solemnity gave way to cocktail party chit-chat. Zol got a few looks sympathizing with his embarrassment at Phyllis's eruption, but no comments.

He approached one of the tables and lifted a dainty sandwich from a plate and examined it — cream cheese and olive on bread that seemed past its prime. He sniffed and wondered whether the family had saved on funeral expenses by dipping into Gus's Waste Not dividends. Surely an outfit like Craig & Lafferty wouldn't allow outside food. What did Colleen think? Did she recognize any of the sandwiches from Gus's rounds? He looked for her but couldn't see her. Her short stature gave her a cloak of near invisibility that made it difficult to pick her out in a crowded room. Lucky her.

"Very nice service," Art said, wheeling toward Zol with a plate of sandwiches balanced on his lap. "But this is turning into too much of a habit — dear Melvin's funeral yesterday, Raimunda's today, and poor Earl teetering on the brink." He paused and looked around to be sure they were out of earshot. "I should have bought shares in Craig & Lafferty. Too late now, I suppose." He scanned the room. "Have you seen Dr. Wakefield? Did he slip in at the back?"

"Hamish has still got his hands full at the Lodge," Zol said.

"I wanted to thank him. Betty's a bit better today. Turning the corner, I'd say."

Zol smiled, sharing Art's relief, then pointed to the sandwich in Art's hand. "Should you be eating that?"

"Why not? I love Italian salami." His eyes twinkled as he touched the side of his nose. "Sometimes Gus sneaks it into the Lodge for us."

"I don't recall you including any deli meats in your food questionnaire, Art."

Art put down the sandwich as a guilty look came over his face. Zol couldn't tell whether the old guy felt embarrassed about his fading memory or guilty about an intentional deception. "I should have told you about tea time in the upstairs library. I'm sorry. I guess I forgot about the snacks."

Zol studied Art's benign face, the permanent sparkle in his clear grey eyes, and chose to believe that the reading-room salami had slipped the dear fellow's mind.

Zol pulled out his cellphone, suddenly blaring in his pocket. The screen said *Trinnock, Peter*. He backed away. The boss was calling from home. On Saturday afternoon. He pressed Talk and braced himself.

"Szabo? What the hell are you up to? I just got another call from the PMO."

"Oh."

"Yes, 'oh.'"

Zol let Trinnock's sarcasm hang between them. That usually stopped it from escalating.

"What can I tell them?" Trinnock continued, his tone not quite so harsh.

"We may have found the pathogen responsible for the outbreak."

"Damn it, man. Why didn't you call me? Let me know immediately?"

"We're still in the process of unravelling the story. And the Feds are so touchy about listeria these days that —"

"Listeria? These old people are dying of listeria? Just like the fiasco last year in that meat-packing plant? For God's sake, Szabo, you better have your facts iron-clad before you —"

"Don't worry, sir. I'm being very careful."

"Is it time to call in the Food Inspection Agency? Let them take over from here?"

The last thing Zol needed was the CFIA descending upon Camelot and Viktor Horvat. Those federal boys and girls would drive Vik and his counterfeit operation into hiding immediately, and no one would ever get to the bottom of his drug scheme. More and more, it seemed the listeria and the phony meds were intimately connected.

"We don't need the CFIA just yet, sir. Camelot meets all federal and provincial food-handling guidelines." Well, except for the recycled salami sandwiches, but he wasn't going to go into the details. He'd sort things out with Gus this afternoon. "We've put a stop to further C diff cases, and . . . and we think we've found a possible source of the listeria."

"You *think* you found a *possible source*? That sort of language doesn't fill me with confidence, my boy."

"I've got our own experts on the case." Colleen was tailing Horvat, and Hamish would soon be using bacterial genetics to prove that the listeria came from the sandwiches misappropriated from Waste Not.

"I want a full report on Monday. Ten a.m. My office. I can't stall the PMO any longer than that."

Suddenly, there was commotion to the right. Two men in grey business suits, taller than Zol, huge mandibles, fresh buzz cuts — one dark, one blond — were plowing their way through the crowd. They locked Zol with their eyes and two seconds later were crowding either side of him, practically standing on his toes. Their breaths were hot with peppermint, but the gum didn't disguise the musky odour of taco sauce and testosterone. Zol closed his phone and dropped it into his pocket.

"We need to talk to you," said the one with dark, deep-set eyes and a white scar above his lip.

"Who are you?"

"Just come with us."

Zol's heartbeat shot up twenty points. Had Hamish caved and called someone, reported Horvat prematurely? Had Horvat fingered Zol to his cronies? Horvat had never seen Zol face to face, but it would be easy to dig up a photo of Dr. Zol Szabo, public-health crusader. Half a minute with Google would do it. Health-unit docs were cited throughout the Internet. That's what the job was about — making waves. He'd been criticized, even vilified, by irate mothers and paranoid politicians. But never threatened by hired guns.

His tongue was so thick he could hardly speak. His eyes swept the room for safety in numbers. "No. I'm staying right here."

They whipped out their badges and business cards. Shoved them in his face.

RCMP.

Oh, no. The PMO was muscling in, just like he'd feared. Their timing was terrible. They were going to ruin everything.

The cards flashed so fast that Zol didn't notice the officers' ranks, though he didn't miss their names. The blond one was Gretzky, the dark one with the scar through his lip was Crosby. They must be aliases; those names would never appear side by side in real life except in a hockey lineup. Were they allowed to use fake ID when questioning a public official? Or was this some sort of covert action, masquerading as RCMP but masterminded by CSIS, the Canadian Security Intelligence Service? Yes, the Prime Minister's Office was behind this.

"In the next room," said Crosby.

"But . . ."

"Let me put it this way, you don't want to make this difficult."

"Okay, okay. But I'm not leaving the building."

The two men guided Zol into the adjacent parlour, marching him between them shoulder to shoulder. The room was deserted. It seemed they'd commandeered it already. Gretzky shut the door and dragged an armchair in front of it.

The room began to spin. Zol could barely keep upright. The back of his shirt felt cold and wet. He steadied himself against a stand holding a spray of flowers. He breathed in the revolting pungency of the lilies — as jarring as smelling salts — but it did nothing to clear his head.

If this wasn't the PMO in action, it must be Francine. Had she sicced the RCMP on him in a bid to steal custody of Max? That was it — she was accusing Zol of fraud or neglect or something worse. Pedophilia? She must be back on the continent. In one of those ashrams in British Columbia, the Kootenays or Vancouver Island. She'd lived in a string of communes in Asia for the past eight years, ever since the day she'd stormed out, leaving ten-month-old Max alone in the house. She hadn't called in months, not since she'd threatened to take Max to Toronto for an unsupervised visit, court order or not.

Gretzky pointed to the sofa and said, "Have a seat."

"We got a few questions," Crosby added, pulling a notepad from his jacket pocket.

"Who's the short babe with the camera and the long ponytail?" said Gretzky.

Yes, Francine was behind this. She'd found out Colleen was staying over. Not that it needed to be a secret. The divorce had come through years ago. The witch must be claiming that Colleen, a private eye, was a toxic influence. No, it couldn't be. For the RCMP to be involved, the allegations must be horrendous. Francine had always had a morbid fear of the devil. Was she accusing Zol and Colleen of Satanism?

Hell, was he *never* going to be rid of her?

"She's . . . she's a private investigator," Zol said.

Gretzky was asking the questions. "And her name?"

"Um . . . Woolton. Colleen Woolton."

"What's your relationship?"

"She . . . works for me."

Gretzky raised an eyebrow.

"Consultant," Zol added. His tongue was so dry that he could barely spit out one syllable at a time.

The men each pulled up a chair and positioned themselves directly in front of Zol. They were enjoying watching him squirm.

"Look," Zol said, "does this have anything to do with my personal life? With my ex-wife?"

Gretzky smirked. "You tell us."

"I haven't seen my ex in eight years. The last I heard she was living in India. She's got nothing to do with . . . with Camelot Lodge."

Crosby shrugged and shot a knowing smile, then looked at Gretzky. They both had exes in their pasts. "Works for us."

"What do you know about Augusto Oliveira?" Gretzky asked.

"Who?"

"Calls himself Gus."

Gus? Oh, of course. "Um . . . He's the son-in-law of the deceased."

"A friend of yours?"

"No."

"Then what are you doing at his mother-in-law's funeral?"

"He's the handyman at Camelot Lodge, a retirement residence. My grandfather lives there."

"Camelot," Gretzky said. "That's the place. Looks like a castle. Fancy neighbourhood at the bottom of the Mountain."

Only Hamiltonians called the Niagara Escarpment "the Mountain." Gretzky was from the local detachment.

"Handyman, eh?" Crosby said. "Lots of construction projects? Major renovations?"

"Not that I know of."

Crosby's scarred lip curled into a sneer. "Come off it. Where's he stashing the building supplies?"

Zol balled the Kleenex in his suit-coat pocket between his sweaty fingers. He could barely stop from pulling out the tissue and ripping it to shreds. But there was no point in showing Gretzky and Crosby how nervous he was. Hell, they could probably smell it off him anyway. "No idea."

"Don't give us that," Gretzky said.

"I've got nothing to give you."

Gretzky stiffened and let out a rumbling sigh. "The goods, man. We know there's criminal activity being perpetrated at that old-people's place."

How much should he tell them? Should he spill everything? Luncheon-meat sandwiches misappropriated from a respectable charity, recurrent listeria infections in a subset of residents tied to a federal political party, empty antibiotic capsules and counterfeit antihypertensives? Then what would these guys do? Stomp into Camelot with their Tasers? Storm into Steeltown Apothecary and ruin any chance of catching Horvat red-handed?

Zol pushed himself back farther onto the sofa and let the cushions take the weight of his back and shoulders. This had nothing to do with Max, the core of his life. It was only about work. He could cope with that. He wiped the sweat from his hands with the ball of Kleenex. He bored his gaze into Gretzky's chiselled face.

"Tell us what you know about Joe Medeiros," Gretzky demanded.

Now that Max was out of the equation, Crosby and Gretzky had lost their bite. Zol shook his head. "Don't know him."

Crosby pulled a photo from his inner jacket pocket and thrust it at Zol. "Sure you do. He hangs out at Camelot."

Zol studied the photo. The face looked familiar, but he couldn't place it. Then he pictured the right eye swollen and blood streaming from the forehead and he knew who it was. "Oh. That's Joe. The nephew."

"Whose nephew?"

"Um . . . Gloria's, I think."

"What do you know about him?" Gretzky asked.

"He's a visitor. From Portugal. Got in a car accident three or four days ago. He's here at the funeral, but you'd never recognize him with his face banged up. You can talk to him yourselves. His English is perfect."

Now that Zol didn't feel like the target, the words were stumbling more easily out of his mouth. He tightened his fists and reminded himself to be careful. Gretzky and Crosby were undercover for some reason, and they could scupper his own investigation.

Crosby flipped his notepad to a fresh page. "What do you know about his frequent trips between Canada and Europe?"

Things suddenly started to make sense. These guys were RCMP drug squad. They must be hot on the heels of that drug bust in Escarpment Country out near Kilbride. The front section of the *Spec* had been full of the story all week. The cops had uncovered a crystal meth factory on a rundown old farm, but hadn't nabbed anyone.

"If you're asking if I've seen anything to suggest that the Oliveiras are in the drug trade, the answer is no." If he was right about the crystal meth connection, neither Gretzky nor Crosby showed it on his face.

"Have you noticed anything suspicious about Joe's behaviour? Or his uncle's?" Crosby asked, his pen poised over his notepad.

Zol clamped his jaw and fixed his gaze on the door, still blocked by the armchair.

Suspicious? Hell, he could give them suspicious. He could spill it all and be done with it. But . . . whether these guys were CSIS, or RCMP, or a couple of thugs from the local criminal families, he was going to keep his mouth shut.

Could he maintain a neutral face and flat-out lie to Gretzky and Crosby?

He'd do his damndest.

CHAPTER 28

An hour later, outside Betty McKenzie's room on the Mountain Wing, Zol shrugged out of the black suit coat he'd worn to the funeral. He rolled up his sleeves, still tacky from the sweat of his interrogation. His tongue was dry as the Gobi. It would have been easier to cave, to spill everything to the two bullies, whoever they were. But he'd put up a wall and stood behind it. Despite their badgering, they had no inkling about Horvat, didn't even mention his name, which had made it easier to tell them nothing about the events at the Lodge that bothered him most.

But how much information would the Mounties turn up on their own? And when would they be back?

"You okay?" Hamish asked him. "You look terrible. Funerals always affect you like that?"

"Just tired, I guess." He was in no mood to tell Hamish about the goons.

Hamish's isolation gown cast a yellow glow of jaundice to his pale skin and bloodshot eyes. Last night's beers, and whatever else Hamish had got up to, had taken their toll.

"That'll be Art," Hamish said as the elevator pinged. "His daily visit with Betty. Will you get him gowned up?"

Zol fastened Art's isolation gown at his neck and tucked the trailing edge between Art's skinny thighs and the scooter seat. More than ever, the old man was showing his age. Funerals did that to you, Zol reckoned, especially when you were over ninety. The solemn service brought you face to face with the possibility that the next person lying in the coffin would be you. And such thoughts were bound to show in the creases on your face.

As Zol followed Art into Betty's room, he was struck by a sudden wistfulness. He'd never known either of his grandfathers. The Second World War had consumed them both, consigned them to unmarked graves somewhere in Europe. No funerals. No burials. Just open-ended grief. Their widows, his grandmothers, had lived the rest of their frugal lives in Budapest, imprisoned behind the Iron Curtain. As a child in Ontario, Zol imagined the curtain as a giant wall encircling his grey-haired *Nagymamas*. In the rare photos sent from Hungary, he'd looked in vain for soldiers and a barbed-wire barricade. The letters with the bold *Magyar* stamps stopped coming sometime in the eighties, before he became a teenager.

Zol handed Art two vinyl gloves and squeezed into a pair of his own, afraid the flimsy things might rip. Large was never large enough, and the nurses didn't put out boxes of XL. Hamish had no trouble slipping on the smalls.

Art took Betty's blue-veined hand. She seemed tiny, swallowed up by the hospital bed. "You're looking a little better, my love," he said.

"Only a little?" She pushed wisps of silvery hair from her pallid cheek, then extended her arm towards Hamish. "How am I doing, Doctor?"

Hamish hesitated, then glanced at Zol and said, "We'll soon have you dining on . . . on filet mignon."

Zol stiffened at the false note in his friend's tone. They both knew she had a long way to go before she could eat solid food.

"Thank you, Dr. Wakefield," Betty said. "I think I'm getting there."

Hamish looked away, then turned his attention to Betty's tubes. Zol could see him subtly checking the labels on the IV bag, the rate of the infusion, the volume in her urine container, the moisture on her tongue, the temperature of her brow, the distension of her belly, the pained look in her eyes when he pressed on the four quadrants of her abdomen. They'd already reviewed her chart and seen that the frequency of her diarrhea had decreased. Only three stools since midnight. Was that a minor triumph or a signal that the intestines were giving up, injured beyond repair?

Zol studied the rainbow of get-well cards displayed on the windowsill. "A lot of fan mail there, Betty. Once you're up and about, you'll have your hands full with correspondence."

Her eyes dipped modestly. "It's nice to be remembered, even after all these years."

"A lifetime of friends and associates in high places," Zol continued.

"Most of the old friends are gone. But the party machine still remembers. And they know I'm writing my memoirs. They must think cards and chocolates will keep me from soiling their reputations."

"For heaven's sake," Art said. "They have nothing to worry about. Your stories aren't salacious. No bedroom scandals."

She touched her finger to the side of her nose as her eyes brightened. "It *is* a minority parliament, remember. So they're nervous over rumours about a certain former PM's noontime indiscretions, which only his former assistant knows about for sure."

Art squeezed her hand through his gloves, the vinyl an ugly barrier between them. But there was no mistaking the love in his eyes. "You're making an important contribution to the nation's history."

"Thank you, Art dear," she said. "But you know how skittish politicians can be. When it got around that the old den mother was writing a book, they became as edgy as a bunch of cats."

"You haven't been threatened, have you?" Zol said.

"Oh no. Though I hear they *are* a little unsettled in the PMO. Wish I'd taken up crocheting afghans instead of writing books."

"Are you still in touch?" Zol asked.

"Myrtle's nephew. He works for the current prime minister. Says the office is afraid of the tidbits I might reveal about the old guard. Afraid my insights will reflect badly on the current generation." Betty pulled her bedsheet up to her collarbones. A moment went by. She looked exhausted. Then she rallied slightly and smiled. "Once I get out of this sickbed, the gang at the PMO will have to put away their champagne."

"Betty, please," Art said, squeezing her hand, "don't talk like that. You've always been beloved."

"Except when I poisoned my prime minister."

"You what?" said Hamish.

"Gave him salmonella," Betty said. "By accident, of course. But they never again let me contribute to the office potluck."

Art's face was full of concern. "How were you supposed to know home-grown sprouts, or whatever they were, could make anyone sick, let alone a prime minister."

"Was he hospitalized?" Hamish asked.

"No, no," she said. "Just a few days of the runs. And antibiotics, if I remember correctly. But when the health unit in Ottawa discovered it was my alfalfa sprouts that poisoned the PM, I was *persona non grata* in the lunchroom for a long time, I'll tell you. But the boss was very good about it. When I retired, he named it the Betty McKenzie Lunchroom and had a plaque placed on the door."

"Makes you a culinary legend, I would say," Zol said.

"But it's got Myrtle's nephew worked up," Betty said. "He's not sure he wants his aunt living in the same residence as Lunchroom Betty. Told Myrtle I must be somehow responsible for the diarrhea around here." She turned to Zol. "Between you and me, I wouldn't be surprised if he called you from the PMO and threw his weight around. Just ignore him. He's a not a very big fish."

She gave Art a demure flash of her eyes, then turned a more determined gaze on Hamish. "So tell me, why did I get so sick and take so long to get better?"

Hamish and Zol exchanged glances.

Hamish clasped his gloved palms together. The gloves were contaminated with the invisible veneer of pathogens that coated everything in Betty's room. He scratched his nose and cheek against his gown-covered shoulder. "You had two pathogens — two germs — at the same time. C diff and listeria. We had trouble . . . well, let's just say we had to find them both, then treat both of them to make you better."

If she'd sensed any evasion, she didn't show it. In the PMO, she'd had years of practice keeping her observations and judgments to herself. Of course, she could voice them later, to anyone, any time it suited her. To the RCMP, perhaps, if they came calling again.

CHAPTER 29

Half an hour later, Zol led the way into Camelot's reading room on the top floor of the turret. The room's best feature was its heavy oak door, which he planned to shut as soon as Hamish, Natasha, and the available Camelot Irregulars got settled. It was past tea time, which meant they wouldn't be disturbed.

The first thing he noticed, besides the room's small size and overwhelming clutter, was the musty odour of stale coffee, old carpet, and heavy drapes. A dusty-rose loveseat and a striped arm-chair sat in front of the windows. Paperbacks spilled out of the curved bookshelves that gave the room its name. Two hardback chairs piled with dog-eared magazines crowded a small wooden table, on which were balanced two insulated carafes, a sugar bowl, a pitcher of milk, and a plate of stale-looking doughnuts. No sand-wiches today. The place looked like an afterthought, somewhere to stash faded chintz, mismatching stripes, discarded newspapers, three garage-sale lamps, and, it seemed, past-their-prime snacks.

"Don't sit on that," Phyllis told Natasha, who was sweeping crumbs from the armchair's frayed cushion. "Its unruly springs poke into one's . . ." Phyllis tightened her lips and continued in a stage whisper: *"Puga pyga."*

"Where would you like to sit, Miss Wedderspoon?" asked Natasha, struggling to keep a straight face.

"I seldom come here. It's not sanitary. I'm not squeamish about bats, but I do draw the line at their droppings underfoot while I'm taking my tea. For some reason, they congregate here. But certainly not for the fine prose on offer." Phyllis flicked her hand at the bookcase. "Just look at those potboilers. *Tainted. Grinder. Darwin's Nightmare.* None of it proper literature." She tugged at her cardigan, checked the floor for bat droppings, and strode to the loveseat. "I obtain my reading material from the public library. The Terryberry branch is a splendid resource. What's more, the parking and Internet are free."

Natasha covered her mouth and nodded politely, her eyes crinkling. She lifted the stack of magazines from one of the hardback chairs. As she sat down, Hamish did the same, and Art completed the circle with his scooter.

Zol closed the door and took a deep breath. He and his *puga*-whatever would have to take their chances with the prehistoric armchair. "Thank you for coming."

"It's about time we had a powwow," said Phyllis. "No one tells us anything."

"Now, now," Art cautioned. "We met two days ago. Zol was kind enough to have us to his office. Remember?"

"Of course I remember," Phyllis snapped. She pulled at a disobedient pleat in her kilt. "But surely, a few *occasiones graves* have turned up in the past forty-eight hours. Come now, you must have at least one significant development to report."

Hamish turned to Zol and raised his eyebrows, his wide eyes replaying their heated conversation of a few minutes earlier. Hamish had insisted they bring Art and Phyllis into their confidence, tell them about Horvat's bogus meds. Zol had said no, it was too early. A tongue might slip and send Horvat covering his tracks. But Hamish — hangover gone, the police reasonably hopeful about the Saab, his passions revived — was adamant. He insisted that Art, Phyllis, and the others laid up with repeated episodes of diarrhea in

the past few weeks had every right to know they'd been fed counterfeit medication. And, Hamish reckoned, Art and Phyllis might
have noticed something crucial to proving Horvat's culpability. Zol
had finally agreed, but only if they didn't include Myrtle. The last
thing he needed was the Prime Minister's Office updated, via
Myrtle's nephew, on the latest commotions at Camelot Lodge.

At Zol's nod, Hamish finished a long draft from his water
bottle, screwed on the cap, then explained how he'd found the
empty capsules.

For a moment, even Phyllis was dumbstruck. She and Art would
have been less stunned if they'd been told Betty had spent the
morning skydiving.

Fire lit Art's face, the patches of rosacea on his cheeks glowing
more crimson than ever. "Outrageous," he sputtered.

"And sorry, Art, that's not all," Hamish said. "It looks like your
Zytopril — your blood pressure pills — are counterfeits, too."

"You mean poisonous?" Art said.

"Heavens, no," Zol said. "Counterfeit in the sense that the tablets
may be perfectly good but come from an unlicensed supplier. At a
bargain price."

"No point in mincing words, Dr. Szabo," Phyllis said, her face
more stern than anxious. "You mean pirated. Pure and simple."

Hamish pulled the ballpoint from his shirt pocket and clicked it
anxiously. "There's no telling what's in those pills. They could contain the genuine drug. Or they could be completely fake, with no
active agent, just filler. How's your blood pressure been lately, Art?"

"Hell . . . I don't know," Art said. "It's been ages since Dr.
Jamieson checked it."

"Did the nurse take it last time you were in bed with the runs?"
Hamish asked.

Art shrugged. "I suppose. Didn't mention it was a problem."

"Well, I'll take it as soon as we're finished here."

"Pirating is big business," Phyllis said. "The Internet is rife with
deceivers. How many other dubious medications is Horvat purvey-
ing?"

"So far, there are only two that we know about," Zol said.

Phyllis scowled and voiced a skeptical *tsk*.

"We have an independent pharmacist working with us," Hamish countered. "A man we can trust. He's checking all the meds Horvat's been dispensing at the Lodge."

"I don't think there can be anything fake about the arthritis meds," Natasha said. "There's a strong link between listeria infection and both Xanucox and Durimab, which means they must be biologically active."

Phyllis pulled the pencil from behind her ear and waved it at Art. "I warned you before, it's not natural to take so many medications." She straightened her back and fussed with her kilt, then pressed her lips together and held Art with her brown-eyed glare. That look must have bolted countless teenagers to their seats until they could decline *murus muri* and *puella puellae* to her satisfaction. "All I ever take is a baby aspirin. Eighty-one milligrams."

"But you haven't been cursed with arthritis," Art said, pointing to his legs. "Nor neuropathy."

Hamish grabbed at his belt and pulled his chiming cellphone from its holster. He flipped it open. "Hamish Wakefield here . . . Hi Ellen . . . You do? We're discussing them right now . . . And? . . . That was fast . . . What's it called, again? . . . Oh . . . Atlanta? Impressive . . . Every one, eh? Wow! . . . Correct, I looked after him . . . That can't be right, Ellen. There has to be a mix-up, a glitch in your new method . . . Oh. Yes, of course, your controls . . . Sorry, I understand. I didn't mean it the way it . . . You do have to admit, this is a surprise. I mean, totally unexpected . . . Yes, I'll share this with the folks at the health unit. They'll be amazed."

Hamish said goodbye, closed his phone, and put it away. Oblivious to the four expectant faces aimed at him, he uncapped his water bottle and sipped delicately. Then dabbed his lips with a tissue and stared into space.

"Hamish!" Zol said, "You're killing us. What's so amazing?"

"That was Ellen," Hamish said finally. He turned to Art and Phyllis. "She's the chief tech in the diagnostic microbiology lab at Caledonian University Medical Centre."

"We gathered that much," Zol said. He thrust his hands into his pockets, but he'd left home without his loonies. Damn.

"Ellen finished fingerprinting the listeria isolates," Hamish continued.

"Pulse-field gels on all of them?" Natasha said. "That's a lot of work. How'd she do it so fast?"

"She didn't," Hamish said. "She used a new technique. MLVA. Got the primers from Atlanta, the CDC. Overnight courier."

The epidemiological whiz kids at the U.S. Centers for Disease Control always had some new wonder toy from the world of molecular genetics. "ML-what?" Zol asked.

"Let's just say it uses DNA amplification technology to examine fragments of a bacterium's genetic code. Much faster than running pulse-field gels, and the results are reproducible from lab to lab."

Hamish explained that such reproducibility was a breakthrough. Different labs could compare their strains from a distance, without testing all the strains in the same lab at the same time.

"You mean they can make the comparison with a simple phone call, a fax, or a file from the Web?" Zol asked.

"That's right," Hamish said. "MLVA is turning the pulse-field method into a dinosaur."

"In plain language?" Phyllis tsked.

Natasha glanced at Zol before explaining. "It's a way of fingerprinting the listeria found in the dozens of stools submitted from Camelot's residents with diarrhea. A way of telling whether the bacteria are identical, like twins. Or close relatives, like sisters or cousins. Or come from different families altogether."

Phyllis nodded and smiled. She liked Natasha's explanation.

"Out with it, Dr. Wakefield," Art said. "Tell us what's the surprise."

"Ellen tested every listeria recovered from Camelot residents over the past two months — from stools, blood, and cerebrospinal fluid. And she examined listeria from a bunch of other patients with no links to Camelot — those were her controls." Hamish stopped and looked from face to face, making sure his audience was with him.

"And?" Zol said, struggling to keep the exasperation out of his voice.

"The Camelot isolates all belong to a well-known strain, serovar 4b. It's the most aggressive listeria, so there's no surprise there. Then she did the genetic fingerprinting with MLVA. All the Camelot listerias came out identical, but completely different from the other patients she tested except one."

"No genetic variations within the Camelot cohort?" Natasha said.

"None."

"A huge set of twins?" Art said proudly, clearly pleased at his grasp of a complex situation.

"Exactly," Hamish said.

Natasha opened her notebook. "The first Camelot isolate was obtained from a stool sample submitted on January eleventh. The most recent would be Earl Crabtree's, grown from his blood culture taken two days ago. Does that sound right, Dr. Wakefield?"

"Correct."

Natasha looked up from her notepad, the wheels turning furiously. "That's a span of sixty-seven days." She paused again, her pen suspended in the air. She looked at Zol for reassurance, as if she needed his permission to voice her opinion.

"What are you thinking, Natasha?" Zol said.

"This has to be a point source," she said, her confidence growing. "And one that's sustained over a period of more than two months."

"Again, in plain language?" Phyllis said. "Is one to suppose that a point source is a single object that's contaminated with the bacteria in question?"

"Exactly," Zol said.

Art dipped his chin to the tea table beside him, his eyes hooded with guilt. "And you think our illicit salami sandwiches are the culprits?"

"Are the sandwiches *always* salami?" Natasha asked.

"Oh, no," Art explained. "Salami is just my favourite. We'll have it for a week, then not see anything but turkey for a while. Then bologna turns up. Then nothing but tuna or egg salad for a few days. Come to think of it, we've had a lot of that soya stuff lately. It may look like bologna, but one bite and I can tell it didn't come from anything with legs."

Zol remembered the outbreak of listeria at the Royal Hamilton Hotel last fall — traced to cheese made from unpasteurized milk. "Was there cheese in the sandwiches?" he asked.

"Occasionally," Art said.

Natasha dashed a few notes into her scribbler, then paused before asking, "Do all the residents eat the sandwiches from this room?"

"Hard to say," Art said. "It's a casual arrangement. You bring your own mug, help yourself to tea or coffee, grab a sandwich, then take it back to your room. As you can see, there's not much space to sit."

"Some of us never come up here," Phyllis said. "Maude, Myrtle, and I make our own tea. And we don't snack between meals."

"As I remember, Miss Wedderspoon, the three of you haven't had any diarrhea," Natasha said.

Phyllis crossed her arms. "Certainly not. *Mea non culpa.*"

Natasha dipped into her briefcase and pulled out a folder. She riffled through it until she found what she was looking for and turned to Phyllis. "In the medication survey, the three of you put down hardly any medicines. You take your baby aspirin, Maude takes only vitamins, and Myrtle takes Zytopril, acetaminophen, and a sleeping pill."

"She didn't listen to me about those sleeping pills, and now she's addicted."

"None of you have bad arthritis?" Natasha asked.

"We exercise together. Regularly. Walk the circuit in Lime Ridge Mall from nine to nine-thirty, three mornings a week."

Zol pictured Art's best friend Earl, fighting for his life at Caledonian Medical Centre. He touched Art's arm. "When would be the last time Earl ate one of the sandwiches from this room?"

"He's fussy. Only eats corned beef. We haven't seen it around here for a month, maybe longer. He wouldn't touch the salami or the fake bologna they've been serving lately."

"I don't think our source can be the sandwiches," Zol said. He eyed the tea things on the table. His mouth was parched. He had half a mind to drink the milk right out of the pitcher. Only half a mind.

"Let me tell you about your sandwiches," Zol continued. "They've been coming to you from all over the place. Colleen followed them here from the Royal Hamilton Hotel, the Convention Centre, Four Corners Fine Foods, and Delia's Donuts in Ancaster." He explained about Waste Not and its roster of volunteer drivers who recycled food to the needy by shuttling leftovers from hotels, restaurants, and caterers. He told them how Gus brought a tray or two of sandwiches back to Camelot Lodge at the end of each run.

"Recycled sandwiches! I ask you," Phyllis said. "What will Gloria and Gus do next to save a few pennies at our expense? I knew there was a reason I never took tea in this room."

"That explains the bread," Art said. "Dry as toast until you slather it with mustard."

"But what's your bacterial genetic whoozits got to do with Gus's misappropriated sandwiches?" Phyllis said.

"There are hundreds of clones of listeria," Hamish said. "Each has a unique genetic fingerprint. It's impossible that one clone, with a single fingerprint, could contaminate so many different sandwiches obtained from diverse sources over a two-month period."

"If the sandwiches were the source," Zol said, "Ellen's new test would have detected a variety of listeria fingerprints among the Camelot samples. But she found only one."

"And the five cases from that outbreak at the Royal Hamilton last fall don't match the Camelot ones. Ellen was clear about that," Hamish said.

"That lets the Royal Hamilton's cheese supplier off the hook," Zol said.

The room fell quiet as Art and Phyllis tried to puzzle out the science, and Natasha studied her notes. Hamish looked like he was chewing on something Ellen had told him. Whatever it was, it had him puzzled. Zol wondered where to go from here. He shifted on the armchair, away from that spring poking him in the ass.

"Tell me about the mustard, Mr. Greenwood," Natasha said.

"What mustard?"

"Didn't you say you have to slather mustard all over the sandwiches because the bread is so stale?"

It looked like Natasha was on to something. "Art," Zol said, "is the mustard in a jar?"

"Oh, yes."

"And is it always the same jar that's set out with the sandwiches?"

Art turned to Phyllis and raised an eyebrow. He was hoping two memories were better than one.

"Don't even think about asking me," she insisted, her arms still crossed.

"Yes," Art decided. "I think it's the same jar."

"Does Gus serve any other condiments?" Natasha asked. "Mayo? Ketchup? Relish, maybe?"

"Just a single jar of that French stuff," Art said. "You know what I mean . . . begins with a D."

"Dijon?" Zol suggested.

Art flashed a tentative smile. "That's it."

Zol pictured a simple kitchen table knife spreading Dijon onto contaminated cold cuts, returning to the jar, then spreading mustard — and bacteria — over the next sandwich, and the next, and the next. A jar of mustard could last for weeks. Was this Natasha's point source, a single strain of listeria doled out over a couple of months?

But could listeria survive in Dijon? Perhaps its white wine and vinegar were too acidic for bacteria to survive in it.

Hamish was staring out of the window as if the conversation were suddenly irrelevant. Was he worrying about his Saab, imagining it in a shed somewhere, dismantled into parts? He finally stood up and tugged at his sleeves. "I'm not sure how much I care about the mustard," he said, "but we can easily check it out. Listen, I've saved the best for last." His eyes twinkled as he ran his hand across his flat-top. But then he paused, suddenly uncertain.

"Go on, Dr. Wakefield," Art said. "What is it?"

"Art and Phyllis," Hamish continued, his voice cloaked with caution, "this is strictly confidential. And I mean *strictly*. I shouldn't be sharing this information with anyone outside the health unit." He looked at Zol, then took a deep breath. "Viktor Horvat — everyone's favourite pharmacist — was a patient in our ICU at New Year's. I looked after him. He had listeria meningitis. And completely recovered."

"Yes," Natasha said. "We investigated, but couldn't find a local source. We decided he'd picked up his infection in Mexico. He'd been there quite often. You know, the business about his son."

"Well, listen to this," Hamish said. "Ellen told me that Horvat's listeria is identical to every isolate from Camelot, down to the very last detail on the MLVA fingerprinting."

Natasha dropped her pen. It rolled off her lap and clattered onto the floor. "Oh my God. His case was reported on New Year's Day." She tugged at the curls at the nape of her neck. "That . . . that makes him case number one. The index."

"*Sacrum excrementum*," said Art. "You mean he brought it from Mexico and gave it to us?"

"Wherever he brought it from," said Hamish, "he's been shoving his stubby, unwashed fingers into something you've been eating."

Zol had a feeling that *something* wasn't as simple as a jar of Dijon, but the kitchen in Gus and Gloria's apartment was about to get a surprise inspection.

CHAPTER 30

At eight-thirty that evening, Natasha pulled her Honda into the lot behind Caledonian Medical Centre. She took her ticket from the dispenser and the gate opened. The pavement ended in the tangled shadows of the Mountain brow. She quickly rolled up her window. In the daytime, the Escarpment's woodland cliff soared above the lake, offering views of two skylines, Hamilton's rising immediately below and Toronto's shimmering in the hazy distance, like an echo. But at this time of night, the black mass of trees and shrubs threatened with the rawness of a jungle.

She checked over both shoulders before turning off the ignition. No lurkers. She opened the door a crack to turn on the light, then checked her teeth and lipstick in the rear-view mirror. She'd flossed away the remains of her mother's curried veggies. Filling up on plain chapattis, she'd only taken a few bites of the spicy dishes, but still those damn okra seeds got stuck between her front teeth. She dug into her purse for two sprays of mouth freshener to cover the garlic, if only for a few minutes while she broke the ice with Ellen. It was a continual struggle to get her mother to tone down her spices, especially the cumin. Natasha had loathed the smell of cumin since grade nine, when she'd overheard two freckled girls complaining that curry stank like sweaty armpits. They were right: too much cumin reeked through your pores. But so did cabbage and red meat.

She showed her health-unit badge to the security man at the front door. He didn't bother to check her tote bag, so he didn't notice the hunk of *chouriço* sausage and the half-full jar of Dijon mustard.

She and Dr. Zol had visited the Oliveiras' apartment immediately after the powwow in the library. Gloria had been resting in bed, but Gus Oliveira's face was full of smiles and crooked yellow teeth as he answered the door. You'd never know from his demeanour that he'd just buried his mother-in-law. But when Dr. Zol asked to inspect the kitchen, Natasha saw apprehension flash into Gus's eyes. He led the way without protest and didn't fuss about handing over the jar of mustard Natasha found in the refrigerator.

"Nice-looking *chouriço* sausage in there," Dr. Zol said, as Mr. Oliveira closed the fridge door. "You make it yourselves?"

"Oh, no," Gus said. The trepidation in his face showed he was aware that deli meats and old people's homes weren't supposed to mix. "A Christmas present. From my cousin in Stoney Creek."

"Must be from that Portuguese butcher. The guy from San Miguel?"

Gus beamed utter surprise and delight at Dr. Zol's knowledge of Azores culture. "You like *chouriço*, Doctor?" His shoulders relaxed and he pulled open the cutlery drawer. "I cut you a piece."

Dr. Zol took a step back and put up his hands. "No thanks, Gus." He glanced knowingly at Natasha and added, "I prefer salami."

"Salami?" Gus shook his head in disgust. "Not salami. Taste like old shoe."

"Only when it gets sliced ahead of time and dries out."

"I stick with *chouriço*."

"And let the English have the salami, eh?" Dr. Zol said with a chuckle.

"They don't know no difference."

"Like my granddad, eh? He's happy with his salami."

Gus nodded. "Always asking for more. But they don't always have it."

"Yeah, I know. The Royal Hamilton is more famous for its chipotle egg salad and Thai veggie wraps."

Gus started to nod again, then caught himself. "Um . . . Royal Hamilton? You mean the hotel?" He shook his head, but his deception was obvious.

"It's okay, Gus. I know all about your charity work. Driving for Waste Not. Feeding the poor."

"But?"

"You've got to stop bringing the salami back here. No matter how much a treat it is for the residents. You know the ministry's guidelines."

"How . . . ?" Gus seemed to shrink in size as his face went pale. "You going to report me?"

"That depends on our investigation. If the residents have been getting sick from the salami and bologna you've been skimming from your Waste Not deliveries, then the ministry is going to find out. If not . . . well, we'll see."

Gus scratched an itch under his singlet and said nothing.

"For now, no more trips for Waste Not. My office will call them on Monday, let them know you're unavailable until further notice."

Again, the man said nothing. Just stared at his slippers.

Natasha opened the fridge again. She couldn't take her eyes off the *chouriço*.

"You're right, Natasha," Dr. Zol said, reading her mind. "We better test that sausage. Exclude it as our point source." He turned to Oliveira. "Okay, Gus, I'll take that piece of *chouriço* you offered me."

Natasha tossed her ID badge into her tote bag as the hospital's security guard picked up his phone and punched in Ellen's extension. He stumbled over Natasha's name, then nodded, grunted, and hung up. He pointed down the hall and waved his arm, left–right–left–left, mumbling the directions. She already knew the microbiology laboratory was on the sixth floor.

Ellen was waiting as the elevator opened. Her fine blond hair was cut in a pageboy style for easy care. She wore a lab coat that was no longer crisp, designer jeans over slim hips, and an Anne Fontaine blouse. Clearly, she was a savvy shopper. Probably made Saturday trips battling the traffic to Buffalo or Toronto. Or did she know a gem of a place hidden somewhere in Hamilton? Natasha hoped so. She'd have to find out.

They introduced themselves with a handshake and agreed it was a pleasure to finally meet face to face after speaking about so many cases over the phone. Ellen led the way down the deserted, dimly lit corridor toward the laboratory. A broad smile crossed Ellen's face as she opened the door into the clear light and soothing hum of her domain.

Her office, tinier than Natasha's at the health unit, was at the back of a large laboratory. They settled themselves in front of Ellen's computer. A department-store photo of a family of four was sitting on a shelf: Ellen with a handsome man and two school-age kids against a pseudo-Hawaiian backdrop. Beside it was a four-photo collage of a huge black dog lounging in various rooms of a house.

"That's Alfie," Ellen said, pointing to the dog. "A great big suck. A Newfoundland. I need to teach him to vacuum his own hair. He's a mess but we love him." She swept her dark jeans with her palms, then gestured at the family photo. "Thank heavens for movies-on-demand. They're watching *Mrs. Doubtfire* at the moment. Won't notice I'm not there until they get a craving for popcorn."

"But you've been here all day doing the genetic fingerprinting."

Ellen rubbed the back of her neck and looked suddenly tired. "Not *all* day. We have a fantastic machine that does much of the work with minimal supervision. It can run a hundred samples at a time, once you get them set up. But I did have to get them done today while the machine was free. It's booked for tomorrow."

"I'm sorry to take you away from your family on a Saturday, but you have no idea what a help it is to know for sure we're looking for a point source." Natasha pulled the sausage and mustard from her bag and held them up, not sure she should put them down on Ellen's spotless desk.

Ellen eyed them skeptically. "What have you got there?"

"We're hoping they're the cause of our listeria. One or the other." After Natasha and Dr. Zol had left the Oliveiras' apartment, Dr. Zol had speculated that either Gus had been secretly sharing his *chouriço* with the residents, or he'd contaminated the mustard weeks ago when making a sandwich. That didn't explain Viktor Horvat getting infected with the same listeria strain as the Camelot residents, unless he had a passion for *chouriço* too. Colleen had traced Horvat's home address to a Croatian neighbourhood in Stoney Creek. Horvat could easily be a customer of Gus Oliveira's Portuguese butcher, whose shop was in the same part of Greater Hamilton.

Ellen slipped on a pair of vinyl gloves and took the sausage and Dijon from Natasha. "Follow me," Ellen said, "we'll take these into the lab." In the lab, she set the sausage on the counter and read the list of ingredients printed on the mustard jar. "I don't know, Natasha. I'm sorry to disappoint you, but there's vinegar in here. You know, acetic acid. The Americans are using an acetic acid derivative to kill any residual listeria in their packaged deli meats. We should be doing the same to our packaged cold cuts, but the government doesn't require it."

"So the listeria can't be living in the mustard?"

"Sorry, but I doubt it. Never mind, we'll culture it and see what we get." Ellen put down the jar and picked up the hunk of sausage Gus had sealed in a clear sandwich bag. "Now this could be your culprit." She sniffed the *chouriço* and made a face. "Do they actually eat this at Camelot? I thought it was a pretty white-bread kind of place."

"We don't know. Mr. Greenwood, Dr. Zol's grandfather, didn't recognize it when we showed it to him. But the time frame is perfect. Gus says he got the sausage at Christmas, and the listeria started showing up at Camelot on January eleventh."

"Well, you've got to cover all the bases, eh?"

"Right now, I need to follow any lead I can find. I'm thinking, if there *is* listeria in the *chouriço*, it may have contaminated the kitchen in Gus's apartment and somehow made its way into Camelot's food chain."

"We'll set up cultures tonight. Of both the mustard and the sausage." She pulled off her gloves and began washing her hands in the sink. "Viktor Horvat is your index case, right?"

"He got sick first, yes."

"Doesn't it make sense that he is the source of the epidemic, not Gus and his sandwiches?" Ellen dried her hands and tossed the paper towel in the waste bin. "Pharmacists don't mess about in kitchens. But they do count pills. Could Horvat be accidentally contaminating the residents' medications when he's preparing their prescriptions?"

"We thought about that," Natasha said. "Did you know I went to his dispensary undercover?"

"Undercover?"

Natasha explained about the wig, the sari, and the fake Punjabi accent.

Ellen laughed. "You've got guts, girl. Didn't know public health required training in drama school."

"Mr. Horvat is a meticulous hand washer. I saw that for myself. And he doesn't touch the pills when he counts them. Uses a stick thingy, then slides them off a tray into the bottle. The assistant puts in the cotton batten."

"And besides," Ellen added, "he must be dispensing meds for clients all over the region. We recovered listeria with his MLVA pattern only from Camelot Lodge."

"Which means there's a unique link between Viktor Horvat and Camelot."

Ellen paused for a moment, then her eyes widened. She went to the computer, clicked the mouse, then began typing on the keyboard. "Let's see what MLVA matches we can find between the Camelot strain and anything else out there on the Internet."

She clicked again, tapped at the keyboard, and pressed Enter. Up came the website of the CDC, the U.S. Centers for Disease Control and Prevention — the granddaddy of epidemiology, central command for outbreaks around the world. After a few false leads she came to the MMWR, the CDC's weekly publication documenting outbreaks and other infectious "fascinomas," as Dr. Wakefield called them.

Ellen typed "Listeria" into the search box. In less than a second, the first of fifty-two citations appeared on the screen, with a clarification: the results were only those items found within MMWR; for a wider search of the CDC website, select "All CDC documents" and search again. Ellen clicked the All Documents button, and up came a list of 1,540 citations.

"Listeria's a popular pathogen," Natasha said, scanning the first twenty citations on the screen. "Look how often it gets into raw milk." There were outbreaks from all over the U.S., and reports involving American tourists who'd visited places like Azerbaijan, Syria, and Sarajevo. "At least we don't have to worry about the milk at the Lodge. I've never seen suspicious-looking dairy products in their fridges."

Ellen clicked in the search box and added "MLVA" to "Listeria." The list narrowed to twenty-five. "That's better. We can handle that." She clicked on the citations one by one. Not all of them involved listeria. A few concerned the MLVA fingerprinting of other bacteria, such as E. coli and staphylococci. When she'd finished making selections, they had four relevant papers. She clicked Print.

She handed two of the printed articles to Natasha. The first one described an outbreak in Wisconsin, a listeria strain 1/2. It was the wrong strain; they were only interested in strain 4b, the one found at Camelot. Natasha tossed the paper aside.

The second paper described a listeria 4b outbreak traced to un-pasteurized goat cheese in Michigan. Her pulse quickened. Michigan was only three hours away by car. A good start, but it didn't prove anything. It was the genetic fingerprint that counted, and the researchers had used two fingerprinting methods, the standard pulse-field gel and the new MLVA. The pulse-field gel looked like a bunch of fuzzy white bars on a black background. How anyone could make sense of such nebulous output, Natasha had no idea.

She turned the page and studied Michigan's MLVA. Now *that* looked like a proper high-tech test: a printout of crisp lines and numbers. You didn't have to be a techno wizard to see how easy it was to compare the MLVA printouts from different laboratories. MLVA's numbers and lines let you compare the fingerprints of a listeria from Hamilton with another down the road or across the world.

"This one looks promising," Natasha said, waving the Michigan paper. "A 4b from Detroit. It's got a nice clear MLVA profile."

"Mine are both 4b," Ellen said. "An outbreak linked to sausages in Brandon, Manitoba, and another involving dairy products in Sarajevo." She opened a drawer of hanging files, walked her fingers along the tabs, and pulled out half a dozen sheets of paper stapled together. "Here are the printouts of my MLVAs." She pointed to rows of lines and numbers. "This is what I'm calling the Camelot strain. You can see that Viktor Horvat's isolate is identical to all the samples from Camelot. And these over here, my controls from anywhere but Camelot, are all very different."

"Check out my Michigan one. Do we have a match?"

Ellen put the papers side by side on her desk and compared them. "Not even close."

"How about Brandon?" Manitoba was a long way away, but maybe Viktor Horvat had connections there.

"No," Ellen said. She picked up the paper detailing the outbreak in Yugoslavia.

It didn't match, either. Of course not. Listeria isolated from a commercial dairy in Sarajevo could have nothing to do with Hamilton, Ontario. Linking Mr. Horvat with Mexico would be a much better bet, but no one had published any MLVA results from Mexico.

Ellen tossed the paper onto the desk. She closed her eyes and sank into her chair, deflated. Tongue-tied by disappointment, Natasha felt awful for having put Ellen to so much work, for having taken her away from her family — all for nothing.

For several moments an awkward silence hung between them. The wall clock ticked away the Saturday-night seconds, mocking their measly efforts.

Suddenly, Ellen sat upright, her eyes wide with renewed enthusiasm. She grabbed the Sarajevo paper and flipped again to the section outlining its results. Her lips mouthed noiselessly as her fingers traced every line.

After an interminable couple of minutes, fire flashed into Ellen's chalky pale cheeks. She raised the paper, waved it, then air-kissed it. "Bingo!"

"What?"

"They've used a different scale, so the lines look shorter and don't seem to match. But, hey, look at the numbers. Just look at them!"

Line by line, number by number, Natasha compared Ellen's Camelot printout with the Sarajevo paper. "Oh my God. They're . . . well, they're very similar."

"Better than that," Ellen said, her voice rising. "They're identical. Well, almost. Only a couple of numbers are slightly off."

"What does this mean?"

"They're close enough to call them a match."

"You're kidding."

"Whatever came out of that dairy in Sarajevo last year made its way to Camelot Lodge. Can't tell you how, but there it is." Ellen clipped the two papers together, the printout of her work and the CDC's analysis of the Sarajevo outbreak. She stared at them for a long moment.

The collective whirr of the computer, the refrigerators, and the incubators grew into a colossal whine in Natasha's ears.

"Horvat," Ellen said. "What sort of name is it?"

"He's got an accent. Eastern European. Polish, maybe?"

"I used to go to a physio called Horvat. Sheryl Horvat. Told me her mother made the best Hungarian goulash."

"How close is Sarajevo to Poland or Hungary?"

"No idea," Ellen said. "I'm not up on European geography. But I do know they held the Winter Olympics in Sarajevo when I was a teenager. Those British ice dancers were amazing. Torvill and Dean. I watched the tape of their gold-winning free dance over and over. I never got tired of the music — *Bolero*. The cassette finally broke and my mother threw it out." She looked wistful for a moment. "After that, Yugoslavia fell apart and there was a civil war."

Natasha had never heard of any Olympics in Sarajevo. To her the place was synonymous with grade eleven history. The start of the First World War, the murder of Archduke somebody or other, and then a long siege in the 1990s. "Wayne Jarvie will know."

"Who?"

"Our pharmacy go-to guy. He knows our Mr. Horvat."

CHAPTER 31

The man sitting across from Natasha at the Nitty Gritty Café the next morning was gorgeous. When she'd called Todd's uncle Wayne on his cell from Ellen's lab, he'd given her a phone number for someone called Al Mesic, said he was a nice guy, late twenties, a walking encyclopedia about Hamilton and its personalities. Wayne agreed to phone Al right away, tell him to expect Natasha's call. They'd set up a breakfast meeting.

Al smiled at her with his amber eyes, his dark-blond hair cut short and spiked as though he didn't care what it looked like but really did. And he had none of that designer stubble on his freshly shaved cheeks. The South Asian guys who let their heavy whiskers grow to stubble looked like terrorists, no matter how nerdy they really were. Natasha had seen them all, every unattached Indian guy under forty within a fifty-kilometre radius, paraded into the living room by her mother. It was going to be a nightmare when Mummyji started working her way through Mississauga, heartland of korma, tandoori, and masala dosa. She had a knack for finding computer geeks with bad breath. Of course, the hot guys didn't need Mummyji's help finding dates or wives.

Al Mesic didn't even *need* to look gorgeous. He could win hearts with his voice — warm and mellow, with just a hint of an accent that kept it disarmingly boyish. But why, she wondered, was a newspaper reporter from the *Hamilton Spectator* hiding his rich tones behind a word processor? He should be on TV, or at least on the radio. He could make you weak at the knees announcing the weather report — gloomy drizzle or full sun, it wouldn't matter.

Natasha had ordered a chai tea — she wasn't going to chance the foam of a latte — and the waiter came with their drinks and set them on the table. He paused and flashed more than a casual smile at Al. They seemed to know each other.

The waiter turned toward the kitchen and flashed his butt, cute and tense under his tight black jeans. He certainly wasn't flashing it at her. He'd ignored her completely.

"You're a regular here?" she asked Al.

He looked around, taking in the Andean posters and bright alpaca weavings on the terracotta walls. "Nice place. But no, this is my first time. My beat is more downtown."

"I've done some reading on the Internet about Yugoslavia," Natasha began, then paused, unsettled by the sudden frown on Al's face, the glow of anger in his eyes.

"Not everything on Wikipedia is accurate. There's a strong American bias, you know. And please, call it former Yugoslavia."

"Sorry . . . um . . . I understand that the owner of Steeltown Apothecary, Viktor Horvat, is originally from . . . former Yugo-slavia." Wayne had told her that much last evening, but hadn't mentioned Mesic's touchiness about his birthplace.

"Yes," said Mesic. "Horvat was a pharmacist in the city of Sarajevo."

"Now the capital of Bosnia and Herzegovina? Did I pronounce it correctly?"

"Close enough."

"They held the winter Olympics there in 1984, when it was part of . . . former Yugoslavia. But then President Tito fell —"

"Died. I suppose he fell, but first he died."

"And then the country started breaking apart. There was civil war." She paused but Mesic didn't interrupt, so she must be on the right track. It was a complex story, and she didn't know how much of it was relevant to her investigation of listeria 4b. "And then Sarajevo was under siege. I don't really understand that part."

Mesic took a long draw on his latte and wiped his lips with the his finger. "It's complicated. So I'll give you the tabloid version."

He explained that Slovenia and Croatia, two predominantly Roman Catholic states within the former Yugoslavia, broke away to form their own republics after Tito's death. That left Serbia, an Orthodox Christian state, as the dominant force in the rest of the brittle union that had been Tito's Yugoslavia. When the state of Bosnia and Herzegovina declared its independence, Serbian forces invaded, claiming that much of the Bosnian lands belonged to a greater Serbia. In simple terms, it became a war of Serb Christians against Bosniak Muslims with a few Croatian Catholics complicating the mix and suffering along with everyone else.

"And that's when the siege started?"

"The longest in modern times. Serb forces encircled the hillsides around Sarajevo. The blockade lasted from May 1992 to the end of February 1996."

"Four years!"

"And not just a blockade. The Serbs bombarded the city with heavy artillery, rockets, snipers with rifles, you name it." Sweat beaded on Mesic's brow. The colour drained from his cheeks. The cheery glow in his eyes morphed to anger. No, something stronger. Hate. "We had no electricity. No running water. Not much food." He stared at his latte. "Just darkness, hunger, and terror."

"You were there?"

Mesic nodded.

"And escaped?"

"With my mother. January 1995. I was fourteen."

"And came to Canada?"

"After a few months in Austria. The Croats and Slovenes, our former brothers, wouldn't let us stay on their Christian soil. We were Bosniaks, ethnically Muslims but not religious in any way." He made a face and shook his head. "We're descendents of the Muslim converts indoctrinated by the Ottoman Turks who invaded our lands five hundred years ago. But really, we're atheists. Can you believe it? I'd never seen the inside of a mosque, and suddenly I was hated for being Muslim."

"What about Viktor Horvat?"

"I really don't know too much about his background, except that he's a Christian Croat who found himself in the middle of mostly Muslim Sarajevo under bombardment. He and his son survived the siege. As a pharmacist he would have been given special privileges. Anyone in health care was especially valuable."

"Sounds like an endless nightmare."

"Ten thousand deaths and sixty thousand injuries. Maybe more. And most of them civilians."

"When did Viktor Horvat come to Canada?"

"I'm not sure. About five years ago, I'd say."

"With a wife and children?"

"Just a son."

"He left his wife behind?"

"Probably in a grave. Unmarked."

"What happened to her?"

"Who knows? A rocket? A sniper? Childbirth under impossible circumstances?"

Natasha did the math in her head. "It's strange he would leave eight years after the siege ended."

Mesic shrugged. "There could be many reasons to leave Sarajevo. Especially if you find yourself a hated minority in a city divided by ethnicity."

"He's done very well here." So many immigrant professionals were reduced to driving taxis or working on construction sites, but Viktor Horvat had Canadian certification and ran his own business. "Wayne Jarvie says Mr. Horvat has exclusive contracts with retirement residences and nursing homes throughout the city."

"That's the Croatian connection."

"How so?"

"The community sponsored his immigration. Set him up in a pharmacy."

"Why?"

"So they could be served in their own language, by someone they trust. You get tired of always being foreign, especially when you're sick. You need someone who understands everything about you. Not just your language." Al rubbed the few drops of coffee spattered on the tabletop beside his mug. Without lifting his eyes he said, "Maybe you know what I mean?"

Her mother would. Mummyji had been in Canada thirty years but said she still felt like an outsider. Didn't completely trust anyone who wasn't Hindu and from Punjab. Natasha's dad was the opposite. He felt more Canadian than someone whose family had arrived three hundred years ago with the Scottish explorers. From her dad Natasha drew her confidence and her courage to stand up to her mother's histrionics.

"But why is his pharmacy over on the West Mountain? You'd think he'd set up shop on the Stoney Creek side of the city. You know, in Little Croatia."

"The building is owned by a Croatian millionaire. Horvat probably gets a big break on the rent. Besides, I imagine he delivers all over the city. Doesn't matter exactly where his store is." Al sprinkled some sugar into his latte and stirred it thoroughly before tapping the spoon against the rim of the mug. There was something on his mind, but he was holding it back. Finally, he put down the spoon and said, "The Croatians aren't happy about Horvat's family troubles in Juarez. He's drawing the wrong sort of attention to their community."

"That seems a little unfair. It's not Mr. Horvat's fault that he and his son are targets of extortion by the Mexican judicial system. It must be awful being a tourist in the wrong place at the wrong time."

Al picked up his spoon and twirled it between his thumb and forefinger. "The Croatians know Vik Junior isn't innocent." Al let that hang there for a moment. "Juarez is no tourist town," he continued. "Punks like Horvat's son go there for only one reason. Well, maybe two reasons. And both are illegal."

The idea of Mr. Horvat's son being guilty of the drug charges had never occurred to Natasha. And she still didn't know how Viktor Horvat's previous life connected him with last year's listeria outbreak in Sarajevo. She was certain that understanding the ongoing link between Viktor Horvat and Sarajevo was the key to pinpointing the source of Camelot's outbreak. One way or another, the pharmacist had carried the Sarajevo strain from his hometown to the Lodge. But how did he pick up that particular listeria in the first place? And how had he transmitted it to his clients at Camelot?

"Can we talk frankly for a few minutes?" she asked.

"I thought we already were."

"If I share something confidential with you, will you keep it out of your newspaper?"

Al smiled, his eyes no longer sad. "I have to warn you. My job is to expose corruption inside City Hall. Starting with the city manager."

"What does Viktor Horvat have to do with City Hall?"

"The city manager, Mike Sage, he's Croatian too."

"That sounds like a British name."

"His name used to be Zelenic. It means green in Serbo-Croatian. He may have changed his name, but not his allegiances, if you know what I mean."

She'd never thought of it before, but it was amazing how changing your name could hide so much about you, alter the way people thought of you. She'd always assumed the city manager, caught in photo ops perfectly turned out in Saville Row suits, belonged to some posh English family. How would people have related to Natasha if she hadn't broken up with Bjorn, but had married him and become Mrs. Jorgensen? To start with, her mother would have had a stroke and never left her couch. Of course, her father would have laughed and said, "But Nina, at least our grandchildren will have what you always wanted — nice light skin." If she introduced herself on the phone as Natasha Jorgensen from the health unit, would she be met with a different reaction because the person thought she was white? She supposed it depended on who was on the other end of the phone.

"Don't worry," Al said. "I won't be writing anything until I have all the facts and my story is . . . iron-clad. And even then, my editor might refuse anything I write about Horvat."

What did he mean? Was he guaranteeing the confidentiality of what she told him, or not? She asked him again, straight out.

He put down his spoon and pushed back his chair. "I'm not going to disclose anything without your approval," he answered. He crossed his arms. "This is just a friendly chat. And that's a promise."

Could she trust him? The pit of her stomach was telling her to be careful. Dr. Zol would never forgive her for sabotaging their investigation with a leak to the press. And rightly so. But she needed the tiny, specific details only an insider could give her.

She stirred more sugar into her tea, then tasted it. It was sweet enough. So was Al Mesic, she decided. She sipped again, took a deep breath, and told him everything about the gastro at Camelot Lodge. She started with last year's listeria outbreak in Sarajevo, which had been traced to dairy products. Then she told him about the identical strain infecting Viktor Horvat and sending him to intensive care with meningitis. Finally, her scribbler in hand, she showed him the details of the sustained listeria gastroenteritis epidemic at Camelot Lodge. She was careful to leave out any references to counterfeit medications.

"I remember when the milk stopped coming," Al said. "I was eleven. Then we ran out of porridge and milk didn't matter anymore."

"Well, the milk is flowing again in Sarajevo. Clearly, Viktor Horvat drank some last year."

"Think so? I doubt it. Not with his son in that Mexican jail. I can't see how he'd have the time or money for trips to the old country."

"Are they big on dairy products in Bosnia?" she asked.

"Not like here, but we do have cheese. Actually, quite a few different kinds. My favourite used to be *Travnicki*. It is a bit like feta, but tastes much better." He held his nose and laughed. "But the smell . . . really terrible. Like wool socks that haven't been washed for forty days. It takes some getting used to."

Natasha laughed with him, then thought for a moment. If Mr. Horvat hadn't travelled to the listeria, maybe it had travelled to him. "How often do you get food packages from Yugoslavia?"

"You mean from Bosnia and Herzegovina. The place of my birth is no longer Yugoslavia." He looked wistful, then added, "Yugoslavia is where the bad guys live now." He drained his latte and fished a packet of Nicorette out of his jacket pocket. A guilty look crossed his face. "I am trying to quit. You can either sing or smoke, but you can't do both." He popped the gum into his mouth. "Food packages? I suppose. By mail, or when someone returns from the old country." He laughed again. "But only if they get past the sniffer dogs at Toronto airport. I doubt that's possible with *Travnicki*, unless it's vacuum-sealed under ten layers of plastic."

CHAPTER 32

After coffee on Sunday morning, Gus
Oliveira helped Art Greenwood into
the Lincoln's passenger seat and secured the seat belt. Then Gus folded
the portable wheelchair and stowed it in the trunk. All the while, his
crooked-toothed smile was missing, even when he waved goodbye.

"Half of me feels terrible about this," Art confided, as Phyllis
backed out of her parking spot. If the mission they were embark-
ing on was successful, Gus's life might never be the same. He and
Gloria might even be incarcerated. "Gus deserves our loyalty. He's
always so good to us, which makes me feel even sorrier for him
today than usual."

"How could you possibly feel sorry for him? That blasted mustard
of his is probably teeming with bacteria. Causing all the fuss around
here. And the deaths. And by the look on his face, he knows it."

"Dr. Wakefield says the mustard's probably okay."

"If it's not the mustard, then it's Gus's recycled, back-door salami.
Really, Arthur. How could you bring yourself to eat such stuff? Week-
old sandwiches on mouldy bread?" She shook her head in disgust.

They'd been through this before, but Phyllis wouldn't let it go. She
was convinced that Gus had been diving in Dumpsters for Camelot's
provisions.

"He works so hard around the place," Art countered, "fixing every little thing that's on the fritz, making sure we're safe and comfortable. But Gloria doesn't give him a lick of credit."

"She *is* the boss, Art. And a marriage works best when the husband knows his place."

This wasn't the first time Art reckoned it was just as well Phyllis had remained a spinster. Was that a smirk on her lips, or were they pressed together in anxious anticipation of the tricky left turn between the six-foot snowbanks? The combined workings of Mother Nature and the city's snowplow crews made negotiating the Eaglescliffe loop devilish by car, and impossible by scooter, from December to April. But there was no way Phyllis would ever consider giving up her driver's licence or the Lincoln, even for the winter season. And thank goodness for that. Her car — officially an antique at thirty-seven years of age — was a symbol of the continued independence of everyone who rode in it. Especially when the sidewalks were rutted with ice and snow.

"Besides," she continued, "you said yourself they may be up to something highly illegal."

"Have you thought about getting the muffler fixed?" Art asked, changing the subject. With Phyllis, that was always the best strategy.

"I rather like the noise," she huffed. "It's full of conviction. And doesn't affect the vehicle's performance."

Her deafness must be getting worse. Either that or she'd turned off her hearing aid before starting the engine.

Art tried a different tack. "I'm surprised Terryberry is open today," he said.

"They only just reversed their Sunday closures. They're still closed on Fridays and Mondays. Disgraceful, really. If we're going to foster a knowledge-based economy, libraries have to open their doors every day of the week."

"Are you sure no one will see what we're doing on the Internet? Don't the librarians —"

"Stop fussing, Arthur. No one will bother looking at our screen. And we need no help from the library staff. I've been using Google and Wikipedia there since they first came out."

"And no one will know who is doing the searching?"

"For heaven's sake. *We're* not proposing to do anything illegal."

Half an hour later they were seated at a terminal in Terryberry's computer room. Phyllis had charmed, or perhaps browbeaten, the teenager restacking the shelves into leaving his post and lifting Art's wheelchair from the trunk. If the lad had balked at first, he was all smiles the moment he spotted the Lincoln. He'd peppered Art for details about the car as he pushed him through the slush, up the ramp, and through the front door. Any answers Art didn't know he made up on the fly, which kept the boy chatting all the way to the computer room. Phyllis finally dispatched him with her Latin-teacher look and repeated assurance that they needed no help connecting to the World Wide Web.

"How do you suggest we start?" Art asked Phyllis after they'd removed their coats and she'd draped her mink over the back of a chair.

"You tell me. You're the man with the ideas. I'm just here to work the computer as your amanuensis."

He opened his scribbler and set it on the desk beside his pen.

"You won't need those," Phyllis said. She pointed toward the end of the room. "We can print anything important on their machine. Only five cents a page."

All the same, he knew he would want to take a few notes. The charisma of electronic wizardry was no match for the comfort of pen and paper.

Phyllis tapped the keyboard, and up came the Google logo, faster than turning a page in a book. Computer speeds and consistency never ceased to amaze him — as reliable as telephone land lines connected to the touch-tone service he'd perfected, but a hell of a lot more versatile, and in living colour.

"So?" she said. Her Latin-teacher look hadn't faded since she'd dismissed that helpful boy, and she looked all the more intimidating in her luxuriant fur hat.

Art's mind went blank. The empty search box taunted him like an exam question. "I . . . I've never done a search before. Earl has always —"

"Don't look so worried. It's quite simple, really." Phyllis moved her chair to give him a better view of the screen. "One just has to go step by step. Tell me again what makes you think Gloria's nephew is not what he's cracked up to be?"

"First, it was his English. A man lives his entire life in Portugal, yet speaks with a perfect Canadian accent? Impossible. Then I saw the Argylls tattoo. That's a Hamilton regiment. What's he doing with that?"

"Maybe he spent his early childhood in Hamilton and has a friend in the Argylls."

"Did you see those two military types at Raimunda's reception yesterday?"

"I didn't like the way they barged in. It was unseemly."

"They made a beeline for poor Zol," Art reminded her, "and marched him out the door. He looked quite shaken." Art's tongue felt dry as he imagined what might have transpired.

"Must be drugs," Phyllis pronounced. "Perhaps they wanted his professional opinion on what they discovered in that raid up near Kilbride. Amphetamines, I believe they were making. In an old barn."

"I'm sure it wasn't drugs. They looked like a pair of MPs — buzzed haircuts, broad, stern, no nonsense."

"Members of Parliament are all fake smiles and glad hands. They don't pair up and go marching into funerals."

"No, no. Not MPs as in politicians. Military police. The only current connection I know of between Camelot Lodge and the Canadian Forces is that Argylls tattoo on Joe's bicep. It says something like *Jason Argylls Forever*. If the MPs were asking about Joe and his tattoo at his grandmother's funeral, his buddy Jason must be in big trouble. A deserter. That's what MPs are interested in when they're making inquiries off the base. Deserters. Jason must be hiding out somewhere, like Ronnie Biggs."

Phyllis paused for a moment. A frown creased her forehead. "The train robber?"

"The bugger hid in Australia and Brazil for decades. Even made trips back home to England, but only with the help of his friends and family. And always in plain sight, bold as brass."

"Caravaggio did the same."

"Who?"

"Sixteenth-century painter. Killed one man, then another, and spent the rest of his life on the run in Italy and Malta. With the collusion of his family and high-placed patrons."

"They finally locked him up."

"No, no. He died free but poor. Some sort of fever."

Art couldn't suppress a little smile. "I meant Ronnie Biggs. They nabbed him and sentenced him to thirty years. But they're talking about releasing him, now that he's a harmless old codger. And dying of cancer or something."

"What's Joe's name? If he's Gloria's nephew, it isn't Oliveira."

"Medeiros. Joseph Medeiros. I've heard him spelling his name when ordering pizza from the telephone in our sitting room. It's spelled —"

"For goodness sake, Arthur, I know how to spell it." She adjusted her fur hat then clicked rapidly at the keyboard. "We'll put *Jason, Joseph Medeiros*, and *Argylls* into the search box. If Jason went AWOL from the Argylls as you surmise, and Joe is mixed up in it, there might be a newspaper story about both of them."

Up flashed a list of ten titles, with the words *Jason, Joseph, Medeiros*, and *Argylls* highlighted in random order. Art ran a finger down the screen and read the titles one by one. There was nothing remotely military in the list; just community newspaper stories about softball games (it seemed a fellow named Joseph Medeiros was a star player), details of a place called the Argyll Centre in Edmonton, Alberta, and a faculty listing from the University of Illinois Department of History.

Phyllis cupped the mouse with her hand. "Let's see what's on the next page of listings."

"How many entries did Google find?"

She pointed to the top of the page: 1,270.

"We can't look at all of those. They'll be turning out the lights and kicking us out before we're half-finished."

"You're quite right," Phyllis said. "We need to refine our search strategy. Let's try *Argylls*, *AWOL*, and *Jason*. Leave Medeiros out of it."

She clicked at the search box, typed in the new terms, and pressed the Enter key.

A new list flashed up. Just fourteen websites in total, but all of them gibberish, mostly lists of words starting with the letter A. And an invitation to something called Facebook.

Phyllis fingered her pearls and gazed past the computer for several moments. When she looked at Art, her eyes were probing. "Are you sure the name was Jason? You barely got a glance at that tattoo. Did you even have your glasses on? Maybe it was Jack or Jake you saw. Or even Adam."

Art felt foolish. Perhaps his eyes, or his memory, had deceived him. "I could have sworn it was Jason."

"Let's delete the name. If it's not correct it will act as a confounder."

She clicked on the search box, deleted *Jason*, and put in *Hamilton, Argylls, AWOL*, and *deserter*.

The first two listings were Government of Canada non-military websites. The third riveted with possibilities: *Hamilton native AWOL from military base in Sarajevo. Corporal Jayson Dasilva missing after accident.*

"My word," Art said. "Can we have a look at that . . . link, is it?"

"I knew you had the name wrong. See — it's Jayson with a Y."

Phyllis did something with the mouse, and a page from the *Hamilton Spectator* filled the screen.

Beneath a September 18, 2003, headline, the item was short and lacked detail. It did say that Corporal Jayson Dasilva, of the Argyll and Sutherland Highlanders of Canada, known affectionately as the

Argylls and based in Hamilton, Ontario, had been charged with impaired driving and dangerous driving causing death after a motor vehicle accident in Sarajevo in August 2003. An unnamed woman and two children died at the scene. While confined to barracks awaiting a preliminary hearing and potential court martial, Corporal Dasilva disappeared. Military sources among Canada's peacekeeping forces in Bosnia and Herzegovina remained confident it was only a matter of days before he was located and detained.

"Goodness," Art said.

"But that news is almost six years old. Anything could have happened by now. He could have been tried and acquitted, or found guilty and already served his sentence."

"Or he's still on the run," Art said. "Can we keep searching? There must be updates to the story."

Phyllis erased the contents of the search box and inserted *Jayson Dasilva*, *Argylls*, and *Sarajevo*.

Up came a short list: four entries from the *Hamilton Spectator* and three from Canada's national dailies.

"Pick that one," Art said, pointing to the third entry. "It has the most recent date."

Another page from *The Spec* flashed onto the screen. January 4, 2004. Sources from the Argylls confirmed that Corporal Jayson Dasilva, age twenty, remained at large. His whereabouts was unknown. It seemed to Art that the brevity of the report indicated the Canadian Forces' embarrassment that one of their number was AWOL five months after being implicated in the deaths of three civilians.

"And that's the most recent update the Web has to offer?" Art said.

Phyllis took them back to the list of newspaper articles. They read each item in detail, but found no news more recent than January 2004, five years ago.

"Any bright ideas are most welcome at this point," Phyllis said.

"Too bad there weren't pictures with those stories. I'd at least like to see what this Corporal Dasilva looks like. Do you suppose he's the guy in the toque and sunglasses? Did he and Joe fall out and now Joe is threatening to expose him?"

Phyllis grabbed the mouse and zipped the arrow to the top of the screen. "Of course. I should have thought of that. One needs to search separately for images. I do it regularly for my art history class. My pension doesn't stretch to the purchase of the recommended textbooks."

The screen filled with four rows of assorted images — photographs and cartoons the size of postage stamps. The photos were too small for Art to identify any of the subjects, and the captions beneath them too brief to make any sense.

"You can analyze Renaissance paintings from photographs this small?" he asked. "Phyllis dear, are you sure you're studying art history, not philately?"

"For someone who was once on the ground floor of high tech, you've turned into a veritable Luddite. Those aren't postage stamps, they're called thumbnails." She waved the mouse's pointer over the photo of a young man wearing a military cap.

A second later, a familiar face filled the entire screen.

"Mother of God," said Art.

"No need to invoke the deity, Art. But this *is* quite the machine." Her face beamed with pride, as though the Internet and all its bits and bytes were her invention.

The caption read: "Corporal Jayson Dasilva, Argyll and Sutherland Highlanders of Canada, Hamilton, Ontario."

Art couldn't take his eyes off the face. The young man had extremely short hair, and there were no stitches above his right eye.

But there was no mistaking his identity.

Corporal Jayson Dasilva, formerly of the Argylls, was pulling a Ronnie Biggs and currently loafing at Camelot, ordering takeaway pizzas.

CHAPTER 33

Shortly before noon, Zol steadied the glass bowl as Max cracked a seventh egg against the rim, his tongue clamped between his teeth. The poor kid was trying his damnedest to separate the yolks from the whites, and he wasn't going to give up. The recipe called for four yolks in one bowl and five whites in other. So far, Max had managed to separate only one egg. Zol had tossed the five others into a plastic container; they'd be having omelettes for supper well into next week.

If a Cheddar-and-basil soufflé was going to rise like a cloud, the whites had to be separated perfectly. Cooking-school dogma said that yolk-contaminated whites wouldn't whip into the requisite soft dry peaks. Much as Zol hated arbitrary doctrines, today was not the day to put the perfect-separation theory to the test.

Producing a soufflé was like uncovering the culprit in an outbreak investigation. You amassed the ingredients like facts, checked them for freshness or accuracy, assembled them with some measure of skill, then served the results for everyone to see. If your work was built out of dubious components, it fell flat. As did your reputation. Zol craved the simple triumph of a feathery soufflé, a golden dome rising above plain white porcelain. Natasha had called with the news that the links between Viktor Horvat and Camelot Lodge appeared more complicated than ever.

"That's great," Zol told Max, who'd finally got the hang of the eggs, managing three in a row without a speck of yellow in the white.

Zol fished the hand-operated beater from a drawer and held it out to his assistant.

Max pulled a face. "Aw . . . Gimme the electric one."

"This is better."

"No it's not."

"Hey, real chefs don't even get to use this. They use a whisk. And a lot of elbow grease."

Max checked his elbows for greasy stains, then realized he'd been outsmarted. "Da-ad."

Zol pressed the beater's handle into Max's right palm.

"Do I have to?"

"Of course. You separated all those eggs, now you get to beat them into submission. It's good practice."

"For what?"

"For your game stick."

"No it's not."

Zol chuckled. The boy was right. The slick manipulation of a video joystick bore no relation to any useful occupation.

Max dipped the beater into the bowl and scowled, first at the instrument, then at Zol. Then, certain that his reluctance had been duly noted, he started cranking. Barely. Those soft dry peaks were a long way off.

"Something smells extraordinary," Colleen called from the front hall, the door banging closed behind her, the heels of her boots clicking against the tiles. "Do I detect basil and garlic? And Cheddar?" Moments later, she burst into the kitchen like a barefoot sunflower, her coat in one hand, a shopping bag in the other. She set the bag on the counter and paused, cocking her head as she tugged off her scarf. She covered her eyes with her hand. "And . . . another cheese? Don't tell me . . . it's . . . um . . . Parmesan."

Zol folded her gorgeous, compact body into his arms. He breathed in deeply, devouring the jasmine, green apple, and hint of musk that enveloped her. He kissed her lips, but only lightly. More would come later. At the moment, Max was all eyes, his beater silent.

"Sorry," Zol told her, "wrong about the Parmesan."

"Give me another chance." She lifted her nose and made a playful show of sniffing like a connoisseur. She shook her head. "It's not Gouda or Stilton."

She slid from Zol's embrace and gave Max a hug, whispering, "Can you give me a hint?"

Max paused, uncertain what to say. "Is it Italian, Dad?"

"That's my boy."

Max seized his beater, puffed his chest, and began churning like a fiend. Zol wondered if he was as transparent as Max when it came to impressing a beautiful woman. Yes, he decided. It was in the hard wiring.

Colleen shot Max her smile of approval, then closed her eyes, sniffed again, and turned to Zol. "I know what it is," she said, smirking. She stuffed her scarf into her coat sleeve and retreated to the front hall.

"So?" Zol asked when she returned, slippers in hand.

"You masked it with sesame oil, which isn't exactly cricket." She slid her toes into her moccasins and crossed her arms. "You're serving Thai salad with the soufflé?"

"And the cheese?" Zol said.

"It's that sneaky relative of Parmesan. Asiago."

He slipped his arm around her waist and pulled her toward the refrigerator, then lifted his prepared ingredients from the shelves. "Right on all —"

The phone blared from the desk beside him. The call display said *Caledonian Med Cent.* Must be the coroner calling from the morgue. Something unusual, with public health implications. No one else ever called him from the hospital.

Colleen shrugged out of his embrace as he picked up the telephone. It was Bill Whitehead, a public health inspector on weekend call for the communicable-disease unit.

"Sorry to trouble you at home, Dr. Szabo," Bill said, "but I've got a Dr. Suszek on the line from Emergency at Caledonian Medical Centre. Says he's reporting three cases of an unusual meningitis and sounds very concerned. I thought it best if he talked to you directly. Can I put him on?"

"Sure." Zol motioned to Max to keep beating the egg whites.

"Thanks for taking my call, Dr. Szabo. It's Jeff Suszek, Caledonian Emerg. I'm cool with one case of meningitis per shift. But three in one day, and at least two with the same weird bug, that's too much. Know what I mean?"

"What weird bug?"

"Dunno exactly. Their spinal fluids were cloudy and the tech's reporting Gram-positive rods. Not your run-of-the-mill cocci. I know what to do with little round bacteria. Blast them with penicillin. But bacteria shaped like rods, they're more your department. Too far along in the textbook for me."

Zol closed his eyes. The coincidence was overwhelming. Gram-positive rods sounded like listeria.

"Do all three patients come from the same family?"

"No, but two are kinda related. They're soldiers. Officers, if that makes a difference. A captain and a major, I think."

Army barracks used to be plagued by epidemic bacterial meningitis until they started immunizing military personnel against meningococcus, the prime culprit. Outbreaks seldom happened nowadays and had never been a problem among commissioned officers, only enlisted men in crowded dormitories.

"You're certain the lab is reporting Gram-positive rods, not negative cocci?"

"I know what you're thinking. I called the lab myself. Definitely not meningococcus."

"And the third case?"

"A boy. Age about ten. Don't have his lab results yet. But I can tell by eyeballing him, it's meningitis all right. Just a sec." There was the sound of shuffling papers at the other end of the line. "Got the name here, I knew you'd want it. Travis . . . Andersen."

The name hit Zol like a smack on the head. "His address?" He prayed it wasn't around the corner on Scenic Drive.

"It's . . . Scenic Drive. I can't read the number. It's smudged."

Yes, it was Travis, Max's buddy with the map-of-Norway birth-mark on his face. Zol had last seen him ten days ago when he drove him home from indoor soccer. Come to think of it, Travis hadn't shown up for the game the day before yesterday.

"Does this sound like listeria to you, Dr. Szabo? I paged the infectious disease doc on call but it's been almost two hours and she still hasn't answered. Afraid she's like that sometimes."

Zol steadied himself against the desk. "Certainly could be."

"The lab tech told me he wasn't allowed to report the identity of the organism from the Gram stains. Supposed to wait a day or two for the final culture results. But he said it looked like listeria to him. The two adults, anyway."

"You know how to treat it?" Zol asked.

"I can look it up. Ampicillin, I think."

"I'll page Hamish Wakefield and get back to you. We'll need his help with this."

Hamish wouldn't be pleased. It was bad form to horn in on a colleague's consultations when you weren't on call. But what the hell. Travis felt like family. And meningitis wouldn't wait for the on-call doc to finally deign to answer her page. This damn listeria business had spun out of control. The only chance they'd have to rein it in was to trace the movements of these new cases and track down their closest contacts as quickly as possible. Would any of them lead to Sarajevo where Natasha's Internet footwork suggested Horvat's listeria had originated?

Zol ended the call and grabbed a glass from the cupboard. He filled it with cold water, chugged it, then looked around the kitchen. Had Travis eaten here lately? Had his hands been in the fridge? Zol swallowed hard. He knew he was overreacting but couldn't help it.

"Say, Max," Zol said, doing his best to keep his voice sounding calm. "Do you know Travis's last name?" Perhaps the kid in the hospital was a different Travis. After all, Scenic Drive was a long street, and Jeff Suszek couldn't make out the number.

"Why, Dad? Is Travis in the hospital? Is he sick?"

"Max, I need to know his last name."

"Dad? What's wrong with Travis?"

"Please, Max."

Max had to think for a minute. "Andersen."

Zol dropped into a chair and drew his son into his arms. "Well . . . the truth is, yes, Travis is sick. He's at the hospital. A couple of other people are there with the same sickness."

"His sister? Jessica?"

"No. No one we know. But I gotta go and check them out."

"At the hospital?" Max pressed. "But you never go to the hospital."

"I know. This is different."

Colleen squeezed Zol's arm. She had a way of sharing her strength by shining it at him. "You go, and I'll page Hamish," she said. "He's probably at Camelot. Can't go far without his car. I'll tell him you're collecting him there, then call you to confirm."

Zol stared at the half-made soufflé. All those eggs separated for nothing.

"Don't worry about the soufflé," Colleen said. "Max and I will finish it. The tricky part's already done, eh Max?"

"We're going to need Natasha. An all-out assault on this outbreak." He pointed to the telephone desk. "Her number's in the little red book. Tell her I need her to drop everything. I should be back in an hour. Tell her we'll feed her."

He pulled Fannie Farmer from the cookbook shelf. "Page three-fifty-one. Wait till Natasha gets here before you put it in the oven. It won't —"

"I know. It won't keep." She handed him two bananas. "Eat these on the way. I'll expect you when I see you. Except . . ."

"Yeah?"

"I have an appointment at five o'clock." She raised her eyebrows and glanced at Max. Her appointments were never suitable for tag-along nine-year-olds. "Please be back by four-thirty at the latest."

"No worries. This should take me ninety minutes, tops."

She threw him a look that said she knew all about doctors: ten minutes meant an hour, and ninety minutes could mean all afternoon.

CHAPTER 34

"You can wrap yourself in this if you insist," Phyllis told Art, handing him a yellow gown from the cart outside Betty's room. "*I* don't need one."

Art slipped his arms into the gown and peered up and down the hallway. He hated Phyllis's blatant disregard for the Contact Precautions warning on Betty's door. "Come on, Phyllis. Follow the rules. If Gloria sees you in there without a gown you'll be confined to barracks for the next week."

"I have no intention of making contact with anything in there. We're here for a quick confab with Betty, that's all. I'm not about to make them waste hot water and laundry soap without a perfectly good reason."

"Then at least hand me a pair of gloves."

She tossed him two gloves, then strode into the room ahead of him. There was a dark smudge of crumbs and chocolate on her cheek from the Tim Hortons doughnut they'd shared on the way home from the library; in his own act of defiance, he didn't point it out to her.

"Hello, you two," Betty said. Her face brightened as she noticed Phyllis in her street clothes and winter hat. "Am I out of isolation?"

She'd combed her hair and put on a little lipstick. A magazine sat beside her on the bed.

Phyllis raised her nose in defiance. "I'm not touching anything." She settled into the chair beside the bed and straightened her skirt.

Betty shot Art a knowing look and said, "Shut the door before anybody sees her. And for heaven's sake, Phyllis, put on a pair of gloves. You don't want to get what I've had, believe me."

"How are you feeling, my darling?" Art asked after pushing the door closed.

Betty's dimples winked on her cheeks. "At this point, chicken broth tastes as good as a rib-eye steak." She extended both hands and squeezed Art's palm through the slippery vinyl of his glove. A moment later her face turned serious as she looked from Art to Phyllis. "What's wrong? I can see it in your faces. Bad news?" She drew back and held her hands against her chest. "Oh no, it's Earl, isn't it?"

Phyllis flicked her hand dismissively, a slim Lady Bracknell, clutching vinyl rather than kid gloves. Her frown deepened. "They won't tell us a *thing* about his condition. We barely know whether the poor fellow is still breathing."

"Dr. Wakefield says he's in intensive care and getting the right treatment," Art said, trying to sound hopeful.

"Then why do you two look like a pair of undertakers crashing a wedding?"

Phyllis glanced over her shoulder. "Major skullduggery," she pronounced. "Right under our noses."

"Goodness," Betty said.

"Our conundrum," Phyllis continued, "is the following: do we contact the Hamilton police, the Mounties, or the Canadian Army?"

"The army?" Betty said. "Phyllis, you can't be serious."

"We *are* serious," Art assured her. "We didn't want to bother you and scupper your recovery, except we decided you were the best one to point us in the right direction — you know, all those years coordinating protocol for the Prime Minister."

"And with everything else that's been happening around here," Phyllis said, "we decided we couldn't dilly-dally. We had to *carpe diem*."

"What 'everything else'?" said Betty. "I feel like Sleeping Beauty or Rip Van Winkle waking up in . . . I don't know . . . *Alice in Wonderland*."

Art paused and looked for a nod from Phyllis. Where should they start? So much had happened while Betty had been cooped up in isolation these past few days. Six deaths at Camelot in the past fortnight. Earl's collapse in Zol's office. Horvat's fake pills. Those big thugs grilling Zol at Raimunda's funeral. Gus's pilfered sandwiches and his French mustard under suspicion.

Between them, Art and Phyllis poured out the facts. The more they said, the wider Betty's eyes grew, especially when Art dug into his pocket and pulled out the photo they'd printed from the Internet — Corporal Jayson Dasilva, a.k.a. Joe Medeiros.

"I'd leave Viktor Horvat and his bogus medicines to Zol and Dr. Wakefield," Betty said, her cheeks flushed, "but the business about Joe — and by implication Gus and Gloria — good grief, that *is* a shocker. And dangerous for all of us." She paused and stared through the window, as if looking for inspiration. She squeezed Art's hand. "Such a situation needs handling by experts. You mustn't put yourselves at risk any more than you have already. You need to speak to the co of the Argylls. Present him with your observations. Let him take it from there."

Phyllis flapped her gloves, which she had yet to put on. Lady Bracknell's confidence vanished from her face. She looked more like Miss Marple with a migraine. "You mean to say we just call up the head of the Argylls and say, Look my good man, we've found your missing corporal, he's hiding out with a bunch of — of batty old folks in their retirement residence?"

Art tried to stifle a cynical chuckle. "Yeah, you think he's going to believe a retired Latin teacher and an ancient engineer who confront him out of the blue with what sounds like a cock-and-bull story? He'll send in the guys with the straitjackets. We have no proof, no recent photo, nothing to show him."

"I may be a bold old dame," Phyllis said, "but I'm not about to jam my camera in Joe's face and say 'Hello Sonny, give me a nice smile.'"

"Well," said Betty, "what about a drawing? Police often use sketches when hunting down suspects. Art, why don't you draw a likeness of Joe, or Jayson, or whatever his real name is? Show him as he looks today — older face, longer hair, and that tattoo you spotted on his arm."

"But that doesn't prove he's here at Camelot," Art said.

"Quite," said Phyllis. "We need to put him in context." She walked to the window and pointed to the parking lot. "I know. I'll snap him from my bedroom window. He goes out to Gloria's vehicle for a smoke a dozen times a day. I'll use my digital zoom. I told you the photography course I took last year was more than a dalliance."

Betty straightened herself in the bed and smoothed the covers. Her clear eyes and upturned lips conveyed benevolence and tenacity. Art could see the influence she must have wielded in the PMO. She cleared her throat with a well-practised little cough and told them, "Presented with Art's close-up drawing of Jayson the way he looks now, with that distinctive tattoo on his arm, and a shot of him in our parking lot, the Argylls' CO will be sufficiently impressed to take proper action."

"Do we phone first?" Art asked.

"What day is it today? Goodness, I've lost all track."

"Sunday," Art told her.

"Early afternoon," Phyllis added. "We've just had a quick lunch at Tim's."

Betty smiled. "I can see that." She caught Phyllis's eye and touched her own cheek, but Phyllis didn't get the hint. "Arrive — unannounced — at the CO's office tomorrow morning with your evidence. I believe the Argylls are based at the Armouries on James Street North, near the cathedral. Mind you, don't tell a soul what you're up to until you speak to the CO. And be sure you insist he protects your anonymity. Who knows how Gus and Gloria are going to react."

Despite Betty's inspiring tenacity, Art could feel second thoughts eroding his resolve. If Jayson went down, so would Gus and Gloria as accomplices to his deception. Then what would become of everyone at Camelot Lodge?

Perhaps it would be better to let Jayson lie like a sleeping dog. The idea went against the grain, but Jayson would return to Portugal soon enough. His visits to Camelot were never very long.

Art glanced at Phyllis, her back straight, her face taut. She'd always lived by the rules, led a life as disciplined as her Latin grammar. She wouldn't sleep until she saw to it that Jayson got what he deserved.

They'd be visiting the Argylls tomorrow, right after breakfast.

CHAPTER 35

Zol followed Hamish through the wide automatic doors and into Caledonian University Medical Centre's emergency department waiting room.

"You stay here," Hamish told him. "No sense both of us traipsing all over the department. It's a wild place and Jeff Suszek could be anywhere. I'll find him and the three of us can talk."

The ten minutes it took Hamish to resurface felt like a week. The longer Zol stood in the alcove beside the chips-and-candy vending machine — doing his best to shield himself from the coughing, the retching, and the bleeding — the more he convinced himself that Travis was dead, or worse. Zol had never met the boy's mother. An older sister always dropped him off at soccer, and no one ever came to the door when Zol drove Travis home. Two women huddled in the far corner of the waiting room, sobbing on the scuzzy vinyl couch. They could be Travis's mother and a much older sister for all Zol knew, but he knew it wasn't Jessica who drove the boy to soccer. He wanted to introduce himself, try to comfort them in some way, but couldn't bring himself to risk an awkward moment with the wrong people.

A skinny young man in an orange jumpsuit and handcuffs, who'd been marched in between two large-bellied police officers, vomited a stomach full of blood on the floor beside the reception window. Zol covered his nose against the stench and looked away. Public health dumped him in political shit often enough, but rarely brought him face to face with body fluids.

Then Hamish came out through the door marked *Authorized Personnel*. With him was a taller man, early forties, wearing blue scrubs. He had a boyish round face. Both men were rubbing alcohol sanitizer into their hands. Hamish introduced Dr. Jeff Suszek, who scanned the waiting room, smiled apologetically at Zol as if personally responsible for the semi-organized chaos, then led the way to a quiet corridor where they could talk in private.

"How's Travis?" Zol asked.

"Meningitis, all right," Hamish said. "Fever, stiff neck, cloudy spinal fluid. The full monty."

"Is he conscious?"

"Be a stretch to call it consciousness," Hamish said. He looked at Jeff for corroboration. "He's responding to painful stimuli with moans and groans. His mother is in there with him, but he's not awake enough to talk. "

"Is he going to make it?" Zol asked.

"They'll be taking him upstairs shortly. ICU," Hamish said. "He'll make it. But whether or not with his brain intact is another matter. Time will tell." There it was again, the bloodless manner that came over Hamish whenever he was concentrating on a difficult case.

"Does it look like listeria?" Zol asked.

"Don't know yet," Jeff said. He checked his watch. "The lab should be sending over the results any minute."

"And the two soldiers?" Zol said. "How are they?"

Jeff scratched the back of his neck. "That's the interesting wrinkle I was telling Hamish about."

Zol felt himself bracing. A wrinkle could be the tidbit of information that led to the listeria's source, or a complication that made his job almost impossible. "Hit me. What is it?"

Hamish looked at Zol and arched his eyebrows like a dog trainer dangling a bone. On the drive to the hospital, Hamish had been troubled that two robust young men had contracted invasive listeria. It didn't make sense. Men strong enough for active military service didn't get infected with listeria. The germ hurt only newborns, the frail, and the elderly.

"Afghanistan," said Jeff. "Both men served there together. A six-month tour, I believe. They're with the Argyll and Sutherland Highlanders, based here in Hamilton."

Zol had done a stint in a travel-health clinic as a resident. He'd learned that tropical viruses, parasites, and bacteria had predictable incubation periods, some short, others surprisingly long. Knowing a patient's overseas return date was critical to making an accurate tropical diagnosis. These guys could be infected with something in addition to listeria, something they'd picked up on their travels, a microbe that made them unusually vulnerable to listeria. Or had they been exposed to a chemical weapon or an experimental vaccine that had wiped out their immune systems? If that was the case, the Canadian Forces wouldn't divulge any details without a fight. "Tell me, when did they get back?"

"Um . . . don't know exactly, but the families can give you the details. They're in the waiting room." Jeff grinned. "Let me know what you think. And Hamish —"

"I know. You owe me. Big time."

Jeff Suszek let out a chuckle and strode back into the fray. He seemed to thrive on it.

Zol and Hamish returned to the waiting room. Hamish grabbed at his pager, suddenly alive on his belt. He squinted at the display. "It's the micro lab. With the results of Travis's Gram stain, I hope." He surveyed the waiting room and mimed a phone with his hand. The only one visible was a pay phone on the other side of the glass entrance doors. He shrugged and told Zol not to move, then strode to the inner sanctum and called over his shoulder, "Back in a sec."

When he returned two minutes later, Hamish's face was grave. Moments before, his eyes had been bright, full of the excitement of the hunt, the clinician-detective in full steam. Now he looked furious. And frightened.

"What's wrong?" Zol said.

The dark clouds deepened in Hamish's eyes. "Not here," he said. He rattled a bottle of pills clutched in his fist, clearly distressed by its contents. "Down the hall. To the cafeteria. It's closed on Sundays, except for the vending machines. We can talk there."

They slid onto a bench in the dimly lit cafeteria, an instant haven away from the noise and stench of the waiting room.

Hamish plunked the pill bottle onto the Formica tabletop. "Look at this, will you?" His face was still full of thunder.

Zol read the label. "It's made out to Travis Andersen. Gabapentin. That's an anticonvulsant."

"One of the nurses gave them to me. His mother forgot them in Emerg."

"I had no idea the boy had epilepsy. His family should have told me."

Zol was beginning to realize Travis's birthmark and epilepsy were probably caused by the proliferation of tiny arteries on his face and in his brain, a congenital condition called Sturge-Weber syndrome. Max and Travis had spent hours alone together in Zol's computer room. The boy could have had a seizure there any time. Or at any of the soccer matches Travis's parents never attended. It was one thing not to mollycoddle the child, but reckless not to have warned Zol about Travis's epilepsy before Zol took the boy for a full day at the zoo on the other side of Toronto.

"Look again at the bottle," Hamish said. "You missed something."

Zol scanned the label. This time he saw the bold letters at the top: *Steeltown Apothecary, Mohawk Road, Hamilton, Ontario.* "I can't believe it. Our friend Vik."

"Care to guess what the micro tech just found in Travis's spinal fluid?"

Zol had never liked being pumped by his professors and was glad he was past those humiliating days as a trainee, when relentless questions demanded picky answers. The answer to Hamish's question was written all over his face. "Gram-positive bacilli," Zol said. "Exhibiting tumbling motility."

Hamish didn't answer. He didn't need to. The fury in his eyes said it all.

At a moment of crisis, your life was supposed to pass before your eyes. But what Zol saw flashing was a headline: *Meningitis Stumps Health Unit's Szabo, Head Rolls.*

"My God, Hamish. We're not in Camelot anymore."

Zol hung back as Hamish flicked on the light in the windowless classroom across the hall from the cafeteria and ushered in the families of the two soldiers with meningitis. Hamish directed everyone to take a seat and beckoned Zol to join him at the front.

"I'm Dr. Wakefield," he began, "and this is my colleague Dr. Szabo from the public health department. Thanks for agreeing to be interviewed together. We hope you'll be able to help us put our finger on how Peter and Gavin got sick."

Zol put on his government-issue smile, the one that was supposed to convey compassion, dignity, and confidence without overdoing it. You lost your audience if they thought you were smug and armed with a load of bull. He could see this was going to be a tough crowd — tired, worried, and hungry. An explosive mixture.

"What's this about a goddamn interview?" a forty-something man called from the back. "We're looking for answers, Doc. Not more hot air." His sour face, heavy winter boots, and oil-stained ski jacket suggested he'd been dragged off the snowmobile trails against his will on one of the final days of the season. "We've been here all friggin' day and no one's told us a goddamn thing."

"Take it easy, Bob," said the blonde woman sitting in front of him. "These are the first doctors we've talked to all day. Give them a chance."

Ski-Doo Bob unzipped his coat, put his feet up on a chair, and leaned back with his hands clasped over his beer gut. The look on his face said *She made me shut up for now, but I'm watching you.*

"We do have some answers for you," said Hamish. "But first I'd like to get a sense of who you all are."

With the practised hand of a tutor leading a seminar, Hamish got each of them to introduce themselves and state their relationship to Captain Gavin Scarfe and Major Peter Legault. There were ten relatives in the room, including the two wives, Peter's teenage son, Gavin's identical-twin daughters, and an assortment of adult siblings and in-laws.

"Let's start with what we know for sure," Hamish said. "Gavin and Peter both have meningitis. That's an infection of the membranes covering the brain."

A murmuring went through the room. "Meningitis?" said Loreen Scarfe. "That's contagious, eh?" Her huge hoop earrings flashed beneath curly red hair as she flicked her head to the left. "Oh my God, we're all gonna get it."

"This is not the highly contagious form of meningitis," Hamish said, waving his hands, trying his best to smooth the waters. "We don't expect any of you are going to get it."

Well put, thought Zol. Fair and reasonably factual, with just the right spin. But a bit of a stretch in light of all the unexplained cases of listeria in the past few weeks, and the fact that the epidemic — yes, it really was an epidemic, not just a curious little cluster in an old-folks' home — was accelerating. Until the source got pinpointed, anyone in the room could be the next victim.

Hamish pressed on, explaining that the exact identity of the germ responsible for the infection would be known tomorrow, and in the meantime the men were getting excellent treatment and should be showing signs of improvement over the next day or two.

"I want to know where they got it from," said Shirley Legault, a compact woman with prematurely silver hair and an intelligent face. She unzipped her pink fleece vest and fanned herself. "Pete's never been sick a day in his life."

"Yeah, same for my Gavin," said Loreen, her head flicking to the left every fifteen seconds like clockwork. "They musta picked it up in Afghanistan. Gavin said the conditions over there were, like, so filthy I wouldn't be able to stand it for one minute."

The twin teenage girls looked at each other and rolled their eyes as if sharing the knowledge that their mother was a neat freak with an embarrassing head-flicking tic and should be ignored at all cost. Poor girls, they resembled their mother far more closely than they'd like to believe — same hair and freckled skin, but without the tic.

Zol fingered the loonie in his pocket and nodded toward Shirley Legault, the silver-haired wife with the intelligent face. "We're as anxious as you to find out how your husbands got this infection. That's why we need your help."

Hamish pulled a pen and notepad from his lab coat. "Let's start with their travel history. When were they in Afghanistan?"

Bit by bit the history came out, peppered with a few false starts and moments of confusion. The five women in the room competed with each other over the accuracy of the details while the men watched from the back, grim and silent. They knew better than to contradict their women. Loreen had the loudest voice and the poorest head for dates and facts. Her twins and her sister-in-law corrected her repeatedly. It eventually got settled that Major Peter Legault and Captain Gavin Scarfe had served together with the Argylls for the past twelve years. They'd spent two terms in Afghanistan, the most recent a six-month deployment ending four months ago. They'd never been injured or required admission to either the base hospital in Kandahar or the NATO facility in Germany. It was clear they hadn't picked up their listeria in an army medical centre.

"Have they served anywhere else overseas?" Zol asked.

"Pete was seconded to the UN in Haiti," said Shirley Legault. "Logistical support for the Mounties."

"And when was that?" Hamish asked.

"Three years ago."

"No, Shirley. It was four," corrected the blonde sitting beside her. "I know, because that was when I had my gallbladder out, on my thirty-fifth birthday, and ended up with peritonitis. Pete sent me a get-well card that was smudged in dirt and took three months to arrive." She turned to Hamish with tears in her eyes and pain all over her face. "Pete's my big brother and he never forgets my birthday." Her lips began to quiver. "Please, Doc. You've . . . you've gotta make him better."

Hamish looked flustered. He never coped well with tears. He glanced at Zol, searching for support, but all Zol could do was return a look that told him, *Awkward, ain't it.*

Hamish pressed on with his questions, focusing on the stony faces of the men. Clearly, he found it easier to cope with testosterone's smouldering anger than estrogen's unbridled grief.

Zol felt the frustration building inside him. None of the families' answers was helping clarify anything. The men had seemed perfectly well until they developed fever and headache three days ago. No gradual weight loss or insidious fatigue suggesting a chronic underlying illness. No rashes, bleeding gums, or hair loss to suggest poisoning by chemicals or radiation. Apart from their military assignments, the two friends led ordinary lives that provided no clues suggesting how they could have contracted listeria. No unusual hobbies that would bring them into contact with the pathogen — no taxidermy, no goat-milking, no cheese-making. No immune-suppressing medications. They never ate raw meat or unpasteurized cheese. Because of listeria's short incubation period, their travel histories seemed increasingly irrelevant. Postings months or years ago in foreign hotspots would have no bearing on any acute listeria infection today.

Out of desperation, Zol asked, "Any other postings in exotic locations?"

The two wives looked at each other for a moment. Shirley Legault raised her eyebrows first. "Just if you count Bosnia."

"And when was that?" Zol asked.

"In 2003. The last year of the peacekeeping mission."

"No health problems there, I gather," Hamish said dismissively, clearly wanting to move on from a travel history six years in the past.

The wives shook their heads.

Hamish looked around the room, a blank look on his face. He'd run out of questions and was still rattled by the blonde woman's sobs and tears. He studied his notepad for a moment then looked up. "I almost forgot. What about medications? Do Peter and Gavin take anything on a regular basis?"

Again, the wives looked at each other as if searching for the right answer in the eyes of the other. For a long time, neither blinked, then they both looked away. They shook their heads. The redhead examined her nails as if deciding which colour to paint them next. Pete Legault's wife fiddled with the zipper on her vest.

Hamish snapped his notepad shut and surveyed the group as if about to dismiss them. Clearly, he was none too pleased with the meeting's paltry harvest of answers.

Zol held up his hand. "Before you go," he said, "I wonder if Dr. Wakefield and I might have a word in private with Mrs. Scarfe and Mrs. Legault?"

Hamish looked puzzled. He'd been the de facto leader and seemed surprised at Zol's sudden initiative.

The blonde woman, her tears dry, said, "We're all family here. If you've got bad news, you better share it with all of us."

"No bad news," Zol assured her. "And it won't take long."

"Come on, Courtney," Ski-Doo Bob said to the blonde. "Leave them to it. I'll buy you a doughnut and coffee." He took Courtney by the arm and steered her out the door with the others, then called back to the two officers' wives, "We'll meet you girls across the street at Tim's."

Zol closed the door after the others had filed out. He checked his watch. Four-thirteen. Colleen had her surveillance job at five. She'd said the timing on this gig was critical, and he'd promised he'd be back by four-thirty without fail. He never asked about her work. Her cases were confidential, and her methods stretched, if not the letter of the law, certainly its spirit. It gave him a kick to think he'd fallen in love with a private investigator, but her safety was a hell of a worry.

He calculated he could make it home in time if he left Caledonian's parking lot at twenty past four — barring unexpected traffic on Sunday afternoon.

He ignored Hamish's puzzled face and pressed on. "I sensed you ladies might have something to tell us in confidence. Something you didn't want the others to know."

Shirley Legault fanned herself then slid into a chair. Neither woman spoke.

"Your husbands' medications," said Zol, watching the women carefully. Loreen's shoulders stiffened slightly. Shirley's lips tightened, and she looked at the closed door as if worried someone was eavesdropping behind it.

Zol clasped his hands in front of him so the women could see he wasn't writing any of this down. "What have they been taking?" he pressed gently. "I sense it's something you don't want others to know about."

Addiction to oxycodone, a prescription narcotic, had become a problem everywhere. In the streetwise inner city and in the well-groomed suburbs, patients turned to dealers when their legitimate prescriptions ran out. In desperation, some injected crushed tablets directly into their veins, risking life-threatening infections like meningitis, hepatitis C, and HIV. Perhaps two terms in Afghanistan, a place rife with recreational narcotics, had turned these soldiers into junkies, weakened their immune systems, and laid them open to listeria.

"Perhaps they're taking prescription painkillers?" Zol suggested softly. "More than what's good for them?"

Hamish flashed him a look of understanding and stashed his notebook in his lab coat. The possibility of AIDS rendering these men vulnerable to listeria was striking him, too. "Oxycodone, maybe?" Hamish said. "You know, for chronic back pain."

"Our husbands aren't drug addicts," said Shirley Legault, "if that's what you're getting at."

"We had to beg to get them to take the medication in the first place," Loreen Scarfe added.

Shirley frowned. Loreen had said too much.

"What medication?" Hamish said sharply.

The women studied their hands, their faces hard as stone.

Zol checked his watch again. He had to be out of here in three minutes, tops. He dug the loonie out of his pocket and wove it between his fingers. The rhythmic action always relaxed him, and he hoped it would have the same effect on the two women. They stopped examining their nails and began watching the coin as it floated from one hand to the other. Loreen's eyes brightened, and Shirley watched intently, as if trying to work out the physics of the floating loonie.

Zol let the coin do its thing until he sensed Hamish was getting fidgety beside him. Taking the plunge, he said, "I'd like to share something confidential with you. Your husbands aren't the first cases of meningitis we're investigating. There've been a few others lately. And —"

"That's why," Hamish pleaded, " if you've got something to tell us, you can't hold back."

Loreen's eyes were as wide as the hoops in her ears. "You mean there's an epidemic?"

"We don't like to use that word," Zol said. "It scares people. But you could call it that."

"Other forces personnel?" Shirley asked. "We noticed a senior officer from the Argylls in the hallway. She said her son was on the way to ICU. If you ask me, that sounds serious."

"Does that kid have the same thing as Pete and Gavin?" Loreen asked, her head flicking faster than ever.

"What's the boy's name?" Zol said.

"Travis," Shirley said.

"Thank you," Zol said, struggling to maintain his composure. "That's very helpful."

Shirley drew her lips tighter across her teeth and fixed Zol with her dark green eyes. "You didn't answer my question, Doctor."

Zol knew if they were going to get the information they needed out of these women, he would have to bend the rules and give them something in return. He took a deep breath and hoped this didn't get back to the privacy police. "We're not supposed to tell you about other patients, but yes, that boy has the same infection as your husbands."

Shirley turned to her friend and said, "I think that changes everything, eh Loreen?"

"I guess," Loreen said, reluctantly. "You start."

"Our husbands came back from their second tour in Afghanistan with . . ." Shirley paused. For the first time, tears welled in her eyes. She dug a tissue from her pocket. "With . . ."

"For heaven's sake, it's shell shock, pure 'n simple," Loreen said. Her eyes stayed dry, as though she'd done all her crying long ago and had no tears left for her husband's post-traumatic stress disorder. Zol noticed her tic had stopped. "Like, you know, a bunch of really bad scenes," Loreen continued. "Nightmares, flying off the handle, screaming at the kids for no reason."

"Our guys finally agreed to see a psychiatrist," Shirley said. "It took a lot of pushing to get them there."

"Gavin and Pete, they thought they could, like, tough it out," Loreen said. "Get better on their own." She rolled her eyes. "Like *that* was ever going to happen."

"The doctor called it PTSD, post-traumatic stress disorder," Shirley said. "He finally put them on fluoxetine. First he tried Paxil, then Zoloft. But neither worked."

"Is the fluoxetine helping?" Zol asked.

Shirley considered her answer, then said, "I'd say so. A bit, eh, Loreen?"

Loreen shrugged and looked away.

"What pharmacy do they use?" Zol asked, his heart rate rising. He could feel it in his chest.

"It's, like, across the street from their doctor's office," Loreen said.

"On Mohawk, at Magnolia," Shirley clarified.

Hamish leaned forward, his face full of anticipation. "Do you remember the name of it?"

"Steeltown something," Loreen said.

"Steeltown *Apothecary*," Shirley said, then handed Zol the bottle containing her husband's capsules.

Zol tightened his fist around the bottle until it nearly burst. "Do you have any friends or family living at Camelot Lodge? It's a retirement residence."

Both women shook their heads. Zol could see the truth in their eyes. They'd never heard of the place.

He checked his watch. Four twenty-five. He pictured Colleen in his front hallway, pacing in her coat and boots.

Oops.

CHAPTER 36

"You're sure you're up for this?" Colleen asked Natasha from behind the wheel of her Mercedes.

No, she was anything but sure about breaking into Viktor Horvat's pharmacy. But she wasn't going to let that stop her.

It was three minutes to five and they were parked opposite a pizza place two doors down from Steeltown Apothecary, which was going to close any minute. They'd driven separately from Dr. Zol's in their own cars, and now they were both sitting in Colleen's, trying not to look suspicious. Colleen said she'd chosen this spot in the strip mall because it gave a clear view of Steeltown's front door without making it obvious they had the place under surveillance. She'd told Natasha to park her Honda at the far end of the mall outside the dry cleaner's. No one would notice it there on a Sunday afternoon.

They'd barely made it here in time. Dr. Zol, red-faced and panting, had begged forgiveness for returning home late, missing their brainstorming session, and making Colleen late for her appointment. He told them he'd been chasing three new cases of listeria meningitis — two soldiers and a child, all linked to Viktor Horvat and his pharmacy. Clearly, this was not a community-wide outbreak. The new links to Steeltown kept the focus sharply on Mr.

Horvat. Natasha had been desperate to stay and hear more details from Dr. Zol, but she'd committed herself to Colleen, and she knew they were about to do the right thing.

Of course, Dr. Zol had no idea what she and Colleen were up to. He thought Natasha was on her way to a Hindu family engagement and Colleen was on a surveillance job. Natasha had had a fine afternoon cooling her heels with Max and Colleen. The soufflé was delicious, and the wine made it even better. Max was an easy kid. Mature for his age and polite. But he sure was hooked on video games. His frenzied, senses-boggling world of online gaming was almost more than she could take.

Natasha found herself staring at Steeltown's front door. She forced herself to look away. She didn't have to stare. It would be easy to spot Mr. Horvat and his staff leaving after closing up. Colleen had said the best time to sneak into someone's place was ten minutes after they left. That gave the target ten minutes to return for something they'd forgotten and gave the operative at least twenty minutes to snoop around without getting caught. Any errand was bound to keep Viktor Horvat away from his shop for at least thirty minutes; he might even be gone for several hours.

"You *are* sure you want to come in?" Colleen said again. "Zol made it crystal clear. He doesn't want any of us sneaking inside Horvat's operation."

There was anxiety in Colleen's voice that hadn't been there a few minutes ago. As soon as they'd arrived, Colleen had slipped into the pharmacy, stayed two minutes, and returned looking worried. She'd seen something inside that had frightened her.

"Zol would have a stroke if he knew I'd taken you poking inside Horvat's lair."

"But you said —"

"The situation is looking increasingly dangerous. Horvat's as mad as a hyena. Something's set him off. His face is bloated and I heard him swearing at his staff."

"So, now what?"

"I should go in alone."

"No way. If it's too dangerous for me, the same goes for you."

"I'm just a consultant. Zol can't fire me for disobeying orders."

"But what if Mr. Horvat —"

"You'll be watching my back. If anyone goes near that front door, you'll ring me on my mobile. I'll slip out the back door and into the alley at the rear."

Disappointment hit Natasha like a colossal wave. She was dying to see exactly how Viktor Horvat was infecting his clients with live listeria. "But I really wanted to have a look inside his operation." She knew she looked too much like her mother when Mummyji put on one of her major pouts.

"Zol's right," Colleen said. "It's no mere coincidence that Horvat and those two army officers were in Sarajevo at the same time. That place was a war zone for a long time. Bound to have left many unsettled scores." She stared at the pharmacy, then pierced Natasha with a pensive gaze. "Something extraordinarily sinister is going on. We must be extremely careful."

Colleen pulled a tiny camcorder from her handbag, hit Play, and peered at the video on the screen. She'd hidden the camera in the store yesterday — at the rear of the toothpaste display — and aimed it at the push-button combination lock securing the rear door. After casing the place over the past few days, she'd figured out that the locked inside door led to the converted garage abutting the rear of the pharmacy. She said the garage's impromptu Jack the Printer sign wouldn't fool anyone with half a brain. The one-storey build-ing was an extension of the pharmacy and had to be the centre of Viktor Horvat's counterfeit operation.

"So you're going to call the police, let them handle it?" Natasha asked.

"They'd need a warrant to go snooping in that garage. But no judge would ever grant them one, especially on a Sunday, without a believable story and reasonable evidence to back it up. I have a feeling that Horvat's activities are coming to a head — he could pull up stakes and cover his tracks at any moment."

It bothered Natasha that none of this made sense. If Viktor Horvat was using listeria to settle old grudges from the ruins of Bosnia and Sarajevo, then why would he target old folks and a child? Nellie, Raimunda, Earl, Betty, and the others at Camelot had no links to Bosnia. She'd checked that out. Furthermore, they'd been retired for twenty or thirty years — long before Yugoslavia had dissolved into war. And what did army officers with listeria have to do with empty antibiotic capsules and counterfeit Zytopril, a blood-pressure medication?

"Aha," Colleen said, lifting the camera. "Here's a shot of Horvat unlocking that door. Yesterday. Ten twenty-seven p.m." She played the scene several times in ultra slow motion before her eyes brightened. "Got it. A six-digit code. 2-0-0-3-0-8. You agree?"

Natasha studied the screen as Colleen replayed the segment. "I suppose."

Colleen nodded at Steeltown's front door. "Don't look now, but here comes our man. With his technician and the cashier. He's in a hurry."

"Looks like he's crying."

Mr. Horvat fumbled with his keys then locked the pharmacy's front door. He wiped his swollen face with the sleeve of his coat, then dashed toward his car with neither a wave nor a word to his staff. A second later he pulled his cellphone from his pocket, scowled at the call display, and pawed at his wet cheeks. He barked three or four words into the phone, flipped it closed, then climbed into his vehicle. Natasha had no interest in cars but took note that it was a black Ford suv with vanity licence plates: *SJJ YHM*.

The pharmacist roared past them, his wheels skidding on a patch of ice. Natasha had seen him gruff before, but now he looked like a grizzly gunning for revenge.

"That's his ten minutes," Colleen said. She glanced in the rear-view mirror then peered through the windows on both sides of the car. "Time to go, before he comes back. Are you coming?"

Natasha's right hand hovered above the passenger door handle. She was desperate to see inside Viktor Horvat's operation, but nothing in her training had prepared her for this cloak-and-dagger stuff. The practice of epidemiology, which she'd always seen as grounded on facts, logic, and mathematical formulae, had taken on an emotional dimension. And that emotion was sitting somewhere between fear and terror. The safest thing to do would be to listen to the cautious, rational left side of her brain and stay in the car.

"Cold feet, Cinderella?" Colleen said. "That's okay. You don't have to come to the ball."

"No, no," Natasha said, doing a poor job of hiding the truth.

Her left arm, controlled by her impulsive right brain, reached for the door and swung it open. A second later she found herself stepping into the brisk March wind.

Colleen led the way to Steeltown's front door, walking with an unhurried purpose that attracted no attention. She produced a key from her coat pocket, took a quick but thorough look for prying eyes, then opened the door. She ushered Natasha inside and closed the door behind them. When Natasha had asked earlier how Colleen had obtained a key, Colleen had said there were certain trade secrets of no concern to the health unit.

Inside, Natasha felt her heart booming in her throat as she waited for the piercing shriek of the burglar alarm. She fisted her car keys and glanced back at the Honda.

The pharmacy stayed strangely quiet, lit only by the failing afternoon light filtering through the front windows. Natasha could barely make out the outline of the shampoo display she'd knocked over when she'd been dolled up in Anjum's sari and wig.

"My sources were correct," said Colleen. She pointed to a box mounted on the wall near the door. It was covered in alarm-company decals. "Horvat cancelled his contract with his security company six months ago. Doesn't want the police sniffing around here on the heels of some burglar searching for narcotics."

Natasha stared at the alarm box, certain it was going to blink and blare to life any second.

The box stayed quiet. Inert and harmless.

Colleen produced a flashlight and led the way past the mouth-wash, dental floss, and toothbrushes to the rear of the store. She stopped and shone the beam at a heavy-looking steel door. It was more imposing in real life than on the video camera's tiny screen.

Colleen studied the number panel below the doorknob and raised an eyebrow. "This is where we find out how often he changes his code. If he were smart, he'd change it every day." She punched in the six digits they'd both memorized.

There was no siren, no snarling Doberman, just a simple click as Colleen pulled the door open and they stared into darkness.

A moment later, the sweep of Colleen's flashlight caught a work-table, a refrigerator, LED lights blinking on a large glass-fronted box, and two dozen cardboard cartons at the back stacked beyond a side door to their right. The place looked like a cross between a window-less workshop and a storeroom. If there'd ever been a wide garage door at the rear, there was no sign of it now. Goosebumps pricked Natasha's neck as Colleen eased the door closed behind them.

A dark shape shot from the shadows at lightning speed. It headed straight for Natasha. She froze, her heart leaping out of her throat. Her knees barely held her.

The thing pressed against her leg. She braced for bite. "What is it?" she whispered. "I can't bear to look. Oh my God. Is it . . . is it a snake?"

Colleen flicked on the lights.

Natasha stared ahead, eyes on the side door. She couldn't look down, not to see a snake winding around her legs.

"Meow," said the object at her feet.

She threw her hands above her head. "I'm allergic to cats."

The tabby looked up as if expecting a treat. It caressed her calf with its tail. Ugh.

"Asthma?" Colleen asked.

"Runny eyes. Sneezing. Shoo it away. *Please.*"

Colleen strode to the middle of the long, rectangular room and knelt down. She called the cat and a moment later it was purring beside her, waving its tail.

"I trust you can tolerate being here for a few minutes?" Colleen said.

"I'm usually okay for half an hour. As long as that thing doesn't sit in my lap and expect me to pet it. I've got antihistamines in the car."

Colleen stood up and pulled her camera from her coat pocket. "We won't be here for any half an hour." She pointed across the room. "Let's start with that table."

A long table was pushed against the side wall to the left. Scattered across its Formica surface were a propane torch, an ashtray littered with burnt matches, a pair of fine surgical forceps, and a short loop of thin wire attached to the end of a metal stick the size of a pencil. Natasha had seen a similar wire loop in Ellen Ballyk's microbiology laboratory. She had no idea what it was for.

On one of two shelves above the table, a photograph in a black frame was propped next to a half-consumed votive candle. The sooty wick stood stark, almost angry against the white wax. The picture showed a youngish woman and three school-age children, two girls and a boy. They had big smiles and were standing in an open field, white-capped mountains rising behind them. Hanging from one corner of the picture frame was a string of translucent beads attached to an ornate silver cross. Natasha's friend Maria once showed her something like this when they'd been listening to rap music in Maria's bedroom after school. She'd called it a rosary and made Natasha wash her hands before she touched it. It had belonged to Maria's grandmother to whom Maria prayed every night.

On the second shelf sat two large, white plastic medication bottles and a box of extra-large vinyl gloves. Natasha reached for the closer bottle, labelled only with a bold letter *V* in black marker.

Colleen caught her arm. "Don't touch anything without gloves on."

"Oh yeah, fingerprints."

"Or worse. You never know what Horvat's been doing in here." Colleen pulled a handful of vinyl gloves from her coat pocket. "Here, put these on. More our size."

They donned their gloves, and after a nod from Colleen, Natasha took hold of the bottle marked *V*.

"What have you got?" Colleen asked.

"Should I open it?"

Colleen adjusted her camera. "That's what we're here for."

Natasha held the bottle at arm's length and unscrewed the cap. No hiss, no bad smell. Nothing jumped out when she lifted the top. Still, the flimsiness of the vinyl gloves made her shudder at her lack of protection from anything really dangerous.

Inside, dozens of two-toned capsules, beige and blue, crowded the bottle.

"What are they?" Colleen said, snapping close-ups.

"They look like vancomycin capsules." Todd had shown her several of the fake vancos he and Dr. Wakefield had found at Camelot.

"Real or dummies?"

"We'd have to open one."

Colleen whipped a notebook from an inside pocket of her capacious coat and ripped out a blank page. She placed the page on the table like a placemat then picked up the forceps, lifted a capsule from the bottle, and set it on the paper. "You do the honours."

"You mean . . . open it?"

"Go ahead."

Natasha pulled at her gloves to smooth the wrinkles from her fingertips. She lifted the capsule and twisted it. The two halves separated with no effort at all. No puff of powder. No smell. No sticky liquid. Nothing.

Colleen leaned in for a macro shot of the empty capsule, then jerked her head toward the other bottle on the shelf. "See what's in that one."

Natasha replaced the first bottle and carefully uncapped the second one, labelled *X 100*. It contained hundreds of bright pink capsules, smaller than the vancomycin dummies. Colleen took her close-up shots, then reached in with the forceps and held a capsule to the light. "Quite pretty," she said. She dropped the pill into Natasha's open palm. "I've always liked a touch of pink."

Natasha rotated the capsule between her thumb and forefinger. "Says 'X 100.' That's all."

"Extraordinary colour. Looks more like candy than medication."

Natasha had seen these before. There was no forgetting that colour, but where had she seen it? Her grandma didn't take anything like these. Her mother's lorazepams were white tablets, not pink capsules. And the Zytopril antihypertensives that Wayne Jarvie had sent to Montreal for analysis were robin's-egg blue.

"What's wrong?" Colleen said.

"I've seen these before, but . . ."

"Yes?"

A picture was coming to her. Rows of pink capsules . . . and other pills of assorted shapes and sizes. She closed her eyes, and the image sharpened. "Got it . . . the blister packs."

"What?"

"The compliance packs Viktor Horvat prepares for the residents at Camelot and a bunch of other nursing homes. Each week's pills in a blister card for easy dosing. Many of the residents had pills like these in their cards. I should have recognized that pink immediately."

"What are they for?"

"If the X stands for Xanucox, then they're an expensive medicine for arthritis." She squeezed the capsule. It compressed like plastic between her fingers then regained its shape without shattering. "Among the Camelot residents with arthritis, there's a strong correlation between taking Xanucox and acquiring a moderate to severe illness that satisfies our case definition of listeria monocytogenes febrile gastroenteritis."

"Sidestepping the jargon, you mean these pills cause listeria?"

"Looks like it."

"Open one."

Natasha twisted the capsule over the paper. It required more force than the vancomycin dummy, but came apart in her hands without splintering. Dry white powder spilled onto the paper.

Colleen snapped a flurry of close-ups of the bottle and the open capsule. "What's he doing with these? Do you suppose they're real or counterfeit?"

"I've learned you can't tell by looking."

Colleen photographed the propane torch, dead matches, and the wire loop, then strode to the stack of cardboard cartons at the rear of the room. She pointed to a large box covered in stickers and labels.

The printing looked like barcodes and acronyms. There wasn't one word on the box that Natasha could decipher. There were strange accents over the vowels and curlicues under the Cs and Ss. "The printing's in code," she said. "And a foreign language."

Colleen studied the carton from various angles. "Turkish," she said, pointing to the top corner.

"You read Turkish?"

Colleen's lips formed a proud grin. "No, but I've been to Izmir. See the return address? ADB? I've been there."

"Where?"

"That's the airport code for Izmir. A resort town in Turkey. Actually, it's a big city. On the Ionian coast."

"You know airport codes?"

"Why not? You know the Latin names of obscure microorganisms. I know airport codes. Like Horvat's vanity licence plate. SJJ YHM — Sarajevo and Hamilton."

"You've been to Sarajevo?"

"No. I followed a hunch and looked it up on the Internet after our first visit here. Your Bollywood debut."

"Don't remind me."

Natasha checked the lettering on several of the boxes and realized they all shared the same destination: YYZ. "I know that airport code," she said. "That's Toronto Pearson." The cartons had arrived there first. And cleared customs.

The cat nuzzled against Natasha's pant leg, purring with wasted enthusiasm. "Shoo!" she said, waving it away. It strolled off and sat under the table, licking its paws, a sly smile in its eyes.

"Turkey," Natasha said, "that's where the counterfeits came from last year. You know, the fake antihypertensives that turned up at that pharmacy in the north end?"

"Perhaps Horvat has tapped into the same obliging supplier. If there are pills in those cartons, they won't be obvious. Probably hidden under Turkish-made shirts and blouses. It's a smart business, smuggling fake prescription drugs. No cocaine or marijuana to set off the sniffer dogs at Canada Customs."

Colleen took shots of a dozen other possibly incriminating cartons, thoroughly taped for the trip from Turkey. They couldn't be opened without arousing suspicion, but Colleen said the photos would pique the Mounties' interest.

Natasha let her eyes wander around the room. The LED lights of what appeared to be an oven caught her eye. A closer look told her it was an incubator. The glass door felt warm to the touch, but when she peered inside she could see only empty shelves.

Next to the incubator was a kitchen refrigerator, a simple two-door job with the freezer on top. She pulled on the lower handle without thinking. The smell of rotting flesh punched her in the face. She slammed the door shut, but not without glimpsing an array of test tubes and petri dishes.

"Careful," Colleen said when she heard the door slam. A second later she covered her nose and mouth with her hand. "What an extraordinary stench."

"Smells like death." There could be body parts in there. It was time to get out of here. Things had moved past epidemiology. Way past.

Colleen raised her nose and sniffed. "Truly extraordinary." She closed her eyes and sniffed again, her head cocked in concentration. She look like a sommelier judging an obscure Merlot at a pretentious restaurant. "No, not putrefaction," she said. "That's the odour of fermentation. Overlaid with cultured mould, the kind they use in Stilton or Limburger." She approached the refrigerator but didn't open the door. "Yes." She nodded after a slow deep breath. "Cheese. A very strong one. Not the sort you pick up at Kelly's SuperMart."

Colleen punched a number into her cellphone. "We've seen enough," she told Natasha. "Better tell Zol. He and his boss need to hold a powwow. Tonight. With the evidence we've got, it's time to call in the boys in blue."

Dr. Zol answered quickly, and Colleen gave him a rundown — where she was and what she'd found. But first, she had to calm him down. It was obvious he was upset she'd gone against his strict order to stay out of Viktor Horvat's operation. Colleen didn't mention Natasha, thank God, and was cagey about how she'd broken in.

"He says to get out of here now," she told Natasha as she closed the phone. "Horvat will be off his head. As belligerent as a bull hippo with a toothache." Colleen closed her eyes and slowly shook her head. "The radio is reporting that his son was found dead in his prison cell today. The Mexican authorities are claiming he hanged himself."

"Oh, how awful. Mr. Horvat did look upset when we saw him closing up. Maybe he'd just found out."

Heavy footsteps crunched on the gravel outside the side door. Natasha froze. She prayed the steps would quickly fade as the person walked past the garage and down the alley.

The crunching didn't fade. It stopped. Abruptly.

A low-pitched voice barked an order.

The cat pricked up its ears, jammed its tail between its legs, and retreated further under the table.

Another man's voice, brusque and angry — and way too close — raised the hair on Natasha's neck.

A key scratched at the side door.

"Quick," Colleen whispered. "Behind the cartons."

Three seconds later the deadbolt on the side door clicked and the shuffle of footsteps echoed into the room.

"Hey. Who is leaving light on?"

Natasha crouched on the floor behind the cartons, imagining her body made of soundless granite. She pictured the man behind that voice sliding pills across a tray, his eyes memorizing her features as he handed her the bag containing her grandmother's Zytopril prescription.

Her knees burned against the hard, frigid concrete floor, but Natasha didn't dare move anything but her eyeballs. Through a crack between two cartons, she could see three men crashing into the room through the door. Viktor Horvat led the way, his face glistening with rage as he shoved a young man in handcuffs onto the only chair in the room.

Horvat tossed his keys and sunglasses onto the worktable and barked at a third man panting beneath a black balaclava. "Remove that thing. You not needing now."

The man pulled off his menacing headgear and swept the room with his gaze. For an agonizing moment he aimed his sightline at Natasha, and she found herself staring at the face of Nick, the hunky chef from Camelot Lodge. When he'd stood at his kitchen counter, a cleaver glinting in his hand and his pecs bulging beneath his apron, he'd exuded professional confidence and a whole lot of sexual magnetism. But here, squinting nervously and fingering a switchblade, he looked like an unpredictable creep who wouldn't know a rasher from a ramekin.

"Give me bottle," said Horvat, then grabbed the litre bottle of Smirnoff Nick tore from a liquor-store bag. Horvat opened the vodka with a practised twist and held the bottle to the lips of the young guy cowering on the chair. "Drink," Horvat demanded. "I know you are liking. Same like all goddamn Canada soldiers."

The young guy coughed and spluttered when he swallowed the fiery liquid. He clutched his throat with his manacled hands. His face turned blue. When he raised his head and breathed in deeply,

Natasha saw the blue-green bruises around his right eye. This was Joe, Gloria's nephew from Portugal who'd stumbled into Camelot's front lobby covered in blood. Something he'd mumbled at the time had intrigued her, something about being the target of a man wearing a black toque and dark glasses.

Crouching beside her, Colleen nodded a millimetre then raised and lowered her eyebrows. She signalled *What's up with the vodka?* then inched her cellphone out of her pocket. Even the buzz of it vibrating would give them away if it came to life with a call or a text. Natasha was glad she'd left her phone in the car. Colleen turned hers off.

CHAPTER 37

Zol hung up the kitchen phone after Colleen's call and dropped into a chair next to Max. He watched his son attacking a pizza pocket and marvelled at the resilience of youth. The moment Zol had come through the door after his trip to the hospital, Max had peppered him with questions, his keen eyes wide but dry. *How's Travis? Is he in a oxygen tent?* They'd read a story about a boy with chest problems; Max had been fascinated by the drawing of a boy sitting inside a clear plastic pup tent on a hospital bed. *How many needles did Travis get? Are they going to give him an operation?*

Apparently satisfied that the doctors and nurses were properly looking after Travis's fever (Zol considered that an appropriate simplification of the infection threatening the boy's brain), Max returned his attention to the pizza pocket. The restorative powers of corn syrup solids, disodium inosate, titanium dioxide, and riboflavin were amazing to watch. Zol tousled Max's mop of curls then rubbed at the warmth of his son's spine through his Star Pirates sweatshirt. If only Zol could capture the boy's optimism and equanimity.

Zol knew he should be elated that Colleen had busted Horvat's operation and likely put an end to Camelot's untimely deaths. But a slew of worries about her safety trumped any kernels of elation he might have felt about the case. He hoped she did as he'd said and got out of there fast.

He wondered what to do. Call Peter Trinnock? Or maybe the Hamilton city police? The Ontario Provincial Police or the RCMP? But without Colleen's crime-scene photos, how could he spark any police officer's interest in Horvat's pharmacy? Come to think of it, how was Colleen going to present her incriminating photos without admitting that she, a consultant with the health unit, had obtained her shots by illegally entering Horvat's premises? Shit. He'd told her not to go in there. Trinnock and the press were going to have a collective fit once the health unit was implicated in unlawful acts. Had she taken a big risk for nothing?

He pulled two loonies from his pocket and ground them into his palms. He should have taken his suspicions about Horvat to the police in the first place, let them handle the investigation. But hell, they'd have made a balls of it, let Horvat walk with only a tap on the knuckles from the College of Pharmacists.

Zol strode to the family room and grabbed the computer mouse. Max trotted behind clutching a bowl of rocky road ice cream. Zol clicked the Track Colleen icon on the monitor and keyed in his password. Three clicks later, the GPS gave him the answer he dreaded: Colleen's cellphone was at Mohawk and Magnolia. Damn. She was still at Steeltown Apothecary. Why the hell was she dawdling?

He looked at his watch. Five-forty. He wished she'd get out of there. She was a smart woman and he trusted her judgment, but she was taking unnecessary chances by staying there so long. He pictured Horvat, reeling from his son's suicide, lunging into his den like a psychotic cougar.

He dialled her cell number from the land line beside the computer. After one ring a recorded voice picked up: *The customer you have dialled is unavailable.* Damn! What good was a cellphone if you turned the frigging thing off or let the battery go dead? He thought about it for a second. No, the battery wasn't dead. The GPS was still working: it knew where she was. She'd turned off the receiver. On purpose. She didn't want the phone vibrating, or ringing, or lighting up. That meant she was in trouble. And she was hiding.

"What's wrong, Dad?" Max asked, his face covered in chocolate.

"Um . . . nothing for you to worry about."

"Then why are you looking for Colleen?"

"Big people stuff, that's all."

"Don't be mad. She's with Natasha."

"What?" said Zol, spinning in his chair.

Max recoiled at the sudden movement and his spoon flew from the bowl. A gooey mass of ice cream landed on the carpet. Max's face crumpled.

Zol reached out and grasped his son by the shoulders, keeping his grip as gentle as his taut muscles would allow. "How do —" He checked himself and lowered his voice. Too much force and Max would clam up. "How do you know that, son?"

Max peered at what was left at the bottom of his bowl, his face full of hurt.

"Please, Max."

"I, um, heard them."

"Talking?"

Max nodded.

"What did they say?"

Max stared at the mess beside his sneakers, then mumbled, "Natasha was, um, only pretending about going straight home."

The phone screeched to life on the desk. Zol closed his eyes and prayed it was Colleen returning his call. "You okay?" he said, his heart pumping a mile a minute.

"I'm still fine. Thanks for asking." It was Hamish. "But Art is in a state, that's for sure."

"Sorry. I thought you were Colleen."

"Don't you have caller ID?"

"I didn't look. What's up?"

"Art and Phyllis. They think they've just witnessed a kidnapping. In Camelot's parking lot."

"Jesus H. Christ. A kidnapping? You're not serious."

"*They* are. Claim they saw two men in dark glasses and balaclavas forcing Gloria's nephew into a black SUV."

"The nephew that got banged up the other day? The hit and run?"

"They swear it was him. Joe. Nabbed outside Art's bedroom window."

"D'you believe them?"

"They say they've got pictures. Phyllis's camera. And part of a licence plate. SJJ something."

Public health involved far more facets of modern life than Zol had imagined at the start of his training. But one thing was for sure: kidnappings were not part of his mandate. "Sorry. I'm drawing the line right here. I can't let myself —"

He suddenly noticed Max's quizzical stare, pupils wide as hockey pucks. The boy was an unrivalled listening machine.

"Just a sec, Hamish," Zol said, then cupped his hand over the phone and told Max to fetch a roll of paper towels from the kitchen. As soon as Max shuffled out of earshot, Zol whispered to Hamish, "For God's sake, I can't get involved in an abduction."

"Art recognized the vehicle. Says it's Horvat's SUV, and the SJJ on the licence is the airport code for Sarajevo."

References to that city were turning up everyplace. "Where would the kidnappers take their victim?" Zol had a good idea but hoped like hell Hamish had a different one.

"I'm not sure. Maybe that garage behind Steeltown Apothecary. Secluded. No windows, back alley, high cedars on both sides."

"Where are you?"

"Still at the hospital. My student's taking care of things at Camelot."

"No sign of your car?"

"Don't rub it in."

"I'll pick you up in ten minutes. Front entrance."

CHAPTER 38

As she watched Viktor Horvat clip Joe's handcuffs to the back of the chair and nearly drown him with another blast of vodka, Natasha decided Joe must have stumbled onto Horvat's counterfeit drug business. He must have been blackmailing Viktor and the pharmacist was retaliating. But could Joe be stupid enough to threaten the man who controlled every medication entering his aunt's retirement residence? Horvat certainly had the upper hand now.

She ran through the list of his Camelot victims. Among others, he'd infected and killed the Prime Minister's aunt, a judge, a history professor, and a hard-working Portuguese immigrant. Was he settling scores against Joe by picking off Joe's grandmother and his aunt's high-profile residents? Was this a warning to a blackmailer or was it a long-running feud? And what about the two men and the boy admitted to Caledonian Medical Centre today with probable listeria meningitis? Zol had told her they had no links to Camelot, but all three were tied to the Canadian Forces.

It made more sense that Joe — and possibly Gus and Gloria — had been in on Viktor Horvat's counterfeit-drug scam and they'd fallen out. Maybe street drugs had become part of the package and complicated everything. The scuttlebutt in the nightclubs of Hess

Village was that Viktor Horvat's son was a dealer, not a tourist, and facing two routes out of Juarez: a slow march in a cut-price coffin or a million-dollar ride in a private jet. Natasha's dad, a pediatrician with a sharp understanding of human nature, always said the mango never fell far from the tree.

Natasha winced as Nick cursed and held his switchblade to Joe's neck, a centimetre from his jugular. Viktor Horvat forced Joe's head back and poured another dose of vodka down his throat.

"You like drink and drive, don't you Corporal Jayson?" Horvat said.

All Joe could do was gasp.

The pharmacist righted the bottle and shook Joe by the shoulder. "Answer me, Corporal," he said, his face luminous with fury. "Is exciting to street race in army Jeep when you're drunk?"

Joe stared straight ahead and didn't answer.

Horvat shook his fist. "I tell you, Corporal Jayson Dasilva. You gonna drink and drive one last time. Superfast down McNeely Road. You know McNeely? Runs very steep down the Escarpment. And on Sundays, very quiet." A wicked smile lit Horvat's face for a second or two, then the hatred returned. "This time, you not kill no one. No mother. No two young daughters. Just yourself. Police find you. Note in pocket. Telling real name. Admitting what you done in Sarajevo, August 2003."

"You're making a mistake," Joe insisted through a string of coughs and wheezes. "Mixing me up with somebody else."

Either Joe was one hundred percent sincere, or terror had turned him into a great actor.

"I not make mistake. I see your face every night. In my dreams. Five years I dreaming. And then I see you. At Camelot Lodge. Pretending to be nephew. How can you be nephew from Portugal? Your English, it is perfect. Not like anyone in ESL classes." He punched Joe in the belly. "You Canadian. You Gloria's son. Corporal Jayson Dasilva."

Horvat let the accusation sit for a minute, then nodded to Nick who uttered an obliging grunt, grabbed Joe's right arm, and sliced through the sleeve of Joe's ski jacket with his switchblade. Horvat ripped Joe's shirt open. He exposed the man's bicep and examined it. He couldn't have looked more satisfied if he'd found the Holy Grail. "There. I am knowing. It say Jayson Argylls Forever."

"That's my cousin. We're buddies."

Horvat swatted Joe's cheek. "Liar."

"*Please*, I'm Joe Medeiros. Never been in the Canadian Army. I'm from Portugal."

Horvat shook his head. "One day I see you. The face of my nightmares talking to Gloria, my best customer. She smile at you like son, not like nephew. Give you sandwich, call you Jayson. You frown, look nervous. I stay quiet, send for your birth certificate. Easy to do on Internet. You born in Cambridge, Ontario. Mother is Gloria Dasilva. Father Sergio Dasilva. Gus Oliveira is second husband, I am guessing. You not have his name."

The vodka was making Joe bolder, his eyes wider. "Some other guy's birth certificate doesn't prove nothing."

"Army told me about tattoo when you escape from Sarajevo barracks in 2003. They promise find you. Send to court martial." Horvat's face filled with disgust. "After six months, Army give up. I beg on graves of wife and daughters, but Army bigwigs doesn't care. Now, I thinking Canada knows you hiding in Portugal, but is easier to leave you there. No trial. No expense. No more embarrassment for Argylls."

Horvat jammed the vodka bottle against the young corporal's teeth, and Nick whacked him in the belly until Joe opened his mouth and gulped like a force-fed goose.

Out of nowhere, Natasha was slammed by two violent sneezes. The cat shot across the floor in front of Horvat, then raced out of sight.

Viktor Horvat whipped around, his face a stew of anger and surprise.

Nick looked up, his switchblade poised for action. "What the hell?"

For a second, Natasha felt buoyed as she watched Colleen's eyes fill with fire. A moment later, the world began dissolving. Colleen's fire had turned to stone-cold fear.

CHAPTER 39

As soon as Max realized he was being left behind at Grandpa Art's place, he began creating an unholy scene. Good thing Hamish was waiting in the minivan and didn't see it. Max yelled and screamed and refused to take off his jacket and boots. Zol braced for a standoff in the middle of Camelot's common room under Phyllis Wedderspoon's cold gaze. It was clear she saw no reason for a small boy to squawk when left to the care of a gaggle of grey-hairs. Things got ugly when Max threw his arms around Zol and screamed, "Don't leave me here. Daddy *please*, don't leave me. That old lady is grinding her teeth again."

Phyllis stood with her arms crossed in rigid judgment, oblivious to vacant-eyed Alice sitting on the sofa pulverizing her molars with robotic determination.

Art tried a few of his old standbys at the piano, but none caught Max's attention. Of course not. What kid had an interest in Stephen Foster and show tunes?

Then Art played the intro to Bob Marley's "No Woman, No Cry."

Stunned by the syncopated reggae notes floating through the air, Max went silent. He stared open-mouthed at the old man's hands working the instrument. Zol was stunned too. He felt Max's grip loosen from his waist. Moments later, off came Max's jacket, and he crept to the piano in his stocking feet.

Reggae was Max's favourite music, by a long shot. He'd memorized every note of Ziggy Marley's "Dragonfly" and "Love Is My Religion." He'd played the CD so many times it was a wonder there was anything left of it.

Two minutes later, Zol gunned the minivan out of Camelot's driveway while the going was good.

At the Queen Street summit, light snow was churning in the icy wind at the top of the Niagara Escarpment. As Zol drove westward along Mohawk Road, just shy of Horvat's pharmacy, the snowflakes got thicker and wetter, as they do in March when the sun begins to strengthen and Canadians fool themselves into thinking winter is over.

At the traffic light at Rice Avenue, two blocks short of Steeltown Apothecary, Hamish tensed and grabbed the dashboard. He closed his eyes and started some sort of ritualistic breathing — in through his nose, out through his mouth.

"No need to get uptight, Hamish," Zol said, after Hamish had taken a few of those strange breaths. "I'm going to cruise past the strip mall first. See which cars are in the lot. If Colleen and Natasha are there alone, we just have to knock on the door and get them out of there. No problem."

"There's a rear entrance, you know. Through the derelict print shop." He mimed quotation marks with his fingers. "Leads from the back alley off Magnolia."

"I know." Colleen had shown Zol the converted garage on the narrow lane behind the buildings fronting Mohawk Road. "We'll cruise along the lane before we make a move. See if Horvat's there. Art gave you his licence number?"

"Starts SJJ. Black SUV." Hamish fiddled with his coat buttons. "I don't like that high hedge. Cuts the place off from the buzz of Mohawk Road."

"Don't worry, I'm not going to stop. But keep your eyes peeled."

The light changed, and Zol eased past the strip mall on their left. Natasha's Honda and Colleen's Mercedes were easy to spot. There were two other cars in the lot, a black Silverado opposite the pizza place and a gold Lexus between the dollar store and the dry cleaner's. Zol turned left onto Magnolia and saw Horvat's SUV as soon as he turned left again into the narrow lane. The SUV was parked on an asphalt pad next to the converted garage behind Steeltown Apothecary. A dusting of snow had collected on the vehicle's roof but there was no snow on the hood. The engine was still warm.

"Change of plan," Hamish said. "No way we can walk in there."

Zol swallowed hard and forced himself to slow right down to get a good look at the building and the vehicle.

Hamish's face was white. "Get us out of here."

Zol eased on the gas and dodged the deepest of the alley's pot-holes while pondering what to do. About fifty metres along, he crept past two guys, late thirties, parked in a silver Cadillac SUV. Smoke and rock music — the Tragically Hip — spilled through the front windows. Since the tightening of the smoking bans, the only place a couple of buds could sit and smoke was in their car. These guys had decked their vehicle out like a rec room on wheels — leather seats, walnut panelling, booming woofers, and a flat-screen TV. They probably had brewskies in a cooler and a few joints under the seat. They nodded and waved as Zol drove by. In the rear-view mirror a moment later, Zol saw the guy in the passenger seat answer his cellphone. The man's eyes narrowed; his face tensed. Bad news. Or maybe just a summons from the wife to get the heck home and take the kids off her hands.

Zol turned right at the first intersection and parked at the curb.

Hamish already had his BlackBerry out.

"Who you calling?" Zol asked.

"The police."

"What're you going to tell them? That a petite private eye and the health unit's whiz-kid epidemiologist broke into a pharmacy storeroom and are now engaged in a tête-à-tête with the owner?"

"You got a better idea?"

"Probably not. But let's walk back, maybe listen at the door. Colleen's a professional. She would've heard him coming and got herself and Natasha hidden. Horvat's not going to stay there long. If I'd just lost my son, I sure as hell wouldn't hole up in a window-less storeroom. Unless . . ." He couldn't complete the thought.

"What's he going to do with Joe? Lock him up there? Kill him on the spot?" Trust Hamish to put it into black and white.

"I'm not dropping Colleen and Natasha in it without taking a closer look first," Zol insisted. "Five minutes, that's all."

The flurries cleared and the sky brightened as they walked along Mohawk, the weakening sun in their faces. They approached the front of the pharmacy and peered through the windows. No move-ment in the dimly lit store. The place was obviously closed. The wall clock said twenty past six. On the right of the building, a wooden gate led through the cedars. Zol peered between the slats and saw Horvat's suv still parked in the small backyard. Zol looked at the sky. It would be dark in half an hour, maybe less.

He opened the gate and took one step inside. Hamish followed and let the latch down silently. They both listened. No voices, no screams, no crashing of furniture. Zol padded toward the door on the side of the garage. The fresh snow was silent under his feet. At a balmy three degrees Celsius, snow didn't crunch under your boots. Emboldened by the silence in the yard, Zol crouched at the door. He beckoned Hamish to join him. Hamish hesitated, his face a mixture of annoyance and fear, then he tiptoed forward. They cupped their ears and listened.

A man's voice boomed through the door but Zol couldn't make out any words. The tone held either anger or terror, he couldn't tell which. Maybe both.

And then he heard them. Colleen's distinctive South African vowels. Calm and assertive, but tinged with a strange anxiety. Zol could distinguish her cadence, but had no idea what she was saying. He put his hands on his stomach and took slow breaths against the bile scorching his throat. In through the nose, out through the mouth.

He knew he'd heard enough. Horvat had Colleen. And Natasha. And probably Joe from Camelot.

Hamish mouthed, "Let's go," and signalled their retreat.

Zol reached for his cellphone. They'd call the police from the safe bustle of Mohawk Road.

Two paces short of the gate, it opened in front of them. All Zol could see were the dark coats of two men approaching. The lengthening shadows obscured their faces.

"Stop right there," the shorter man barked.

The latch clanged as the taller one pulled the gate shut.

Zol found himself composing an innocent excuse for their presence in the yard.

Then he saw the gun.

"Hands in the air," the shorter guy said.

The tall one told Hamish to toss him his BlackBerry. The guy caught it and turned it off, then looked up, and his eyes met Zol's. A flicker of recognition passed between them. Zol pictured smoky blue haze and walnut trim. This was the driver from the Cadillac suv, a gorilla standing six foot five and two hundred seventy pounds. "Your phone too, Mr. Piece-of-Crap Minivan."

"Turn around, both o' youse," ordered the short guy with the gun. "Now over to the door, the one you were snoopin' at."

They'd only taken a couple of steps before a young man in handcuffs stumbled out through the door. The man swayed and fell to the ground. Colleen and Natasha shuffled out behind him, hands tied behind their backs, their feet shackled with some sort of twine. Colleen's hair was a mess. She'd put up a fight. His heart ached at the sagging defeat in her posture. Natasha's bloodshot eyes loomed with terror and were brimming with the tears he knew damn well she was struggling to suppress.

A stocky man with a large Slavic head came out next. Zol recognized him from his photo in *The Spec*, in which he'd seemed a fierce opponent to the Mexican judicial system. Viktor Horvat's face was bloated, his back stooped, his eyes wary. On his tail was a tall man with a shaved head. He was holding a knife and seemed to be threatening Horvat with it, but Zol couldn't be sure. Maybe he just had it at the ready. The guy glanced nervously around the yard as he exited the door and pulled it closed behind him. Zol saw who it was. Camelot's cook, Nick.

"Hey boys," Nick called to the two enforcers behind Zol and Hamish. "What you got there?"

The short guy waved his gun. "Got your hands full too, eh buddy?"

"We can handle it," Nick said. "Plenty of room in your Caddy."

Shorty jammed his weapon into Zol's spine. "Anybody bleeding? You know how much I hate getting blood on my Moroccan leather."

"Not yet," Nick told them. Zol pictured the scabby tattoo under Nick's jacket, the menacing thunder of Niagara surging down his right arm.

"Come off it," Colleen said. "You really think you can silence six witnesses?"

Horvat straightened up, glanced around the yard, then stepped away from the group by the door. "Only five." He sneered at the man crumpled on the ground in handcuffs and hoofed him twice in the gut. "Or maybe four." The man moaned but didn't move.

"Sorry to tell you, Viktor," Colleen continued, "the Family doesn't take kindly to loose ends. And you're as loose as the rest of us."

Before Nick had a chance to acknowledge or refute Horvat's favoured-member status, Horvat forced a nervous smile and pulled a revolver from beneath his jacket. Spittle oozed from his lips as he aimed the weapon at the man on the ground. His eyes seethed with festering hate. He shook his head and spat in the man's face, then pulled the trigger.

The yard roared with the thunder of three shots.

Shorty's gun dug deep into Zol's spine, the searing pain nearly buckling his knees. He knew if he went down, that would be the end of him. Horvat would dispatch him too. And the others.

"What you doin', asshole?" Shorty called to Horvat. "Want the whole neighbourhood to know you can pull a trigger?"

Nick put out his hand to Horvat. "Gimme the gun."

Horvat didn't budge. He stood over the body, the gun wobbling in his hand. He looked disappointed, as if the killing hadn't settled whatever bitterness had been rotting between them.

Natasha was staring too, shoulders heaving.

Colleen sought Zol's face with her unblinking gaze. Without a coat, she was shivering. Natasha too. Colleen tightened her lips, but Zol could see they were quivering. The crinkles around her eyes said she was sorry, she'd miscalculated, she should have stayed out of Horvat's hole. Tears welled in her eyes.

Another wave of bile stung Zol's throat. His arms felt like lead above his head. He forced down the bile and did his best to flash Colleen a forgiving wink. They couldn't die with unresolved regrets.

Nick fixed his scowl on Horvat and raised his knife. "I said, give me the gun."

Horvat studied the revolver, turned it over in his hands. Then he nodded as if he'd come to a decision. Cold indifference masked his face, a look more frightening than anger and hate. He hooked his finger on the trigger and aimed at Nick's chest.

Shorty whipped his gun out of Zol spine. Zol's relief was instantaneous, but replaced by the terror of two guns poised for action. He braced for the gunfight no one would win, and fixed his eyes on Colleen's.

A vehicle lumbered up the alley. Everyone stiffened and turned to the approaching sound, a throaty engine with a hole in the muffler.

Horvat lunged at Colleen, threw his left arm around her, and pressed the gun into her back.

Nick scowled hatred at Horvat and palmed his knife.

Shorty rammed his revolver against Zol's spine.

A moment later, a white Lincoln pitched into the yard and ground to a stop beside Horvat's suv.

"Not a word out of any of youse," Shorty said, "or Mr. Minivan here gets a hot lead souvenir." He turned to his mate. "Get rid of them."

The gorilla guarding Hamish told him not to move a friggin' muscle, then strode to the Lincoln's front passenger window. The tinted glass rolled down, and an old man's face appeared.

In a loud, clear, speaking-to-the-elderly voice, the gorilla said, "Lost, aren't youse?" He smiled honey into his face and pointed to the alley behind the Lincoln. "If youse return the way youse came and turn right, you're gonna find Mohawk Road. Can't miss it." He swept the scene with his eyes. Zol thought the thug couldn't have helped realizing how incriminating it all looked. The thug scratched his head, pawed the ground, then made a show of checking his watch and looking surprised at the time. "We're, like, um, rehearsing a movie here. Need to get through this scene. One more time before dark. So if you'll excuse us . . ."

"We're not the least bit lost," Phyllis called sharply, climbing out of the driver's seat.

No one moved. They all watched her stride in front of the Lincoln.

"I know this neighbourhood *capite ad calce*," she continued. "Used to live two blocks south, so I know these back alleys head to toe." She approached the gorilla. "Of course, a fellow like you never saw the inside of a Latin class. You'd have favoured detentions over declensions."

"What the —" the gorilla said.

Phyllis stabbed the air with her bony forefinger. Her hat feather waved fearlessly in the wind gusting through the yard. "Yes, I dealt with your type every day at North Hamilton High."

Shorty twisted slightly so that Phyllis couldn't see his gun digging into Zol's spine. "Ma'am, I really must ask you to leave." He looked at the darkening sky. "We're up against a deadline here."

"And what sort of deadline involves Mr. Horvat over there?" Phyllis asked, her finger thrust toward the pharmacist. "The arrival of another shipment of phony pills?"

Phyllis crossed the yard. She stopped in front of Horvat, who was still holding Colleen. "Unhand her this instant."

Horvat's face remained impassive. Beside him, Nick stood tense and rigid; he had no idea how to respond to this brash old woman who sent back his overdone broccoli and refused his lukewarm soup.

"In plain English, Viktor," Phyllis said, "let go of her." She reached out with both hands and grabbed Horvat's left arm.

His right arm swung out. His gun fired.

Phyllis collapsed at Colleen's feet.

The blast tore through Zol's ears. The sharp smell of cordite bit at his nostrils.

No one moved.

And then a voiced boomed from beside the Lincoln.

"Two down. How many to go? Six? Seven? Eight?" Art Greenwood was out of the Lincoln and leaning on a cane. "Still plenty of us left at Camelot. Going to finish the job there as well?"

"Get back in the car, old man," said Shorty.

Art took three breaths and started across the yard. Zol had never seen him walk more than two paces. Each step was a marathon, but he lumbered through the slush, his gaze fixed on Horvat. Everyone watched, mesmerized by the determination in the old man's face.

Shorty's gun eased its pressure on Zol's back. The pain lifted a little, and his knees strengthened. But a moment later his mouth turned to dust. Where was Max? Art and Phyllis must have left him with the Oliveiras. They'd be filling him with Waste Not's leftovers — sandwiches and dirty dishes teeming with listeria. No, he told himself. The food at Camelot was fine. It was Horvat, not Gus, who'd brought the listeria into Camelot. Gus and Gloria may not know much about keeping preteen boys amused, but Max was safe. Better bored at Camelot than embroiled here in this mess.

Hamish tensed but stayed rooted next to Zol, their hands still raised, as Art shuffled forward, occasionally stopping for breath and leaning on his cane.

"We know what you're up to, Vik," Art said. "Empty capsules, counterfeit blood pressure pills, and by the looks of things —" he motioned toward the enforcers "— transactions with the stars of our city's informal economy."

Horvat opened his mouth but nothing came out.

Art moved forward a few more steps in the stunned silence, then paused to catch his breath. After a moment he continued. "Haven't figured out exactly how you poisoned us — and yourself — with that listeria bug. I figure you forgot to wash your hands." He jerked his cane toward the body slumped on the snow. "Now, about that corporal there," he said, wrinkling his nose. "Was he reeking of vodka before or after you and Nick nabbed him from our parking lot?"

Horvat threw Colleen to the ground, then lunged at Art, taking the old man in a bear hug. He jammed his gun into Art's temple. "Enough."

Zol bounded across the yard, half expecting Shorty's gun to pick him off. "Your party's over, Horvat," Zol said, forcing himself to ignore Horvat's gun. "Seems you got some sort of beef with old folks and the Canadian Forces. Don't know exactly how you did it, but I know you polluted their prescriptions."

Hamish dashed across the yard and crouched beside Phyllis. He tugged her coat open, pulled up her skirt, and slammed into doctor mode. Ignoring Shorty's curses, he called for something, anything to stop the blood gushing from Phyllis's thigh. Zol knelt next to Hamish and held his bare hand on the wound, but simple pressure didn't do much to stem the tide. Hamish took Zol's scarf and wound it tightly around Phyllis's leg near her groin. The bleeding slowed to a trickle. Zol grabbed Phyllis's wrist. Her radial pulse felt rapid and weak, but at least she had one.

Colleen heaved herself out of the slush. "Use my coat. As a blanket. It's inside the —"

"Well, well, well," said Shorty, three paces behind Zol and waving his gun. He nodded toward the Lincoln. "What have we here? The ultimate hostage, wouldn't you say?"

Zol turned but couldn't see what Shorty was referring to. They say the eyes see only what the brain has prepared them for. And there was no way Zol was prepared to see his son standing beside Phyllis Wedderspoon's Lincoln. But there he was, with his ski jacket unzipped, clutching his game gadget.

"Oh my God, Max," cried Zol. "How did —"

"Are you really in a movie, Dad?"

"No, Max. I'm afraid this isn't a game."

Max returned his *I thought so* look and gaped at the enforcers.

Zol caught Shorty's gaze and narrowed his eyes. "It's okay, Max. They never shoot boys." Zol gripped Phyllis's bony hand and wrist, his finger on her galloping pulse his only connection with reality. He knew if he let go, his world would explode.

Shorty held up his weapon. "You wanna see my gun, kid? Come over here."

Max looked at Zol, his inquisitive face asking for permission to check out the revolver. Had video gaming desensitized Max to the danger? Was he confusing the sanitized gore of shoot-'em-up games with the irreparable devastation of real weapons?

Zol didn't know what to say. If Max could stall the gangsters — charm them even — maybe . . . No, he told himself, that was pure denial. Hoping a nine-year-old gamer could outwit heartless criminals was ridiculous. He felt ashamed.

Max clamped his tongue between his teeth and took a step toward Shorty.

"Hold it there, kid," Shorty called. "What's that in your hand?"

Max froze. "Um, my, um, game gadget."

Shorty looked at the gorilla then at Nick. "What the hell's that?"

"For computer games," Zol explained. "Kids' stuff, like Super Mario and Pac-Man."

"It got a phone or WiFi?" Shorty asked.

"No," Zol answered quickly. "It's just a toy."

"Throw it to me, kid," Shorty said. "I wanna see it."

Max stared at Zol, his eyes filled with the terror of a boy caught in a life-altering lie.

"I said toss it over," Shorty demanded.

The sun was fading quickly, the shadows deepening with every passing second. Zol could barely see Max's face, but there was no mistaking the screen glowing in his son's hand. That wasn't a game gadget. That was Max's cellphone.

Max planted his feet in the slush and fixed his eyes on the ground. The phone didn't budge from his grasp.

Zol swept the yard with his gaze. Everyone was riveted by Max's fist, aglow in the light of his Aladdin's lamp. Was it too late to hope for a genie, or was it already out of the bottle?

Zol's heartbeat pounded on his eardrums as he stood shivering in the dark, his eyes darting back and forth between his son and the gunman.

The seconds ticked by. Wishful thinking, fuelled by desperation, toyed with his senses, prickled his ears with an eerie whine.

The noise rose steadily. When it eclipsed the throbbing in his ears, he realized it was no illusion; it was real.

It wasn't the throaty blare of fire-truck horns.

Nor the high-pitched wail of an ambulance.

It was the piercing yelp of police-car sirens — two, maybe three of them — their pitch distorted by the speed of their approach.

Max heard it too. He looked at Zol and very slowly raised his hand. His cellphone lit the whites of his eyes, the lift of his eyebrows, the hint of satisfaction on his lips.

Only a dad could understand that look.

CHAPTER 40

Ten days later, about quarter to four on Wednesday afternoon, Natasha stopped at the Nitty Gritty's front counter to check on the arrangements she'd made with Marcus, the proprietor.

"Yes, miss," Marcus said, "the maple-glazed coffee cake is ready. D'you want me to set it out now?"

She glanced at the health unit's table. Marcus had done a nice job with the colourful plates and festive serviettes. "The others will be here soon. Please wait until you've served our coffees. Then bring in the cake and we'll sing 'Happy Birthday.'"

"A bit tough having a birthday on April Fool's Day," Marcus offered.

"He got teased about it at school. So, let's not —"

"Don't worry. I won't mention it. Say — did they find his car?"

"Yes. In Niagara Falls. The interior's being deep cleaned. Some sort of special process."

"Excellent."

Natasha hoped everything about this afternoon would be excellent, although Dr. Wakefield might not feel like celebrating his birthday. He'd told her he'd broken up with his boyfriend, Ken, on the weekend but had confided few details. Still, there was much to celebrate. Professor Crabtree was out of the intensive care unit. Betty McKenzie was back to eating normal food. Phyllis Wedderspoon was walking on her fractured femur, stabilized with screws and a plate. Travis and the army officers were recovering from their listeria meningitis, so far with no major complications. And Viktor Horvat was in jail.

The past week had been exhausting, but enlightening. Natasha and Dr. Wakefield had spent most of the last seven days sequestered at Camelot Lodge and Steeltown Apothecary with two RCMP officers and a forensics team. A separate team was investigating the medications Viktor Horvat had dispensed to his other clients across the city.

Wearing crime-scene suits, rubber boots, masks, and gloves, they'd inspected and replaced every pill in the Lodge, combed through every shelf and drawer of Steeltown's dispensary, and examined every millimetre of Horvat's infamous garage. The only sign of the cat was its feces piled in a corner. At first, it was difficult to face that dark, windowless place again, but Dr. Wakefield showed her how he calmed his anxieties with his version of yogic breathing — in through the nose, out through the mouth, out first from the abdomen, in first to the chest. She'd let the rhythm overtake her, and it worked — well, the breathing *and* the academic process of sifting through the evidence.

The petri dishes she'd spotted in Horvat's refrigerator turned out to be loaded with listeria bacteria. Ellen from Caledonian's microbiology lab confirmed they bore the same genetic fingerprint as those recovered from Viktor Horvat's spinal fluid when he had meningitis at New Year's. They were also identical to the listeria in Camelot's gastro stools, young Travis's blood, and both soldiers' spinal fluids. Of course, all the microbiologic tests were being repeated in government forensic labs elsewhere, but Natasha was confident Ellen's results would hold water.

It was Hamish — he'd asked her to call him that, though his intellect was sometimes so commanding that *Dr. Wakefield* felt more natural — who figured out how Viktor Horvat had infected so many people. He knew right away the purpose of the propane torch, the forceps, and that wire loop thing.

Horvat was facing a string of charges, including the first-degree murder of Jayson Dasilva, the second-degree murder of at least half a dozen Camelot residents, the attempted murder of Travis Andersen and the two army officers, and the willful sale of counterfeit medications. Nick the cook had been charged as an accessory to kidnapping. The two gang enforcers — she never did learn their names — were awaiting bail on alleged weapons offences. The police were building the case for charging them with conspiracy in a counterfeit drug ring. The cops had developed the theory that one of the local gangland families had made Horvat one of those offers you can't refuse: be the pharmacist front man for our new venture into counterfeit prescriptions. The mobsters could see that fake drugs were easier than cocaine to get past Canada Customs and their sniffer dogs, and could be almost as lucrative. The RCMP had impounded the Cadillac SUV parked in the alley behind Steeltown and were pulling the vehicle apart, piece by piece. So much for the short guy's Moroccan leather seats.

One thing was for sure: Max would never get into trouble over his cellphone again. The dispatcher had used the GPS to pinpoint Max's location the moment he'd called nine-one-one from the back seat of Phyllis's Lincoln.

Dr. Wakefield set his fork on his empty plate and fixed Natasha with his wide blue eyes. When he beamed that boyish smile of his, it was easier to think of him as Hamish. "That was the best birthday cake I've ever had," he told her. "Thank you, all of you. Very much."

"For a while there, I thought we weren't going to see it," Dr. Zol said.

"The cake?" said Hamish.

"No, your birthday."

Colleen dipped her eyes and pressed a few final crumbs onto her fork. She was still recovering from the shock of watching Viktor Horvat pump those bullets into Jayson, right at her feet. She wasn't the kind of seen-it-all private eye they showed on TV. She'd come all this way from South Africa to escape violence, and the shootings had left her contemplative for a few days, despite her clear-headed courage under stress.

Colleen had been right about the terrible smell in Steeltown's refrigerator. It wasn't rotting flesh, but *Travnicki* cheese sent from Bosnia and Herzegovina six months ago. The postmark on the paper wrapping left no doubt about its origin and mailing date. Ellen Ballyk's cultures showed it was teeming with listeria bearing a genetic fingerprint matching all the others. Whether Horvat had ordered the contaminated cheese from Bosnia with criminal intent, or if he'd seized the serendipitous opportunity of a present from the old country, they would probably never know.

"Yes . . . well . . . Here we are." Hamish lifted his plate. "Care to cut me another piece, Natasha?"

"Was it only Xanucox capsules that Horvat laced with listeria, Hamish?" asked Dr. Zol. "Did you find any other contaminated medications?"

"Just the Xanucox," Hamish said. "He plucked listeria colonies from his petri dishes with the tiny wire loop we found on his work table." Hamish demonstrated by skimming a smidgeon of maple glaze from his coffee cake with the tine of his fork. "Then he placed the colonies inside real Xanucox capsules. But not every capsule. That way, the infections appeared at random and were distributed over time."

"Extraordinary," said Colleen. "He made it seem like a problem with the kitchen. Unrelenting food poisoning. A clever way of discrediting Gus and Gloria to force them out of their livelihood."

It had worked. Gus and Gloria Oliveira were out of Camelot Lodge like a shot, replaced by a team from a temporary employment agency. Camelot's owner didn't like the idea of his managers having harboured an alleged murder fugitive. Besides, Jayson's death meant the Oliveiras were in no shape to look after the Lodge. They'd be mourning Gloria's son for a long time.

If the Oliveiras had stayed on any longer, Dr. Zol would have been forced to publicly expose Gus's misappropriated Waste Not dividends. The man hadn't been exactly Dumpster diving, and according to Ellen Ballyk his Dijon mustard and *chouriço* sausage were in the clear, but stealing from a registered charity was the final blemish on the Oliveiras' record. They would never work in long-term care again. At least not in any place near Hamilton.

"Art says the food is better already," Zol said. "The veggies are fresher and the soup is piping hot. I phoned Waste Not, by the way. Suggested they might like to remove Gus Oliveira from their list of volunteers."

Natasha was learning that with a phone call you could pass along sensitive information without making a federal case of the details, and leave no paper trail to answer later. She'd made a note to see about making Waste Not's operation more secure, perhaps with bonded drivers and rules about faster door-to-door delivery times. Maybe the well-meaning charity could learn from the cut-throat pizza delivery business. No one liked lukewarm pizza.

"And the propane torch?" Colleen asked. "What was that for?"

"Sterilizing the wire loop after he used it to inoculate the capsules," Hamish explained. "But he must have forgotten to use the torch once or twice, and got a big dose of listeria on his fingers. He probably licked them when he snuffed that votive candle beside his wife's photo, and infected himself."

"Was anyone a specific target of his contaminated capsules?" Dr. Zol asked.

"My guess is Raimunda, Gloria's mother," Hamish said. "All the others were just taking the wrong meds at the wrong time, so to speak." He shook his head and looked rueful for a moment. "Betty got her contaminated Xanucox from Raimunda. An informal trial to see if the drug would help her arthritis." He raised his finger and wagged it assertively. "If she'd listened to her doctor . . ."

Dr. Zol fidgeted with his fork, and an embarrassed look came over his face. "What about those goons who gave me a hard time? You know, at the funeral?"

"I asked our RCMP buddies about them," Hamish said, enjoying the moment. "Laughed their heads off. Said you should have twigged to the Gretzky–Crosby routine."

Dr. Zol's ears flushed red. "What do you mean?"

"You were fed fake IDs. Those guys were probably enforcers with the construction company Jayson was working for."

"Pilfering from job sites is a big problem," Natasha added.

"I don't get it," Dr. Zol said.

"It's kind of complicated," Natasha explained. "But Jayson Dasilva — that's Joe's real name — wasn't living in Portugal after all. He was working in Toronto, pretending to be an illegal Portuguese construction worker named Joe Medeiros."

"He wasn't in Canada illegally?" asked Dr. Zol.

"Not as an illegal *immigrant*," Hamish said. "But as an illegal *army deserter*. AWOL from the Argylls while awaiting trial on a drunk-driving homicide charge."

Natasha shuddered and was careful not to catch Colleen's eye as she relived those three deliberate shots Horvat fired into Jayson's crumpled body. One bullet each for Horvat's wife and two daughters.

Colleen asked, "Any news about Horvat's blood-pressure tablets? Has the drug company finished running its tests on them?"

"Oh, I meant to say," Natasha said. "Wayne Jarvie from Lakeview Pharma called today and left a message on my phone. Not a trace of active ingredient in any of Steeltown's Zytoprils. Just brick dust."

"Brick dust?" Zol said. "How does . . . . Never mind."

A warm presence approached Natasha from her left, then crouched beside her and whispered in her ear. "Are we permitted to join you now?" Al Mesic asked. She nodded, then watched wistfully as he aimed his sexy smile at Hamish, a wrapped present in his hand.

"Happy birthday, Dr. Wakefield," Mr. Greenwood called out. He wheeled eagerly to the table and explained, "Betty's at the hairdresser. Having an afternoon at the spa with Maude and Myrtle. They'll be coming by taxi when they're done."

Hamish was radiant with a mix of pleasure and shyness. He touched Al Mesic on the arm and jumped to fetch him a chair. Dr. Zol shuffled the seats to make room for the guests and placed Colleen beside him. He flashed her an intimate smile when he thought no one was looking.

Mr. Greenwood looked around. "Say — where's young Max?"

Dr. Zol explained that Max was at home with Ermalinda, competing with his nanny to see who could make the awesomest thin-crust pizza from whatever they could find in the refrigerator. Coming face to face with real gangsters had dampened — for the time being, at least — the boy's enthusiasm for his vast library of shoot-'em-up video games.

For Natasha, the end of a case induced an almost physical craving. While it was great to solve a complex puzzle, she missed the high stakes, the lurking unknowns, the heart-racing adrenaline.

And today held another kind of longing. It was wonderful to be treated with respect and kindness by a boss like Dr. Zol, but watching the two couples at the table made her yearn for more than a respectful workplace.

She couldn't help thinking about Kostos, the surgery resident who'd taken her phone number at that Hess Village dance club on the weekend. She hoped he'd call again, as he promised. He had a nice ass, gorgeous dark curls, a great sense of humour, and a sensitive manner that seemed sincere. Perhaps her mother might not swoon if she brought him home. A Greek guy holding a plateful of chicken korma and a stack of chapattis could almost pass for Punjabi.